Mr Frisk

R. D. Berg

Dedication

This story is written for the windswept tumbleweeds who have no specific destination yet feel a need to direct their paths toward shelter. This story is also written for the potted plants that sit on the windowsill behind a safe pane of glass as they watch the rolling tumbleweeds. This story is also written for all those in between who wonder why.

In Memory

This book is authored by R. D. Berg. One of his last wishes, in July of 2014, was to have his manuscript published. It is with great honor and everlasting memory that I am able to fulfill his wishes with the publication of this novel, Mr. Frisk. It is a great and notable achievment to write such a novel and his family is very proud. R. D. Berg was, in many ways, similar to some of the characters in this book, leading a simple life while preserving the values of family and God. His intellect, advice, insight, and life experiences will be greatly missed. ~ Your son.

Contents

And have no fellowship with the unfruitful works
of darkness, but rather reprove them.
—Eph. 5:11 (King James Version)

Oh, the ascetic wanderer
Forbidding carnal paths
Barefoot, feeling the pebbles beneath
Seemingly seeing past the veil
Past the world of images
Through the abstraction
Inwardly gazing in deep meditation
Correcting, perfecting
Self

Oh, the ascetic wanderer
Flawed gemstone
Washing clean in the river of virtue
How difficult is your journey?
How will you survive the hidden snares?
How will you survive the covert brambles?
How will you manage the deceptions?
Surely you will be affected!

How will you rise above?

Who is the foe that spreads the seeds of discontent?
Who is the antagonist of virtue?
Who is the enemy of humanity?
Where does the enemy reside?
Reader, Beware!

For we wrestle not against flesh and blood, but against principalities,
against powers, against the rulers of the darkness of this world.
—Eph. 6:12 (KJV)

I

Mr. Frisk

The alarm clock sprang to life at the stroke of 6:00 a.m., but no one was there to turn it off. Mr. Frisk lay dead in his bed, never to rise again.

Mr. Frisk was a very particular man. His day started at precisely 6:00 a.m. Of course, his mechanical alarm clock would notify him of the appropriate hour at which to start his daily routine. He would arise and proceed to the kitchen—coffee and toast, every morning. Once in a great while, Mr. Frisk would buy a box of Raisin Bran for variety, but for the most part, it was always coffee and toast. Frisk prided himself on economy. The way he figured it, coffee and bread are about the cheapest form of breakfast a person could possibly consume. And besides, he enjoyed the simplicity of it all.

After the coffee was busy percolating, he would shower: just a dab of shampoo and a sliver of soap would do the trick. The shower would have to be quick so as to save the hot water. Most people have no idea how much it costs to heat water—a small fortune, for sure! Mr. Frisk kept a strict account of his utility use, as well as all his expenditures.

After his shower and breakfast, he would dress himself in the usual wardrobe: dress slacks, dress shirt, tie, black shoes. The shirts and slacks were all the same brand, but different colors for each day of the week. If it were up to Mr. Frisk, he would wear the same color clothes every day, but people would talk, hence the various colors.

He would then drive his light blue Honda Civic sedan to the post office where he worked. His car was twelve years old and had on it not one speck of rust nor dirt. Mr. Frisk cleaned it most every evening, after work. If, by chance, the roads were sloppy from rain or snow, he would skip breakfast and walk the two blocks to the post office.

At the post office, Mr. Frisk had a small, insignificant office in the far corner of the second floor, hardly noticeable. He was in charge of filing certified letters and ensuring the post office had verification of all these important documents. Mr. Frisk took his job very seriously. Once, the Eighty-Ninth District Court demanded verification of a certified letter to prove notification for jury duty for some unsavory character who was trying to squirm out of his civic duty! Upon request of the court, Mr. Frisk promptly and efficiently produced the perfectly correct documentation, proving that the jury duty notification had certainly been sent and delivered.

Mr. Frisk was currently in the process of transferring the millions of certified letter files to the mainframe computer. This was tedious work, but very rewarding. There was a certain sense of accomplishment in perfectly transposing a hard-copy, handwritten document to a digital, electronic format. Mr. Frisk felt a slight surge of euphoria when each document was perfectly recorded. He always kept a running record of his daily, weekly, monthly, and annual progress, strictly justifying any setbacks or delays. He once estimated that he could record all of the certified letters, including the recent ones, in precisely twelve years, four months, and eleven days, estimating and compensating based on statistical averages taken from his personal data.

Mr. Frisk worked alone and undisturbed. His supervisors had much more important things to do than check on Mr. Frisk. After all, Mr. Frisk had an impeccable work ethic and was a very dedicated employee. Everything always ran like clockwork with him, so there was no need to monitor his activities. There was no time for Mr. Frisk to fraternize with the other employees. He stayed focused and perfectly on schedule. He took no coffee breaks because he did not think it was healthy to overindulge in the caffeine-rich brew. One cup in the morning was enough and seemed to promote a balanced diet of sorts.

Lunch break was a ritual. Mr. Frisk always had a desk drawer filled with cans of Campbell's condensed tomato soup, which he would buy on sale. At precisely 12:05 p.m., he would retrieve his microwave-friendly soup cup from his desk drawer and mix a can of soup with an equivalent can of water. He had bought his own used microwave, so there was no need to leave his office, which was very convenient. Nobody could see or bother him. Each day, the hot soup seemed refreshing, not only refreshing his nourishment but also his sense of economy. You see, Mr. Frisk figured that tomato soup was both a drink and a food. Therefore, for only thirty-three cents a can, he could enjoy an entire healthy meal—at minimum cost to boot! Also, there was some medical speculation that tomatoes prevented cancer.

The end of the workday was at 5:00 p.m. Mr. Frisk worked precisely up to 5:00 p.m. Then he tidied up his small office and made sure everything was in its correct place. After that, he turned out the lights and locked the door.

Mr. Frisk always made sure that the following day's order of work was well prepared for in advance, lest his schedule suffer from an unforeseen setback. Yesterday, after locking his office, he marched to Marcia Gratchett's office, which was located on the third floor, overlooking Sunnyside Park. He firmly intended to remind her to send last month's certified letters to his office no later than noon the next workday. Mrs. Gratchett had been working at the post office for seven years. Her office was always in disarray. Family pictures, loose paperwork, and trinkets of art that she collected were all scattered in helter-skelter fashion. Her bright, colorful clothes never seemed to match. She looked like Pippi Longstocking, but with an earring through the side of one nostril!

When Mr. Frisk arrived, she was chatting with a colleague, something about teenagers and skinny-dipping. An embarrassed and appalled Mr. Frisk waited for eye contact and acknowledgment before speaking.

"Mrs. Gratchett, I would just like to remind you to make sure the certified letters for last month are sent to my office by noon tomorrow. My work will require them to be available no later than noon."

"Certified letters?" Mrs. Gratchett pondered. "Oh, oh! Yes, of course, the monthly letters. I'll have my aide haul down the boxes for you. Where is your office again?"

"Second floor, all the way in the back, in the corner, next to the janitor's closet."

"Oh, yes! I'll write a note to myself, so I do not forget."

"Thank you, Mrs. Gratchett."

"You're welcome, Mr. Fik."

Mr. Frisk recognized Mrs. Gratchett did not recall the correct pronunciation of his name. While he considered correcting her error, Mr. Frisk decided it would likely not be worth the effort.

After Work

Mr. Frisk's daily work routine rotated from day to day in splendid accuracy, like the sweeping hands of a well-oiled clock. Any deviations in the least were always compensated by tweaking the perfectly balanced schedule in such a fashion so that it would fall back in order.

Upon leaving the post office, he flicked through his personal organizer to verify the day's agenda. Today was Thursday. His after-work duties included going to the bank to verify his direct deposit accounts and then getting his car's oil changed.

Efficiently and effectively, Mr. Frisk drove his light blue Honda Civic to the Wal-Mart automotive center. He had discovered that he could get an oil change there for three dollars less than any other place in town. Also, while he waited, he could do his banking at the bank located within the supercenter. And if that was not enough to justify his actions, he could get a free cup of hot coffee in the employees' break room even though this was in addition to his usual morning cup. Mr. Frisk allowed himself this special indulgence, mainly because the cup was free.

Mr. Frisk loved Wal-Mart. To him, it was the greatest feat in retail engineering that the world had ever known. All the employees had an assigned area and an assigned responsibility. Everyone was an expert in his or her own area. Just excellent! Most stores were open twenty-four hours, with a merchandise selection that could not be matched, not to mention the low prices.

Upon arrival at Wal-Mart, Mr. Frisk registered his car with the appropriate attendant, and he was told that his car would be ready in forty-five minutes. Mr. Frisk wrote the exact estimated time down in his personal logbook and then proceeded to the banking area.

The bank teller was a younger-looking girl with long blond hair. Her blue eyes sparkled as she smiled while joyfully chatting with each patron.

"Well, hello, sir! What can I do for you on this beautiful day?" she said and smiled.

"My name is Robert Frisk. Here is my account number: 227918. That's 227918. These are my personal direct deposit forms from my employer. I would like to verify that these transactions are correct. I would also like a hard-copy verification of that fact, complete with today's date and your signature, for my personal records."

"Wow! You are really on the ball! Half of the people who come here either can't remember or can't find their account numbers. Do you bank here often? I've only been here a month or so, and I just love it. The people are so friendly, and you learn so much just by chatting with them. Why, the gentleman just before you told me that he just flew in from Africa! He was inspecting a diamond mine for an investor. Can you imagine? A diamond mine! He might have had a diamond stuck on the heel of his shoe, and you could be standing on a million dollars!"

"My paperwork is straightforward enough. If you will be so kind as to verify and document this information for me," droned Mr. Frisk.

"Oh, yes! I have the information right here. Let's see…Yes…No, wait a sec…OK. I think that's it. Does this look right?"

Mr. Frisk glared over the paperwork, quickly assessing that the transactions were indeed correct.

"Everything is in order," stated Mr. Frisk. "If you would be so kind as to sign and date this form."

"Okeydoke," cheerfully replied the teller. "Glad to be of service to you."

"Thank you," replied Mr. Frisk.

"Oh, you're very welcome," the teller said with a smile. "Oh, I almost forgot to ask you; I am supposed to ask all the patrons, and I keep forgetting. It's probably because the people who come in here are so interesting that I just get sidetracked and—"

"Please, I'm very busy. What is it?"

"Oh, I'm sorry. There I go again," the teller said and laughed. "We are collecting donations for the Harper family, whose little boy has terminal cancer. You've probably read about it in the paper. Anyways, would you like to donate a dollar to help out the family?"

"Yes," stated Mr. Frisk.

"Oh, thank you," beamed the teller. "We are hoping to fund a trip for the whole family to Disney World or anywhere they would like to go. They say that little Jimmy has only about a year left, and he still gets around fairly—"

"Thank you and good day. I really must be off," abruptly stated Mr. Frisk.

"Thanks again! And have a great day, Mr. Frik!" the teller said with a gleam in her eye.

Mr. Frisk glanced at his watch while walking toward the auto center.

"Thirty more minutes," he muttered to himself.

Stopping at the counter, Mr. Frisk stood and waited for recognition from the attendant, who was apparently busy at the moment. The attendant was a middle-aged man wearing a dark blue work shirt, half tucked into his blue jeans. Smears of grease lined his sleeves and hands. He was busy staring at the computer. He glanced up briefly at Mr. Frisk and then back at the computer.

"Damn it!" the attendant barked.

Mr. Frisk waited patiently. It was quite obvious that the attendant was preoccupied with his business, as all good employees should be. Mr. Frisk remained contently motionless for five minutes.

"Whut kin I git fur ya?" the attendant said.

"My car is getting its oil changed, and it will take another twenty-four minutes. I was wondering if I could wait in the employees' area until it is finished," said Mr. Frisk.

"Sure, go ahead. We'll gitch ya whin it's dun. Wuz that the green Ford?"

"Light blue Honda," stated Mr. Frisk.

"Gotcha. Hep yurself to sum hot coffee, if ya like."

"Thank you," replied Mr. Frisk.

The employees' waiting room was a mess. Tan, steel folding chairs lined the small room's soiled walls. A cardboard box full of magazines was just below the stained coffeepot. A once-yellow mop bucket stood idle in the corner, half empty with black water. The coffeepot was turned off, and the cold coffee that remained seemed the consistency of molasses.

Thumbing through the magazines, Mr. Frisk found absolutely nothing to suit his interests. He reluctantly settled for a *Good Housekeeping* magazine and took a cold seat in the far corner of the room.

As he mindlessly flicked through the pages, he noticed an advertisement for a bank that happened to be geographically located somewhat closer to the post office where he worked. He considered the possibility of closing his account at the Wal-Mart bank and transferring his funds to the closer bank. He pondered this idea for some time, lost in deep thought. The idea appealed to him. He wondered why he had not thought of it long ago. After all, it was much closer to his job, and he could—

"Car's done!" yelled a girl with curly, dark hair through the open door. "C'mon up to the counter, and we can straighten up," she bellowed.

Mr. Frisk placed the magazine exactly where he'd found it in the pile of other magazines, third from the top, and marched to the counter, while glancing at his watch.

"Forty-three and a half minutes," Mr. Frisk thought with delight.

The curly-haired attendant looked over the paperwork, minimized the solitaire game on the computer, and quickly punched a flurry of keys on the keyboard.

"Let's see. Robert Fisk…Honda Civic sedan…oil and filter…That will be sixteen fifty-seven," stated the attendant.

"Thank you," said Mr. Frisk, as he handed her the check.

"Front tires are worn," the girl said. "Kind of dangerous driving around on bad front tires. I can set you up for some new ones if you'd like."

"How much?" questioned Mr. Frisk.

"Let's see," the girl said as she stared at the computer screen. "Tires, balanced...Goodyear...One eighty-eight, seventy-five."

"Is that for all four?" questioned Mr. Frisk.

"Nope, just the two."

"I will have to think about it," stated Mr. Frisk. "I will let you know."

"OK, suit yourself," replied the attendant.

"Thank you," said Mr. Frisk.

"Yup," said the girl.

Mr. Frisk drove silently toward his apartment building. He wondered whether he should stop at McDonald's for dinner...or not. Traditionally, he always stopped at McDonald's after his oil change; however, this time was a bit complicated. You see, usually he had a cup or two of coffee in the employees' waiting room, which means that he would have had plenty of liquids; thus, he would not have to order a drink at McDonald's. His usual order would be two small hamburgers and no drink. But now, he was thirsty. This was a conundrum that plagued his thoughts.

After a laboring assessment of the situation, Mr. Frisk identified his weakness and labeled it as temptation. He gathered his wits about him and defiantly motored past the golden arches.

Mr. Frisk felt a dash of accomplishment as he defeated the evil one with his arsenal of restraint. Still, he knew very well that this was but a small battle in the raging war. The enemy was all around him—planning, calculating, smiling, coaxing, and using any tricks at his disposal. Oh, yes, the enemy was not to be taken lightly. Mr. Frisk thought about his wound at the bank and shuddered. The teller had used the perfect opportunity to strike. How could anyone refuse a dollar for such a cause? The enemy had found a chink in his armor! How devious—and accomplished with a smile! Of course, after all, are not they the tools of the evil one? Smiles...handshakes...gleeful advertisements? Even Eve must have coaxingly smiled at Adam.

As Mr. Frisk pulled into his parking spot next to the light post with the burned-out bulb, he swore a personal vow of alertness.

Instinctively, Mr. Frisk opened the trunk and retrieved the car-cleaning utensils for his evening ritual. First, he vacuumed the interior, top to bottom, with a twelve-volt Dustbuster, and sucked up every crumb of lint.

Then, with a spray bottle of Spiffy's Car Shine, he proceeded to spritz and wipe down the entire car, top to bottom. While merrily wiping and polishing, he noticed the worn front tires and lost his gleeful tone. Mr. Frisk sensed the enemy and slipped into a solemn, meditative trance. He felt the enemy laughing at him. Mr. Frisk knew very well that the battle would eventually be lost. The fiendish enemy would simply use attrition. That dastardly demon! Mr. Frisk pondered the inevitable and assessed his battle plan. There was no feasible way out. Trapped! His only course of action was to delay the unavoidable.

He marched to the trunk of his car, strategically replaced the cleaning kit, and retrieved his tire jack and lug-nut wrench. Pulling the wrench out of its nylon sheath, Mr. Frisk resembled the image of a samurai. With his car jack and a jack borrowed from his landlord, he rotated his tires. He worked feverishly, in precise military fashion.

"I may lose the battle," he thought to himself, "but I sure as hell am going down fighting!"

At the end of the fighting, he sheathed his tire wrench, replaced his weapons in the trunk, and defiantly slammed shut the lid. Raising his eyes and his fist to the sky, Mr. Frisk declared, "Take that!"

The battle-worn soldier marched directly into his barracks.

Reverend Daniels

Mr. Frisk was glad to be home, safe in his sanctuary—an island of sanity amid the chaos of the world. He changed his clothes, cleaned up a bit, and then pondered what to have for supper. His schedule was drastically off! The strategic plan was to dine at McDonald's and be home by 6:30 p.m. Now, due to the conversation about the tires, it was well after 7:00 p.m., and he had not even begun supper. And to make matters worse, the food he had stored in the pantry and refrigerator were already scheduled on the menu for the latter days of the week. Mr. Frisk contemplated the various procedures for rectifying the situation. He decided to prepare next Tuesday's meal, consisting of pork and beans, buttered bread, and a hot bowl of ramen noodles. He could replace the various food items on Sunday's trip to the supermarket, after church services. This plan was plausible and pleased Mr. Frisk immensely.

Suppertime was always quite a celebration for Mr. Frisk. His splendid table was always impeccably set, as for a festive celebration fit for royalty. The china was of the finest import. The glassware was fine, hand-etched crystal. The polished cutlery glistened under the single, white candlestick that burned brightly, perched upon its crystal throne in the middle of the table. Mr. Frisk valued his collection of fine dinnerware as it was a family heirloom and very valuable. Mr. Frisk often thought of putting the china and glassware under lock and key, but that would require purchasing new dishes. Instead, Mr. Frisk reasoned that using the china on a regular basis and taking the risk of an accidental break would far outweigh the wasteful spending of purchasing additional dinnerware.

With the table precisely set, Mr. Frisk began the task of creating supper. He had no sooner begun when the doorbell rang. Mr. Frisk shuddered. "Who could it be?" he mused. "Should I answer it? Maybe they will go away."

The doorbell rang again.

"For goodness's sake," Mr. Frisk thought in a panic, "whoever it is is sure to see my car out front. They will think me an irrational recluse if I do not answer the door, and I am so busy with supper. What a time for this to happen. If only I would have taken a shower before supper, I would have been under a noisy stream of water and would not have heard the doorbell. Then I would have not known anyone was here. But now, I know."

The doorbell rang again.

"Coming!" shouted Mr. Frisk as he blew out the candle on the table.

He unlocked both dead bolts, leaving the custom chain lock fastened, just so he could crack open the door. Outside the door stood a short, elderly man carrying a jet-black briefcase and wearing a gray sport coat, black tie, and matching hat.

"Reverend Daniels, what brings you out this evening?"

"Hello, Robert. May I come in?"

"Actually, I was right in the middle of my supper. In fact, I—"

"I shan't be long, Robert," interrupted the reverend.

"Yes! Yes, of course," stated Mr. Frisk, "please come in. Please take a seat on the sofa. Can I get you a glass of iced water?"

"Yes, Robert, a tall glass of iced water would do splashingly," the good reverend said with a grin.

Mr. Frisk retreated into the kitchen. He frantically browsed his collection of glassware, looking for just the right one. "None of these will do," he thought to himself. "Ah! I know!" Mr. Frisk opened the cabinet door under the kitchen sink, where he had placed a tall tin cup to catch the few drops of water that constantly leaked out of the sink's drain. He briefly washed the tin cup to satisfaction, filled it halfway with tap water, and then dropped in one ice cube.

"Thank you, thank you," beamed the reverend as he drained the simple beverage in one gulp. "Ah! There is nothing as refreshing as the purity and simplicity of a cup of sparkling water wrung out of the clouds and filtered through the earth's crust. It's enough to lift one's spirit unto the clouds themselves."

Immediately after his brief speech, a tranquil pallor glazed over the good reverend, who was, no doubt, reflectively realizing the possibility of incorporating those words into an inspirational sermon for his congregation Sunday morning.

Mr. Frisk sat at the other end of the worn sofa, staring at the transfixed reverend. Only a few seconds must have passed during this time, but it seemed as though time had stopped. Mr. Frisk wondered if, perhaps, the reverend had seen a vision, or perhaps he'd seen God himself! Of course, no one can actually see God and live; it says so somewhere in the good book. And if the reverend never actually saw God, how did he know, for sure, that there was a God or that the god he worshipped was, in fact *the* God? It seemed to Mr. Frisk that there were distinct differences between faith, belief, and knowing, the dangerous element being the "knowing." After all, who can really know without actually seeing? Sure, a person's belief and faith can be unshakable, but can it be pure, without knowing? Does true "knowing" come only after death? Or must we receive a supernatural encounter, like Job, to satisfy and transform our belief and faith into the solidity of knowing for sure? What if a person believes that he or she "knows" when he or she only has a strong belief and faith? Are not the radicals spawned from this mind-set?

"Oh, excuse me," apologized the good reverend as he pulled himself out of his transcendental state and back into the reality of Mr. Frisk's living room.

"Now, then, Robert, I will get right to the heart of the matter without dallying about. Our church records indicate that you have not missed a single Sunday service in years. Your loyal dedication to the word is exemplary to say the least. Why, after all the sermons you've heard me preach, you must command a good comprehension of the scriptures. Therefore, the word of the Lord has, no doubt, infused itself into the essence of your very being. You may not be consciously aware of it, but your thoughts are steeped in the Holy Spirit! The Holy Spirit shines its light with you, Robert; however, that light should be placed high on a lamp stand in order to cast its joyous beams in every direction for all to see! Does a person turn on a flashlight and place a basket over it? Does an electrician install lighting in the floor of a room? No! No, I tell you! The light goes in the highest place. If the light is in the floor, it is not efficient. If the light is under a basket, it is not efficient. If a light sits in the back pew, next to the door, it is not efficient!"

The reverend worked himself up into such an emotional state that beads of perspiration formed on his forehead. Mr. Frisk wondered if he should offer the reverend his handkerchief, lest the beads of perspiration turn into blood and stain his sofa.

"Robert," continued the reverend, "I am sure you noticed the empty pews in the front of the church on Sunday morning. Every year the number of empty pews increases. Our church's membership is declining, slowly eroding, slowly deteriorating. The abasing force that erodes the pillars of our church's membership is none other than that eroding force of passivity. Passiveness, I tell you! Let me ask you this, Robert: what does a man throw on a fire to quench its fiery destruction?"

Upon hearing his name phrased in the form of a question, Mr. Frisk was jolted to attention. His mind had drifted to the odd topic of stain removal for some reason unknown to him.

"Water," replied Mr. Frisk.

"Yes! Yes, of course—water!" bellowed the reverend. "And do you know why? I'll tell you why. Because water opposes fire—that's why! Water is the opposite of fire, in a sense. Thus, we need the same method for combating passiveness. We need its opposite—its opposite, I say! Do you understand, Robert? Do you see the logic laid out before you? Can anyone dispute these words?"

"Would you like some more iced water?" asked Mr. Frisk.

"Robert, I am afraid that the mere properties of physical water will not quench the destructive erosion of passiveness. What we need is action—action!" repeated the reverend. "Action is the opposite of passiveness, and it has the power to counter the idle corrosiveness of passivity. Action, Robert, action!"

At this point in the sermon, the reverend paused as he looked directly into the blank gaze of Mr. Frisk.

Suddenly, the veil was lifted from the eyes of Mr. Frisk. The purpose of Reverend Daniels's visit had made itself glaringly apparent. He was not after a donation of money, but a donation of time: time and work, which is the same as money, in a way—how devious! Mr. Frisk now saw clearly the trap that was laid out before him, and he frantically contemplated an escape route.

"Robert," continued the reverend, "I am in the process of orchestrating a war on passiveness by implementing action to thwart its complacent corrosion. I have decided to reinforce the dormant pillars of our congregation with an arsenal of action in the form of active duty. Robert, you are one of those pillars! With duty and action, you will have the tools to lead a frontline attack on the enemy. No matter how fierce the battle rages, your efforts will be noticed by the parishioners. They will see. You will be an example, a model, an inspiration. Others will follow! They will see, and they will follow, strengthening the army, strengthening the cause, strengthening the congregation into a unified mass of spirit that will beam as a brilliant beacon of light atop the highest mountain! Yes, Robert, action will spread among the parishioners like ripples on a lake, a dormant lake that the wind wakes from its slumber on a warm summer morning. It's time, Robert. Like the dormant morning air, you are called to awaken from your slumbers and blow the placid people into waves of action as a mighty wind. You are called, Robert, called by me and, more importantly, called by God Himself!"

Mr. Frisk suddenly felt the snare snap him helplessly off his precarious footing. He was contemplating various excuses or, at least, various ways to put off the good reverend in an attempt to buy more time to consider a plausible maneuver. However, the wolf had cunningly planned his trap well! He'd waited for the innocent sheep to be home alone, where he would be the most vulnerable. Then he'd carefully lay out the snare, camouflaging it with honeyed words. Then, he'd craftily seal off the exits and spring the snare!

How could he validate an excuse now? How could he speak against a call from God Himself? Mr. Frisk's only feasible escape route would be to lie and say that he was planning to transfer to another church. However, he did not want to change his traditional schedule. Furthermore, his current church was conveniently located. Changing churches would complicate his schedule immensely. Mr. Frisk briefly contemplated defeat.

"What did you have in mind?" asked Mr. Frisk.

Reverend Daniels smiled. "Robert, you have just taken a step, a step in the right direction, and in this new direction that you have accepted, you can take further steps. It's up to you." The reverend snapped open his briefcase and retrieved what appeared to be a sheet of parchment with black scribbling on it resembling calligraphy. He held the parchment gently with both hands as he solemnly bowed his head and mumbled a few queer noises.

Mr. Frisk assumed the reverend was speaking in Greek, Latin, or Arabic. Obviously, the words on the parchment were important, or at least important to the good reverend.

Mr. Frisk imagined the reverend penning the words on the Holy Parchment, while entranced by the Holy Spirit. Perhaps the inspired words were transfused from heaven through the earthly conduit of the meager minister! Or, was the wily wolf conjuring up a precise, covert ambience in which to camouflage yet another snare? Would the relentless fiend dare to implement such a devious ploy? Mr. Frisk doubted that the reverend was consciously aware of the underlying motives of the subconscious. In fact, the man before him, dressed in sheep's clothing, was probably oblivious to the fact that the deceptive tools he was using were not of heavenly design. The intriguing element of the whole affair was—

"Oh, pardon me," said the reverend. "It's high time I had out with it. Robert, in my hand is a carefully constructed plan to get our church back on a progressive spiritual path. I have, with great deliberation and inspiration, devised duties for a select group of soldiers. These individual duties are strategically designed to work in unison to further our glorious cause. Robert, I have assigned you to the gift committee. Your responsibility is to actively implement a progressive agenda for the collection and promotion of congregational gifts. I would expect a precise account of everything accomplished by the committee. You will report directly to me, every week. Robert, your efforts, as well as the efforts of those on the committee with you, are paramount for the growth and expansion of the church. With increased gifts, we can actively provide more services, thus promoting God's work, here in this veil of tears. You and your committee are the cornerstone on which our church can flourish! Hopefully, with the help of God, our combined efforts will bloom into a spiritual maturity that will encapsulate the hearts and minds of not only our own congregation, but also the people of our community, with a dynamic outreach program that could touch people throughout the state! The nation! The world! The world, I tell you!"

Beads of perspiration were glistening again, as the good reverend caught hold of his emotions and tamed his enthusiasm.

"Robert, I am requiring each new recruit to sign his or her name on this parchment, as a formal seal of your pledged commitment to this endeavor."

The reverend gently handed Mr. Frisk the parchment and a unique-looking fountain pen that seemed to hold some sort of mystical qualities from antiquity within it.

Mr. Frisk stared at the strange parchment, which was written in a style or language that he could not decipher. There were six other names of parishioners who had previously signed. Their commitments were permanently documented in their signatures in a dark red ink that Mr. Frisk could not place. In all other respects, the parchment resembled the familiar elements of a contract, in which Mr. Frisk immediately felt a spark of defiance and renewed sense of confidence, being on familiar footing.

"Well," replied Mr. Frisk, "I cannot sign anything until I have had appropriate time to consider my role in such a commitment. This is all much too sudden and will require a great deal of thought. To tell you the gospel truth, I was recently considering transferring churches. It felt quite awkward to bring up the issue tonight, but under the circumstances, I feel it is necessary. Surely you understand my dilemma. How can I be committed to an active role in a church when I may not be committed to that same church in the first place?"

The good reverend stared directly into Mr. Frisk's eyes, successfully encouraging maximum discomfort.

"Why," continued Mr. Frisk, "signing that parchment now would be a travesty if my heart was not completely infused into such a worthy commitment. Would God not want me to act out of the spirit of my heart, instead of out of the guilt of the noncommittal? And if I did sign under such circumstance, would I not be as hypocritical as the condemned Sadducees and Pharisees?"

Reverend Daniels raised his brow; perhaps he had underestimated Mr. Frisk. He sensed the distinct aroma of a countersnare being laid out in front of him, and without any camouflage at all!

The battle lines were clearly drawn. Reverend Daniels pondered that perhaps the blitzkrieg was inappropriate. Perhaps a brief retreat would be best, before he was surrounded.

Mr. Frisk, sensing the success of his coup de théâtre, grew confident and pushed onward toward total victory.

"Reverend Daniels, I appreciate your dedication and determination in regard to this matter; however, I feel that it is spiritually imperative that I decline this nomination. To accept such a position would be a deceit—a deceit to me, a deceit to you, a deceit to the church, and a deceit to God Himself! Pure honesty must be fluxed from society's corruption and shine its bright beams to light our paths. This light of honesty should be set on a hill, not under the dark veil of social manipulations. It should not be stifled. Honesty makes straight the path to the Lord!"

Reverend Daniels was shocked and dumbfounded at such an intense oration as this. It was as if the meek parishioner before him was temporarily reincarnated into John the Baptist himself! Surely, spiritual forces were at work, crippling his frontal assault and scattering his troops. Retreat was imminent.

"Robert," spoke the reverend as he solemnly placed the pen and parchment gently back into the jet-black briefcase, "I will take my leave. You have made your position as clear as purely refined gold. I only ask that you contemplate a question over the next few weeks. And after you've given it much thought, write me a letter explaining your rationale pertaining to the subject."

Mr. Frisk sensed danger, but agreed to the compromise offered by the defeated general. He nodded.

"We are all sinners, Robert, you as well as I. We are as stained and corrupt as used rags. Lord knows, my thoughts are not always pure, and my motives may not be appropriate. However, we, corrupt and dirt-ridden dredges that we are, must promote and spread the good news, which is pure and holy. Do you see the dilemma here, Robert? Do you see the question? How can a congregation, composed of sinful rags, promote holy purity? And furthermore, what should be their specific roles in the congregation? It is quite obvious that you are somewhat knowledgeable in the holy scriptures. Can I, at least, count on a written response to the questions I have given you?"

"Yes...I will consider your question," replied Mr. Frisk, as he reluctantly accepted the challenge of continuing the skirmish on the literary battlefields.

"Thank you," said the reverend, who smiled as he snapped the gold clasps on his briefcase, propped his somber gray hat atop his head, and marched toward the door. "I will be looking forward to your letter," he stated as he opened the door to leave.

"Good night," stated Mr. Frisk.

"May God help us both, eh, Robert? Good evening to you."

Mr. Frisk stood in the open portal, watching the solitary, war-torn soldier limp off into the blackness of night. He remained standing at the threshold, looking at the minister's path forging into the reality of the unknown. Turning away, he gazed into his apartment's warm ambience of security, shining its tranquil, artificial lights, beckoning him back. Mr. Frisk remembered his sacred supper and closed the door.

Mr. Frisk replaced the worn tin cup under the leaky sink and then relit the solitary candle on the kitchen table and prepared his long-awaited supper. When the boiling and microwaving were complete, and the table impeccably set, Mr. Frisk bowed his head in reverent prayer. "Come, Lord Jesus, be our guest, and let these gifts to us be blest. Amen."

The hot soup and cold beans never tasted as good as they did that night. Even the hard crusty bread, when dipped in the soup, tasted heavenly! "But of course it tastes heavenly," thought Mr. Frisk. "It is not necessarily what you eat, but when you eat it. It's all about appreciation—appreciation and commitment. The greatest foe of appreciation is luxury and excess. If people have plenty of any particular commodity, they will be prone to overlook its true value; however, if, for some reason, that commodity is unattainable, a hunger for it builds, a want, an appreciation. In fact, people would actively seek to fill the void left by the missing item. Thus is the cycle. In this land of milk and honey, we are tiring of the milk and honey! We are losing appreciation, which breeds erosion to contentment. Our loss of contentment is then remedied by corrupting ourselves with earthly pleasures of various sorts, which immediately nourish, but only temporarily sustain us. Thus, we seek out more earthly pleasures for sustenance, for contentment, temporary as it is. Soon, our appreciation for the greatest gifts of life is replaced by an earthly desire to be entertained, either by show, activity, trinkets, power, or whatever else our fancy. Of course, that's the way of it," reflected Mr. Frisk. "From the beginning of recorded human existence, the cycle repeats itself. The solution seems to stem from appreciation—appreciation and thanksgiving...through fasting, perhaps..."

Mr. Frisk mopped up the remaining gravy on his now-vacant plate of pork and beans with the remainder of the stale bread, savoring the last mouthful of this divine supper.

The flame flickered on the single candle, perched upon its glassy throne, reflecting its majesty on the mirrorlike supper plate. Mr. Frisk stared at the solitary flame and was mesmerized by thoughts pertaining to the good reverend's question.

Of course, the question itself was nothing more than the equivalent of a lifeboat, poised for the sole purpose of redemption sprinkled with a dash of guilt as a garnish. Also, supposed Mr. Frisk, the question was left as a lifeline, a connector of sorts, to take back up the issue at some preordained time convenient for the reverend. In fact, the reverend's question was elementary in a way. Any half-wit Christian knows that all people are corrupt sinners striving to steer their lives on a somewhat holy course by allowing the Great Pilot to direct them. What people really need to focus on goes back to the beginning. After all, human beings were unblemished in the early days. In fact, in those days, evil and corruption were not even conceived of! How could they? They had not manifested…yet. It was quite impossible to do anything but good—that is, as long as restraint was utilized. Restraint! Yes, in the garden we were informed of a "negativity," and we had the gift of free will, to choose righteously. Free will can only be kept in a pure state by utilizing restraint. It is mandatory! However, people are weak willed, like tumbleweeds that are blown every which direction the wind happens to be going. It is so tempting to just eat the delicious fruit that pleases the eye and tantalizes the tongue, instead of strengthening the will to avoid what we know does us no spiritual good. Thus is the defensive side of the battle. Defense must come first! It is paramount that the troops stay safe and on course by keeping the enemy at bay, by not allowing him to sleep in our tents, by keeping the front lines exposed. Yes, restraint is our defense and must be fortified! Reverend Daniels's offensive maneuvers will face grave challenges without the fortified walls of restraint.

Mr. Frisk, still staring deeply into the candle's hypnotic gleam, noticed its brightness dimming. The glow diminished to a small drop of iridescent blue before extinguishing into a tiny speck of red…and then…blackness.

Mr. Frisk, suddenly overcome by fatigue from the day's strained deviations, decided to retire for the evening. However, life's chores must take precedence over rest.

He flicked the kitchen light on and gathered the supper dishes from his hallowed shrine. He placed the dirty dishes in the sink and ran the hot water. He only used the highest quality soap for his personal china.

"Everyone should clean their own dishes," he thought to himself, "but it is imperative that they use the correct soap as the mediator between the water and the grease!"

With the kitchen satisfactorily in impeccable order, Mr. Frisk double checked the locks on the front door and then prepared for bed.

The Enemy

The bedtime ritual consisted of a celebration of sanctuary. "There is hardly any place on earth that is more peaceful that the security of the unconscious world while under warm blankets," said Mr. Frisk to the shadows, as he hung up his trousers and shirt.

The initial shock of the cold covers on his bare skin quickly faded into an oasis of warmth. The alarm clock did not have to be set, for it was always set in the morning, precisely it rang and accomplished its daily mission.

Mr. Frisk had always gotten up at 6:00 a.m. for as long as he could remember. It seemed an appropriate hour to begin his daily schedule. And why deviate from a system that is logical and pragmatic?

Sleep was a mystical world that refreshed the body, recharged drained energies, and revitalized the soul. Mr. Frisk felt the familiarity of sleep engulfing him. Sometimes, he fought against its captivity with a feeble attempt to prolong the enjoyment and fascination of being between the two worlds, but sleep is a mandatory temptation that eventually must be indulged.

Sleep opened its slumbering doors and received Mr. Frisk.

Somewhere in the darkness, Mr. Frisk consciously became aware that he was sleeping and attempted to awaken himself, but to no avail! He tried to muster the mental strength to pull himself from sleep's grasp, frantically swimming for consciousness as a submerged man swims for the surface of an inky-black sea. He dared not breathe the suffocating blackness as he swam. His burning lungs screamed for air. The surface seemed nonexistent. Some…thing…some force was holding him. He pooled all his psychological strength in a desperate attempt to burst free from the engulfing blackness. Spontaneously, his strangled lungs breathed in a blast of thick darkness as he shot up in bed, shaking and sweating!

He was in his bedroom. Was this a bad dream? The illuminated numbers on his alarm clock displayed 1:47 a.m. It was a dream—a nightmare!

"Robert Frisk."

"Aaaaahhh!" screamed Mr. Frisk. "Who is there? Who are you! State your name! What is your business here?"

"Your front door's locks were opened, so I thought I—"

"My door was locked. Don't lie to me! Do you think me a fool? Who are you? I demand an answer!"

"You really should invest in a better quality door lock," spoke the voice out of the dark room. "Mechanical ones are always fallible in one sense or another."

Mr. Frisk flicked on his reading lamp next to his bed and stared at the man seated near the door to his room, in the shadows. The man seemed of average height and build, as far as one can tell when assessing the physical appearance of a sitting man. He wore dark trousers and a leather sport coat. His clean-shaven face shone brightly, reflecting the lamplight.

"You mind if I smoke?" the man casually asked.

"Who in the hell are you," screamed Mr. Frisk, "and what are you after?"

The man struck a stick match across the wooden floor and lit his cigarette. He blew out the match and tossed it on the bed. "Just calm down and relax, Mr. Frisk. I am in control now."

"A common thief, are you? Well, you've chosen a poor residence to ransack; I can assure you that! I have absolutely nothing of value here. Look about you, for Christ's sake! Did you not notice the old, dingy furnishings? Why, the value of everything in this room alone would not equate to the work and bother required to steal it. Obviously, you have chosen a random mark, which, as it has turned out, will have little benefit to you!"

The man sat contently on his chair, smoking his cigarette, listening.

"Why do you not speak?" questioned Mr. Frisk. "Do you expect me to believe that you have broken into my residence to enjoy a comfortable smoke? Which, I abhor, by the way. I ask that you leave this instant. I demand you go! I will call the authorities and have you arrested!"

"Do you have any photographs?" calmly asked the man.

"Photographs? Photographs of what? I do not even own a camera. What is it? Do you think I am a spy or perhaps a blackmailer or some such foolishness? You've made a mistake of some sort. I have nothing of value. Nothing, I say!"

"I like photographs," said the man as he lifted his smoke to his lips, "especially old ones, you know, like of family or friends—that sort of thing. People seem to have a need to document their lineal existence in some fashion or another. Some write in diaries; some create scrapbooks. Some save boxes of memorabilia in their attics, but most find it convenient to save photographs."

"I demand you identify yourself and your intentions here!" bellowed Mr. Frisk.

"My intentions? My intentions! Yes, I have intentions," said the man as he inhaled a drag of smoke. He pursed his lips and exhaled a near-perfect smoke ring, followed by two others. The rings eerily drifted upward, bending and curving, distorting with the draft of the room and then dissipating into oblivion. "Did you ever see a perfect smoke ring, Mr. Frisk?" said the man as he stared at the point in space where the smoke ring had vanished.

"That is your intention—to make smoke rings in my presence? Are you mad? I fully intend to call the—"

"I am here to kill you, if you must know," said the man as he crushed out his cigarette with the heel of his black shoe, grinding the freshly extinguished mass into the hardened wood of the floor.

Mr. Frisk mentally recoiled from the blast of the blunt statement. "I have fine china in the kitchen. The set is worth over two thousand dollars. Take it and go."

"Dishes? Dishes?" The man laughed as he kicked the dead cigarette butt across the floor. "You barter your life with dishes? Tell me, does a quality soap come with those dishes?"

"An antique crystal candle holder is on the kitchen table. I have not had it appraised, but it is sure to have value. Take it and leave me. I implore you!"

"I find it interesting," reflected the man, "how quickly people have a change of heart. I suppose it's a natural reaction, when one realizes his situation or environment has changed. Why, just a minute ago, you were preaching to me of how nothing you owned had any value. However, after you realized that I am here to take your life, you miraculously remember items of value with which to barter. I wonder how long it will take for you to offer me the two thousand dollars in cash you have hidden under your bread box."

Mr. Frisk sat motionless.

"No," said the stranger, "I do not want your money or dishes. I have no desire for such trivial distractions. That seems to be the trouble with people. They are so distracted with things, schedules, knickknacks. Don't they realize they are going to die? Look at your sorry self. You live meagerly, while socking away money in various bank accounts, diversifying your hidden fortune for security's sake. You, a wealthy man, playing the public role of the miser!"

Mr. Frisk sat motionless.

"Cat got your tongue?" the man said and laughed. "Mind if I have another smoke?" He chuckled as he scratched the second stick match across the floor. He lit his cigarette and then flicked the lit match at Mr. Frisk. The match extinguished itself in midair before striking Mr. Frisk in the chest. "Look at you," continued the man, "you sorry bastard. You're a dead man. What was it all for? Your life, I mean. All your effort...for what? A cold can of pork and beans?" The man laughed hysterically.

Mr. Frisk glared at the man.

"It's sinking in, isn't it?" the man said with a grin. "Oh, I know the protocol quite well. First they are frightened; then they are defensive; then they barter; then, finally, they either soberly assess their situation, or they lunge at me in vengeance, at which point I am forced to end the deliberations quicker than I would like to. I am glad to see you are reflecting. I really enjoy this part. I mean, I really never know, for sure, what they are going to say. Some grovel and beg for their lives, as if it were worth anything. Some even cry! I suppose they are grieving for themselves a bit early, since they won't be present at the funeral. What are you going to do, Mr. Frisk? Nothing to say? No declarations?"

Mr. Frisk blankly stared at the smug stranger, as he contemplated his predicament. "Sir, I have nothing to declare to you or anyone else. I see no reason to. I have lived my life deliberately and honestly. I accomplished my work that was given me to the best of my abilities."

"And what was the fruit of your labor?" interrupted the stranger. "Living in a dunghill like this, while the bankers are getting rich off your deposits? Did it not occur to you to spend some of your hoard while you had the chance? Did it not occur to you that you could die tomorrow?"

"Yes," replied Mr. Frisk, "I have, indeed, thought about the future. The question I have contemplated is not 'what if I die tomorrow?' but 'what if I live tomorrow?' If I die, my journey is done; a dead man can have no regrets! But if I live, what then? Who will pave my road into old age if I do not plan and accrue the means while I have my health and am able? Will the physicians comfort my physical aches and pains that come from old age without payment?"

The stranger casually smoked his cigarette, listening, smiling.

"Why not put your faith in God?" said the man. "After all, He takes care of the birds of the air. They do not have to stow their wealth in barns or, in your case, banks. Where is your faith? You go to church every Sunday, just like an oiled clock, right on time, yet your faith resides in yourself. In fact, the reason you go to church is born out of stagnating tradition and your dependence on your almighty, mechanical schedule! You blandly sit in the congregation, next to the door, listening to the preacher's words, but the words are hollow and useless unless they are put into practice. You pretend to be a Christian, yet you are born of the devil! You crawl to your pitiful job every day and senselessly file certified letters because your boss has nothing important for you to do and is keeping you busy until retirement, and then they will eliminate your useless job. And then, after a mindless day at work, you come home and make love to a supper of scraps unfit for a dog. Then you retire to your crypt and welcome unconsciousness as a respite from your dreary existence. Why, you would be better off in hell!"

The stranger stood up and kicked the wooden chair over with such force that it shattered into splinters.

"I have faith in God," spoke Mr. Frisk in a solemn, reverent voice.

"Ha! You?" the stranger said and laughed. "Where is your compassion for your fellow man in which God resides? What have you done for people lately, for anyone? No, Mr. Frisk, you alienate yourself from society. You avoid interaction with anyone on a spiritual plane. You speak only business, facts, and figures. You depend on no one but yourself. You trust no one but yourself. You believe in no one but yourself. You worship no one but yourself!"

"I follow the scriptures," Mr. Frisk quietly said.

"Scriptures!" screamed the stranger, kicking the broken splinters of wood across the floor. "You follow the bible of Mr. Frisk! You have handwritten each page of your small, insignificant text. And each pitiful chapter repeats itself. You have been living in hell for years, and you are oblivious to the fact. Scriptures!" The man laughed. "You do not even know the difference between the book of Malachi and the book of Matthew. You worship your lousy job and praise your stale food scraps."

"'It is written,'" quoted Mr. Frisk, "'A man can do nothing better than to eat and drink and find satisfaction in his work. This...is from the hand of—'"

"Shut up!" yelled the stranger as he pulled a silver handgun from under his black sport coat and pointed the ominous barrel directly at Mr. Frisk. "Shut your damned mouth, you useless son of a bitch. You dare to quote the Bible to me? You stinking worm. Do you honestly think that the book of Ecclesiastes has any merit standing alone? You bank your illusionary salvation upon the words of some ancient, spoiled-rotten king, who spent his life pondering wisdom and then failed to listen to his own words? You sicken me! It's going to be a pleasure to blow you away and watch you die like the decaying vermin that you are."

Mr. Frisk stared at the revolver's barrel and the evil force behind its penetrating stare. "Armageddon," thought Mr. Frisk.

The stranger smiled. "To battle is of little consequence if you lose the war. Don't you agree, Mr. Frisk?"

"'The Lord is my shepherd,'" solemnly said Mr. Frisk, "I shall not be in want. He makes me lie down in green—"

Blam! The gun propelled its seething bullet through the right side of Mr. Frisk's abdomen. He buckled over, shocked with pain. He forced himself upright, staring at the smoking gun barrel and the smile behind it.

"Even though," struggled Mr. Frisk, "I walk through the valley of the shadow of death, I will fear no—"

Blam! Another stream of fire ripped through his left shoulder, knocking him backward against the blood-smeared headboard of his bed. He glanced at his torn shoulder and the red bone fragments protruding from the gash, staring with disbelief that it was actually a part of him. The pain seemed to drift into a sullen numbness. He pulled himself upright with his able arm, while grasping his thigh for support.

"You prepare…a table…before me…in the…presence…of my… enemies…You anoint—"

Blam! Another shot of stinging venom pierced his ear, ripping it to shreds, renewing the numbing pain to an unimaginable intensity.

"Surely…" whispered a struggling Mr. Frisk, "I will dwell…in the house…of…the—"

Blam! Blam! Blam! Blam! Blam! Blam! The gun fired, forcing six bullets through Mr. Frisk's now-bloody chest.

II

Benjamin

The alarm clock sprang to life at the stroke of 6:00 a.m., but no one was there to turn it off. Mr. Frisk lay dead on his bed, never to rise again. The buzz of his eternal alarm droned on.

Two weeks passed. At the post office, the backlog of work was attributed to Mrs. Gratchett's third vacation of the year. Thus, it wasn't until a neighbor, Mr. McFarland, noticed a foul smell in the building one day that anyone suspected something may be amiss. He had noticed it before, faintly, but it seemed to be growing in intensity, culminating in a reeking stench that was quite intolerable. The odd thing about it was that the whole building seemed filled with the rank odor at about the same intensity, so it was hard to pinpoint the location of the source. Mr. McFarland roused the other tenants and formed a makeshift detective team to prowl and inspect every nook of the entire building if need be.

Finally, by an organized process of searching, sniffing, and inquiring, the mob came to the door of apartment 7A. They rang the doorbell and knocked on the worn wood of the door, but no one answered. No one was sure who even lived there. A single man, they said, a "Mr. Frish" or "Fish," something like that, but that was really all they knew about him—a loner.

Mr. McFarland crouched on his hands and knees and stuck his nose close to the crack at the bottom of the door. He boldly inhaled and immediately started gasping and choking, while scrambling to his feet with his hands clasped over his mouth. His contorted face was a queer green hue that no one had ever seen before, at least on a person's complexion. McFarland, intent not to vomit in front of his neighbors, ran down the hall, out of sight.

The landlord was immediately informed of the situation pertaining to apartment 7A.

"Hmm, 7A, you say?" questioned the landlord. "Mr. Frisk's apartment. Strange…he is my best tenant. Been here for years. Never any trouble. Hardly hear a peep out of him. Always right on time with the payment." He glanced at the parking lot, upon the light blue Honda Civic. "No one answers the door, you say? Strange. He borrowed my car jack a week or so ago. He seemed a little on edge. Hmm…strange. I have a master key for his apartment."

"Well, we have to get in there," complained the tenant. "The stench is so goddamned bad it just about knocked old McFarland on his ass. I never saw a man turn so many shades of green! He looked like—"

"I'm calling the police!" interrupted the landlord. "They can formally investigate the matter. For all we know, he could be dead in there… probably is."

The tenants were grouped together like a flock of cackling chickens, abuzz with the flurry of the moment's excitement. The lead rooster, the recuperated Mr. McFarland, ushered two policemen to the door of 7A, explaining the situation in speculative detail. Sergeant Franks procedurally rapped on the bland door while simultaneously ringing the doorbell.

"Mr. Frisk?" he bellowed. "Mr. Frisk, open up. This is the police. Mr. Frisk, we have the key to your apartment and are coming in!"

Sergeant Franks opened the lock and turned the doorknob, but the door would not budge. "Inside locks!"

"Whoever went in there is still in there," stated Patrolman Davis while turning to the landlord. "Is there any other way to get into this apartment?"

"Maybe the windows," suggested Mr. McFarland, firmly establishing his authority as chief rooster in the investigation.

"We already tried," admitted a tenant. "We wanted to peek in, but the blinds are down, so we checked all the windows. They are all locked."

"Wood door," observed the sergeant. "We'll need a one-and-a-half-inch drill, pry bars, and the Sawzall."

"Got it," replied Patrolman Davis as he scurried off to the squad car.

"I will need explicit documentation of any damages," whispered the landlord to Sergeant Franks. "Feel free to demolish what you need to," he said, his voice rising to a confident forte. "I do not care what it costs! Whatever it takes to ensure the well-being of every tenant living under my supervision. My only concern is for Mr. Frisk. I only pray he is away, and the foul odor is that of spoiled cheese or some such thing! Safety and well-being take precedence over…"

Patrolman Davis returned with the tools. Sergeant Franks immediately began to operate on the door with the precision and skill of a seasoned surgeon.

"Drill!" he commanded.

"Drill," Davis repeated as he handed Franks the instrument.

Franks placed the inch-and-a-half auger about six inches above the doorknob and a foot toward the center of the door. The large drill bit slowly spun its way through the old wood, sharply shaving paper-thin curls as it bore. As the auger broke through the other side, a distinct whiff of pungent air mingled among the crowd of tenants as they whispered and speculated.

Sergeant Franks kneeled down and peered through the hole and then stood up.

"Sawzall!" he commanded.

"Sawzall," Davis repeated as he handed him the reciprocating saw.

Franks inserted the saw's blade into the hole and proceeded to cut an opening large enough for his arm. With the hole cut, he held his nose and peered into the vacant room. He then inserted the full length of his arm, feeling for the inside lock. "Two of 'em!" he stated.

"Two of what?" questioned the rooster.

The tenants shuffled and murmurs of "two something" echoed through the crowd.

"Got 'em both," stated Franks as he retracted his arm and turned the doorknob, pushing the door open just enough to briefly look in. A gust of rank air fell out and into the hall, scattering the onlookers toward any window or opening with fresh ventilation.

Sergeant Franks looked at Davis. "Stay here," he stated. "Don't let anyone beyond this point."

"See here," chirped the rooster, "we live here and have every right to—"

"No!" interrupted Franks, glaring at Mr. McFarland. "No one is to interfere with this investigation beyond this door! Is that clear?" Not expecting an answer, Franks placed a handkerchief over his mouth and nose and entered the eerie stench, closing the door behind him.

Patrolman Davis guarded the door like a Roman centurion, dedicated only to Sergeant Caesar. The crowd of spectators was growing as passersby noticed the red-and-blue flashing strobe of the patrol car, which Davis had flicked on when he'd retrieved the tools and which piqued their curiosity and desire to be a part of a live disaster of some sort—as long as it did not involve criminals with guns. Patrolman Davis always felt somewhat like a celebrity on these occasions. He was a relatively young man, who wished for more action. He dreamed that someday he could use his gun. He watched the spectators, with his ear close to the hole in the door and his hand on his holster, just in case.

Sergeant Franks scanned the living room, which was in perfect order. However, the shades and curtains were covering the windows, allowing minimal daylight to penetrate, giving the apartment a dismal ambience.

"Mr. Frisk! Police!" declared Franks as a precautionary measure.

A faint noise, hardly audible, seemed to emanate from the dreary dungeon. Franks, still holding the handkerchief with his left hand, drew his gun with the other. Slowly, he stepped across the hardwood floor and peered into the adjacent room, which turned out to be the kitchen. Again, everything seemed to be in order, except for a narrow glass decoration of some sort glistening in the middle of the table. It seemed out of place for some reason, even though it was standing perfectly in the center of the table.

The odd noise was almost imperceptible from the kitchen, yet, when Sergeant Franks held his breath, it was ever so slightly audible, heard only between the beats of his heart. He walked back into the living room and listened. Yes, it was slightly louder. It was not a constant sound, almost like breathing—raspy breathing!

Sergeant Franks shuttered and flicked the safety off on his .38 police special. "Better not take any chances," he thought to himself. Franks had nine months to go before retirement—thirty-five years with the force. He was looking forward to spending time with his two grandchildren. He felt an uncanny premonition of danger. He cautiously approached a closed door, presumably a bedroom or bathroom door, just off the living room. With his ear to the wood, he was positive that the intermittent, raspy breathing was coming from behind those walls. He listened breathlessly. There was movement, or at least noises that sounded like movement of some sort. Someone was in there. That was for sure. It was as if a person was moving about, unconcerned…yet, that shallow, raspy breathing!

Sergeant Franks's mind was flashing all sorts of imaginary scenarios as he flattened his back against the wall, next to the door. He stuffed the handkerchief into his pants pocket and gripped the handgun with both sweaty hands. He paused to catch his breath, while thinking of his wife, his garden, that trip out west they were planning. This was supposed to be a routine call. Why hadn't he accepted that desk job—dammit!

"OK, Franks," he thought to himself, "get that shit out of your head. Focus, goddamn it, focus!"

He took a deep breath and slowly exhaled while mouthing an inaudible prayer, mustering his stamina. He drew another long breath.

"This is the police. Open up!"

Crash! A startling noise, resembling breaking glass, instantly erupted from behind the door.

"They're making a run for it," screamed Franks. "Davis, get outside, by the window—now!" he yelled as he simultaneously burst open the door with his body.

A flash of moving gray!

Blam! Blam!

Patrolman Davis was scrambling through the crowd toward the door when the shots rang out. He was able to get out the front door before the panic-stricken tenants streamed out of every exit like stampeding cattle. The rooster hid in the utility closet.

Davis ran toward the general area where he thought the appropriate window might be. Both hands were on his revolver, and the safety was off. He sprinted around the corner and dropped to the dirt, on his belly, using the ground to steady his trembling aim at the row of windows before him, ready to blast anything at the slightest sign of movement.

Back inside, Franks had realized his mistake. "Rats! My God, rats!" he shouted.

He lowered his artillery as the last rat jumped off the bed and scurried out of sight. He quickly scanned the room. A dead man lay in the bed. A broken, intermittent raspy noise whispered from the tired alarm clock on the nightstand. Franks drew a deep breath, and holstered his firearm. He edged closer to get a look at the corpse. The grayish, rotting flesh on its face was half gnawed off! The nose was completely gone.

"Well, Mr. Frisk, how are you today?" spoke the sergeant under his breath.

There did not seem to be any sign of a struggle or foul play. Everything else in the room seemed to be in impeccable order. He sat down on a wooden chair by the door, temporarily collecting his composure, assessing the blunder of his gunfire, which he would have to explain to the chief.

He stood up and walked toward the bedroom window, intending to signal his rookie partner. He stopped in midstride as a rat darted out from under the bed and ran behind the window's curtain. He hated rats. Spiders…snakes…anything but rats! Even dead bodies did not seem to bother him. Lord knew he'd seen his share of mangled bodies in his day. Franks grabbed his portable two-way radio.

"Davis…Davis…Davis, you there?"

"Go ahead," Davis replied.

"All clear."

The Funeral

Detectives were called to the scene, and proper police procedure was observed. All evidence pointed toward a heart attack.

"Died in his sleep…lucky bastard," noted the aged detective.

The case was closed. The body was transported to the morgue. And the gawking tenants had a story to tell at social gatherings.

At police headquarters, Sergeant Franks was immediately promoted to a desk job by an unamused chief. His first duty was to notify the next of kin for the Frisk body, which was a relatively simple task to accomplish but difficult to administer. He hated to be the bearer of bad news.

"Damned rats!" he thought to himself.

A background check revealed one surviving relative: a son, Benjamin, living at 1067 Hillsdale Drive.

"Damn it!" swore Franks. He was hoping that the next of kin was in a different city or, better yet, a different state. It looked like he would have to do the dirty work in person—the sooner, the better. He jotted down the address.

The drive to Hillsdale was short—too short. Isn't that the way of it? When you look forward to an event of some sort, time drags all the slower with the increase of positive anticipation, and vice versa for unsavory events, such as being the jolly, lucky fellow to inform a person that his father is dead. "Oh, by the way, sir, your father's face was gnawed off by rats, since he died two weeks ago and no one even knew till his rotting carcass stunk up the whole damn building!" Sergeant Franks tried to divert his mind but to no avail. "Goddamn it," he cursed, "get ahold of yourself."

The house at 1067 Hillsdale was nothing fancy: white siding, brick trim, black shingles, small garage. It was about the same as the other homes on that block. The only noticeable difference was that it didn't have a fence around the yard like the others. A dark blue, four-wheel-drive pickup was parked in the driveway, indicating that the occupant was home.

Sergeant Franks reluctantly began his journey from the unmarked patrol car to the front door. His professional gait matched his gaze, just as he had mentally rehearsed during the drive over. Halfway to the door, his foot struck an object, and he tumbled to the ground. "Shit!" he spontaneously exclaimed. He scrambled to his feet, casting his eyes across the immediate vicinity, ensuring that no one had observed the ballet. He brushed himself off, noticing the brick that had interrupted his mission. There were some other bricks scattered about. Apparently, the brick trim on the house was under construction. He continued his journey, unaware of the deep brown smear on the side of his trousers.

Franks rang the doorbell while simultaneously rapping with his knuckles. Immediately the house erupted with howls, growls, and yelps. There was no need to knock again.

"C'mon in!" a muffled voice beckoned from within.

Franks cracked the door open enough to observe a set of paws and a wet, black canine nose greeting him with a snarl.

"C'mon in. She won't hurtchya. Barney, go lie down!"

Franks swung the door open, and the greeter ran a few feet off, barking viciously, tail wagging.

"Barney, go lie down!" a young man said firmly to the mongrel that resembled a beagle.

The young man was holding an apple core while chewing his last mouthful. He was of common height, about six foot, dark hair, no glasses—seemingly average. He wore older jeans and a dark burgundy T-shirt. He was covered in white stains from head to toe, even on his sneakers. And from the looks of the bare room, he had been attempting to drywall.

"Sorry, Officer," he said while wiping the apple juice from his chin and tossing the core into the trash can. "She didn't do any harm," he continued, "and besides, the darn cat was in *my* yard. Why, a beagle can't help its genetics. It's like an automatic force. She was just being a beagle and defending her turf. That cat's lucky it didn't get—"

"Your dog's name is Barney, and it's a she?" interrupted Sergeant Franks.

"Yep," smiled the young man. "And that cat's lucky it didn't get—"

"I'm sorry," interrupted Franks again. "I am not here due to a complaint about your dog."

"Oh? Oh! Ohhh..." observed the young man.

"My name is Sergeant Franks, and your name is?"

"Benjamin," replied the young man.

"Benjamin Robert Frisk?" asked Franks.

"That's right. What's up?"

"Your father is Robert Frisk?"

"Yeah."

"I'm sorry, but your father has died—an apparent heart attack. I'm sorry."

Benjamin stood silent with a pasty, waxy stare, like he was being mentally transported back in time, reflecting, revisiting old thoughts that balled themselves up in an instant. The impact seemed to melt his vibrant, concrete spirit into a puddle of liquid, without form.

"We found his body this morning," continued Sergeant Franks. "He was in his apartment, in bed. The coroner has to confirm the heart attack, but we are quite positive the death was from natural causes. We should know by tomorrow. Mr. Frisk? Mr. Frisk, perhaps you should sit down."

Benjamin sat down on an unopened pail of drywall mud, blankly staring toward Sergeant Franks, but yet looking past him, far off.

"The actual time of death was approximately two weeks ago."

"What? Two weeks? He's been dead for two weeks?" said Benjamin as he was thrust into ice-cold reality.

"The body was decomposing. The tenants in the apartment building complained about the odor. That's how we found him. We have positively identified the body with past dental records."

"Two weeks, and no one knew," whispered Benjamin. "I try to call once a month, just to touch base…two weeks!"

"The body is at the county morgue," said Franks. "You are the only living relative on record. Arrangements will have to be made."

"What? Oh! Yes, yes. What? How? A funeral?"

"I suggest," stated Franks, "that you contact a funeral service and any religious organization he was affiliated with. They will inform you of your options. There are also legal matters pertaining to the estate, which you will have to address, perhaps after the funeral. That's up to you. Are you all right? Is there anyone I can call?"

"No, no, thank you," said Benjamin, drifting back into a ghostly reflection.

Sergeant Franks grasped the pause to implement his exit strategy. "Well, I had better get back to the station. I'm truly sorry about your loss."

Benjamin was cleaning fish with his father and did not want to be disturbed.

"I'll just let myself out. Again, I'm truly sorry."

Sergeant Franks made his getaway. Stepping out of that house felt like he stepped out from under a mental winepress. The sun shone bright. The air tasted delicious. It was really a nice day. He hadn't noticed. He walked to his patrol car, carefully scanning the ground for bricks. It felt great to get back in the driver's seat as he shut the door. "Maybe I'll swing by McDonald's on the way back," he thought to himself as he drove off in a direction opposite the station.

Benjamin sat on his pail of white mud, resembling a replica of *The Thinker*. His father was dead. Dead! How strange life is, an amalgamation of joy and sorrow, health and sickness, leisure and work, ups and downs, all ending with an exclamation point...or a period.

Benjamin had been close to his father, yet in a way distant. After he'd graduated from high school, his parents divorced, which was probably for the best...or not. He wasn't sure. He wasn't sure about a lot back then. Seven years! Had it been that long? Life seemed so joyful between his parents while growing up. Once, during Christmas, his dad proved the existence of Santa Claus beyond a shadow of a doubt at a point in Benjamin's life when doubts were mounting. Benjamin was skeptical as his father placed the note on the kitchen table next to the full glass of milk, the huge home-made chocolate chip cookie, and the Polaroid camera. The note read: "Dear Santa, enjoy the homemade cookie and milk. I hope you like chocolate chip. Please take a picture of yourself with the camera if it's not too much trouble. Thank you." The next day, Christmas morning, Benjamin woke to an oasis of merrily wrapped gifts stacked under the glimmering, tinsel-clad tree. And on the kitchen table was a half-full glass of milk, cookie crumbs, and a photograph. And on that photograph was the kitchen table and the glass of milk, but the cookie was floating in midair—invisible!

Christmases were big in the Frisk home. Benjamin's parents seemed so jubilant. Of course, they always seemed happy, right up to the divorce, or at least his father did. There were secrets that he kept hidden inside, secrets that his father was unaware of while he was away at work.

Secrets in a marriage are like dribbling vinegar into a soup. The secret may be hidden, but the flavor of the marital soup is forever soured. Too many secrets or too large a secret makes the soup impossible to eat. How does one get vinegar out of a soup? It would be difficult if not impossible. Benjamin's father would have eaten the corrupted soup and worked hard to throw in new broth and solid, clean vegetables, eventually diluting the vinegar's sour effect. But there was no will in the heart of Benjamin's mother. She had tasted the bitter sour of the soup long before her husband noticed it, for it was her hand that fouled the recipe. For years, she smiled and drank the soup she smilingly fed her family, secretly dribbling in vinegar behind closed doors. She longed, in her heart, to throw out the foul soup that was increasingly becoming detestable. She hated the sour taste that languished after each spoonful. It made her stomach churn with despair. Sometimes she would vow to stop corrupting the soup. She truly wished she could stop. Her feeble attempts seemed futile. The timid battles always ended in defeat, always overpowered. She was tired with the conflict, tired of the raging war. She longed to surrender, to give up or to give in, to just throw the putrid marital soup out the window or leave her husband wallowing in it. Anything would be better that these constant battles that were always lost...in the end. Therefore, she was ripe for the seeds of infatuation, which sprouted and quickly took root on the fertile, shallow soil carefully cultivated by the enemy. This was the point when she left her family. Benjamin's father reluctantly agreed to the departure. By this time, he tasted the vomit-inducing vinegar in his soup and understood the need to allow his wife to ride into battle alone. It was hard to let her go, but go she did, and with no armor!

Benjamin's father dawdled on for some time, hopeful that she would see through the enemy's delicious, temporary spices, but it was not to be. She did hold her ground, but only briefly. The tempting spices were tantalizing, especially to one who was starved under a forced diet of boredom soup, laced with vinegar! She drank deeply from her shiny, new bowl, savoring the enticing, erotic flavor, which left her hungry for more.

Gorging herself drunk, she willingly allowed her crumbled walls to fall. Laughing and carefree as the walls crashed, she set torch to all bridges leading back.

The fires of divorce consumed Benjamin's known family. He attempted to make some sense of it all as he watched his father sift through the ashes, collecting any charred remains that could possibly be salvaged. Life was the same, yet somehow twisted, abnormal, and he and his father were the only ones in this warped world, something like Alice in Wonderland, everything was upside down or backward or sideways. Benjamin's father absorbed the role of cooking supper and keeping the house bearably clean. Benjamin began having longer, deeper discussions with his father, usually after supper or early in the evening. In a sense, his father was partially fulfilling the traditional role of the wife. The oddest part of the new social order was his mother's new role. She briefly lived in a rented house before moving in with Ned, or "deadhead Ned" as his father dubbed him. She had virtually no contact with his father, almost like their previous life had never existed. But he existed! How would he fit into her world, a world that was foreign to him? Would she want him to visit on birthdays and Christmas? How should he react to Ned? How could he react to Ned? If he did forge a workable relationship with the new couple, would it be breaking allegiance with his father? It was like his mom wasn't his mom anymore. Sure, physically it was the same person, but the person he'd grown up with had died in the fire of divorce. And now this new person expected him to continue their relationship like nothing had happened! In fact, it seemed like she wanted him to substitute Ned for his father and continue on. This was bizarre! All of this twisting and bending of identities and roles left his world scattered. What if his father found a girlfriend? What if the girlfriend had little kids? Then how would he fit in? His known family would be dead—yet alive…yet dead. He would be alone.

Divorce is a strange demon. It infiltrates lives and ransacks households, robbing people of the treasures they hold dearest. It consumes hearts and souls, choking joy with a fierce grin. Surely, this demon is feared by all people. Is it not true that if a neighbor or relatives are in trouble, everyone rushes in to help? If an intruder breaks into a house, the police can come to the rescue. If a home is on fire, the volunteer fire department rushes to snuff out the blaze. But when divorce creeps into a household, while the family is sleeping, and attacks with its bloody daggers, no one comes to help fight the fiend. When the alarm is sounded, people passively stand by and watch the gory murder.

"Oh well," they say, "these things happen…Pass the peas."

Then, after the murderous torturer has finally killed the created person that marriage has united and forged into one, there is silence, smothering silence. There will be no funeral, no social support for the surviving members. No formal grieving ceremony. No casket. No encouraging words by a preacher dressed in black. What there will be is avoidance. Neighbors will whisper to each other, but dare not speak a word of it to the survivor. The immediate family members, flirting with a tinge of guilt, feel obligated to address the issue and ease their consciences. Once the awkward deed is accomplished, the topic is shelved.

The opening lines are usually generic. "We were shocked. How did this happen? So sorry." Then the finale, "Oh well, these things happen. Life goes on…Pass the peas."

Barney whimpered an inquisitive bark, yanking Benjamin from his nostalgic stupor into the horrors of the present. Beagley eyes were staring into his, with a puzzled head cocked to one side.

"C'mon, girl," Benjamin coaxed while encouragingly patting his lap. The two embraced.

The funeral was a surreal affair. The few neighbors and work colleagues present played their splendid roles with great subtlety and solemnity, all cast in black. A distraught Reverend Daniels was the officiating minister over the proceedings.

"Friends and neighbors," the reverend began his sermon. "Today is a dark day indeed. The sun has been blotted by the shadow of death. Our brother, neighbor, and father, Robert Albert Frisk, has been taken from our presence. We will never see him in this world again, and we are saddened by his terminal departure. And thus, we grieve. We grieve of our loss. We grieve of the great chasm that separates us from a man we so dearly loved. But! We need not fear any discrepancies while contemplating where he has gone. For he is in a place that is so joyful and bright with heavenly love that our greatest day here on earth would seem but a black, grimy speck in comparison. Yes, the dark veil has been ripped from the soul of our dear Robert, and he now wears a robe of white, washed spotless with the blood of the Lamb."

The reverend strategically paused, closed his Bible, removed his reading glasses, and seemed to gaze directly into tranquility itself.

"Robert," he continued, "was a Christian. Many people go to a Christian church every Sunday, but I dare say they are far from being a Christian. But Robert was a true Christian, in the truest sense. He was right here, sitting in that seat right there—" he pointed to Mr. Frisk's seat "—every single Sunday for as far back as my memory recalls. He listened reverently to the word. But not with idleness did he listen. He did better than just listen. Robert heard!"

The reverend paused.

"Yes, Robert heard!" bellowed the reverend while slamming his fist down on the wooden pulpit. "He listened, and he heard the word just as surely as if God Himself were speaking to his soul. You might be wondering how I know this. How can I be sure Robert heard the message? Well, I'll tell you. I know because Robert told me so himself. In fact, the very night he died, I visited Robert at his home, possibly hours before his death. And we talked. We talked about church and what it means to be a Christian—an active Christian, active in duty, active in spirit. We talked of the demonic force of passiveness that corrupts our congregations and robs our bright, spiritual flame of its brilliance, eventually dimming its gleam and eventually snuffing it out to a smoldering, decrepit wick. Our brother Robert was contemplating an active role in this very church, in this very congregation. He felt a need, a compulsion to forge ahead in the battle for good, to forge ahead in the battle for honesty, to forge ahead in the battle for truth, to forge ahead in the battle for love—to forge ahead in the battle for God!"

The reverend paused.

"Yes, Robert knew of the battles—the battles that we all face. And now, our soldier is gone. The mysteries and wonders of God that work together toward ultimate good have taken our brother from our midst. But we remain. We remain to carry on the fight, the struggle—the war! We must not—we *will* not allow the work of our comrade, now fallen asleep, to go unfinished. Let Robert's death not be an end, but a beginning—a beginning for an active commitment for the work of the Lord, a beginning to unite and push onward!"

The reverend paused.

"There is a time for everything under heaven. And may you all be called for a time of action! Just as there is a time for action, there is a time for sorrow, a time for grieving. Today, we grieve. But let us make no mistake. We grieve today for ourselves and *our* loss. Do not grieve for Robert! Robert, as sure as I am standing in this pulpit, now stands in the glories of heaven, basking in a reverent joy that is beyond all human comprehension. All tears are eternally wiped from his eyes. For he is with God Himself! Amen.

"Now, may the peace of God, which surpasses all understanding, keep your hearts and mind with Christ Jesus unto life everlasting. Amen. Please turn to hymn number 658, and together we will sing 'Onward, Christian Soldiers.' Immediately afterward, we will walk directly behind the church and have a short committal prayer at the gravesite. Any monetary memorials may be donated to this parish by request of Robert's son, Benjamin. God bless you all."

The reverend continued standing as organ music erupted from the balcony, forecasting the melody of the song. Reverend Daniels led the small choir of mourners by fervently belting out each musical syllable directly into the pulpit's microphone. The words he sang were correct but so far off key that the meager choir had difficulty following the lyrics. Benjamin plowed through the hymn as best he could. The others chimed in on the chorus, but for the most part lip-synced the rest.

The casket was rolled outside the church and across the paved parking lot, where it was transferred onto what resembled a miniature, motorized wagon. The funeral director started the sputtering gasoline engine and guided the rickety craft toward the far end of the cemetery, where the hill gently slopped downward. There, the casket was slid over the perfectly rectangular hole onto a lowering device. The band of mourners shuffled around the hole as Reverend Daniels began his grand finale.

"Ashes to ashes, dust to dust." The reverend paused. "Glad it was him and not the hell us!"

Snickers of suppressed laughter drifted among the small crowd. Reverend Daniels broke out in a roar of laughter as he kicked the mechanism that was suspending the casket over the hole. As a result, the casket, as well as the mechanism, fell headlong into the grave with a crash, landing with the casket almost standing upright. The group of mourners could not hold it in any longer; they exploded with an all-consuming laughter that left them buckled over holding their stomachs while tears streamed down their cheeks. Benjamin was appalled. He stood in shock, stunned, frozen, unable to speak, unable to move, transfixed with the bizarre proceedings. The reverend, doubled over with laughter, attempted to regain his composure as he lifted his robe, unzipped his trousers, and began urinating in the hole. At the sight of this, the group roared all the louder. Some fell on the ground, frenzied with laughter, hardly able to breathe.

"Take that," the reverend jubilantly exclaimed between fits of suppressed chuckles.

Benjamin used all the strength he could muster to break free of the mental restraint that held him as captive—as a statue. "Stop it!" he yelled. "What the hell are you people doing? Have you lost your minds? This is a funeral, for God's sake!"

The roar of the crowd diminished. Revered Daniels zipped up his pants while coldly staring into Benjamin's eyes. All eyes were fastened on Benjamin. The tears of merriment that once streamed out of those eyes turned to glares of hate.

"Benjamin," Reverend Daniels calmly spoke, "you must forgive us, for we know not what we do. But we try; we really do try. However, I am not wholeheartedly sure that we can forgive you. You have interrupted this solemn service and purposely broke the sanctity of this holy ritual. And, I, for one, will not stand for your miserable lack of tolerance!" Turning to the group, the reverend lifted both hands in the air and asked, "Shall we punish this belligerent devil who dares condemn our services? Or shall we sit passively and do nothing? Should we bury our heads in the sand and allow him his leave?"

"Kill him," someone in the crowd shouted.

"You order death?" asked the reverend.

"Kill him!" they chanted. "Kill him!"

"Well, then," stated the reverend, "it is settled. The people cry for death. The grave cries for a body. Even the stones cry for death, and by stones shall the villain die!" The reverend turned and faced Benjamin; looking sinisterly into his eyes and slowly raising a pointed finger, he shouted, "Stone him!"

The men instantly pulled stones as big as their fists out from their pockets. The women dumped the contents of their purses on the ground—all stones. They greedily grabbed stones with both hands. They looked at Benjamin with palled faces fused with lust, as if under a spell. They inched toward him. Benjamin turned to run, but lost his footing and had somehow fallen into the grave! The metal casket was cold on his face. He looked up and saw the blank faces of his executioners smiling into the hole while a shovelful of black dirt fell on his face, into his eyes, and down his mouth onto his tongue. He spit and gasped as another shovelful fell about his neck. He struggled with all his inner strength, but he could not break free from the darkness that held him prisoner.

Another shovelful of blackness covered his eyes and face. He couldn't breathe. He couldn't move, surrounded with the cool weight of the smothering earth. Life was ebbing away. Fear and panic struck deep into Benjamin's heart. With a final explosion of inner strength, he thrust through the black, his lungs silently screaming for air. Suddenly a great weight fell on his stomach. He jolted his body upright while drinking in a breath of life.

"Barney!"

Upon hearing her name, Barney jumped off Benjamin's stomach and onto his chest, frantically licking and nuzzling his face.

"Barney, cool it! I'm OK."

Benjamin flicked on the light next to the sofa where he had fallen asleep. It had been two weeks since his father's funeral. He thought he was over the initial shock, and he had been, until tonight. "Damned nightmare," he muttered. "So damn real!" Benjamin shuddered as the reality of illusion and life took leave of their merger.

III

Cindy

The dusky morning appeared with a new luster, sparkling and fresh as the reddish-blue horizon gave way to a commanding orange sun slowly rising to its glory in a cloudless sky. It was spring, and the flavor of spring was thick, like honey. Benjamin opened the front door and sat down on a pail of drywall mud. The sharpness of the morning air mingled with his senses as he mulled over a hot cup of coffee. Birds were chirping to their mates as they invisibly fluttered about singing a symphony of love. A squirrel chattered a playful harmony, at which Barney tore out the door like a bullet, yelping at high speed. Benjamin smiled at the antics of man's best friend. How odd it is, he thought, for animals. What do they think? Barney was now merrily barking in a furious tone at the base of the old maple tree near the driveway, while staring up into its branches. Why do beagles chase squirrels, or rabbits for that matter? They are bred for such things; that's true, but it still makes little sense. It is almost impossible for a beagle to catch either a squirrel or a rabbit. And they bark while chasing their prey, allowing the hunted to know exactly where the hunter is! It must be genetics. They are just programmed through slight variations in their genetic code through various generations of breeding. It would seem that if a beagle was placed in the wild, in a forest, genetics would demand that he chase a rabbit or some such varmint, barking at the top of his lungs until exhaustion. Then he would limp off and eventually die of starvation. His genetics is his guide, but his guide is a false prophet. How much are we humans controlled by genetics? How many squirrels do we foolishly spend our lives chasing up trees? Do we follow an order, or are we ordered to follow?

"Excuse me!" erupted a far-off voice from outside, near the roadway, startling Benjamin out of meditation. "Excuse me!" repeated the voice, which seemed to emanate a tone of sharp directness.

A young woman was now marching toward the open front door in abrupt military fashion. Her short blond hair bounced with each stride, as one hand clasped the front opening of her long, light blue bathrobe, firmly holding it tight to her slender body, giving some indication of the curves that lay shrouded. Her other hand firmly held a rolled-up news-paper. Benjamin sipped his coffee as the puzzling spectacle made her approach to his front door. He wondered if approaching a dog owner's house with bare feet was the wisest of choices.

"Excuse me!" the woman reiterated as she glared.

"Good morning," courteously replied Benjamin, remaining seated on the throne to his palace. "It's not mine."

"It's not?" she said, taken aback with hesitation.

"Nope! I don't even subscribe," said Benjamin. "I usually just catch the news on the radio, driving in to work."

The woman's face reddened with a hue about the same color as the morning sunrise, but not as friendly. She clenched her hand, squeezing wrinkles into the rolled-up newspaper as her glare increased to an inten-sity of lasers.

"Is that your dog?" she growled.

Barney had been actively initiating her method of squirrel hunting, which required constantly barking at the base of the maple tree in an attempt to wear down the varmint.

"What dog?" asked Benjamin while enjoying a sip of coffee.

"You know damned well what dog! I've been living here for two weeks, and every morning at the butt crack of dawn, when most intel-ligent human beings with any sense at all are sleeping, your dorky dog is outside barking at the top of his lungs, waking up the entire neighbor-hood. And I am sick of it! Do you hear me? Sick of it! Some people work midnights. Did that ever occur to you? That some of your neighbors may get home from work in the morning and go to bed and *try* to get some sleep? No, of course that didn't occur to you! You are too busy banging your hammer or running the noisiest tools you can find. And if that isn't enough inconsideration, you allow your mangy mutt to bark uncontrollably like a spastic, every morning while you sit on your ass drinking coffee!"

Benjamin was amazed at the flare and sheer agility of the young woman. Her singlehanded gestures were artfully executed, slicing the air with the newspaper as if it were a machete to accentuate each climactic syllable. Her other hand masterfully held the blue robe secure. Her short little feet mimicked a slight kick with every swing of the newspaper baton. Her voice seemed to raise in accordance to the height the newspaper was swung. She almost resembled a wild conductor of an orchestra while performing *Flight of the Bumblebee*. Benjamin slurped a short sip while reflectively pondering the amazing performance.

Barney had heard the commotion at the front door building to a crescendo that eventually trumped the genetic force that held her centurion at the tree trunk, and she barreled toward the blue fuzzy squirrel standing at the open threshold of the front door.

"If you do not keep that fleabag under control," she thundered, "and keep its yapper shut, I am going to strangle—Aaahh!"

Barney had clenched her teeth onto the blue squirrel's fur and was fiercely growling while pulling backward with all her might. Upon the initial tug, the robe's front opened, exposing female parts that are usually hidden. The woman immediately dropped the newspaper while simultaneously grasping the widening opening in the front of her robe with both hands, all while screeching at the top of her lungs and performing a mystifying dance with an intensity that was electrifying and a dash erotic.

"Do something!" she yelled as the tug-of-war proceeded with great effort on both sides.

Benjamin looked serenely into his coffee cup and said with deep sincerity, "Ma'am, you'll have to quiet down. You'll wake the neighbors."

Her face was now a deeper shade of red, almost like that of a fiery beet. Her eyes boiled out a penetration of pure hate as she yanked the tail of her majesty's train with a fierceness that sent Barney sailing into the house, sliding across the floor and tumbling into some empty drywall mud buckets, sending them scattering like bowling pins.

Her silent, glassy glare was sinister as she gathered her robe about her, turned sharply, and walked majestically, chin up, out the door, slamming it with a force that shuddered the shingles. Benjamin immediately arose from his throne and peered out the small window on the front door. Her majesty was leaving the palace grounds with great determined strides, when she suddenly stopped cold and looked down under her bare foot. Benjamin sipped his coffee and pondered the situation for not more than a fraction of a second. He then opened the front door wide, looked at Barney, and coaxed, "Squirrel!" pointing wildly out into the yard. Hearing the familiar word automatically triggered the beagle into a hysterical ball of barking canine fur as she rocketed through the doorway, making aim directly toward the blue squirrel. Benjamin slurped the last of his coffee as he observed the squirrel make a mad dash toward her nest. She was a fast runner—good form, nice legs. The consistent screeching was a bit annoying, but it let Barney know that the chase was going well. The noisy, high-speed parade disappeared out of the yard and down the roadway. Benjamin whistled a piercing, high pitch. The barking immediately stopped, and shortly thereafter, Barney appeared, merrily trotting toward home, wagging her tail in triumph, dragging a ragged strip of blue fur as a trophy. "Good girl," Benjamin said as he grabbed one end of the tattered cloth when Barney crossed the threshold, encouraging a lively game of tug-of-war, sending more empty drywall buckets rolling across the floor. Benjamin laughed.

Work

Benjamin poured another cup of coffee while Barney chewed on her prize. Ben retrieved four slices of bread from the bread box and slathered on some butter and a plop of mustard on two slices, flapping a medium-thick slice of bologna on the yellow paste. He pressed the two bare slices on top of the meat, squeezing yellow drips around the fringes. Both sandwiches he wrapped into a ball of cellophane with an edible center and tossed it into his black, beat-up lunch pail along with a candy bar and a bag of chips. Glancing at his watch, Benjamin chugged down his coffee, grabbed his pail, and headed out to meet the rest of the day.

The blue sky shone bright on the drive to the docks. The weather man on the radio forecast increasing temperatures all week. Benjamin had a fleeting inspiration to resume the brick work he'd abandoned last summer, but quickly replaced the notion, remembering that he had an appointment with Brian Peters, the attorney who was handling the transfer of his father's estate. It seemed such a bother. Such a beautiful day! It seemed a shame to waste any portion of it.

The old, blue pickup rambled down the familiar road, finding its way to the employees' parking lot next to the loading dock. Most of the vehicles and everything else was coated with a reddish hue, stained from the red dust created from the transfer of tons of taconite pellets from the huge stockpiles on the docks into the cargo holds of freighters, filling their hollow bellies with iron ore destined for some distant steel mill. It was a good job, with good pay. All the unionized jobs on the dock were good pay.

Benjamin grabbed his pail and shuffled across the parking lot and into the lunchroom with the rest of the men on his shift. He slid his dingy pail in the center of the long lunch table, adding to the collection of dingy lunch pails that'd come before him. The other men were sitting around the table on hard wooden benches. Some were reading crumpled newspapers. Most were sipping coffee. The lunchroom chat was usually the same. The topic was normally work related, unless there happened to be a current event that deemed itself worthy of mention. Most of the chat amounted to nothing more than bitching about the way the company ran things or perhaps the way the government ran things, especially those goddamned Republicans! Today, however, was solemn as everyone awaited the foreman's cheery arrival with the day's work orders, while each man mulled over thoughts of the past weekend or thoughts of the coming weekend five long days away.

Benjamin, as well as the other men in the lunchroom, strictly worked the day shift, Monday through Friday, unlike the majority of the employees who worked a shift rotation seven days a week. They were the cleanup crew. The tools of their trade consisted of an arsenal of shiny hand shovels and a fleet of bent-up wheelbarrows. When taconite pellets are transferred from one conveyor belt to another, the marble-sized round pellets love to hop off the carnival ride and dance across the floor, congregating into piles of work for the manual laborer. If everything runs smoothly, each man on the cleanup crew gets assigned a specific area to take care of. And without too much sweat, they can keep their specific areas clean. Of course, the men with the highest seniority in the union chose the easiest jobs. Most had the same jobs every day. Each man was keenly aware of the "better" jobs in the hierarchy. Benjamin was the lowest on the totem pole, being the "new kid" at the facility. This was his third year.

The foreman skipped into the lunchroom whistling the chorus of "Jingle Bells."

"Mornin', men!" he said.

"What's so gaddamn good about it?" a worker proclaimed.

"Oh, c'mon. It's a beautiful day. Spring is in the air. And the weather report says summertime's a-comin'! I trust you fellas had a good, rested weekend."

"Mine wasn't worth a fiddler's fuck in hell," responded Jerry Winters, who was usually the self-proclaimed spokesman for the group. "The old lady got the kid to join band in school, and now he's honkin' on the gaddamn, fuckin' horn every fuckin' day and fuckin' night. It's about enough to drive a fuckin' person fuckin' crazy!"

"Gee, Jerry," the foreman said with a smile, "I would think that a worldly scholar such as yourself would enjoy some fine, formal music."

"I'm ready to stick that horn up his ass. Or, better yet, the old lady's ass!"

The other men kept their eyes on their crumpled newspapers, casually sipping their individual cups of ambition.

"Well, I'm glad you brought up the subject of music today," the foreman said with a grin, "because, to start off the week, we're going to need a couple of volunteers to put on a little concert down in T-2 tunnel, underneath pocket number fifty-nine. There is only room enough for two men. So who wants to grab their banjos and head down there?"

"What the hell happened in T-2 tunnel?" Jerry asked.

"The steel plate on the back of fifty-nine pocket rusted through enough to allow the taconite pellets to trickle out, and they've been trickling all weekend. The millwrights caught it Sunday night and plugged the hole, but there is a pile eight feet high."

"Those stupid motherfuckers!" Jerry stammered. "I reported that rusty gaddam plate two fuckin' weeks ago. Tell those fuckin' millwrights to clean up the fuckin' shit. They're the ones who shoulda fixed it two weeks ago. Them cocksuckers don't do a fuckin' thing but sit around with their finger up their ass, and you, gaddam foremen, don't say a gaddam thing. Well, I sure as fuck ain't going down there. They can just kiss my ass!"

"Well, regardless of all that," said the foreman, "we have to get that mess cleaned up before quittin' time. We have a boat scheduled to load out of that tunnel at five thirty. Gotta get her clean enough to run."

The lunchroom was as quiet as a morgue, except for muffled slurps and an occasional cough.

"No takers?" the foreman questioned. "Now why doesn't that surprise me? Mark and Ben! Looks like it's you two again. I can give you guys a lift to the tunnel. The banjos are already down there. Everything has to be shoveled off the floor and onto the conveyor belt. I'll get you a walkie-talkie so you can call the control room to jog the belt ahead once you get her loaded up. From the looks of the pile, you'll have to jog her quite a few times."

"That gaddam conveyor belt is five feet off the ground!" Jerry piped. "You really expect two guys to shovel iron-ore pellets five feet in the air all gaddam day? Their ass'll be draggin' after two hours!"

"Hey," said the foreman, "we can only do what we can do, and the whistle blows at five o'clock. The rest of you can go to your areas. You know what to do. Well, that's it. Everyone have a safe week. I don't want to be filling out any accident reports on you clowns." Turning to Benjamin, he said, "I'll grab a walkie-talkie from the office. Be back in a second to give you guys a ride down."

Not more than a moment after the door closed after the foreman left, the room erupted in a vociferous, declarative assessment of the orders for the day.

"Stupid assholes!" said one man. "Shoulda had that fixed last year already. The goddamned thing was bad last summer."

"They don't give a shit," chimed in another man. "All they do is play solitaire on their damn computers all day."

"I wouldn't even go down there if I were you guys," stated a high-seniority man to Benjamin.

"They better go down there," said another, "or they will get their ass fired."

"Well, no shit, dumb ass," replied the first man. "What I mean is, go down there, but don't bust your ass. Take a shovelful or two; then take a break. Take another shovelful; then take a break. They can't do nothin' to you just as long as you're on the job working, so just work dead slow."

"They shoulda fixed that last year," said another. "Just like that big spill under T-3 last month. Any asshole with any sense could've prevented that goddamned mess. But no, they're too busy worrying about their own ass instead of putting some money into this place to keep it running half-assed efficiently. That spill alone must've cost this company five thousand dollars in lost production." He turned to Mark and Benjamin. "You guys busted your ass on that spill, and what did you get? Nothing but an 'atta boy,' just like an old, stinkin' hound dog after running forty miles of circles through the snow chasing a rabbit for his master—a master that sits on his ass all day! Hey, I give you guys credit. But you shouldn't be busting your ass. Pretty soon they will expect all of us to bust our ass. Then we'll be doing that kind of shit every day. The quicker you guys clean up the mess, the less incentive they have to fix the problem before there is a problem."

"You got that gaddam right!" agreed Jerry. "You guys get that pile cleaned up before five o'clock, and I guarantee you another mess in less than two weeks. Them bastards only know money! You guys just take your time down there and make sure they can't run that conveyor at five o'clock; that way, that ship can't be loaded, and the shipping company will fine this Mickey Mouse outfit a bundle for the delay. That'll make 'em get their shit together!"

A solemn hush immediately crushed the conversation as the fore-man entered the room with the walkie-talkie. Everyone gradually rose, placing their fluorescent orange hard hats on their heads.

"Let's go, fellas. We're burnin' daylight," commanded the foreman to the workers as Benjamin and Mark left with him out the door.

No sooner than the door closed, someone said, "Them dumb fucks are goin' to bust their ass. Just wait and see."

"They're fucked," stated Jerry.

The foreman dropped Mark and Benjamin off at the entrance to the long concrete tunnel that burrowed underneath mountainous stockpiles of taconite pellets. Fluorescent lights gleamed over a thin film of water covering the concrete floor as the two men sloshed their way to pocket number fifty-nine.

"Holy shit," Mark exclaimed, "look at the size of that spill! It's right up to the roof. I don't know about you, but I sure as hell don't feel like doing a damn thing today. Went to a concert over the weekend. Man, did we get fucked up. I was doin' OK till someone broke out the Beam. The rest was a cloudy haze. Woke up at my girlfriend's apartment. Man, was I wasted! Great time, though." For a few seconds, he was nostalgically reliving some of the finer moments of his weekend, savoring the memory of true freedom that was ushered in by the removal of all inhibitions or restraint, via alcohol. However, the mental illusion quickly dissolved as the reality of the black mountain firmly established itself directly between him and quitting time. "How in the hell are we going to get all this shit shoveled up by five? No goddamned way!"

"Well," said Benjamin, "looks like we're the chosen ones. And those iron-ore pellets aren't going to jump on that conveyor by themselves. I think if we start shoveling on the walkway on each side of the conveyor, most of the high material will slide down in the front of the pocket, where it's the easiest shoveling. How about I go on the other side and you take this side? That way we won't be tripping over each other."

"Whatever blows your hair back," replied Mark as he lit a cigarette.

Benjamin began scraping the marble-sized balls off the walkway and into the mountain's base, creating a safe shoveling area free of the devious ball bearing–like pellets that can get under the soles of a person's work boots, instantly transforming them into roller skates. He then slid the blade of his shovel along the concrete and into the mountain, retrieving the first fruits of his labor. The shovelful was heaved five feet up while pellets rained off the shovel blade like hail until the load was discharged into the deep-trough conveyor, where the impact scattered the marbles, leaving them rolling every which way. The first shovelful was to be repeated for the rest of the day. Millions of shovelfuls, each carrying but a fraction of the mountain, would gradually foster progress.

Although Benjamin did not really recognize it, he knew the recipe for moving mountains. The foundation of the endeavor rested on attitude, planning, and action—all fused together with balance. Balance was the key—the glue that bound everything together and fostered a feasible progression toward the ultimate goal. He knew that working too fast would only cause rapid fatigue, undermining his capabilities. No, working fast to move a mountain is foolhardy. Steady! That is the trick—steady, like a marathon runner. He would develop a pace that was achievable and maintain the progression. Careful attention must guard the attitude from the attack of outside as well as inside influences. Because if the attitude is hindered or corrupted, it may corrode the action, which inhibits progress, further diminishing the attitude, causing a negative, repetitive cycle that would spiral downward toward heart-hardening failure.

Benjamin established a shoveling pace that was tentatively acceptable and settled into a comfortable routine. Shove. Lift. Dump. Repeat! Shove. Lift. Dump. Repeat! Familiar beads of perspiration slid down the side of his face, collecting into one large, salty drop that dangled on his chin. Shoveling was hard work, but also liberating in a way. Benjamin found that his mind would wander and wonder about all sorts of life's mysteries. His mind was already delving into the abstraction of society and how the laborer's place in the puzzle interlocked with the other parts. Laborers, he thought, were an essential, foundational element for any society. Work—that's what has to be done! The work! Managers, superintendents, foremen—whatever the title—are people who organize the work, but without the work itself actually being performed, their occupations are as useless as being a king of an empty prison in a desert, in which the king would have to perform some sort of work to feed himself, or die. Work itself is an interesting entity. What are its origins? Why couldn't all people live in a warm climate and live off a utopia of wild berries, fruits, nuts, or anything that could be harvested, compliments of Mother Nature? People would not need clothes, shelter, or food. All would be provided for. Work would be obsolete! When one felt hungry, one could just pick a grape or avocado. Of course, the act of picking the avocado could be considered work. Then the person who actually did the work of picking the avocado would claim ownership of it because he or she was the one who went through the trouble of picking it. And what if someone would take that avocado away after he or she did the work of picking it? It would seem that the picked, but uneaten, avocado could be considered as wealth. And taking a person's wealth without doing any of the work, or at least paying for it, is a great wrong, because the ownership of the item lies with the person who performed the work. Therefore, it would seem that ownership is a fine thing indeed, as long as the owner performed the work, at least at some point in his or her ancestry. Anything else, be it exploitation of goods or even the conquering of nations, would seem to be on the same level as stealing. That seems to be a motivating force in modern society—to find ways of acquiring wealth without actually performing the labor. No matter how you slice it, it's a form of stealing—or exploitation, which is really stealing in a sense. Suppose Eve hadn't chosen the forbidden fruit. Would human beings just lounge around in utopia with no need to farm, no need to fish, no need to do anything? What would people do? Surely not shovel taconite pellets!

"Ben...Hey, Ben!"

"Huh? What?" said Benjamin as he was yanked out of his musings.

"This sucks," said Mark as he opened a round can of chew. He pinched a wad of the black tobacco with his thumb and index finger. It looked like coffee grounds. He packed the wad between his bottom lip and his gums, causing a deformed bulge. "We'll never get this done today."

"Oh well," replied Benjamin, "we can just chip away at her a little at a time." He began shoveling again.

"Hey!"

"What?" answered Benjamin again, stopping the noisy operation so he could hear his colleague.

"You ever ask Beth for a date yet?"

"No, she's not my type. Besides, she's with Jeff," stated Benjamin.

"Who gives a shit about Jeff?" Mark said and laughed. "He's a damn wimp. You could take him."

"It isn't right to hone in on a girl if she's committed to another guy," Benjamin declared. "It just isn't."

"Chicken ass!" Mark said and smiled as he spit an amber-brown stream of tobacco juice that hit the floor with a splat, then wiped his mouth on the cuff of his sleeve.

Benjamin resumed shoveling.

"Hey," said Mark, "how's your truck running? Is that an automatic or a stick?"

"Stick," replied Benjamin while continuing to shovel.

"I like sticks, too, better on gas," said Mark. "But Nancy hates 'em; that's why I got an automatic, for her ass." Mark leaned on his shovel, watching Benjamin work. He then looked at the black mountain to his side, blocking the rays of a fluorescent light, casting its shadow of gloom. "You think we should go find some portable lights to brighten it up down here? Ben? Ben!"

"What now?" said Benjamin between strokes.

"I'm going to walk up to the shop and see if I can find an extension cord with a light. It's too damn dark on this side. You need one for your side?"

"No," replied Benjamin with a grunt as he heaved another shovelful, adding to the growing pile on the conveyor belt. "It's bright enough on my side." Benjamin could hear Mark's fading footsteps echoing away as he sloshed out of the dark tunnel. Benjamin slightly increased the pace of his shoveling.

Benjamin had thrice loaded the conveyor belt to capacity and radioed the control room to start the belt in order to clear it off, when Mark came back with the light. The time was 11:21.

"Holy crap!" exclaimed Mark. "You're damn near done with that side. I might as well set the light up over by you, and we can finish that side together since it's almost lunchtime. I would've been back sooner, but Bill wanted me to give him a hand in the storeroom."

"Foreman give you a ride?" asked Benjamin.

"No. Hell, it's not that far. I just hoofed it." Mark climbed over the belt and plugged in the extension cord, dangling the bare lightbulb over a suspended length of electrical conduit. "We should be able to get this side cleaned up before lunch," he said as he dug his shovel into the small hill of marbles.

The two men finally scraped the last of the mountain into a pitiful pile and scooped it away. They moved the operation to the remaining mountain on the other side before heading to the shop for lunch. Mark spiritedly led the way, while Benjamin lagged on after him. Outside the tunnel, the foreman was waiting for them in the company pickup. "How'd ya's do down there?" he asked.

"Not bad," Mark immediately replied. "We got the south side done, and we just moved over to the north. I think we got the worst of it."

"Good, good," said the foreman. "If we don't get that shit cleaned up by quittin' time, them assholes in the main office'll have a shit fit. The good news is that the boat may be delayed a bit when docking. They called in, said they have bow-thruster problems, have to come in slow. That'll buy us a few minutes. I hope you know that you guys'll have to stay over if it's not finished at the end of the day. Well, here we are. Pick yous up at twelve thirty."

The lunchroom was as quiet as a church. The workers were turning the crumpled pages of newspapers, slurping coffee, and chomping on whatever was in their pails. The room smelled of coffee and sweat. Benjamin and Mark found a vacant spot to sit on the oak plank and dug into lunch.

The solemnity was broken only once when a worker asked, "How far'd yous guys git down in T-2?"

The crumpled papers stopped shuffling. After a pause, Benjamin finally spoke. "Not that bad down there. We should be able to finish it," he said between mouthfuls of bologna sandwich. The papers resumed their usual shuffle, but a bit louder than normal.

At 12:24 the foreman bounced in. "You two banjo pickers ready for a grand finale?" he said with a smile.

Mark and Benjamin closed their pails as they scarfed the last remnants of their feast and followed the foreman to his pickup. The back
tires flung a shower of gravel as they sped toward T-2. "You guys did
a good job down there," the foreman said. "I went down there during
break. Hell, you're over half done. Should be no problem at all finishing
before quittin' time." Mark had the passenger door partially open before
the pickup came to a complete stop at the entrance to T-2. "I'll be back
to check on you birds, see how your comin'," said the foreman as he
spun off, showering the men with gravel and a choking cloud of dust.

The two sloshed their way back to the remaining mountain, where
the bare lightbulb hung near the summit, like a lighthouse beacon.

"This sucks!" said Mark as he pulled his round can out of his front
pocket. "I would've called in sick if I had known I was gonna do this shit
all day. And now, old ass eyes expects us to finish before quitting time.
A person can only shovel so many tons a day. Did it ever occur to him
that shoveling all morning may have burned us out? And maybe it would
be smarter to get two other guys to bust their ass for the afternoon. Hell
no! We get stuck with all the bullshit work. If the foreman wasn't such
a chicken shit, he would get his head out of his ass and get them other
guys down here. Bet he won't. And you know why? Because he knows
damn well that those other guys won't do a goddamned thing—that's
why. And he knows that we will. You know what I heard him tell Marvin
about us? He said, 'When you get a good horse, you run him.' Then he
laughed. But we're not horses. We're more like dogs. And that's what he's
doin'—runnin' his dogs. Man, I hate this job! I wish I could win the lottery and buy this place. The first thing I would do is fire all those assholes
in the office. Or better yet, I would 'promote' them to tunnel shovelers.
Tunnel rats! But you think they would do this shit? Hell no! They would
starve or commit suicide before they would shovel for a living. That's for
goddamned sure!"

Benjamin started shoveling, allowing his mind to drift into deep
thought as the endorphins kicked in. He wondered why Mark resisted
the duty so vehemently. It did little good to complain. Sure, shoveling
was not much fun, but it was a chore that they were hired to do. The
best course of action would be to shovel up the mess and try to prevent

the mess from happening again, which is the basic "live and learn" philosophy. Maybe that's what was really griping the guys in the lunchroom at the beginning of the day. The idea is that the company doesn't pay enough attention to preventative maintenance. But that is not the worker's responsibility, or is it?

Benjamin wondered whether he should enroll in college. His father had wanted him to go to college, had even offered to pay for the first year, but his dad had never really pushed him. Many parents push and push hard. They start teaching their children at infancy. They sing the ABC song and chant "Old McDonald Had a Farm" while still in the cradle. Of course, they fail to mention that Old McDonald cheats on his taxes, is sleeping with Farmer McCoy's wife, and is going to chop the bloody heads off those "duckies" and eat their flesh carnivorously with gusto. A child's world can surely be a utopia, shielded from all the negativities of life, especially hard work. "I suppose that's why parents push their kids to do well in school," thought Benjamin out loud, barely audible over the din of scraping shovels. "Parents want their kids to avoid hard work in order to have an easier life, so they push them in school; they push them in academics. So, in a sense, the parents, as well as the children, are really working hard to avoid hard work. Yet, someone has to shovel. Who will be the lucky ones? I suppose they do not think of it as working away from a negative. It's more like, in their minds, working toward the gold ring, or 'something better.' Then, competition and/or conniving determines who gets the prize—if it is a prize. Maybe the competitive force is—"

"Ben...Hey, Ben!" yelled Mark from the other side of the mountain.

"What?" said Benjamin.

"I gotta walk up to the shop and take a dump. Be back in a little bit."

"'K," replied Benjamin as he looked at his watch—1:39.

Benjamin rested on his shovel handle as he watched Mark's image fade away down the length of the tunnel, until he was just a tiny speck at the very end. He heard the clank of the large steel doors at the entrance of the tunnel slam shut, sealing him alone in the tomb. He radioed the control room and ran up the loaded belt, which he considered a break from the shovel. The mountain was smaller now, but still a mountain. He looked at his watch—1:54. He resumed shoveling. His pace was slower. His Jell-O arms acted mechanically. His mind seemed to forfeit all thought as he pressed onward, proceeding with the marathon. The finish line was the motivation now, but the finish line was a long way off. "If only everyone would contribute," he said as his mind flickered with a thought. "If everyone would do an equal share of the hardest work, the work would be made easy, even enjoyable. If everyone would pitch in, everyone would have a taste of bitter wine to contrast the sweet, fostering an appreciation that they may have never known. They would realize a deeper appreciation for the sweet cup and deeper appreciation for the laborer. Yes, all should taste of the laborer's cup to intensify the flavor of life."

Benjamin's thoughts continued to ramble and bounce off the interior of the expanse of his mind in abstract fashion, colliding with each other and forming profound ideas that would instantly dissipate into oblivion like a forgotten dream, only to have another take its place. He was unaware of his fatigued body's motions as the progression unfolded. His shiny, wet face carried a palled gaze, as one hypnotized. The shovel plodded onward.

Benjamin was leaning on his shovel handle, resting, when the distant clank of the tunnel door sounded. A small speck of a man was walking toward him with splashing footsteps that echoed eerily off the concrete walls and ceiling. It was Mark.

"Almost got 'er, eh?" said Mark. "Looks good. Would've been back earlier, but I noticed a spill building up outside the process building. Good thing I caught it in time. That mess would've started coming into the door of the building pretty soon. So I hopped on the small payloader and cleaned it up. It was a bitch, too, getting around all those angle irons and braces without hitting them with the bucket. Tell you what, I'm glad that job's over with." Mark glanced down on the tunnel floor. "Is that little pile all that's left down here?"

"Yup," said Benjamin. "That's the last of it."

"Great," said Mark as he grabbed his shovel. "Well, let's hurry up and finish 'er off. It's damn near quitting time. The foreman's gonna shit his pants when he sees we're done."

The men scooped up the last of the taconite and headed for the exit. Mark led the way while Benjamin trailed behind. Mark burst open the rusty steel doors with a kick, revealing the blue-skied, sunny warmth that had been shielded from them. Benjamin drank the sunshine. His mind was immersed in the bright blue of the sky as the warm spring breeze caressed his wet skin. A chorus of seagulls screamed out a melody as they hovered above, almost motionless, like they had been painted there. The waterfront sparkled greenish blue, as the ripples danced and winked twinkles of glittering sunshine. The air tasted alive.

The foreman's dingy pickup was heading toward them, spewing up a cloud of dust, and occasionally spraying thick mud when it bogged through the low spots on the dirt roadway.

"Fellas done?" the foreman asked as the two men climbed into the cab.

"Yup, clean as a whistle," quickly stated Mark.

"Well, you guys must've busted your asses down there. I really appreciate that. If I would've sent any of them other birds down there, those piles would still be sitting there. Then I'd have to explain to the main office why we can't load the boat on time, and those assholes don't like delays. They would've chewed my ass. They don't have a damn clue what goes on down on this end. Anyways, I really appreciate it. Oh, I almost forgot. I need you guys to stay over a couple of hours. There's a damn mess outside the sample station that really should be shoveled up. Should only take a couple hours. It's a hard place to get a payloader into. I was thinking that one of you birds could get the payloader and place the empty bucket as close to the mess as you can; the other guy can shovel into the bucket. You guys up for a little OT?"

"Sure!" snapped Mark with enthusiasm. "Why don't you drop me off by loader thirty-seven, and I'll head down there right now?"

"I can't," said Benjamin.

The conversation immediately ceased with the utterance of the refusal. The pause lingered with smothering disappointment, crushing any positive note of praise that had been previously issued.

"I have an appointment with an attorney right after work," Benjamin explained. "It's about my father's estate. I really have to go."

The pause continued.

"What time you have to be there?" the foreman asked, breaking the silence.

"Five thirty."

"Shit!" exclaimed the foreman. "Well, let's see. It's almost quitting time now, damn near five. Can you go down there and shovel for an hour? I could call your lawyer and tell him you're gonna be late."

"No," Benjamin stated. "His office hours end at five o'clock. He is already working late for my convenience, since I work till five. He's already waiting for me the way it is."

"Well," contemplated the foreman, "maybe I can rope one of those other guys into driving the loader for you, Mark."

"Oh shoot, you know what?" said Mark. "I just remembered. I have a dentist appointment after work today. I can't believe I forgot. And I have to go. I already canceled the last two. I'm surprised that dentist doesn't tell me to take a hike. Man, I'm really sorry about that. It just slipped my mind."

"Damn it," said the foreman. "I really wanted to get that cleaned up today. Well, maybe I can let 'er go till tomorrow. I'll take another look at 'er after yous leave. Well, here we are. Yous guys have a good evening, and I'll see you bright and early tomorrow morning."

Benjamin walked briskly to the company men's room while glancing at his watch. After his visit with the urinal, he went to the wash basin and scrubbed his filthy hands and face in an attempt to make himself somewhat presentable. He had never had a meeting with a lawyer before, or anyone else that high up on the food chain. The paper towel dispenser was empty again, so he wiped his wet hands on his pants and his face with the sleeve of his shirt. Normally, he would have replenished the dispenser with a full roll of paper, but there was no time. It was near five o'clock already, and he did not want to be late for his appointment.

Benjamin walked to the lineup of waiting men impatiently standing in front of the time clock, and filled in the end position.

"How's she looking?" a worker said to the lead man in the line.

"Let's see," the lead man said as he peered into the small digital display of the time clock. "Minute and a half."

"Minute and a half?" someone stated with disgust. "My watch says five. The damn company clocks are fast at starting time and slow at quitting time. That's how they program 'em."

"What do we got now?" another man asked.

"Forty-two seconds," the lead man announced.

"Goddamn it, that last minute takes an hour!"

Mark was near the front of the line, growing more impatient by each fraction of a second. "Is that clock broke or what?" he yammered. "Jesus Christ!"

"Nine more seconds," was the official report.

All eyes were fastened on the lead man's raised arm, which was resting atop the handle of the time clock. His time card was already inserted into the worn slot. All focus was on that raised hand, as the muffled chitchat evaporated to quiet, thick anticipation. It was like starving dogs watching someone opening a can of dog food. Suddenly, the lead man's arm slammed the lever home, and the line came alive as each man mechanically punched out, like a well-oiled machine. One man dropped his card by accident, which temporarily disrupted the progress of the line. Voices erupted with vicious protest.

"Get to the back of the damn line if you can't hang on to your damn card!"

"Hurry it up, up there!"

"Hey, we ain't got all goddamned day here!"

"Oh, hang on to your asses," the man said as he finally positioned his card in the slot and pulled the handle. "You guys'll get to your beer soon enough."

"It's never soon enough," declared two men simultaneously.

By the time Benjamin punched out and walked to the parking lot, most of the vehicles were accelerating through the exit, like horses through the starting gate at the Kentucky Derby.

Benjamin opened the door of his pickup and tossed his pail on the passenger's side as he climbed in. The interior of the cab was warm, almost hot, from the mild intensity of the sun's rays magnified through his windshield. He paused for a moment, drinking in the warmth while allowing his fatigued body to completely relax as he stared into the blue vastness of the sky. Once the parking lot was free of the rushed, chaotic exodus, Benjamin took his leave.

The Lawyer

The lawyer's office was located inside a huge brick building that must have been an old warehouse or department store at one time. The side facing the street was paneled with fine oak and expensive trim garnished with polished brass to give the impressive look of gold. The whole building was divided into various law offices of various firms, all under one roof. Benjamin was amazed at how so many different law firms could work so closely together in complete harmony with their competitors.

His lawyer's name was Mr. Scully, whose office was supposed to be on the second floor. Benjamin had conferred with him by telephone numerous times since his father's death, but had never actually met the man. Mr. Scully was the man whom Benjamin's father had hired to draft his last will and testament. He'd phoned Benjamin after the funeral and offered to administer any legal requirements or implementations of the will, and any monetary or property transferals. Benjamin was thankful for anyone offering to help out, especially because Mr. Scully had worked with his father and must have been trusted by him. It was good to have someone to trust, someone who could at least offer sound advice.

The only close relative Benjamin had was his mother, and she was on an extended vacation in Paris with Ned, who had business dealings abroad. She usually called every couple of weeks, just to keep in touch, but she hadn't for over a month. He hated to phone her about anything. He felt like he was intruding on her life with Ned. However, he had to inform her of his father's death. He did not know how she would react and was hesitant about how to initiate such a conversation. Benjamin recalled the awkward call.

"Hello?"

"Hi, Mom. How's it going over there?"

"Oh, Benjamin, it's you! We were just on our way out to dinner. Wow, I'm impressed; you never call. Is anything wrong? You're not in any trouble, are you?"

"Well, there is some bad news."

"Oh? What on earth is it?"

"Well, it's my dad. He had a heart attack."

"Oh, my God. Is he all right?"

"Well, no…He died."

Benjamin did not know how to put it delicately without prolonging the agony of it all. He felt it best to just come out with it.

"Oh, my God. Poor Robert. When did this happen? How did this happen? I can't believe it. Oh, my God. I feel just awful."

"He died in bed. Dad's minister is handling the funeral; it's going to be in a couple of days."

"Oh, my God. Should I come back for the funeral? I can hardly leave. Oh man, this is too much. I can hardly think. Ben, do you think I should come back?"

"I don't know. It's up to you, I guess."

"Do you think you can handle it? I feel I should be there for you. I really do. But Ned and I are hosting an outdoor dinner in three days and all the planning we did—"

"I can handle it. The preacher and the funeral director are really doing everything."

"Are you sure? I feel really terrible about this. I feel really terrible."

"I just thought you should know."

"Yes, of course! I feel really bad. Poor Robert."

"Well, I had better let you go to your dinner."

"Oh, that? We're going to Flannigan's. It's really fancy. But I hardly feel hungry after hearing news like this. Wow, talk about a shock. Are you sure you're going to be all right?"

"Sure, I can handle it."

"We should be back in the States in a couple of months. I'll keep in touch. OK?"

"OK."

"Oh, Benjamin, I feel really bad about this."

"No problem. We'll see ya later, then."

"OK. I'll call you tomorrow."

"'K. Bye."

"B'bye. Love ya."

Benjamin had received many phone calls from his mother since his father's death, one almost every day, and then one every other day; now it had been three days. She offered Ned's advice on the legal matters; he advised Benjamin to get copies of everything he signed.

Today's meeting with the lawyer was simply to finalize everything, to sign the papers. He was the sole heir to whatever his father owned. Most of his father's material possessions had little worth, except the Honda Civic, which was in great shape for its age. However, there were investments of some sort. Mr. Scully said they were sizable, clearly over a hundred thousand dollars. Of course, after the smoke cleared, hard telling what would be left. Surely, it was some oversight or mistake. The meeting today would clarify things.

Benjamin found Mr. Scully's nameplate on the wall in the small but elegant lobby. The shiny nameplate was engraved in bold, cursive print with an arrow pointing the way to the stairs. The lobby walls were textured and painted with a rich, off-white color that enhanced the hand-painted copies of Monet, Cézanne, and van Gogh that hung strategically where the light complemented them. The stairway leading to the second floor was wide and had a polished, chrome-plated railing on each side, resembling the finest sterling silver. The treads were carpeted in a thick, plush burgundy; however, they creaked when Benjamin's full weight was placed on them, emanating a hollow sound.

At the top of the stairs was another nameplate and another arrow, which pointed the way to another nameplate hanging on a closed door. Benjamin opened the door to the vacant room. Mr. Scully had told him on the phone that his secretary would have left by the time he arrived, but the office door would be open for him.

The office had a rich, new look to it. Two huge bookshelves lined one wall, perfectly filled with horizontal rows of thick, black books that reached to the ceiling. They all looked brand new. The adjacent wall was tastefully decorated with various diplomas and notable awards for outstanding citizenship. On another wall hung a large painting of George Washington wearing his white, curly-haired wig. On one side of the portrait drooped an American flag; on the other side hung the state flag. Every item in the room created an aura of intellectual elegance, and everything was perfectly in place. It almost seemed like he was standing in a photograph from *Better Homes and Gardens* magazine. The secretary's empty chair looked a little frazzled, but the rest of the room appeared impeccable.

"Mr. Frisk, I take it," boomed a voice so loud that Benjamin jumped with fright at the sudden explosion of sound, shattering the tranquility of the mouse-quiet room.

"Jesus!" Benjamin said while simultaneously spinning around in midair.

"Ha! Scared you? Sorry about that," said the lawyer as he grinned from ear to ear, trying his best to suppress laughter.

He was a short, round man, wearing light tan pants, polished black shoes, and a bright white shirt accented with a thick green tie. He was bald with a strip of salt-and-pepper hair that stretched above one ear to the other. A fat, unlit cigar protruded from the side of his mouth, clenched between his back teeth, which flashed hints of gold dental work when he smiled.

"Clarence Scully," beamed the lawyer, sticking out his chubby hand.

"Benjamin Frisk," said Benjamin as he firmly gripped the hand, formalizing the traditional greeting between two negotiating people.

"Glad to finally meet you face-to-face," the lawyer said with a smile. "Come on into my office and take a seat. My, but you do resemble your father. Not completely, but I notice a bit of him in you. It's the eyes. Yes, that's it—the eyes. Your father and I did a little business periodically, nothing serious mind you, just updating his will. It was an annual event with him, almost an obsession. Why, I even suggested to him that he wait every other year to update the will, you know, to save money. But he wouldn't hear of it. We even argued about it a bit. Finally I said to him, I says, 'Look, Richard, if it gives you peace of mind, then it's probably worth it for you personally, even though it's going to cost you a few shekels.' But, you know, it turns out that he was probably right. Hindsight has a way of judging previous actions. Oh well, it was a good thing everything was updated."

"Robert," said Benjamin.

"What?" said the lawyer, losing his train of thought.

"It's Robert. You said 'Richard.'"

"Did I? No! Hmm, maybe I did. Oh well, I tell you it's been a long day, and I'm just beat to the bone. I was so darned busy today. I didn't even have a chance to take a full hour for dinner. To tell you the truth, I had Sheila try to get a hold of you to cancel today's appointment on the chance that you might have been home for dinner, but no one answered the phone. Well, anyways, let's see…Where was I? Oh yes! I have all the official documents drawn up for you to sign." The lawyer opened a large manila envelope and retrieved an indexed file. "It is really clear-cut. Your father listed all his assets in his will and clearly specified you as sole beneficiary. Let's see…" The lawyer scanned over the table of contents of the file. "Hmm." The lawyer's unlit cigar shuffled from one side of his mouth to the other as he flipped over the pages. "Where to start?" he stated. "Well, got to start somewhere. Might as well be the apartment. The rent for your father's apartment is paid up until the end of next month. You own all of the personal belongings in the apartment except the kitchen appliances, which go with the place. It's up to you to remove all personal effects. Next, the car needs to be transferred to your name. All the directions and paperwork are in the file here. It's very simple. You just go down to the Secretary of State's office, just like you do when you get plates for your vehicle. They will know what to do. Then there is the bank account. Your father dealt with National Capital bank. They have a branch located in Wal-Mart downtown. His checking account had two hundred thirty-six dollars and twenty-seven cents. The savings account had fifty dollars. Also, there are three twelve-month certificates of deposit, each worth roughly thirty thousand dollars. They come up for renewal in January, May, and September, consecutively. The forms are all here, along with a copy of the death certificate. Just fill out the forms at home and then go to the bank with the death certificate and three forms of personal identification. There was also a life insurance policy from North State Insurance Group for twenty thousand. Let's see…" The lawyer turned the page of the file. "I've sent them the obituary and the death certificate. All you should have to do is await the check. And that about does it. Of course, you are required to pay all income and inheritance taxes, which are listed on the back sheet of the file. It's all in the file, very clear-cut. There was no real estate involved other than the car and personal belongings. The bulk of the estate was just numbers in a bank account, just black ink. Now the black ink is yours." The lawyer peered across the file at Benjamin, awaiting a response.

"Well," responded Benjamin, "I'm a little overwhelmed by all this. Thirty-thousand-dollar certificate?"

"Yes," said the lawyer as he placed the file in front of Benjamin and pointed at the correct statement. "Three CD accounts, each for thirty thousand. That's ninety thousand total. A CD is really nothing more than a fancy savings account that pays a higher rate of interest: the catch is that you can only withdraw the money at a certain time, or you pay a penalty. It seems your father had the three twelve-month CDs strategically spaced throughout the year to ensure quicker access to the money, minimizing the risk of penalty."

"So, there is ninety thousand dollars in this account?" said Benjamin.

"That and a twenty-thousand-dollar life insurance check," stated the lawyer. "Hundred and ten total liquid assets. It's really clear-cut."

"One hundred and ten thousand dollars," Benjamin repeated.

"That's right, son. All yours," the lawyer said and smiled. "You go ahead and take this file home with you. Look over the paperwork. Read the explanations. I think you will find everything in complete, impeccable order. Sheila is the best. By the way, my fee is on the light green sheet in the very front of the file. Everything is itemized to avoid any discrepancies and confusion. You will find everything in splendid order, I'm sure. Now, if you'll excuse me, I really have to get some supper. It's been a grueling day, just grueling."

The lawyer stood up and stuck out his chubby hand. Benjamin stood up and completed the ritual, ending the negotiation of entities.

"Thank you."

Home

The drive home was slow, and Benjamin was reflective. Benjamin pulled into a fast-food drive-through for some supper. Any energy that the bologna sandwich lunch had provided was depleted.

"Welcome to McDonald's. May I take your order?"

"Eight quarter pounders and a large Coke!"

"Would you like cheese on those?"

"Sure, why not."

"Would you like fries with that?"

"Sure, go ahead."

"Would you like to supersize the drink and fries?"

"Supersize? Sure."

"I'm sorry; was that a yes on the supersize?"

"Yes."

"I have eight quarter pounders with cheese and a supersized Coke and fries. Is that correct?"

"Yes."

"Your total comes to seventeen dollars and two cents. Please pay at the first window. Have a nice day."

Benjamin motored up to the first window, while simultaneously fishing through his wallet.

"Hi. Seventeen and two cents."

"Hello," said Benjamin as he smiled and handed the young girl eighteen dollars.

"Ninety-eight is your change. Thank you and have a nice day."

Benjamin idled up to the next window.

"Sir, would you like salt or ketchup today?"

"Uh…no…No, that's OK."

"Here you go, sir. Thanks for choosing McDonald's. Have a nice day."

"You, too," said Benjamin as he tossed the warm bag on the passenger's side atop the folder the lawyer had given him. The truck accelerated into the line of traffic, heading home.

Benjamin's hands slid into the paper bag, as his eyes stayed focused on the traffic. His probing fingers felt the shape of a warm burger and extracted it from the bag, unwrapping the stubborn waxed-paper covering with one hand, glancing intermittently at his progress. A blob of ketchup squeezed out and smeared the file folder under the bag of food. Finally, with much finagling, the burger was free of its shroud and was lifted to its glory and also to its demise.

Benjamin was munching down his second burger as he pulled into his driveway, noticing a police car parked out front. He opened the driver's door, grabbed the sack of food and folder with one hand and the half-eaten burger with the other, and gently kicked the door shut with his foot. A police officer appeared from out of nowhere, so it seemed. His appearance startled Benjamin. It was the same man who'd brought the bad news of his father's death. Benjamin froze as he approached, his mind racing, his stomach turning into churned butter. "Mom!" he thought.

"Hello, Mr. Frisk," said the policeman.

Benjamin stood motionless like a statue.

"Sorry to bother you, but we received a call about a dog attack. You know anything about that?"

Benjamin started breathing again with relief. Noticing the policeman's name tag, he said, "Sergeant Franks, how are you?"

"Fine, just fine. Nice day, isn't it? Beautiful day for a drive. I was stuck behind a desk all day; glad to be out in the world for a change. The station got a call this morning—complaint about a dog. Says the dog owner lives at this address. She's saying the dog attacked her. No cuts or punctures were reported, but the dog apparently ripped her clothes up pretty good. Now, I know you have a beagle."

"Clothes ripped to shreds, you say?" questioned Benjamin. "And not even a scratch? That's one lucky lady."

"You saying you don't know anything about it?" said Franks.

"Well, you have the right address, and I plead guilty as charged," said Benjamin, fondly remembering the incident while scarfing down the rest of his burger. "This morning Barney treed a squirrel, and the neighbor came over complaining about the barking. And she was mad, came completely unglued; gave me hell. Then I had Barney escort her home. You should've seen her run!"

"I see," Sergeant Franks said with a smile. "Then you're saying there wasn't any actual attack?"

"No. Barney just latched on to her robe and ripped a chunk out of it for a souvenir. I've got the piece in the house."

"So, there was an attack?"

"I'd hardly call that an attack. It's a game Barney plays. She's as friendly as a good salesman. You've seen her. C'mon in the house and take a look." Benjamin walked to the front door. Sergeant Franks followed him.

Benjamin opened the unlocked door with his free hand. Barney instantly exploded out the door, jumping and prancing on her hind feet with joy, sniffing Benjamin, sniffing the blue man, and especially sniffing the bag of food.

"Hi, Barney!" Benjamin said. "Got something for ya!" He reached into the paper bag and retrieved two quarter pounders and unwrapped them as the beagle danced and squealed and whimpered impatience fused with unimaginable ecstasy. He set both burgers on the grass, just outside the door. Barney proceeded to woof them down, tail wagging. "There's the fierce killer. Look how she attacks those burgers!"

Sergeant Franks smiled. "Look," he said, "I have to make out a report here. You understand, don't you? It's obvious that Barney is no pit bull, but your neighbors have a right to a little peace and quiet in the morning."

Benjamin thought hard for a moment. "You're right. To be totally honest with you, it was all my doing. When that beautiful sunrise was in my eyes this morning, and Barney took off chasing that squirrel, it just seemed like something broke loose, like life began again, fresh new life. Sounds kind of weird, I suppose. I can hardly explain it. It was almost like a happy illusion. And then that woman came over, mad as a hornet, bent all out of shape. Guess she didn't fit in my illusion. So I sicced Barney on her. I admit it. It was my fault, and I did it willfully. Now, I know Barney wouldn't hurt a flea, but she loves to chase things, and she sure chased that woman." Benjamin laughed reflectively. "Oh, you should have seen them go—it was great! I don't know what got into me. Not really my nature to do something like that. But I sure did it. And I shouldn't have. It was wrong. I know it was. I knew it at the time I did it. But I'd be lying if I said I was sorry for doing it. I'm sorry for being the type of person who would want to do such a thing, but I'm not sorry for doing it. Anyways, it was my fault and not Barney's."

"Well," said Franks, "any suggestions how we should handle this to keep the peace here?"

"I admit my guilt," confessed Benjamin. "I ask the most severe penalty—jail time, a fine, whatever it is. Give me the maximum sentence. I do respect the law, and I definitely broke it. Did it on purpose, too. Give me the maximum penalty. I only ask that you hold me accountable and not Barney here."

"Well," reflected Franks, "I don't think it will serve anyone's best interest to lock you up and hang you. My intentions here are just to keep the peace, keep the harmony. We all have to get along together."

"Exactly!" cried Benjamin. "That's why I demand my due punishment. If a person does wrong, he should make restitution. I believe in it, and I demand my fine. It's the right thing to do."

"Listen, nobody's getting a fine here," said Franks. "This is just a little dispute. No one was hurt. It's just—"

"I demand it," interrupted Benjamin. "What good is the law if we do not follow its rules? What good is the law if we disregard or bend its perimeters? The law is the law, stringent and concrete. We have to stay within its structure and simply live within its barriers or pay the penalty for going through those barriers. No, Sergeant Franks, it is your duty to give me the maximum penalty since I knowingly broke the law with willful intent."

"Listen, Mr. Frisk, nobody's getting a goddamned fine here! This is just a dog complaint. And to be honest with you, I do not want the extra paperwork, nor do I want to explain to the chief why I would throw the book at you for something so trivial. I respect your respect for the law, but there are not going to be any fines or penalties over this. If you really care about the law, you have to understand what the law is for in the first place. The purpose isn't to fine people that break it. The purpose is to ensure peace and harmony between people who have to live together on the same planet, country, state, county, city, or neighborhood, like this one. A simple fine may be a form of restitution, but it is not the best form. The best form is for you to feel remorse and trot your butt over to your neighbor's house and apologize."

"Apologize?" Benjamin said with horror.

"That's right. Paying a fine is the easy way out. Going over and apologizing takes courage, but you have to mean it. It has to come from the heart, or else it's a lie, and the lie would be worse than the crime itself. What do you say, Mr. Frisk? So do you want to keep the peace, or do you want to simply pay a fine and let the animosity continue between you and your neighbor, allowing it to build up to another confrontation in the future? I'll leave you to decide your own fate. I think there already are enough Hatfields and McCoys in the world, don't you, Mr. Frisk?"

Sergeant Franks turned to go. "Sure is a pretty day," he observed, looking to the sunset. "Hope it's just as nice tomorrow." He walked to his patrol car while Barney, who was finished with supper, bounded along at his heels, nipping at a loose shoelace.

Benjamin called Barney into the house as the patrol car slowly edged out into the street and disappeared around the corner. He tossed the sack of food in the refrigerator—tomorrow's work lunch. Barney followed him, keeping a keen eye on the bag. Benjamin's aching arms and back reminded him of the day's work as he trudged into the living room and unenthusiastically gazed at the half-finished drywall job that was taunting him. The new sheetrock was all hung with the seams taped and mudded. Now came the hard part, the drudgery of tediously sanding the dried seams, which had to be done with elbow grease and sweat. The only piece of furniture in the entire room was a bright blue beanbag that was spattered with white speckles, and it seemed to lure Benjamin from his duty, coaxing him to stray from the work before him, just for a minute. Was there any harm in just a few minutes of rest?

Benjamin scrunched down into the blue vinyl, forcing the hidden beads away from his weight and creating a perfectly molded chair. Barney sat on her haunches, directly in front of her master's gaze, staring directly at him.

"What are you looking at?" Benjamin said as Barney lifted her ears and cocked her head with penetrating eyes. "Can't a person sit down for a minute? I don't have a dog's life, you know. Or maybe I do." He laughed. "What? You think I should get to work sanding? Why don't you start? You didn't do anything but sluff off all day, didn't you?" The beagle cocked her head the other way, staring intently in a most puzzling way. "Or do you want me to go apologize to that girl? You think

I should?" He laughed again, while remembering the morning's antics. "You sure had her hooves flying. I can't say that I feel very sorry. In fact, I feel sort of happy about the whole affair. Anyways, she doesn't know it yet, but I have given her a great gift today. She now has a memory, a story of today that will be revisited and retold the rest of her life. A humdrum, ordinary day that would have otherwise been forgotten will now live in infamy, for both of us. So, you see, Barney? We really should be congratulated for our brilliant, strategic maneuvers this morning. We make a great team, don't we?" Barney looked more puzzled than ever, which Benjamin interpreted to communicate firm agreement. "Besides, if I go over to her house to apologize, it would not be right; it would be phony. OK, I shouldn't have—we shouldn't have done it. I know that. It just created an anger in her that will burn all the brighter each time you chase a squirrel." At hearing the *s* word, Barney pranced to the door with anticipation while whining and looking enthusiastically back at her master. Benjamin laughed. "Girl, looks like your squirrel huntin' days are over, so just get it out of your head." Barney's tail wagged all the faster at the second confirmation of the word. "Oh, damn it. I suppose Sergeant Franks is right. We all have to live together. And I am sorry for being the kind of person who would do such a thing and take such immense pleasure from it. I guess that's the way of it sometimes, maybe all the time. Fighting against some things that I want to do but know I shouldn't. It's funny how some of these things that are ultimately negative in the long run seem so enjoyable in the present, almost luring us, tempting us." Barney was still by the door, prancing on her hind legs, looking at Benjamin and then at the doorknob and then back at Benjamin.

"What? You think I should go groveling over to her? Or do you just want to chase a squirrel?" Upon hearing the *s* word mentioned for the third time, Barney begged and danced with all her might, with her squeals bursting out into agonizing barks. "Maybe you're right," continued Benjamin. "I guess it wouldn't be hypocritical, since I am sorry for enjoying something I shouldn't have done. That counts as remorse, doesn't it?"

The comfort of the beanbag was coaxing the path to sleep, but guilt nagged and gnawed, wrestling for righteousness. Finally, Benjamin hoisted himself out of his deliberations with the verdict and walked out into the front yard toward the street. Muffled yelps of Barney's protest faded with each step toward the young woman's house.

Benjamin approached the house with reservation. It was now twilight. The western sky was ablaze with retreating orange and scarlet as the dark, navy blue from the east forged forth. He stopped in front of the small, white house, scanning the yard and driveway for clues to ensure that this was indeed the correct house. He realized that he just assumed she lived in the second house to the west of his, but did not know for sure. The yard had a white picket fence surrounding the tiny estate. The house itself was quite unique. Its story-and-a-half roofline swept down and jutted out at the eves with a slight convex curve, resembling an Alpine cottage or a gingerbread house. The windows were decorated with colored paper from the inside. He couldn't tell exactly what the oval paper images were, probably silhouettes of Easter eggs. In the driveway, a vehicle was parked. It looked like a dark green Pontiac of some sort, maybe a Grand Prix. On one side of the drive was a small piece of torn cloth, but there was not enough daylight to tell what color it was. He walked closer and examined the blue shred, tucked it in his pocket, and stepped onto the front porch and rang the doorbell.

Benjamin could hear music playing from within, perhaps a radio. He rang the doorbell again while simultaneously rapping with his knuckles. The music abruptly stopped. He knocked again. Shuffling noises could be heard, and the drapes behind the front window overlooking the porch wiggled. He knocked again.

The door opened about two inches, held fast with a gold chain from the inside. "Who is it?" questioned a female voice.

"It's just me, your neighbor, the one with the dog. I believe we met this morning."

"What do you want?" she stated with a slight emphasis on the word *you.*

"I'd like to have a few words with you, if you don't mind."

"I have nothing to say to you, nor do I care to hear anything you have to say. I've called the police, and you can take the matter up with them. Now, if you'll kindly leave…"

"Yes," agreed Benjamin, "an officer was at my house when I came home from work. He asked a few questions. He sort of suggested that—"

"Please!" she interrupted. "If you have something to say about the matter, call the police department, and they will relay any relevant information to me. Under the circumstances, I do not think you and I can be civil. Let the police mediate this dispute. Hopefully, we can come to an amicable settlement. Now, if you'll please excuse me..."

"Don't you think we could just settle this between the two of us and be done with it? It seems silly to have hard feelings between neighbors, especially if it can be prevented."

"Prevented? Prevented?" Her face was changing to that familiar deep reddish complexion again. Her sharp eyes forecast an eruption like a steaming volcano. She slowly removed the chain that held the barrier between them and opened the door, fully exposing her wrath and the broom in her hand. Benjamin was in awe at how quickly he had managed to reach her boiling point, and without even trying. She stood in the doorway, now holding the broom like a pitchfork, pointing its bristly tines threateningly at the unwelcome guest.

"Prevent?" she repeated for the third time through clenched teeth, as she poked menacingly at the air between them. "Mr....Mr....whoever you are, get off my porch and off this property. You have the nerve, coming over here after you humiliated me in the most demeaning fashion. I bet you had a good laugh this morning, didn't you? Well, so did some of the other neighbors who heard the commotion. I suppose they were amused by a near-naked woman playing tug-of-war with a beagle, after your mutt yanked my robe off me. Well, guess what? I'm not laughing, and you won't be either!"

She worked herself up into a boiling mass of fire and smoke, but the mother of eruptions was held in restraint, but just by a thread. For a fraction of a second, Benjamin considered the amusing idea of severing that thread. A simple comment like "Yeah, did you ever look funny. I wish I had it on video" would ignite a real fireworks display. But on second consideration, the fruit of that endeavor, no matter how tasty it seemed at the time, would surely sour in the long run. The young woman was now reeling off all sorts of gibberish at lightning speed, waving that broom like a cannibal's spear. He let her rant and rave, in sheer awe of the energy and diverse vocabulary exerted. He decided to wait for a break in the waterfall of wrath, and then he'd dam the currents of anger with agreement, stopping the raging flow and hopefully creating a tranquil, placid backwater where peace could flourish.

"And furthermore," she continued breathlessly, "I'll see you in court, and I hope they take that dog away from you and throw that beast in the pound. Did you know that I stepped on some broken glass while your dog chased me? Oh no, of course you didn't because you were too busy laughing your ass off. We'll see how you laugh when you get the doctor bills for the stitches and the bill for my lost time at work and the bill for my grief! We'll see how you laugh then. People like you should be sent to the moon or farther. Yes, farther! Pluto, maybe…or another galaxy. But no, we honest citizens are stuck with you and have to have our lives tormented by your inconsiderate, idiotic, asinine, moronic—"

"I agree," said Benjamin, realizing that she might never stop talking.

"Agree?" she snapped. "Agree with what? The fact that you're an inconsiderate barbarian?"

"Yes," said Benjamin, "I admit that my behavior was certainly not appropriate, and I will make no excuses. When you came over this morning, I was amused with your anger and the whole situation. I even coaxed my dog to chase you home and enjoyed the show. This was wrong of me. You came to me with a valid complaint, and I did not respect your perspective. When you did not get satisfaction from me, you went to the authorities, which is exactly what a person should do when a conflict arises between neighbors. I do respect you for coming to me first. And, yes, I acted like an ass by not treating you seriously and with respect. I'm here to apologize and tell you that I am sorry for being the kind of person who would disrespect a neighbor. However, I realize that words are hollow without something to back them up with. Therefore, I promise to try to keep my dog from barking in the morning. That's not to say she won't slip out every now and again, but I will try to minimize the occurrences. Also, I will pay for any damages, whatever they are. Just send me a bill."

"Send you the bill, huh?" she scowled. "What about my robe and my agony and my stitches and my limping for the next month? Are you going to pay for that?"

"Yes," said Benjamin, "just let me know, whatever it is."

"And who is going to determine the cost of grief?" she questioned.

"You can. I'm sure you'll be fair. Whatever you come up with will be fine. Just let me know, and I'll write you a check for the damages."

"It could be thousands."

"Whatever. All I ask is that the price be somewhat fair and reasonable."

"And where, may I ask, are you going to get that kind of money? If I can't walk on this foot, I may not be able to work, and I'll need rent money. Quite frankly, the looks of your naked living room this morning gave me the impression that you cannot even afford furniture!"

"I'm remodeling. And, to tell you the truth, I just came into a little money today."

"Oh? Now I suppose you're going to tell me you hit the state lottery."

"Well, no," he said and smiled. "Actually, my father recently passed on and left me with an inheritance."

"Oh! Well...I'm sorry...I had no idea. I'm...I'm sorry."

Benjamin noticed the change that came over her. He was embarrassed that he'd even mentioned his father's death. He did not want sympathy to interfere with his attempt at restitution. Her cold exterior seemed to instantly melt into the warmth of compassion, which startled and confused him. The firm foundation on which his visit stood was shaken. He stood mute, as he regained his composure.

After an awkward pause, Benjamin finally said, "Maybe we should start fresh." He held out his hand. "Benjamin Frisk."

She looked at him cautiously. "Cindy Granger," she said as the two grasped each other's hands in the customary way.

"I hope I'm on the road to amends," he said with a smile.

"You certainly are on the road," she replied. "Time will tell if you continue the journey."

"You can count on it. And if there is anything you need, don't hesitate to call."

"Well, Mr. Frisk, you certainly are changing my impression of your character. But as you previously said, words are hollow until they are backed up with deeds. We'll wait and see what becomes of your good intentions."

Benjamin noticed the bright fire of compassion and sympathy fade into small flickers, doused with doubt. He glanced at her bare feet, one of which was wrapped in a gauze bandage. He wanted to say something, but couldn't find the words. True remorse was creeping in. She noticed his glance and his silence, while studying his eyes.

"Ten stitches," she said while holding up her foot. "I can walk lightly, but cannot put my full weight on it. However, if I walk on my heel, I can get around with no crutches. Of course, the limping isn't very becoming. I suppose my students will get a kick out of it."

"Students?" said Benjamin. "You're a teacher?"

"Yes, third grade. You sound surprised. Did you think that someone as mean as me couldn't hold the occupation of a teacher of children?"

"Oh no!" replied Benjamin, sensing danger and pondering the wisdom of venturing out on thin ice. "It's just that…well…"

"Well, what? Spit it out, Mr. Frisk!"

"Well…This morning you said you worked the midnight shift," hesitantly said Benjamin as he slid farther out on the thin ice, testing its integrity.

"I did nothing of the sort!" she blurted in a defensive tone. "I merely said that *some* people work midnights, and it would be courteous to think of other people instead of yourself!"

"You implied that you just came home from work and were trying to get some sleep," corrected Benjamin. "Now, before you get bent all out of shape trying to prove you're right and I'm wrong, let's just be honest with each other and get to the work of being civil. It starts here and now or ends here and now. It's your call."

Her reddening face forecast a tsunami, but the storm in her eyes restrained itself. "Mr. Frisk, it has surely been an interesting day. First you inconsiderately woke the neighborhood up at an atrocious hour; purposely encouraged your dog to attack me, which sent me to the hospital; and then you waltz over here and say you're sorry: 'here's a check for your trouble.' And if that isn't crass enough, now you are somehow turning the guilt of this whole affair to point an accusing finger at me, the victim of this massacre. Personally, I doubt that you and I are ever going to get along very well. However, I do appreciate you taking the effort to offer to pay my expenses, an offer I fully intend to utilize. Now, if you will excuse me."

At this point in the conversation, Benjamin saw no feasible path to appeasement. He had made much headway, but the foolishness of venturing out on thin ice paid a wet dividend. Retreat was imminent.

"Yes," he said, "I will take my leave. I think we can work through this. Again, I surely will make good my promise here tonight. Good night, Cindy Granger."

Benjamin turned to step off the small wooden porch and make his way home when his first step landed on a screeching mass of living hell. He jumped in fright, petrified by the surprise attack. His ankle bit with pain as he flew back into the threshold of the doorway and spilled onto Miss Granger's floor. A brownish varmint scampered through the doorway, trampling across his chest with sharp, extended claws. "Ahhhhh!" he screamed in terror at the sight of the furry attacker.

"Oh, my God!" cried Miss Granger. "Are you all right? What did he do to you? Come here, Muppet. It's OK. Mommy's here."

Benjamin lay on the floor, holding his bloodied ankle, while Miss Granger consoled her cat and thoroughly inspected its furry appendages for signs of damage.

"You're OK, honey," she said to the frazzled fur ball. She took Muppet in another room and quickly returned, observing Benjamin pulling up a blood-stained sock and hiding it with the pant leg of his trousers, while scrambling to his feet.

"Why, Mr. Frisk, I didn't know you could dance," she said and laughed. "Oh, I'm sorry. Forgive me!" she chuckled in hysterical fits. Her face glowed a happy pink from failed attempts at suppression. "Are you hurt?" she squealed in a high pitch, while simultaneously bubbling out chirps of laughter. "Please…I'm sorry…but…but…the look on your face!" She burst out in yet another uncontrollable fit of humor.

Benjamin was shaken by the turn of events and amazed at the sheer range of emotional diversity displayed by a woman in such a small segment of time, from raging anger to sympathetic compassion, back to anger, and now to ecstatic humor. He was not positive that the doubled-up woman, gasping for air, standing before him, was completely sane. He looked around the room to make sure that the damnable varmint was not in the vicinity and walked out her door and into the night. He could still hear shrieks of laughter when he reached the street. He paused, reflecting on the evening's strange events. "How ironic people are," he muttered to himself. "Must empathy be born out of circumstance? Are we too emotionally daft to truly understand another's perspective? The irony of life."

Benjamin glided through the sharp night air. A dog barked eerily in the distance, echoing a forlorn complaint. A rushing pain emanated, not so much from his ankle, but from the crooning laughter, the laughter from a fellow human being who was quite delighted and amused witnessing another person's suffering. He was appalled at the wretchedness hidden deep in the heart of people, so deep that it was hidden from consciousness, so deep that it was hidden from view, so deep that it was unrecognizable, masquerading in the nonchalant form of triviality. He remembered the morning's events. How cute it was to watch Cindy Granger run in terror! He remembered feeling refreshed, sanctified. And now the tables were turned. He was at the brunt of his own devices.

"How emotionally reckless people are," he thought to himself. "For every action there is a reaction. Can we not be sensible enough to administer action that will cause positive reaction? I suppose it would be impossible for all actions to have a positive outcome, but many could. People are just crazy. That's the cold hard truth of it. And if everyone is crazy, then I myself am just as loony as the rest of them, yet I do not see my own lunacy. It is shielded from me like the stars on a bright summer's day. We are an entangled mass of thoughts and desires guided by our own physical needs and the drive to fulfill those needs. But what good do desires such as hate and humor provide? What good do they accomplish? Do we humans emotionally feed off such desires? The Roman's built huge coliseums where rows of spectators jubilantly watched animals kill fellow human beings, and they went home to their families and made merry over the exciting events of the day. Yet, if the hungry lion was chasing around that very man or a loved one from his household, his merry outlook would be replaced with fear and horror. Have we learned anything at all from the past, or do we relive these horrors in an endless cycle? Today's world is of little difference. Wars rage on as soldiers laugh and celebrate the massacre of those damned gooks, Japs, sand niggers, and those pompous American infidels. What joy was celebrated as the Twin Towers fell into bloody rubble! Like the Romans, we entertain ourselves with human suffering. Theaters are packed once again to witness the horrific illusion of a tsunami or earthquake or hurricane or tornado or asteroid or war or space aliens or nuclear bomb. People scan the airwaves for any word of a local disaster, such as a fire, and speed along the highway hoping for a glimpse. We watch home videos broadcast on television consisting of people injuring themselves as we munch buttered popcorn and roar with laughter. And children still smuggle their squirt guns and water balloons onto the school bus like amateur terrorists."

Benjamin remembered his own childhood. "Hey, let's jump on our bicycles and ride like the wind, just as fast as we can fly. Then when we get in front of Old Man Brady's house, we'll hit the skids on that tar patch in front of his house and lay some rubber. The squeal scares the old coot to death! Just about jumps right out of his skin. He chased Billy and me with a shotgun once. C'mon, let's see if we can get him going!"

Benjamin poured himself into his house, quite exhausted by the day's activities. The greeter was at the door, whining and wagging her tail with the euphoria of her master's return. Barney's inquisitive nose sniffed furiously, sensing the scent of a recent playmate she had chased up a tree.

He fell into the blue beanbag, took his shoes off, and administered to his wounds. He gently removed the bloody sock to reveal deep scratches and puncture marks where the villainous cat had feasted on his flesh. "Damn, I hate cats," he said out loud while shuddering. "Snakes, rats, spiders, or bats—anything is better than stinkin' old cats, eh, Barney?" Barney did not pay any attention to the familiar rhyme; the bloody sock demanded all her focus. The wounds on the ankle were superficial enough, and the bleeding had stopped. He would live.

The beanbag's comfort coaxed him to lose his grip on reality and to float off into the illusionary world of sleep. He fought the temptation, but his fatigued body persuaded him otherwise. As he drifted toward the mysterious chasm between the living and the dead, a dreamlike bee appeared in his mind's eye, flying in helter-skelter fashion, buzzing its frantic, invisible wings. The buzzing was strange and eerily echoed a chant that was hauntingly familiar…Phone!

Benjamin yanked himself from his stupor, still slightly drunk from the cobwebs of sleep, and scrambled for the telephone.

"Hello?"

"Hello! How's everything on your side of the ocean?"

"Oh, hi, Mom. Things are good here. You still in Paris?"

"Yes. We'll be here for quite a while. The company wants Ned to stay here all summer, maybe even into the fall. It's anybody's guess right now. How did your meeting with Mr. Scully go?"

"Good, good. He went over the assets of the estate. Said it was very simple, since there was no real estate or mortgages…that sort of thing."

"Did he have you sign anything?"

"No, not yet. Actually, he gave me a folder to review with all the information. I haven't had a chance to look at it yet. It's basically just some furniture, the car, and whatever was in the bank. Mr. Scully said it is really cut-and-dried."

"What was in the bank account?"

"Oh, I'm not really sure. It's in the paperwork somewhere. To tell you the truth, I'm not even going to look at it until tomorrow after work. I'm kind of beat."

"Rough day on the docks?"

"Just a busy day is all."

"Benjamin, I'm sure that Ned could find you a better job in the company somewhere. You don't have to scrape out a living like a common layperson."

"Mom, I *am* a common layperson. Besides, I like to work with my hands. It's a good job—honest work."

"Honest work, huh?" she sarcastically quipped. "It seems to me that your definition of honest work is the equivalent of hard labor. It's been my experience that the people who perform all the hard labor get paid the least. And besides that, it's dirty and dangerous. Lord knows what kind of dangerous equipment you're working around."

"Don't worry," he said. "I can take care of myself."

"But I do worry, Benjamin. If anything happened to you, I would fall apart. I would feel terrible. I would feel so much better if you would work in an office or something. I wouldn't have to worry, and you would be safe. A person can hardly be seriously injured by staplers and paper clips. I will speak to Ned about it, just to see what is available. You never know, maybe there is a job that will appeal to you."

"Mom, I really wish you wouldn't. My job isn't glamorous, but it's mine. I like the idea of working with my hands, making my own way. Besides that, I can work my way up in the company. In a few years, I could be a ship loader or maybe a millwright. The company even has a training program for an electrician's apprentice. I could learn all about wiring and maybe get a job on the side."

"Electricians get electrocuted," she snapped. "You remember what happened to Mrs. Meyers, don't you?"

"Mom, she was curling her hair with an electrical appliance while taking a bath. That's hardly—"

"The point is," she interrupted, "that electricity is a powerful force, and it is subtle. It is so subtle. People forget that it is even there. And what makes it even more devious is that it is invisible, just like a demon waiting to pounce when you least expect it. You can only see its end result. And for Mrs. Meyers, the end result was a casket."

"Oh, for crying out loud." Benjamin chuckled. "You're talking like electricity is the devil himself, waiting in the weeds, out to get me the minute I drop my guard."

"Hey," she defended, "do you realize that no one on earth knows exactly what electricity is? It's just like the force of gravity. Everyone knows it exists, and we can try to control its force, but we can only theorize what it is, which means that controlling its force always has the element of danger in it. You're dealing with the unknown."

"That's why there are checks and balances in the government," said Benjamin.

"What?" she questioned. "What on earth are you talking about?"

"Oh, nothing," Benjamin said with a laugh. "I think you're blowing this way out of proportion. The bottom line is that I'm sticking with my job on the docks. It's a simple life, and there is something clean and pure about a hard day's work."

"Benjamin, I only want something better for you, something financially and physically secure, something where you will be happy. Then I won't have to worry."

"I am happy, Mom."

"You know what I mean," she said.

"Yeah, I know what you mean."

"Good. Well, I better get going. Take care of yourself."

"Good-bye."

"How strange parents are," thought Benjamin as he hung up the phone and sprawled himself out on the sofa, which was jammed into the kitchen. "As soon as babies are born, parents try to educate them. For many children, this process continues and evolves into their midtwenties. They push for education; they push for more knowledge, more skills, always striving for one thing—more, always more, more and to be 'better.' Competition—that's what it is, a competitive social filter to strain out the culls. Isn't that a jolly definition of schools? To separate the wheat from the chaff! Parents would sell their souls to have their precious treasures make the grade, to be the wheat of the earth. Therefore, they push, they coax, they establish college funds twenty years in advance, and the race is on.

The winners receive the trophies of prestige, wealth, and security. They receive fringe benefits, such as handsome accommodations and health insurance, and they can afford first-rate schools and tutors to perpetuate the kingdom.

The losers are chained to the shovel in one fashion or another. They are the servers, using their labor to accrue all the wealth of which only a fraction is given them.

Therefore, parents push their children in education, so they will be winners of trophies, instead of the lowly servant, who is commonplace and whom the world shuns. Of course, there is a wide margin between the lowest and the highest, filled with increments of various degrees and levels. And parents only want the best 'increment' for their child. And so the educational battle rages on.

Benjamin yanked down the knitted comforter that was draped across the back of the sofa and covered himself in its drowsy warmth; then he flicked on the alarm clock that was sitting on the floor. Barney was curled up by his feet and did not complain of the close quarters.

As Benjamin tumbled into sleep, he wondered about raising a child of his own. Would he do anything differently? Would he not start teaching his son or daughter the ABCs as soon as possible? Would he not try to educate his offspring to the best of his ability? Is not that the duty of a parent? Even so-called unintelligent animals train their young before setting them adrift in the treacherous seas of the world, to ensure their survival and well-being. There really is no ethical alternative. He supposed that was the key—ethics. As long as ethics was the foundation, the educational ship would be a good thing to pilot. But what should the cornerstone of ethics be? Every person or group of people has a different perception of ethics; and some are as twisted as the führer's. Yet everyone believes that their particular ethics are the genuine article. One thing is certain: a person cannot be so naive to think that his or her personal ethics are the gospel truth. But then, what is?

Dreams

Dreams of flowers and colors and cars blossom out of illusion and into unrestricted thought. The mind, unchained from physics, creeps out of the channeled corridors and roams through the earth, going back and forth in it. Who controls what thoughts it feasts on during its nocturnal reign? The random menu seems to be born out of input. The player's familiar, but the action bizarre.

—∽—

Trains, bustling through clouds, with no tracks and no engineer, carry passengers over mountain tops and across deserts, instantly transforming into whales and plummeting to ocean's depth, only to vomit their bellies' digested pilgrims into a new perspective, or revelation.

—〰—

Ships, tossed by white-crested green mountains, shake real terror in the trembling heart, as the folded hands of ghosts pray furiously that the storm will subside. Waiting, waiting, waiting. The vessel creaks and thumps and shudders with the slam of each wave on its wooden hull made by the hands of men. The captain wears the face of your mother. She is in the sanctuary of her cabin, playing checkers with her life vest on, and doesn't want to be disturbed.

Pirates climb the mizzen mast and yell, "Land ho!" Then throw harpoons at the praying deckhands, who, upon hearing the baited words, came out from their hiding. Horror grips the heart. The waves slash. The harpoons fly. The waiting, waiting, waiting. The waiting!

—〰—

Pink skies burn with heat as happy pedestrians ride to work on unicycles in an attempt to save fuel for the war effort. Skateboarders are the terrorists, and road crews are busy spreading a fine gravel over the pavement and sidewalks. The police chief smiles in approval as you pass, when you suddenly realize that he is actually the president of the country. You turn to affirm, but in his place stands a naked woman, a former lover, laughing and giving you the finger. Your anger burns as you turn and proceed, only to realize you are on a skateboard. This was her doing! You dodge the gravel land mines while rolling downhill at high speed and with no brakes, only to crash into a pyramid of empty metal trash cans. Your seventh-grade science teacher laughs with delight as he kicks over the remaining trash cans.

"Out for a skateboard ride?" he screams in anger.

"No," you lie to him. "It was the woman. She gave me the fruit, and I ate it."

—⟋⟍⟍—

Thoughts roll into others, bouncing, accumulating, separating into parts, reforming into new abstractions. The physical boundaries are reorganized into mayhem, with little earthly reason of construction. Physical reality is the myth. Emotion is king here. Emotion rules the illusionary empire of sleeplessness, deep within sleep itself.

The alarm clock droned its mechanical buzz, chasing away sleep's phantoms and ushering in the physical world and a new day.

Benjamin flicked the electronic rooster off while stretching sore muscles. The house was dark, but the birthing of the new day was beginning its miraculous transformation from the black of night to morning. The coffeepot gurgled and belched its aromatic steam as the first glimmers of light appeared in the east, chasing away the stars. Piping hot oatmeal, smothered in brown sugar, was the traditional celebratory feast of the morning. Barney waited patiently for the leftovers, staring impolitely while licking her chops. The coffee was hot; its welcome bitter sting promoted an ambitious meshing with reality. Frosty window panes whispered premonitions of the outside temperature, and the orange-red east forecasted clear skies.

"Red sky in the morning, sailors take warning!"

Barney busily lapped the remaining kernels of oatmeal, as she nosed the bowl across the kitchen floor. The sun peeked about the trees, shedding its red dress and adorning itself with robes of brilliance and radiance, cascading down the raw energy that ultimately fuels the earth and all life on it.

And there was light.

The outside air was crisp and fresh with the aroma of spring as Benjamin scraped the icy glaze off his windshield. He started the engine to warm up the motor oil and then went back into the warm house. Barney, who was answering nature's call, decided to stay outside and patrol the grounds for any fresh signs of squirrel, sniffing at everything and anything in the yard that seemed out of place from the previous day. Suddenly, she stopped dead in her tracks with nose to the ground. The cold, brown grass emanated the hot fresh scent of varmint! She sniffed and snorted as genetics grasped control of her being, pulling her down the invisible scent trail as if being willingly pulled by a rope. Around the corner of the house, a flash of bounding fur, a hysterical howl, and the chase was on.

The bushy-tailed nut monger defensively headed straight for the large maple tree with the offense yelping in hot pursuit.

Benjamin, who was in the bathroom answering his own call, cut his mission short and hurried toward the commotion. Barney was at the base of the tree, barking wildly while staring into the bare branches. She was unaware that the maple tree's large branches intermingled with the neighbor's tree's branches, offering a safe getaway for the furry trespasser.

Benjamin clipped the leash onto the metal ring on Barney's collar and pulled her toward the front door. Barney, frantic with vocal protest, fought against the cord that held her captive, choking her fierce war cry.

Safely in the house, Benjamin shut the door and released the frustrated canine. He poured the remaining coffee into his cup and stood by the window, waiting for the truck to warm up and half expecting a visit from a larger squirrel.

Driving to work is always a somber occasion. A person is not excited or in dread, just neutral, and this feeling of neutrality has a calming, numbing effect.

The day on the docks consisted of the usual drills: the foreman pushing for more work and less ass time; the workers taking all the ass time they could get away with, striving for a minimum of physical work. Somewhere, the two entities usually found a balance amid the turmoil, and the work always seemed to satisfactorily get accomplished. But the laborer's work is never truly finished. The pile of spillage shoveled up one day is replaced with an identical pile the next day. One machine repaired and back online just focuses attention to the five other broken machines in the welding shop. It's like chipping a foot of ice off the face of a mile-wide glacier, only to have it advance two feet the next day. The work may be hard and monotonous, but at least the company provides a safe work environment.

"Safety is number one!" they say.

"I don't give a damn about profits when it comes to the safety of the workers."

"We need to hit our numbers, fellas; we're twenty thousand tons short this week. What the hell is going on? Faster, faster! And be safe."

"We don't want any lost-time injuries; our insurance rates will triple!"

The drive home at the end of the workday was always positive, with a fulfilling feeling of closure. The chore-laden hours were in, and the occupational worries were completely severed by the final punch of the time clock. The daily due was paid in full with sweat and blood, and now to revel in the reward, which is freedom. Freedom for all the workers to go home to their affordable kingdoms and bask in the budgeted luxuries of their choosing: drinking a cold beer, rebuilding that engine, casting for trout, rolling a strike, grilling that burger.

Benjamin swung his pickup into a Subway, to revel in the fruits of his labor, which was a foot-long club sub, toasted, with Swiss cheese, black olives, lettuce, tomato, onion, cucumber, green pepper, and sprinkled with red wine vinaigrette dressing, a supper fit for a king.

He fully intended to take the sandwich home and devour it in the comfort of his bag of beans, but the tempting aroma of melted cheese and dressing persuaded a quick bite—just one bite, just a taste. Of course, one bite only paved the enticing invitation for another, as a wolf-ish hunger demanded immediate appeasement. Before he came to his senses, half of the sub was ravished. He wrapped the remainder with the cellophane wrapper from whence it came and motored out of the parking lot toward home.

No sooner were the remnants of the last mouthful swallowed did the power of the leftover sandwich demand to be eaten now, not later. "Why deny yourself pleasure now?" it coaxed. "Indulge yourself while you have the opportunity. Feed your immediate passions! Why worry about the future? Throw reason and restraint to the wind and feed your nature. Let the future take care of itself!"

Benjamin fumbled with the cellophane wrapper with one hand while driving with the other. The sandwich was gone as he pulled into the drive, as was his temptation and his hunger. It was good to be home, satisfied.

Barney was ecstatic when the front door opened, dancing on her hind legs as her master's presence filled her world with sheer joy. She was not expecting a reward of food, nor did she want any food. No, her motives to praise her master were not born of selfishness in any way. It was simply a longing for his love and to be in his presence once again. She was willing to do anything that pleased her master. However, it was difficult to understand her master's will, for she could not comprehend the many words he used. Still, she could understand the tone of the words, which emanated emotion or spirit. She had little difficulty recognizing the spirit, and it was the spirit she communed with. The very purpose of her whole life was to be in her master's presence, doing his will.

After Benjamin's daily after-work frolic with his good and loyal servant, he sized up the unfinished living room with a keen eye. Sanding all the drywall seams was dusty, tedious, and laborious, but the job had to be done, and now was as good a time as any. He proceeded to drape curtains of clear plastic over the doorways leading to the other rooms of the house, so as to contain the imminent dust bowl to the living room. Barney nipped at the edges of the dangling plastic, inventing a new sport.

Benjamin strapped on a dust mask, resembling a doctor preparing for major surgery, and began applying muscle to the sandpaper. Soon, the room was a hazy, white fog, which coated everything with a snowy dust, including the maker of the storm. The sweaty snowman worked feverishly, rotating the sandpaper, feeling for bumps and hollows, and eyeing up the contours, as the noisy abrasions made the rough surface flat. Time seemed to dissipate, as well as thought itself, as the focus of the work blotted out everything but the task at hand. Consumed with his noisy work, he hardly noticed the light tapping sound, like a windy willow branch tapping the siding of a house before a summer storm. He stopped sanding and listened keenly to the silence. Barney listened, too, ears perked, aware that something was amiss. A light rap at the front door solved the mystery. Barney erupted with a howlish growl at the potential intruder.

"Barney, go lie down!"

Barney immediately deciphered these words to mean that the intruder was friendly and that she should welcome their guest.

Benjamin, not bothering to remove his dust mask or attempting to make himself the least bit presentable for company, opened the door wide. Cindy Granger stood in awe as the unexpected spectacle before her eyes shocked her speechless. Barney immediately sniffed her ankles, detecting the unmistakable stench of cat. In an awkward moment, the scene was frozen in time, neither person knowing exactly how to proceed.

Benjamin searched Cindy's surprised eyes for any telltale signs of her visit's purpose, while simultaneously searching his thoughts for recent offenses. He removed his dust mask, revealing a large oval of clean, damp skin around his mouth and nose, contrasting the rest of his powder-white face and hair.

"Hello," said Cindy while puzzling over the snowman and the blizzard of dust that spun to life from a gust of wind due to the open door. "I see this is a bad time."

"I'm just sanding my walls, getting them ready to paint. It's messy, but that's how it's done. Is there something…"

"Oh, no…I mean, yes…I mean…I was just thinking about the other day…you know, about your pet and my pet and well…How's your ankle?"

"Fine, just a scratch," replied Benjamin, who was quite surprised that she knew about his wounds. "How's your foot?"

"Better," she said, looking down at her shoes. "I'm not even limping much. It's really not as bad as I thought. I think the blood just gave me a scare."

"Well, I meant what I said about the doctor bill," stated Benjamin. "Whatever it costs—just let me know."

"Actually," she said, turning her eyes form his, "to tell you the truth, I didn't really see a doctor at all."

"I see," he said. "And the stitches?"

"No stitches," she confessed. "I'm sorry. I'm so sorry. I guess I was angry and wanted you to feel guilty. Then when you came over to apologize and Muppet scratched your ankle, I realized that I had been a bit harsh. Perhaps anger had gotten the better of me. Anyways, I have come to offer my apology and ask you to forgive my unruly behavior. Also, I would like to invite you over to my house for pizza, as sort of a peace offering. Maybe we can get on the right track."

"Pizza, huh?" said Benjamin. "Well, I thank you for coming over and leveling with me, but I really should keep the sandpaper moving. As you can see, I've got—"

"I have already called in the order," she interrupted. "The pizza will be delivered in twenty minutes. Now, I saw that you've just come home from work, which means you did not have supper yet. So, why not clean yourself up and come on over?"

"You're very insistent," said Benjamin with a smile.

"Twenty minutes, then," she said and smiled and turned to leave. But before going, she patted Barney on the head and then walked briskly away.

Barney would have escorted her new friend to the edge of the yard, but Benjamin held her by the collar as they both watched the messenger leave.

Benjamin looked at the unfinished walls of his living room. His work would be put on hold once more, compliments of Cindy Granger, who seemed to change moods as fast as a person changes socks. However, he would go to her pizza party. He had little choice. It was purely a political mission, and the utmost diplomacy would have to be observed in order to establish a firm foundation for neighborly relations. It would probably be best to play it quiet and let her do the talking. A few well-placed words are perceived with respect and are assumed to be born of wisdom, rather than a Niagara of words that are sure to magnify a person's faults and eccentricities. The plan would be to create a warm greeting and then get to the pizza as soon as possible so as to end the mission with deliberate speed. It would be wise for him to take mental note of the frilly details of her home's decor. For some reason, women like men to notice insignificant frills and knickknacks in a house and couldn't care less about the quality of their shingles or heating system, which provide the very functions of comfortable shelter that houses are built for. Women were surely mysteries who are best left in their own world. Of course, the mystical forces of biological gravity pull the female and male worlds together, which can lead to either a glorious meshing or a cataclysmic clash. Sometimes, the glorious meshing was only a catalyst for a lengthy chain reaction, which camouflaged and developed into an ultimate clash many years down the road.

Benjamin thought of his parents' divorce. How happy they all had seemed to be, years ago. Who can trust relationships in today's world? Today's relational philosophy seems to be based on fun and enjoyment. When these superficial illusions fade from the realities of life, the participants in the relationship simply terminate the old and replace it with a fresh, new, vibrant illusion.

Benjamin shook off his rambling thoughts in the shower, as he prepared his body for the sacrificial offering. After showering, he adorned his carcass with a brand-new pair of blue jeans, a fresh-washed T-shirt, and squeaky-clean sneakers. "Might as well make a good impression," he thought to himself. So, that was it, then. He gazed into the mirror to ensure his uniform was an accurate depiction of his character and class. He glanced at his watch and rushed out the door, across the lawn, and to the roadway, where he stopped and turned to observe his house. He glanced at his watch again while pretending to be deep in thought. A car appeared down the road a ways with a business logo displayed on the door. He then began a slow pace toward the vicinity of the lion's den, making sure the stage was set before arrival.

He approached the theater with apprehension and a twinge of fear, which was not just stage fright, but something unexplainable, perhaps a premonition of sorts. There also was the matter of Muppet to consider. He hadn't given that scene any thought at all. He would just have to wing it with some impromptu gibberish. With a careful survey of the immediate vicinity, he stepped onto the creaky wooden porch, drew a deep breath, and rang the doorbell, half expecting the building to explode as he pressed the button.

The vault's entrance opened wide, exposing a smiling invitation to enter. She had changed her clothes since their previous interlude. Her short blond hair and light complexion in contrast with the jet-black blouse and light beige dress slacks projected a smart look of professionalism, but yet, somehow, reminded him of a spider waiting on the edge of its web.

"Come in. Come in!" she coaxed.

Benjamin stepped through the threshold, and she closed the door behind him. The aroma of spicy pepperoni lingered as the opening act commenced.

"I thank you for your invitation," said Benjamin. "You really didn't have—"

"Oh, it was a nothing. Come in. Sit down! It's getting cold. There's nothing worse than cold pizza. Hold out your plate, and I'll give you this big slice. You're probably famished."

"Thanks. Wow, it really looks good," said Benjamin while remembering his foot-long sandwich.

"It is good," she said. "I have Coke or milk. What'll you have?"

"Coke is fine, thank you. You really have a nice place; I mean, it's fixed up nice."

"Thanks. I'm renting with the option to buy. It's cozy and close to the school. But I don't know…Maybe it's too small, not much room for expansion."

"Oh, I wouldn't say that," beamed Benjamin. "You could extend the south gable up to ten feet of the property line, and it would be a cinch to add on to the west side of the building. You could even build a second story on the addition if you wanted to."

"Really?" she said, smiling with wide eyes.

"Sure, it would take some doing, but it's certainly possible. However, to be honest, I do not really think you need the extra room. A big house means more cleaning, upkeep, heating, and cooling. Smaller homes are much more practical and efficient."

"Well," she said, "I was thinking of the future. You never know if and when you may need more room."

"You thinking of starting a home business or something on the side?"

"No, no," she said, laughing, "not a business. How's your pizza? You're just nibbling at it. Don't you like it?"

"Actually, I'm just not very hungry. After work, I stopped off at a Subway and devoured a foot-long club. I tried to tell you, but you already had the pizza ordered, and I didn't want to impede your attempt to build a bridge. People do have to find ways to get along with one another. So, I accepted your invitation, regardless of my full stomach. And I certainly appreciate your efforts toward appeasement."

"I see," she said. "Well, you're honest, and it's always best to be honest, I suppose. How about I put the pizza in the refrigerator and you show me how to turn this house into a castle fit for a princess?"

Benjamin hardly noticed the door that had opened, either spontaneously or deliberately. All he knew was that he was on firm footing, as he commandingly plunged forward into his field of expertise. He spoke of dormers and headers, shingles and trim. Both imagined fireplaces, dens, patio decks, and sun rooms. Benjamin's thoughts concentrated on the practicality of building, the costs, and the structural integrity. Cindy, however, imagined only the finished product and pictured herself amid the ambience of the dreams she was creating. And the dreams were intoxicating. She imagined herself reading by the fireplace, sipping hot chocolate as the crackling fire cozied her nest, wrapped in a colorful, soft blanket, with Muppet snuggled alongside. She imagined dinners in the kitchen, perhaps with family or friends. There would be laughter, smiles, and stories, but then the visitors would leave, and she would remain... Well, there was Muppet, at least.

Benjamin was totally unaware of the metamorphosis that was occurring, oblivious to the warming glow in Cindy's eyes and how she responded to his words with a growing reverence, even adulation at times. His only concern was to revel in the firm footing of his topic, to show his leadership and knowledge of the art of carpentry. Unbeknownst to him, he was playing the role of the alpha male—at least, in this particular sphere of influence.

Cindy's wide eyes saw the firmness of the leader, a strongness in his words, a sureness that was secure, and it warmed her. She knew little of what he spoke; she knew not how to accomplish, how to create, how to make a material reality out of mere ideas, out of mere dreams. She knew only of the finished product and an idea of how to use it.

Hours passed as the two roamed from room to room, both unaware of time.

"Well," said Benjamin, "I suppose I had better get back home... workday tomorrow."

"Oh...oh yes," said Cindy, looking at her watch. "I had no idea it was getting on so late." She suddenly remembered the stack of student papers in her briefcase that required correcting.

"I hope I didn't keep you from anything," said Benjamin. "I guess I got carried away. I just love to build or remodel things. I just love it."

"Oh no!" lied Cindy. "I had absolutely nothing to do tonight. And besides, it was I who invited you over for dinner, and it was I who encouraged you to paint me your imaginative pictures of how to turn a house into a home. And, I must say, you are a fine painter of dreams."

Benjamin was a bit puzzled as they both instinctively walked to the door. He really didn't have any idea of Cindy's speech of pictures and dreams. As far as he was concerned, he simply spoke of how to remodel her house, just the mechanics of it, nothing more.

"Well, I must thank you for the pizza and your hospitality," said Benjamin at the door. "I hope we can keep up the goodwill between each other...as neighbors, I mean." An awkwardness suddenly came over him—an awkwardness that frightened him a bit and threw him off guard. He foolishly held out his hand, in a friendly gesture, as he would have done during a formal business transaction.

Cindy took his hand and held it, while looking into his eyes. "Benjamin," she said, "I truly enjoyed this evening, and it is my sincere hope that we can live together...I mean...amicably...as neighbors, of course." She smiled.

Her hand felt like the softness of warm down, and her eyes accentuated her smile. For the first time, Benjamin noticed that her eyes were as blue at the ocean's sky, and her smile made them sparkle with a curious intensity that mystified him. Benjamin briefly paused, still holding her hand, and gazed as if in a trance.

"Good night," he said and turned into the blackness of night and exited her light. Cindy closed the door and locked it for the evening. She lingered a bit by the door, deep in thought.

Benjamin walked slowly through the darkness that hung like the very blackness of space: space between two homes or two people compared to the space between two distant planets. How strange it was to visit an alien environment! There, he was a visitor, an abstraction, temporarily gazing into her world. She was an anomaly to him, a comet perhaps, blazing through his sky, with a brilliance that commanded his attention.

Oh, the unfathomable stellar forces that dictate our fates! What cosmic notions are brewing, unbeknownst to the individual inhabitants of this spinning speck? Who, in the galaxies, plants the seeds of alteration? Whose hand modifies what has been set in place, constantly adjusting its mechanisms? Who orchestrates the movement of the planets and the stars?

Benjamin stopped between her house and his, between her planet and his. He gazed deeply into the night sky, illuminated with a billion flecks of light spangling the black. A thought entered his meditations, a curious thought, or perhaps a premonition. Then he thought of how the planets all have their solitary orbits and are quite content within those orbits. To orbit any faster would hurl them into icy space. To orbit any slower would plunge them into the fiery sun. Everything seemed to have its unique place. To tinker with these celestial mechanisms could have cataclysmic ramifications, perhaps a collision of worlds, or worse; a planet could be thrown out of orbit and out of the entire galaxy, into the abyss of a black hole, away from the known world of light, and into a cold loneliness beyond comprehension.

As Benjamin stared at the stars, lost in thought, a shooting star arced a dazzling white arch to the west, focusing his attention away from the breadth of the cosmos and onto that particular spot in the heavens.

"How glorious," he said out loud, "to die so brilliantly, to lighten the heavens, ever so briefly," contradicting his previous thought.

He then smiled inwardly and laughed out loud, shaking his head as he proceeded homeward, back to his planet, where he belonged, where his trusted beagle was, no doubt, waiting for him with an unconditional love that could not be questioned. And his work was waiting for him also. These were things he could rely on, things he could trust unequivocally.

As Benjamin landed at his home planet, the sole canine reception committee erupted with whimpering jubilance at her master's return; she merrily danced on her hind legs with a euphoric intensity of raw joy and then ran to her empty food dish and back, wagging her tail in expectation.

IV

Camping Trip

The rest of the work week rolled through smoothly and methodical-ly, fusing the daily routines and procedures into the ever-changing stream of life, breeding familiarity into the chaos, supporting a founda-tion on which a person could stand with some degree of confidence. Change would always creep into the clockworks; it was unavoidable. However, as long as the changes were subtle, they would be absorbed into the adjusted schedule in such a fashion as to quickly convert the destabilizing change into the daily or weekly routine, fostering an aggre-gated mixture that would eventually harden into a foundational cement that one could work with and eventually stand on.

Saturday was a wild-card day, in Benjamin's eyes. A person could do anything under the sun, anything one wished or desired, and have the finances from the previous work week to do it. Of course, Benjamin's life palette consisted of colors of the simple variety. To him, the trea-sures of life resided in such things as experiencing the golden orb of a cloudless sunrise, magically suspended over a sun-kissed mountain lake, sparkling like a billion diamonds, alive with shimmering brilliance, alive with a beauty so pure and so intense as to have the power to transcend and mesh one's soul with the eternal. Things such as these were an awe-inspiring elation, an inspiration deeper and more reverent than any man-made church could hope to mimic.

"Well, Barney," said Benjamin, sitting on the front porch while sip-ping his coffee in the darkness of early morning and staring solemnly toward the brightening east, "looks like it's going to be a great beginning to a great weekend."

Barney paid little attention to his master's yammering. She was busying herself sniffing the dewy grass, searching for any indication of a foreign scent, particularly that of varmint.

"Girl, how would you like to pack up the ol' truck and head to the backcountry, up in the hills, just you and me? All we need is the pup tent, a sleeping bag, a fishing pole, and some hot dogs."

Upon hearing the word *hot dogs*, Barney immediately stopped her patrol and cocked her head in an inquisitive manner, staring intently at Benjamin while licking her chops in a salivating fashion.

"What are you looking at?" Benjamin said and laughed. "Would you like to go camping in the hills? Are you interested in catching a fish? Or do you just want a hot dog?"

Upon hearing the *h* word for the second time, Barney dashed in front of Benjamin, prancing intently on her hind legs and whimpering in desperate expectation.

"Well, that settles it," said Benjamin with the confidence of a judge who had just assessed hard evidence for an obvious case. "I'll get the gear together."

Benjamin stood up in reverence to the rising sun, which was peeking its way over the horizon and smiling warmly on the new day. He drank the last of his coffee and walked into the house, toward the refrigerator, with a jubilant Barney bounding before him.

The drive into the wooded hills was always a solemn affair. It was as if a person was in a mobile time capsule, rolling into the yesteryears of long ago, into a time of simplicity, a time shed of the suppressing responsibility of schedules and jobs, a time shed of the mind-frazzling electronic paraphernalia of a world gripped with hysteria, a time shed of the maddening scurry of people, who were geographically condensed like busy ants trapped on an overpopulated ant farm.

Far from the paved road, the old truck rolled down the dusty two-track road, away from the world, deeper and deeper into an existence that always was, and still is, for those who still have virgin eyes.

Progress slowed considerably after the two-track road gradually diminished into more of a forest trail than a road. Still, the time travelers continued. Each mile created a wider gap, a deeper void, separating them, isolating them. Here, they would be alone. Here, they would find respite—respite from the artificial world created by the hands of men and women. Here, they would find peace and experience its delicacies, drinking in its spiritual waters, nourishing the heart, intoxicating the soul to a joyous contentment beyond any word's description.

The trail ended at a clearing at the base of a steep, wooded hill, which acted as a barrier to prevent further mechanical intrusion. Benjamin parked the truck under the protective limbs of a large oak.

"Here we are, Barn, ol' girl," he said while exiting the truck.

The air tasted fresh and sweet. The bright sunshine filtered through the rustling green leaves overhead, exposing intermittent splashes of clear blue sky. A red-winged blackbird inquisitively eyed up the new arrivals, singing a warbled greeting, while periodically preening itself in nonchalant fashion. From somewhere high in the oak, a squirrel was chattering in a high-pitched scold, which commanded the direct attention of Barney, who immediately began circling the base of the tree, staring up into the greenery, trying desperately to get a glimpse of the enemy, who she could not see but knew was there.

Benjamin busied himself by collecting the loose camping gear and fastening it onto his backpack frame.

"Well, Barney," he said, "we've got about a mile of hiking to do—that is, once we get over this hill." Barney paid absolutely no attention to his words. "We should get to the lake in an hour or so. I think we'll set up camp in the same place as last year. There's some good campfire wood there, and the swimming is great. Let's go, girl!"

Benjamin started up the sandy path that led up the hill. "Come on, Barney. Let's go!" he yelled again, this time with more authority.

Barney was still intently staring into the greenery of the bushy oak, in a valiant attempt to wear the enemy out with attrition.

"Barney!" screamed Benjamin at the top of the hill.

Barney reluctantly gave up her post, scampered up the hill, and joined the expedition. From their lofty vantage point, they could see creation as God intended, lush with life, painted mainly in a kaleidoscope of various shades of green, accented with the staccato sounds of birds and chipmunks, gently softened by the melody of the whispering breeze.

Turning and looking back down at the base of the hill, the old truck appeared as a tiny speck. It seemed an abomination of sorts, out of place, not welcome. Onward the travelers trekked, turning their backs on the last remaining relic, the last tie to the present, and forged deeper still, away.

The sandy trail wound through the huge oaks and pines, which stood like ancient centurions guarding the entrance to Eden. Other steep hills and deep ravines added to nature's defensive strategy.

Benjamin walked slowly, stopping periodically to reverently gaze at the majesty about him. He paused to listen to a heat bug, who was invisibly buzzing away from somewhere in the boughs of a white pine tree. He paused to pick a bright red wintergreen berry, plucking it from the contrasting dark green of its leaves, tasting its pungent flavor. He stopped to take off his shoes and socks, continuing barefoot. He loved to feel the warm sand between his toes. Somehow, walking barefoot made him feel more intimate with nature, more connected to creation, more connected to life. Benjamin gazed deeply, participating with all, becoming all, deep in awe, deep in an enchanting wonder. He picked up a particular stone that caught his eye, feeling its heat absorbed from the energy of the sunshine, wondering how old it was, marveling at its colors and shape, curious whether anyone else had ever laid eyes on it or walked on it or bothered to pick it up and really "see" it. Maybe it had once been fashioned into an ancient tool by some primordial tribesman. Or perhaps it had traveled hundreds of miles, courtesy of the prehistoric glaciers of the ice age, which deposited it here, in this place, to be discovered. Benjamin put the stone in his pocket.

Barney did not seem to share in the same reverence toward nature that infused her master. She simply enjoyed her immediate situation without concern—running to and fro, sniffing, and bounding about in merry fashion; stopping occasionally to scratch and dig at the entrance to a gopher hole or some such folly or to curiously nose some new bug that might be inching its way along the sticks and leaves of the forest floor. Whenever her master would stop to stare at a flower or stone, she would venture farther off the trail, exploring the immediate area in more depth while keeping an eye on any hint of Benjamin's movements, at which she would bound back near the trail, near her companion.

The two meandered through the woods, following the foot trail worn in by others before them, others who, perhaps, had sought the same inspirations. The last hill was quite a climb; the rains had washed out the original trail and had left a steep trench of stones and boulders, too dangerous to climb for fear of a rockslide.

"Well, Barn, ol' girl," said Benjamin, "we better go around this mess. We can't afford to get conked on the head or even sprain an ankle, not here. No one even knows where we are. And hard telling when another hiker might happen down this trail. We'll just angle our way up the hill along that deer trail and then cut back next to that stand of maple," Benjamin said and pointed.

Barney, knowing the tone of her master's voice, stood motionless, staring in the general vicinity of where her master pointed, wondering the importance of it all.

The climb was hard, but liberating. As the steepness tapered off near the summit, Benjamin veered over to the original trail, ending the detour. He continued on toward the top of the hill, where he paused in reverent silence as he gazed upon the glistening, aqua paradise through the pines at the declination of the hill that sloped into the beauty and serenity of the lake, the treasure of their journey, the prize.

It's a strange fact, indeed, why people are drawn to water. What invisible force is at work to pull one to the edge of some body of water, just to be there? It is not for drink or to necessarily be utilized in any particular way. Many people do not even use a lake for fishing or swimming. It is just for looking at, just for being near it, for being near the substance necessary for life, a substance which, in a sense, is life or, at least, a symbol of life.

Benjamin and Barney made their way down the hill, down the sandy trail, barefoot, to the water, to life.

"The first thing to do," stated Benjamin in the contemplative fashion of a wise sage, "is to get baptized." He then leaned his backpack onto a basswood tree and commenced to strip naked. He quickly ran with all his might, splashing into the water until the increasing depth enveloped him. He dived under the surface and into the life-giving liquid. Underwater, he swam, submerged, away from one world and into another. His existence immediately changed—breathlessly quiet. He continued on with all his strength until his mortality forced him to break the surface and gulp the freshness of joy into his begging lungs.

The baptism was complete. His soul was now washed and cleansed. He lingered in the water, after catching his breath, enjoying the cool on his nakedness, feeling the sunshine, tasting its energy.

Barney felt no desire in the least for swimming. She was intent on exploring the beach and its strange inhabitants. She discovered a frog that had foolishly ventured too far inland and was apparently making a run for the lake and the safety that the water provided for such creatures. Barney blocked the frog's path and made a great sport of this new game, barking ferociously, in jubilance. The frog's futile efforts at hopping toward escape were abruptly met with Barney's superb counterblocks. The frog eventually abandoned his aggressive strategy for escape and refused to participate in the antics. This annoyed Barney. She barked all the more ferociously, nosing the frog, coaxing him to make a run for it. But the frog would not budge. Finally, Barney grew bored of the situation and busied herself with further investigations. The frog then hopped into the water, silently making his getaway.

Benjamin arose, out of the water and into reality. His breeze-cooled, bare flesh glistened with a fresh vigor and intensity that radiated outward, like light from a sparkling star. He lay on the dry sand of the beach and rolled in it, absorbing its warmth, absorbing its energy into his body. He lay on his back, closing his eyes from the intensity of the hot, smiling sun. Then, turning onto his stomach, he studied the grains of sands on the beach, billions of them, usually gone unnoticed, different colors and shapes, some as clear as diamonds, some as red as rubies. He scooped up handfuls and let the grains sift slowly through his fingers, forming an insignificant mound. A picnic ant wandered by apparently unaware of the giant in its midst, on its way to its own business of life, whatever that might be.

"How odd it is to be alive," thought Benjamin, "to be a creature on this earth, human or otherwise. To be born into existence at all is nothing short of a miracle. Where were we before our birth? What is the purpose of it all? Just to survive, like the ant? Is that all there is? Or do we have a higher purpose? All we really have to do is to find food and shelter—the rest is rather superficial. Suppose our basic needs were somehow mysteriously met and our stomachs were perpetually full and we lived in such a favorable climate as to never need shelter or clothes: what, then, would we do? What lofty goals could there be in a utopian environment, where all people were content and had no desire or advantage to work? In such a situation, people would probably dedicate the bulk of their time to games and amusement, entertaining themselves with one folly after another, all done in a supposed quest for happiness, for fulfillment of the soul. But can one achieve true happiness from games and entertainment? At best, these endeavors can only produce "fun," which, in turn, is only a temporal illusion, representing a false sort of happiness. Once the "fun" wears off, we are left with nothing but a letdown, a void. Then we desperately seek another infusion of fun, as an addict seeks a drug, to foster yet another imitation of happiness. Therefore, if mindless fun does not breed true happiness, what does?"

Benjamin pondered these thoughts as he set his mind free, drifting through the clouds, drifting over the hills and valleys of consciousness, into a peace that only sleep can bring.

Another Dream

Dreams blended with the breeze and swirled into eddies and voids of thought, mixing with a reality that only the imagination can create. He was climbing a mountain, high into the clouds, following a path. There were steep crevasses on each side of the wearying trail as he continued upward. While crossing a plateau, he came across a deep gorge that resembled the Grand Canyon. He was shocked to see Cindy Granger down at the bottom. She was busy shoveling taconite pellets into a wheelbarrow and then dumping them over a ledge, into a black pit.

"Hello," said Benjamin.

Cindy did not respond or acknowledge him in any way, but continued shoveling, filling the wheelbarrow only halfway and then struggling with the load to the edge of the cliff, lifting the handles and showering the pellets into the blackness. She wore a once-white dress that was soiled with black dirt and maroon taconite dust. Benjamin noticed tears and rips in the fabric as he approached; these imperfections were patched with tape and glue. Although her clothes were haggard, her face appeared clean and bright, radiant, like a summer's day. Her blond hair glistened and bounced with every shovelful.

"Hello," repeated Benjamin.

"Oh," Cindy replied, "it's you." She paused briefly, glancing at Benjamin, only to resume shoveling.

"Can I give you a hand?" he asked.

Cindy laughed hysterically, with a rude demeanor. "You? You want to help me? That's a laugh. Wouldn't the neighbors have something to chat about then? Maybe you should just watch. Would you like to watch?"

"I feel guilty, just watching," said Benjamin.

"Ha!" exclaimed Cindy with a sinister grin. "Well, I can't have you helping out. A girl has to draw the line somewhere, you know. Besides, I enjoy my work. Do you hear me?" she screamed with a fire so intense that Benjamin was dumbfounded. "I love my work!" she continued. "But you don't understand that, do you? No, of course you don't. How could you? Just go away and leave me."

"Please allow me to help," pleaded Benjamin. "This work does not suit you; it's too dirty and rough. Please…I can help…"

"You stupid ass," Cindy said and glared. "I like it rough, did you know that? This is the work that I was born to do! And I love it. I wallow in it. I crave it. I would sell my soul to the devil to keep it," she said and hatefully laughed. "In fact, I think I have."

Fear and anger gripped Benjamin's heart as he aggressively grabbed at her shovel. Cindy defied his grasp, clutching the shovel defensively.

"Cindy, put the shovel down," commanded Benjamin. "You're coming with me, right now. I'm taking you out of this godforsaken pit. I'm taking you home—even if I have to carry you." Benjamin wrestled the shovel away from Cindy's hands. She flailed her arms in defiance as he held her close. She hopelessly pushed him away with all her strength, but he held her fast.

"Damn it, Cindy! Why do you fight me? Come home with me. Everything will be all right. Just come home with me."

Cindy stopped resisting and broke down, sobbing. The two embraced. Cindy had melted into his will. She turned from her tormenting spirit and feebly clung on to his. She blandly looked into his eyes and kissed him. "I'll go with you," she said. "If that is what you want, I'll go with you. But if I go, I will die. If you take me away, you will be killing me."

"I don't understand," said Benjamin. "I can't just leave you here. I can't! You have to come with me. I'll help you. I'll help you climb out. It will be all right. Once we get out of this canyon, it will be better—you'll see. Trust me."

She turned away from him, staring blankly at the tattered wheelbarrow. "Then I will die," she said. "Surely, I will die."

"Tell me this," Benjamin said. "Why would you want to stay in this filthy pit anyways? It must be miserable. Does the work you do here provide you with any shred of comfort or joy? No! It cannot! Yet you long to stay. Why? Tell me why. Is it something I have said or done that offends you? If I leave you here, your life will be ruined; if I physically force you out of this pit, you claim you will die. Why will you not come out on your own, by your own free will?"

"Oh, Benjamin," she cried, "truly, I wish that I did not want to stay. Truly, I do. With all my heart, I do. I wish I did not want to, but I do want to, and it torments me. I am not like you, Benjamin. I am not as strong. Do you see now? Do you see why I need to stay?"

"Cindy, don't you see? Don't you see that I cannot leave you here? If I left you here, on your own, I could not bear the thought. I could not carry the burden; I would be crushed. I am not strong enough. Please don't force me to leave you here. Come with me. Come with me on your own! Or at least give me a reason; give me something, anything, so that I might live with some sort of peace. Please, I beg of you, give me a reason."

Cindy, still looking away from him, said in a thin, weak voice that was barely audible, "You're too nice for me."

Benjamin heard the words, but did not immediately speak, standing in silence, deep in thought.

"Then I must leave you and go on alone. I have no choice."

As Benjamin spoke these words, it was if a huge, depressing weight was instantly lifted from Cindy's soul, transforming and fastening its entire weight to Benjamin's shoulders, almost smothering him. He slowly turned from her and began his morbid walk away from her. His steps were unsteady under the load as he inched his lonely way up the path leading out of the canyon. The sun had set, and blackness had engulfed him. Still, he proceeded in the dark, stumbling along like a drunkard. Even the dim stars offered no light; the clouds had shielded them from his eyes.

Benjamin soon grew weary and lay down just off the trail to rest. In the gloom, it began to rain, slowly at first but steady. It would be a rain that would last a long time, a relentless rain, a rain that would paint each day a brooding gray, blotting out the sun.

He closed his eyes in the darkness, allowing his mind to fade, allowing his will to fade, allowing death to enter, if only death would have him. Death, it seemed, would not be unwelcome, if it only happened now, in this place. It would serve as a comforting bed, as opposed to the alternative of life, which had manifested itself into a depressing, uphill climb out of a dismal canyon, treading on a now-muddied and slippery trail, shrouded in gloom. Death would be a way out, an escape.

As Benjamin lay in the muddy dirt, the light rain gradually increased in intensity, soaking him to his core, as he drifted...drifted into death... nearer and nearer...to death's portal...to escape...to peace...His breathing grew shallow...then ceased...His eternal heart beat its last... Through death's door a light shone brilliant and warm, beckoning to his soul. He reached with both arms outstretched, opening his eyes for the first time, to a blazing intensity of light that blasted him into consciousness. He jolted his gaze away, simultaneously thrusting himself upright, confused, bewildered.

He was naked, on a beach.

Barney was trotting down the shoreline with a clam in her mouth. Periodically, she would stop and toss it in the air and then circle it as if it were a prisoner thinking of escaping, growling and nipping all the while. Then she would pick up the creature and continue the game.

Watching Barney's antics was a joy. She had no inhibitions, no responsibilities, and no history, really. She just lived for the moment, enjoying the present.

"What do you have there, ol' Barn?" asked Benjamin, smiling. "You find a clam for supper?"

Barney paid no attention to any distractions; her mission dictated her immediate attention, and she had no time for foolish drivel.

"Should I build a campfire and cook that clam for you? Myself, I'm going to have a hot dog."

Upon hearing the *h* word, Barney released her prisoner on good behavior and sprang toward her master and chef, running full tilt.

"Just hold your horses, girl. We'll have to collect some firewood first. And that's just what we'll do, as soon as I get some clothes on. I must have dozed off for a minute," Benjamin said and chuckled, totally oblivious of reality's departure, of evaporated thoughts that instantly dissipate, eternally erased from one's memory, as if they never existed at all.

Building a fire, just like most endeavors in life, is rather easy, as long as a person goes about it while utilizing a proper procedure. Choice wood must be collected of the desired variety: dry birch bark, for ignition; dry twigs, for immediate combustion; dry sticks to sustain the smaller flames; larger sticks to bring the mass to a blaze; and then larger pieces of dried stumps, limbs, or driftwood to top off the bonfire, adding longevity.

Soon, a crackling fire blazed where there once was none, providing warmth and light for the day's eve as the white, penetrating sun changed into its evening clothes, dressed in a serene yellow robe, garnished with orange lace, adorned with scarlet and violet ribbons, cordially reflecting its fluorescent attire in the calm mirror of the lake.

Benjamin whittled the end of a green willow stick to a sharpened point. He then speared four wieners, horizontally, through their centers.

Roasting wieners is a delicate procedure. If any degree of perfection is to be achieved, it is imperative to keep the flames from actually touching the meat until they are thoroughly heated and smoked. The wise outdoor chef will utilize a makeshift prop of some sort to hold the hot-dog stick in the appropriate place, thus diminishing fatigue in the arms of the chef. Only after the dogs are dripping and well cooked should the chef incinerate the wieners in the flame, blackening them to the desired consistency. Once finished to perfection, the dogs should immediately be inserted into a hot-dog bun, smothered with ketchup and onions and then eaten, savoring each mouthful. The familiar flavor of this traditional delicacy acts as a catalyst to connect and intertwine past memories into a blissful unity, memories of hot-dog roasts from long ago, memories of simple pleasures, of camping trips, of family get-togethers—sort of like a traditional prayer, like an om.

Benjamin, lost in deep meditative contemplation, dined on his supper, sitting cross-legged, with the sacrificial fire before him as the setting sun glorified the ritual, glorified the temple.

Barney, on the other hand, cared little if her hot dogs were cooked or not. In fact, she preferred them raw, because it was much quicker and, in her opinion, much easier. She had quickly gobbled up her four raw hot dogs in mere seconds, gulping them down in massive chunks, barely chewed. Not only was this method of dining efficient, it provided extra time to beg for a portion of her master's supper, which she did, drooling earnestly. She watched her master's hot dogs, perched near the flames, staring directly at them, unflinchingly. Only briefly would she turn her gaze toward Benjamin and then back to the wieners, as if trying to will them to fall off the stick, contaminating them, condemning them to be unworthy for her master and given to her.

Benjamin, as if in a trance, peacefully and tranquilly ate the last of his supper, oblivious of the two penetrating eyes that were keenly fastened on his every move. Even the agonizing whimpers that were intended to arouse sympathy had gone unnoticed, as the last morsel disappeared from existence, the staring ceased; the expectation ceased; the tension was replaced with contentment. Barney lay down near her master.

The night sky unveiled its spangling of stars, illuminating the heavens, reflectively dancing on the glassy lake. Croaking bullfrogs and chirping crickets harmonized along with a symphony of other night sounds, building into a crescendo of nature's song. A raccoon edged his way along the shoreline, just yards from the flickering fire, gazing with reflective eyes. Every so often, a solitary splash echoed from the waters, a bass perhaps, surfacing for a tasty black bug or a plump green frog. There was no moon tonight, just stars, billions of stars, and just as many mosquitoes, doing their best to interrupt the serenity and ambience of the setting. Benjamin, who was annoyingly scratching at his wrists and ankles, moved closer to the exhaust of the fire, in the smoke just enough to deter the buzzing cannibals from staging another assault.

After the initial stages of darkness had settled in for the evening, most of the mosquitoes dissipated to wherever mosquitoes go when they dissipate; perhaps it's the same place they go in daylight hours. Tranquility and peace returned to the tiny camp.

Visitor 1

"Ahoy, the camp!" shouted a man's voice out of the darkness, startling Benjamin that he almost fell headlong into the fire. Barney sprang to attention, growling and staring out into the blackness of the lake. Faintly, a black shape could be seen silently gliding across the surface, approaching out of the darkness.

"Ahoy, the camp!" shouted the voice again. "Permission to dock on your beach?"

Barney furiously barked at the mysterious force that was making its way into their world. Between the angry growls, Benjamin could hear the soft splash of a canoe paddle, as the craft made itself visible, faintly illuminated by the firelight.

"Hello," said Benjamin, feeling a bit uneasy. "Come on in."

"Thank you kindly," said the man as the canoe gracefully slid onto the sand, coming to a stop.

"Barney, go lie down!" commanded Benjamin as the beagle toned down her fierce barking into a menacing growl, displaying her lack of faith and demonstrating a devout skepticism in the integrity of the stranger. "Pay no mind to my dog," Benjamin said, smiling. "She's just surprised to see anyone way out here, and to tell you the truth, so am I.

"Benjamin Frisk," greeted Benjamin while holding out his hand as the man pulled his canoe farther onto the sand.

"Hello," the man replied as the two gripped hands in customary fashion. "Saw your fire from the other side. Thought I'd paddle on over and talk a spell. Not every day a man gets company out here in this godforsaken wilderness. Have to take advantage of situations, situations like these here. Or else, they'll pass you by, wouldn't you say, Mr. Frisk?"

"I suppose so," said Benjamin, releasing his grip. "I'd offer you something, but all we have is water and a few hot dogs; however, you're welcome to them if you like."

"No, no. Just the fire and your company are fine. To tell you the truth, I'm so goddamned sick of hot dogs that I nearly puke just thinking of them."

Both men walked to the fire and chose the most comfortable-looking firewood logs to sit on. The stranger was a stout man, middle aged, clean shaven, with short black hair and matching moustache. He wore wire-framed spectacles that hauntingly mirrored the fire's flames. His attire did not seem to fit the setting at all. He wore a light-colored, long-sleeved dress shirt and dark trousers. If he would have had on a tie, he would have passed as an executive.

"So, Mr. Frisk," said the man, staring across the flames and into Benjamin's eyes, "what brings you to these parts?"

"No reason really," answered Benjamin. "Barney and I usually come here a couple of times a year, just to relax and take it easy. We decided that this weekend was as good a time as any to do a little camping, since the weatherman forecast clear skies and warm weather. And what about yourself, Mr.... What did you say your name was again?"

"Veil," said the stranger. "Heath Veil."

"Doing a little camping yourself, Mr. Veil?"

Mr. Veil laughed. "Yeah, I suppose you could say that I've been camping all right, for about six goddamned weeks, over on the far side of the lake, over there." He pointed out into the blackness. "Not really here for recreation, though."

"Oh?" inquired Benjamin.

"Nope, I'm a surveyor. I was hired by an investment firm to subdivide the lakeshore into a bunch of sixty-foot lots. They're going to bust this lake into a thousand pieces. In a few years, there'll be a city of houses and cottages right here where we sit. People will be swarming over this area like flies on honey. There'll be so many goddamned speedboats and Jet Skis on that lake it'll make your head spin."

"How are people going to get here?" asked Benjamin. "It's at least a mile hike from where I parked. And that's after driving about ten miles on barren two tracks."

"That's always been the problem," said Mr. Veil. "This goddamned lake is so damned hard to get to; it's in the middle of nowhere, and there's so many hills and valleys protecting this place that it's near impossible to feasibly put in a decent highway. But we think we solved the problem. You see, on the west side, there is a huge barrier, solid rock. But behind that fortification, the land gradually slopes for about twenty-five miles or so, all the way to a main highway. It'll still be tough going, but the pot of gold at the end of the trail will be worth it."

"What about the rock barrier?" asked Benjamin.

"That was always the biggest problem—that damned rock. It's over three-quarters of a mile long and just as deep. It's like a huge, granite gate that prevents us access. Well, we've got a plan. We can't go around it, so we're going to blast a road right through the center of that son of a bitch! We've got a blasting crew contracted from Australia. They claim they can blast a road through the entire length in just over a year!"

"I see," said Benjamin, staring into the dying fire, into the glowing orange of the coals.

"Tell you what, Frisk. There's going to be a shit pile of money to be made—that I'll guarantee you. If I was you, I'd think seriously about buying some of these lakefront lots. The company is going to liquidate the first batch they sell in an attempt to get people to start building, just to get the ball rolling. I'm going to buy up all I can. The way I figure it, the price will triple in no time at all. This is choice lakefront. It'll go fast."

Benjamin sat silently, staring at the embers, remembering a time when he was a young boy. His father had taken his mother and him to this lake for the first time. They had tied some logs together, creating a makeshift raft, and then poled themselves about a hundred yards from shore, out to a tiny island, no bigger than the infield of a baseball diamond. There they pitched their tent, roasted hot dogs and marshmallows, cast their lines from shore, and patiently watched their bobbers for a telltale twitch or ripple. He remembered that during the night, his family was awaked by loud splashes outside their tent. *Kerplunk!* It sounded like someone was throwing a large stone into the deep water every so often. Benjamin clung on to his mother while his father left the tent to investigate. He imagined bigfoot monsters lined up on the mainland, hurling boulders at the tiny island, with hateful, hungry eyes. He imagined an octopus-like creature arising from the deep, thrashing its angry tentacles, periodically crashing one arm onto the surface of the water. Fear gripped his soul as yet another loud splash erupted from the darkness, louder and closer than the rest, and then quiet—a quiet as still as death.

"Beavers," said his father, standing just outside the tent.

"Beavers?" questioned Mr. Veil. "What the hell do beavers have to do with it?"

"Oh, I'm sorry," blurted Benjamin. "My mind was somewhere else."

"Say, I've got a proposition for you, Mr. Frisk. You see, I've been surveying out here in the boondocks for six weeks. Originally, I had thought that I could split, stake, and record all the land divisions in about eight weeks' time, but I was mistaken. In fact, I'm only half done. That means I'll be here another six weeks, minimum. Six weeks, goddamn it! I should have hired a helper, but I figured I could handle it. Now I'm singin' a different tune. I just want to get the hell out of this tree-infested jungle and get back to civilization, get some concrete under my feet. So how does this sound? You stay here and help me survey. I'll make it worth your trouble."

"Can't," said Benjamin, shaking his head. "I don't think my company would think too kindly on the idea."

"Where do you work?"

"I work at a raw materials facility. We mine and ship taconite. It's used to make iron and steel."

"You work at US Taconite, then?"

"Yes, that's it. Only been there a while."

"I see," said Mr. Veil. "I know a little bit about that place. My father worked in a place like that, and his father before him. They both died young. That's a union job, isn't it?"

"Yes, it is," said Benjamin. "We get paid pretty good. I wouldn't dream of giving up my job. It's a miracle that I even got hired in the first place. I bet there are a thousand guys just waiting for a chance to get in."

"Yeah, yeah," said Mr. Veil, in a disgusted tone. "I hate to burst your bubble, but my advice to you is to get the hell out of there. Run like the wind and don't look back. That place is nothing more than a prison, and you're a slave, a slave forced to do all the bullshit that the owners and managers find undesirable. Here's how it goes. They look to hire people who are half-assed smart and reliable but not educated enough to find a better job. They also look for family types, the kind that will get married and have kids, the kind that will get mortgages and car payments. Then they hire you and pay you just enough to keep the wolves away, certainly no more than they have to, just enough to keep you locked in. You're never allowed the opportunity to really get ahead in life. Sure, if you work your asshole off for fifteen years, they might make you a foreman, who is nothing more than a higher-paid flunkey. You'll never be allowed to cross the line—never. They don't want you in their world. They'll hire college graduates for those positions. Those are the people who will make the big bucks and live in nice homes and be respected in the community. But not you! You'll work your ass off, doing the same boring routines for ten years. At that time you will grow to hate your job and want to quit, but you won't be able to. And you know why? Because you'll be strapped in debt, and there won't be any other available job that's much better. That and the fact that you'll have ten years' seniority, which means you'll probably get out of the hardest bullshit jobs and into bullshit jobs that are a little easier but twice as boring. And they'll give you another week of vacation and maybe even a tiny, miniscule raise. That, along with your benefit package, will be your ball and chain that will sentence you to thirty years, at least. After the first ten years, you will grow numb and accept your fate and trudge through your weary days, blandly, mindlessly, waiting for the weekend and vacations, so you can actually live for a few days a year. Of course, the weekends won't be much of a life either. You'll probably have to spend your time fixing the lawn mower or replacing that transmission in the work car or fixing some other piece-of-junk machine that you own, since you can't afford a new one. You might as well forget about bettering yourself with college at that point. You'll probably end up working overtime or taking on another job just to stay afloat. The last ten of your working years, you'll dream of retirement. That'll be the golden ring that will keep you packing your pail with stale bologna sandwiches every day as you sell your life away, eight hours at a time."

"It's really not a bad job," interrupted Benjamin solemnly.

"No?" Mr. Veil said, laughing. "Forgive me, but you sound like Boxer in the novel *Animal Farm*. Don't be fooled. You're just a number, a tool—nothing more. They will use you to make themselves money, and that's the end of it. Any patriotism or allegiance to the company is all an illusion created to keep you chained to your position. You know, the scenario that I'm painting here is a best-case scenario. It could be a hell of a lot worse. Once you're there for twenty years, you'll be forty or fifty, at the age of no return. Your kids will be in college, with the hope that they will not have to live the miserable existence of a laborer, and you'll be shelling out a bundle of cash to help them out, and then what? Well, you better not have an accident or hurt your back or some such thing. If you do, your 'friendly, loyal' company that you've given all your years to will turn on you like a rabid dog. You see, then you will be a liability to them, a cost, and they will do everything in their power to eliminate the cost, eliminate you. Then what will you do, if you lose your job at the ripe old age of fifty, with a bad back, to boot? Or what about this? Let's say you work to age fifty and the company decides to downsize. Where does that leave you? Laid off and looking for work? At age fifty? Your best hope would be that they keep you on as a dirt shoveler for the rest of your days, until you retire or die. And in my opinion, the company would rather just send you to the glue factory like an old horse that outlived its usefulness. It's a shame, too, a damned shame. You know why? Tell me this: did you ever read *The Grapes of Wrath*, by Steinbeck?"

"No," replied Benjamin.

"Well, goddamn it, you should! Because that's just how it is. Supply-and-demand economics has its place, but not when it's applied to humans, not to the labor force. Nope, your best bet is to get out of the whole mess; wash your hands of it before it's too late. Hell, you're young! You should get out of there and take a crack at every opportunity that lands on your doorstep. And that's exactly what I'm offering you, an opportunity. Why, if you team up with me, you'll be learning a trade, a damned good trade, a well-paying trade. Why, hell, you should be paying me for all the surveying skills you'll be learning. What do you say, Frisk? It's your choice: you can either choose life or stay and continue building your prison walls."

"I couldn't," replied Benjamin. "I couldn't risk losing my job. I won't risk it. If I went with you, I'd be giving up a sure thing, giving up a potential lifetime of good work, giving up security for only six weeks of survey work, a job that offers no security or benefits. No offense to you, Mr. Veil, but all I want out of life is a secure job, a secure source of income, enough income to pay the bills and afford to get married someday, get married and have a houseful of kids, and then—"

"Oh, for Christ's sake," interrupted Mr. Veil, breaking out in laughter. "You're brainwashed to the core! Married? Ha! That's it. There you go—get married. Yeah, go ahead and get married. Go and walk up the aisle with your sweetheart and live happily ever after. What you don't know is that you'll be walking to the gallows with your hangman to live in torment. Listen, Frisk, marriage is just another prison—a trap. You'll end up working your ass off for your beloved and hand her the paycheck every payday, so she can buy doilies for the house or maybe some new clothes. You'll probably have to take on a second job to pay for all that crap. And when you manage to find a spare hour, she'll have some job for you to do while she watches soap operas or polishes her nails or goes to aerobics classes, so she can look more attractive—and don't think for a second that she's trying to be more attractive for you. Did you know that the divorce rate in this country is over fifty percent? And that's not including all the longer term relationships that failed, which are really marriages without a marriage license. I tell you what: if you're thinking of getting married, you'd be better off tying a big stone around your neck, rowing out in the middle of that lake, and jumping in. It would save you from a lot of suffering."

Benjamin laughed. "It can't be that bad. There are plenty of happy marriages. Anyways, it's not just about being married to a woman that appeals to me. It's the whole family thing."

"Oh," sneered Mr. Veil. "The whole family thing, eh? I get it. You're going to be the 'man' of the house. The dog is going to bring you your slippers in the morning, while you smoke your pipe and read the paper in a comfortable easy chair. Then you and your family will have breakfast together: bacon, eggs, toast, and orange juice. The kids will all kiss and hug you and your wife as they happily bound out to the school bus, while you and your wife look on in a loving embrace. Is that it? Is that the picture that's painted in your mind? You've got to get that crap out of your head and get into the real world. Here's how this one will go. You'll get married, and things will be great for a few years. But then, familiarity and complacency will set in. You'll both develop specific routines and roles. Even sex will become routine. The kids will come along, bringing more routines and roles. Everyone will act their part, like following a script in a play. The erotic glamour of your marriage will be dulled by these ever-boring routines and roles that have imprisoned each of you. The kids will fight and argue. They'll always want something, even though they are spoiled rotten. They will probably hate school and, at best, think it is a bore. Then, as teenagers they will want to go out with friends and probably experiment with drugs, booze, and sex, looking for some kind of escape from the boredom of the prison that society and family has locked them into. And, of course, you, a concerned, loving parent, will try to keep them from straying, and your kids will resent you for it. You will argue with them, and they will be a thorn in your side. Then you will resort to using power struggles in an attempt to control them, forcing them to stay in their roles, their places, the place that you've created for them. You'll start with threats and then punish them by grounding them or taking away their allowance. Then, when they are a bit older, you will use the car keys for leverage. During these trying times, you'll find out your wife is screwing the mailman while you're at work and now wants a divorce. She'll get the house and the kids, and you'll get child support, alimony, and babysitting duties on the weekends, while the mailman and your ex fly to Cancún and drink piña coladas on the beach. Near the end of your life, if you're lucky, your kids will care for you enough to throw you into an old folks' home, where you'll rot away your remaining days, while your loving children wonder how they can spend their inheritance. And that's the cold truth of it. That's reality."

"You paint a bleak picture, Mr. Veil."

"No, I paint a realistic picture. Life isn't a Disney movie. In real life there are tigers and bears just looking for a meal. There are wolves and vultures, waiting to prey on your dead carcass. There are also beautiful plants that are poison to the touch. Don't be a blind optimist, clouded with euphoric illusions. Look at the thing squarely, and deal with it accordingly. Don't be a dumb ass."

Both men stared into the last lingering flickers of the campfire, quietly meditating on all that had been said.

"I don't know how the hell I got started on marriage," said Mr. Veil, chuckling to himself. "I don't give a shit if you want to get married and raise a family. That's your goddamned business. I just need a helper to finish up this surveying job. And I'll pay you good—damned good. What do they pay you at US Taconite these days? Twelve, fourteen dollars an hour? Hell, I'll give you triple that. Let's see...at fifteen an hour... eight hours a day...That comes to a hundred and twenty...times three... three hundred and sixty a day...Oh, hell, I'll pay you four hundred a day, daylight till dark. So, for the next six weeks, that would be...Let's see... That would be over sixteen thousand dollars! How's sixteen thousand smackers grab you, Frisk?"

"Sixteen thousand dollars!" exclaimed Benjamin. "For six weeks' work?"

"You're goddamned right," said Mr. Veil, smiling. "You've found me in a bind. I need a helper, and you're the only one available. This means that old Mr. Opportunity has landed on your doorstep and is knocking. All you have to do is get up off your ass and let him in. And, who knows, if you work out all right, I'll keep you on for other jobs. I'm booked up solid till next year. Of course, I won't be able to pay you four hundred dollars a day, but you'll do a hell of a lot better than you're doing now, that's for goddamned sure. And you'll be learning a trade, to boot."

"Jeez, I don't know," said Benjamin. "That's a tempting offer... damned tempting."

"Sure it is," agreed Mr. Veil. "That's because it's a damn good offer, the offer of a lifetime. You've sort of reached a fork in your road of life. You can stay on your same old dreary path, along with most of the population, or you can choose something better for yourself. Hell, if you work for me, in just a few years, you'll know enough to go it alone, own your own surveying company. Then you'll be an owner, a true player in the game, not just a pawn."

"Owner?" questioned Benjamin. "What do you mean 'owner'?"

"Listen, Frisk, it's all about ownership; that's the holy grail of capitalism. Once you own something significant, something that others want but can't afford, you lord it over them in return for their life, which equates to dollars earned. Don't you see? People like you have to work for owners. Tell me this: do you own a house?"

"Yes, I do," replied Benjamin.

"Do you have a mortgage on the house?"

"Well, sure I do, just like everybody else."

"Then the bank owns the house, not you. They're loaning you the house for a fee. And you're going to work every day to pay off the owners of your house. You'll probably be paying triple the original price by the time you're through. I bet you never even calculated how much you'll be paying by the time you're finished. You know, the same goes for your car and anything else you buy on credit. The owners get rich on your labor. Even where you work, at your job, you're working to make money for the owners of the company."

"Well, sure, I make money for the owners," said Benjamin. "But in return I get to have a house to stay in and a car to drive."

"Sure you do," Mr. Veil snapped. "But when you work at your job, you're helping to create something. You're helping to create iron ore, and in doing so, you are creating wealth, actual wealth that can be traded or sold."

"I don't see your point," said Benjamin.

"The point is that labor creates one hundred percent of the tradable wealth, and for whom? For the owners, that's who. Then the owners pay you only a miniscule portion of the very wealth that you yourself created, and then they pocket the rest."

"It's not like they keep all the profit by doing nothing," defied Benjamin. "They have to manage the business and deal with all the problems. And they have to put a lot of money back into the business for renovations and upkeep." Benjamin threw a few dry sticks on the glowing coals, encouraging a flicker of new life in the fire pit.

"Sure, they put money back in, to perpetuate the chain gang in order to make more money for themselves, while they sit in air-conditioned offices, wearing white shirts and black ties, giving you just enough crumbs of wealth to keep you working for them and broke enough so you can't quit. The only way out is to cross the line, to become an owner yourself. Then you can afford to own a business or an apartment complex or whatever and then charge others to use what you own. Instead of you having to pay for such things, people will have to pay you. Even if you start a business, the workers are really paying their employer in a sense. Listen, if owners weren't making money off you, they wouldn't hire you."

"You mean, like you hiring me?" said Benjamin, looking away from the fire and into Mr. Veil's eyes.

"Sure! You're damned right!" screamed Mr. Veil. "I'll be making a hell of a lot more off you than fifteen thousand dollars, that's for goddamned sure. I'll probably make double that, just for what you accomplish, and I'll pocket the rest. All I'm saying here is that if you stick with me, you'll be able to afford to be an owner of a business or whatever and make money off other people's labor and get rich doing it. I'm offering you the pathway to fortune. And when you achieve fortune, people cater to you like you're a king. Fortune and fame, Frisk. But you have to pursue it on your own, with your own free will."

"So," said Benjamin, "then I'll get rich screwing over my fellow man. Is that it?" Benjamin tossed some larger pieces of wood on the fire, igniting a healthy blaze. "I'm sorry, Mr. Veil, but I'm content where I am at right now. I'm not interested in a pile of money and all the headaches that accompany the type of ownership you're talking about. I just want a simple life. Enjoying this fire here tonight is enough for me at the moment."

Mr. Veil's puzzled gaze focused on the image of Benjamin, as if he was assessing a strange new phenomenon for the first time. He stood up, turned from the light of the fire, and walked away, into the blackness. "It's your funeral," he muttered.

Through the darkness, the watery sounds of the retreating canoe faintly disappeared into the shrouding mist.

Benjamin was troubled by the conversation. His thoughts turned and tumbled as he lay closer to the fire with his back to the cool sand, gazing at the stars. "Life has many directions," he thought to himself. "Who knows which direction is best? The best direction may not necessarily be a painless one, but then again, who would knowingly choose a direction laced with pain? Choices are strange phenomena. Can we really direct our paths? Or does our intrinsic nature make the choice for us, only falsely leading us to believe that our own intellect made the choice? Why does a person have to choose at all? Isn't it better just to stay on the path that you're on and let destiny direct you, sort of just go with the flow? Or should a man pilot his own course? And take charge of every situation as much as possible. Row against the current, if need be. Who knows? If I just go with the flow, the current of life might take me down a rocky rapids or over a waterfall, to my death. But, on the other hand, the flow of life may be a peaceful journey, with little frustration and few worries, as long as you stay in the current, just stay in the current, making the best of each day. And the current is truly beautiful," thought Benjamin as he drifted off to sleep, under a blanket of stars glittering in the heavens.

Visitor 2

The morning sun awakened a chorus of birdsong, hidden in the trees. Chattering melodies filled the crisp, fresh morning air, gently waking Benjamin to the day, into the current. He stood up, shaking off the sand.

"Guess we didn't need to haul that sleeping bag and pup tent back here," he said to Barney as he put the remainder of the firewood on the smoldering vestiges of the campfire. "We might as well have breakfast." Once the fire got going, the two campers roasted the last of their food supply and enjoyed the simple breakfast.

The calm lake shivered as the first morning breeze rippled across its surface, causing a jillion sparkles to dance in joyful sunlight. A family of mallards graced the shallows of the shoreline, but quickly paddled to deeper water as Barney ran to greet them with a friendly, good-morning bark.

The day warmed itself under a cloudless blue sky. The fishing would be best while it was still early. Benjamin gathered his pole and tackle and began walking through the woods down a familiar trail that followed the shoreline, heading toward a small bay where he'd had good luck fishing in previous years. The trail was scattered with last year's acorns as it wound its way through the oaks and jack pine. Chipmunks scurried across the dry leaves as Barney skipped after them, their furry tails fleeing up the tree trunks and into the safety of their sheltering branches. There, they would chatter in a high-pitched, scolding tone as the intruders passed by. Benjamin absorbed the essence of the setting, the essence of the natural world, lost in the sights and smells and sounds, lost in the ambience of peace itself. As he proceeded, a movement caught his eye immediately in front of his next step—snake!

"Argh! Goddamn it," he shouted while spontaneously jumping backward like a coiled spring instantly releasing its powerful burst of energy. He tumbled over, but immediately sprang back on his feet as the snake slithered down the trail and toward the water. Benjamin grabbed a large stick and screamed a hysterical war cry as he uncontrollably chased the hated serpent, crashing a blow on its midsection. It turned its now-squirming body away from the lake and toward its enemy, striking the stick with its pink open mouth. Benjamin instinctively swung the club again and again, dashing the brains of the snake to a pulverized oblivion. Benjamin spastically continued beating the dead carcass violently in fanatical fashion, driven by adrenaline, bashing the crushed, bloody skull again and again and again, while gritting his teeth and droning out a primeval growl, resurrecting an inner spirit that evolution had nearly erased.

Finally, his hysteria subsided enough to stop beating the tangled corpse. As he gazed at the dead, twitching body, shivers ran through him like iced lightning.

"Goddamn you," he yammered, gasping for breath. Benjamin looked away from the site of the murder, trying to get a grip on his composure. He walked a safe distance away, where he could still see the mangled cadaver, and leaned his wobbly body on the trunk of a large pine, allowing himself to slide down to the ground, exhausted.

The snake had done him no harm. It had just been in its home, just in its own environment, enjoying the day, probably looking for breakfast. In fact, it was he who was the intruder; it was he who was out of his element. Yet, the murder was not premeditated; it had been spontaneous. It had been born out of an ancient past that genetics had fused into him, perhaps from the beginnings of creation itself. It was not he, not his own mind, who had killed the snake; it was something else, something programmed within his being. Perhaps it was the very face of nature, brutally releasing its power.

Benjamin sat in numb contemplation with his eyes fastened on the crime scene. Barney, confused and frightened with the intense spectacle that manifested itself before her, inched her way toward the bloody mess, inquisitively sniffing.

"Barney, get away from that!" yelled Benjamin as he sprang up, running. Barney, sensing an odd tension, darted a safe distance away. Benjamin retrieved his killing stick and used it to pick up the dead snake, its headless length draped over the end of the stick. He walked it away from the footpath over to a bushy area and deposited the creature among the shrouding branches of the thickest shrub. As the body slid off, he allowed the stick to fall from his hands. The deed was finished. He walked back to the footpath, collected his scattered fishing gear, and continued on his way, keeping his eyes glued to the path immediately in front of him.

The path wound its way around a large hill and continued through slight valleys and depressions where the ground was unstable and a bit muddy, only to emerge on high ground again. Finally, he arrived at the familiar clearing at the back of the bay. It hadn't changed much since the last time he was there. In fact, it hadn't noticeably changed at all. It was as if time didn't affect this place. He laughed to himself to think such a thought—that time doesn't exist here! What a foolish notion. Certainly, these were not the same ferns and blades of grasses from last summer. Time has every known thing in its lineal grip. We are placed into the stream of it when we are born and are only allowed one way to exit. The same goes for plants, as well as all living creatures. Even the stones are not permanent. But where do the stones come from?

Benjamin picked up a small, flat stone and approached the water. He skipped it across the surface, amusing himself at the various splashes and ripples that he himself caused. The sun was well into its morning climb as he cast his line from shore, hoping for something out of the deep to happen his way. The hours passed without a single nibble. He frequently changed lures and baits, but to no avail. The fish just didn't seem to be interested. This was somewhat of a dilemma, because he was out of food and had anticipated a hearty fish dinner before packing his gear and hiking back to the pickup to begin the long trek homeward. The sun had already reached its zenith, and hunger had begun its nagging complaints.

"Well, girl," said Benjamin, looking at Barney, "looks like we're skunked. It doesn't pay to keep fishing. Its already high noon, and the sky is as clear as glass; the chance of catching a fish now is slim to none. That means we're out of luck and out of food. We might as well head home."

Benjamin took one last cast, slowly reeling in the line, hoping for a fairy-tale ending to his fishing expedition, but with no success. He gathered his equipment and retreated down the same path that had brought him to this place.

The intensity of the noontime rays brightened the return trip. All the different shades of green seemed to glow as if phosphorescent. The various plants seemed to emit a sense of joy, jubilantly celebrating the day. Benjamin robotically followed the worn path all the way around the large hill; the idea to climb over its peak never even occurred to him. He eventually made his way back to the murder scene; he cringed as the crouching memory sprang to life, seizing him in an instant of terror. He quickened his steps.

Upon approaching his campsite, he smelled the distinct aroma of cooked food. As he approached the fire pit, he saw two good-sized fish and two potatoes lying on a large, flat stone in the middle of the hot coals. Benjamin looked around him for a telltale clue to this riddle. He noticed footprints in the sand. He followed them to the lakeshore, thoroughly puzzled. There were no fresh canoe marks in the beach sand, not even one from the previous night, just fresh footprints. Returning to the campfire, he sat and pondered the situation. The food seemed like it was nearly cooked. Should he eat it? Did Mr. Veil somehow leave this as a gift? Or is someone else expecting to return to their lunch?

Just then, some brush cracked from within the woods, startling Benjamin. A man came walking out with an armful of dry sticks. He was an old man with grayish hair and a long, white beard. As he came closer, Benjamin noticed his attire. He wore a long-sleeved flannel shirt and jeans that were worn in the knees; the rips were patched with a green fabric of some sort. The old leather on his work boots seemed well broken in from years of use, but the leather itself was sound, and the soles looked brand new. As he silently approached the fire, he set down the bundle of sticks, turned to Benjamin, and held out his hand.

"John's the name," he said with a smile, "just John. Don't have a last name."

"Benjamin Frisk," said Benjamin as the two shook hands. "I never met a man who didn't have a last name."

"You probably won't ever again, I reckon. Never really had a use for a last name, at least, not today...Well, sit down there, young fella, and we can have us a fish dinner fit for a king. That there's fresh walleye, and those spuds may look innocent a-lying there on that stone, but them's blue potatoes. The seed come all the way from Germany, long ago. They're some of my best. They ain't actually blue, mind you. The flesh is actually yellow. Don't know how they got themselves named 'blue.' The skin is actually more of a purple color. Grow 'em in my garden, along with everything else. Oh well, we're going to have ourselves a feast, that's for sure. Got some wine, too. I love to make wine, just love it."

"Well, I thank you for your hospitality. I certainly appreciate your invitation. To tell you the truth, I was out of food and just came from trying to catch my lunch...unsuccessfully. You caught these fish off my beach there?"

"Yeah, they sure are some nice ones, aren't they? Ain't nothing like fresh walleye baked on a hot stone with a little wood smoke for seasoning. There just ain't anything like it in the world. It's as unique as an apple compared to the tree it was picked off of. Smell those potatoes? They're nearly done! You're gonna love them blue potatoes. You just wait."

"I don't see your fishing pole anywhere. I'm curious, what did you use for bait? I couldn't get as much as a nibble."

"Oh, I don't bother with poles and lines…all the tangles and such… too complicated. The trick is you just have to figure out where the fish are; that's the trick of it. Ain't no sense trying to catch fish where there ain't any fish, now is it? You gotta figure, just like a fish would figure. Once you find 'em, ain't nothing to coax one out of the lake, 'specially walleye—they're very agreeable."

Benjamin inwardly smiled at the old man, who was obviously adhering to the largest commandment in the fisherman's bible: that of secrecy. Not to say that fishermen are a greedy lot, far from it. They will share their bounty with anyone in need, even a cat. However, to tell another person a particular secret of catching fish is a sin. Some things in life must not be freely given to another. An act of such would belittle the thing itself and kill the seed of appreciation, as well as the seed of respect. No, a person should inspire another to seek out answers on his or her own, to encourage by fanning sparks of interest, but allowing him or her to do the burdensome work alone. Only then will the person truly learn—not only the thing, but the entire discipline. During the course of the study, a deep respect and appreciation will set in, a joyful reverence for the thing, whether it be catching fish, building a house, or some other. However, a person cannot just go through the act of learning by participating in a mechanical fashion, following directions like following a road map. A person has to participate—wholly participate—with body, heart, and soul. One has to be immersed in the thing, intimate with the thing. Out of this total intimacy is where love itself is born. Once born, it will flourish and grow in intensity, as long as it is reinforced with more intimacy. This is the true formula for love. And it applies to everything—all people, places, and things, even ideas. You just have to immerse yourself in the groundwork, participate body and soul, be intimate.…

"About finished?" asked the old man.

"What, uh…What did you say?"

"About finished with your thought? You seemed to be thinking a thought. And I hate to interrupt a person when they are thinking. Especially if it was an important thought like yours was. Interesting, isn't it…how thoughts just conjure themselves in your head…Of course, they're just thoughts until they're forged into something tangible by your own hand. Then the fruit from the tangible transforms to the intangible again, but now has fermented into a fine wine. I love to make wine, did I tell you that? Just love it…Oh, where are my manners? Here, take a fish and a potato. They're cooked just right. Wait till you taste those potatoes…blue potatoes…all the way from Germany. Be careful, they're hot. Hey, I've got some birch bark here that we can use as plates. I'll just set your dinner on here, like that…There you are—fish dinner, set for a king. Go ahead now. Don't be shy. We'll have to use our fingers. Careful now, it's hot."

"Thank you," said Benjamin as the old man served him his dinner and set the makeshift plate on his lap. The fish was golden brown, whole, with the head on. Benjamin peeled back the bronze skin, exposing the steaming, virgin white flesh. Lifting the fish to his mouth with both hands, he ate. It was delicious. He then peeled the purply skin from the potato, exposing the yellow flesh, and ate. It was indescribably delectable. The tastes of both the fish and the potato seemed to accentuate each other's flavors, mingling with each other, marrying each other, unifying into one distinct taste.

The old man eyed up Benjamin's facial expressions as he watched him eat his potato, waiting for an affirmation of praise.

"My God!" exclaimed Benjamin passionately. "These potatoes are great. I've never tasted any with this unique flavor. And the fish! They're out of this world!"

"Ha!" said the old man. "What did I tell you? Them's blue potatoes. They're my best. Glad you enjoy them. German seed, you know. Go ahead now, eat up. Yup, grew 'em myself, along with everything else. I love to grow things. My garden has just about everything in it that's imaginable, and even a few things that aren't imaginable…for some folks. Take these potatoes, for instance. I love to plant them in the spring and watch them sprout and break the surface of the soil, taking root as they absorb the sun's energy. I tend them every day, watering their roots, plucking out the weeds, picking off the potato bugs. I just love it, especially in the fall, during harvest time. That's when the plants have finished one of their lives and provide the seed for another. Oh, I love my garden. I tried a new sort of tomato this year, sort of a delicate variety, but it didn't work out; they didn't do what I expected they should. So I pulled all the plants out and burned them—had to. But then I had a bare spot in my garden. Well, that bothered me quite a bit. I don't like any wasted space in my garden. So I planted some squash, some plain old thick-skinned squash. And you know what? Those squash took root and grew like crazy. The vines grew clear out of the garden and up and over the hedge that I have around the perimeter. There were so many big, plump squash hanging from those vines that it made my eyes shine with delight! Who would've thought? Squash, of all things? Just goes to show you never know.

"Last fall," continued the old man, "I had a lot of peppers. There were reds, greens, yellows—every kind you could think of. Seemed to have an overabundance of hot peppers, jalapeños."

"Jalapeños?" exclaimed Benjamin, while finishing the last of his dinner. "I hate jalapeños, too hot for my taste."

"Oh no," solemnly stated the old man, "*hate* is a strong word. You know what I do? I mix and store them with other vegetables. That takes away their sharpness and actually acts as a mellowing agent, binding all the flavors into something unique and beautiful. In fact, that's why I grow so many peppers. They may be a sassy lot, but they sure add color and flavor. Yes, sir, they surely do. Life would be drab, indeed, if it weren't for a few peppers here and there."

"I sure do thank you for the meal," said Benjamin. "It was great; I loved every bit of it."

"You're most welcome. I'm glad you enjoyed it; I truly am. But we're not quite finished yet. We're going to top off this feast with some home-made wine. Did I say that I love to make wine? I just love it. This here bottle is fresh. I know I should age it for a while, but this is a special occasion."

"What's the occasion?" asked Benjamin.

"Why, it's Sunday, of course!" stated the old man in a surprised tone. "Sunday only comes but once a week. It's a day of rest, and it's a day of celebration—and for good reason, too. Just look at that bottle of wine. You see how clear it is? Hardly no sediment at all. I try to sift out all I can by straining the mixture through a finely woven cloth. Yes, sir, I surely love to make wine."

"What kind of wine is it?" questioned Benjamin. "When I was a kid, I used to make rhubarb wine. It never turned out very good."

"This here is grape wine," replied the old man, "made with genuine wild grapes. Handpicked each one myself."

"Wild grapes?" said Benjamin with a puzzled tone. "I've never heard of wild grapes."

"No? Why, they're all over the place. You just have to know what to look for and where to look for them. These particular wild grapes are sort of a natural *baco noir* variety. They're a hearty bunch; the vines are sturdy, woodsy, full framed. The fruit is a bit acidic, a bit sour if you were to taste an individual one. But when you get a bunch of them together and ferment them with a little added sugar, they transform into something special. I try to pick the grapes when they are just ripe enough. Then I press them, using a large vat, squeezing the fragrant juices out of them. After I add the sugar, I turn the whole shebang, every day—every day, mind you. That's important. During the turning process, I add my own special yeast. Then, I just keep turning as she ferments, as she works. You've got to let her work. The more she works, the better she is. The fermenting process is vital; it's actually a transformation process, a changing from one substance into another substance. Some folks would call it a miracle. Funny thing about miracles, though: people witness miracles every day of the week, but they don't recognize them as such. I guess they'd prefer me to pull a rabbit out of a hat. Oh, I'm sorry. Where was I? Oh, oh yes. Let's see, then, once the wine's done working, I strain her out and let her sit a week or two, to settle her down. Then I strain her out again—and again if I have to." The old man uncorked the bottle. "Here, take a swig."

Benjamin tipped the bottle to his mouth, mostly in a friendly gesture to salute the old man. The wine was a bit tangy, almost sour, but it had a warmness to it, indicating a high alcohol content. "Tastes good," said Benjamin politely, handing over the bottle.

The old man took a hefty mouthful, allowing the liquid to coat his entire tongue, allowing the red fluid to linger, absorbing every bit of the flavor, before swallowing. He helped himself to another long drink, similar to the first. "Tart," he said after he swallowed. "Needs aging…five years at least…maybe ten. A few years in the cellar will soften the acidity; it's a bit harsh as it is: not suitable for the kingdom, not as it is. A few years in the cellar for this batch; then we'll check it again." He handed the bottle over to Benjamin. "Might as well finish it."

Benjamin took a deep drink. "That's enough for me. Thank you. Thank you for everything. This was really great—and a great surprise. I surely didn't expect to see any people way back here, and you're the second man I've met since I've been here."

"Is that so?" said the old man as Benjamin handed him the bottle.

"Yup. A surveyor came to visit me last night. Said he'd seen my fire from the opposite side of the lake. Veil was his name—Mr. Veil. I don't know if he told me his first name or not. Says he's subdividing the lake, breaking it up into small lakefront lots. Says he's even going to put a highway in to get people back here. Says there's going to be a lot of money to be made. He even offered me a slice of the pie."

"Is that so?" said the old man. "That's quite a bit of knowledge to be walking around with. I suppose one could say that knowing what you know could make you a rich man. I suppose you have been given the opportunity to have it all: fortune, fame, then power and prestige, then women, everything—the works. It seems that you've been offered the door that leads to all the things desired by most men. You're one lucky fella. You have the whole world in front of you, ripe for the picking." The old man took a quick drink and then corked the bottle.

"Nope, that's not for me," said Benjamin. "I don't want anything to do with it."

"Why's that?" said the old man, keenly eyeing up Benjamin.

"Life isn't about fortune, fame, or power and prestige. If you ask me, those things are nothing more than bait for a trap. Once people bite into any one of those things, they just hunger for more; then they finally build themselves up into such a consuming hunger that it controls their lives, eating them up in the process. No, I believe a person has to show integrity, do what's right, not just what's notable in society's eyes or profitable. And to tell you the truth, I don't think it's right to split up this lake and sell it off. Right now, this lake is free for anyone to use, anyone who cares enough to make the effort to make the trip. It's beautiful, just as it is, just as it was created. Why, anything that people would do to it, in an effort to 'improve' it, would be to its detriment. The best thing that people could do to this place is to leave it alone and live in harmony with it. Yup, if you ask me, this place is like heaven just as it is. But the people will come, sooner or later; the people will come and try to buy a piece of this heaven and try to own it. They'll put up fences and No Trespassing signs; they'll build their summer homes and cottages, filling the lake with all the noise and commotion of a city. Then they'll form a 'lake association' of some sort and try to control everything, even the fish."

"What's wrong with that?" asked the old man. "Shouldn't people be allowed to be caretakers of nature's gifts?"

"No!" quickly responded Benjamin. "Well, yes, I suppose…maybe. I don't know. It's just that this lake is pristine right now; it's perfect just as it is. And who's been taking care of it? Who made it this way? The good Lord, that's who, certainly not the hands of men or women. Men and women will only contaminate nature's delicate balances, balances that have been put in place thousands of years ago. Nope, if you ask me, the only thing people will do is take advantage of the seemingly inexhaustible natural resources, the way they've always done and will continue to do so until they've discovered the damage they've caused. At that point, the best-case scenario would be that humankind would realize the damage they've created and try to reverse the situation—to get things back to their original condition. They would have been better off to just leave it alone in the first place."

Benjamin and the old man sat in silence.

"I don't know," continued Benjamin. "Maybe it's me who is greedy. Maybe I'm the selfish one. I come here a couple times a year and have this all to myself—well, mostly all to myself. Maybe I just don't want to give up what I have. Maybe it would be good to get other people up here to experience what I've been experiencing all these years."

"And what exactly have you been experiencing all these years?" asked the old man.

"Peace, I guess," answered Benjamin. "Treasures maybe."

"Treasures?" asked the old man, laughing. "You find gold up in those there hills?"

"Yes," replied Benjamin. "Yes, I believe I did. The truest treasures in life, for me anyways, are the simple things: a cup of hot coffee in the morning, an honest day's work, a surprise fish dinner with a stranger, enjoying places like this lake and those hills. This is a place where a person can just be, a place shed of all the distractions of life, a place to recharge, to refuel the spirit. I tell you the truth: when I leave this place, I feel like I've been rejuvenated, like I was born again. I just love it here. It bothers me to think what it will be like in years to come, after Mr. Veil gets through with it." Benjamin turned his gaze from the lake, toward the old man. "You must come here often. To catch those fish as quickly as you did, you must've known about a secret fishing hole or something of the sort."

"Oh, I've been around," said the old man. "Been around for a long time."

"Did you ever come across Mr. Veil?"

"Mr. Veil…" said the old man deeply. "Oh, I know of Mr. Veil. He always seems to be on the opposite side of the lake from me, been that way for a long time now. Oh well, it's necessary. He's necessary. You have to have a contrast; you just do. Once a contrast is created, the playing field of free will is born. It's all about choices…among other things."

"I suppose," responded Benjamin, not fully understanding what the old man had just said.

The old man uncorked the wine bottle. "Take and drink," he said.

Benjamin half expected the old man to hand him the opened bottle, but he held it close to his body. Their eyes met. Benjamin reached out and took the bottle, lifted it to his lips, and drank. The wine tasted different, somehow sweeter, mellower than he remembered. Puzzled, he looked at the bottle in disbelief, assessing whether it was indeed the same bottle. "This wine seems changed," he said.

"Well, sure it has," said the old man, laughing. "That's the miraculous thing about wine. It's changing all the time." Benjamin handed back the bottle. The old man helped himself to a healthy drink, savoring and assessing the flavor in his usual, ritualistic manner. "You know," he stated, "maybe this batch doesn't need as much time in the cellar as I previously thought." He corked the bottle and stood up, placing the entire bottle in the front pocket of his trousers. "Well," he said, reflectively smiling, "best be moving along now, back up the hill. No more to do here. Been a pleasure, Benjamin."

"The pleasure is mutual, then," said Benjamin. "Again, I thank you for the food and the wine, as well as the hospitality. I've really enjoyed your company. I'm leaving myself. Heading west about a mile. That's where I parked. You're more than welcome to walk with me if you're heading in the same direction."

"No," said the old man, shaking his head. "You don't know what you ask. Anyways, that's not really possible at this point. It's best you travel down your own path. You're on your own now."

The old man turned away and walked silently into the woods, into the trees, disappearing from sight. Benjamin stared at the spot where he departed from view. A strange feeling of sadness came over him, a feeling of separation, an aching of the heart, similar to the feeling experienced when a loved one is separated from you for a knowingly great length of time, a period that seems like forever. Benjamin remembered the camping trips that he and his family used to share in this very spot. Benjamin remembered his father.

Just then, Barney appeared in the exact spot where the old man disappeared from view, startling Benjamin. She was happily bounding toward her master in a nonchalant fashion. He knelt down as the dog approached. She jumped and pranced on her hind legs as she joyously celebrated the reunion.

"Hey, girl," said Benjamin between licks on the face. "Where've you been?" He tried to hug the frantic dog as best he could. He suddenly realized that Barney had been absent during the whole encounter, the whole time since the old man had appeared. How odd it was that he hadn't thought of his dog during that entire expanse of time! He attempted to think into the past, to when he last remembered Barney being with him. It was sometime while he was on the return trail to their camping area. She was with him then, he was sure of it. She must have wandered off sometime before he'd approached the campfire and met the old man. However, it wasn't like Barney to wander off for any length of time—especially with the scent of food around. Maybe she'd ventured back to the forbidden bush. Benjamin cringed at the thought.

"Let's go, girl," he said. "Time to head back home." He walked to the beach and filled a plastic bag full of water to douse what was left of the campfire. The lake sparkled a friendly smile, a loving smile. He stood there on the beach, as if in reverent prayer. Then, turning abruptly, he marched to the fire, doused it, and walked away carrying his gear. He didn't look back. He kept his eyes focused ahead of him as he headed forward, yet simultaneously, unbeknownst to him, he was heading backward, backward in time, back to where he came from.

Back Home

The winding drive home was like traveling out of a consciousness, out of an entirely different world and into another, out of the real world of life and into a man-made world, an artificial world, a world constructed with dead materials, materials that needed constant repair and upkeep. Everything was held together by rules and regulations. Every person was socially held in an order, intertwined within a maze of walls and corridors, not able to see his or her direction clearly or the direction of others, all bound into a social and physical interdependency in which any semblance of harmony depended solely on which foundational principles the whole construction was built upon.

The winding two-track road eventually straightened itself into a two-lane gravel road, and the two-lane gravel road, into pavement. The pavement grew into four lanes as it expanded its concrete-like surface past its boundaries, forging itself into sidewalks and brick buildings fortified with steel, smothering an entire area under a sea of hardened stone. The reality of the true earth lay hidden somewhere underneath.

Benjamin pulled his pickup into his driveway. He felt a bit strange, a bit alien, like he had been away for months or years instead of one night. Yet this was his home; this was where he was supposed to be. This was his place in the scheme of things, or so it so strongly seemed.

Benjamin hesitated exiting the truck, allowing the moment to linger, not in any hurry to sever the psychological thread that still connected him to the recent excursion; however, he realized that it was inevitable. After a time of reflection, he left his time capsule and entered his house, disconnecting the last filaments, making the transformation complete.

V

The Dog Issue

The familiarity of his home instantly surrounded him like the feeling of water after diving into a warm pool. His old life was there, intact, waiting for him with unfinished business. Empty drywall buckets were scattered across the floor; the kitchen sink was full of dishes; the plastic lunch pail rested on the table. Barney ran to and from her empty dog dish with begging eyes. Yes, he was home. He was immersed back into his existence, his slot in the flow of time. Tomorrow would bring the beginning of a new workday, a new workweek. He would go to the plant and fulfill his daily obligations with an accepting heart, paying for his sins, as well as the sins of others. His life would roll onward, forever onward, until plucked from the stream of it all.

Near the telephone, the answering machine was blinking, indicating that one call had been recorded. He pressed the Message button.

"Hi, honey. It's just me, checking in. You must be out, I guess. Hope you're doing OK. I've got some good news. Ned and I are going on a trip to Japan! Can you believe it? We are leaving in two weeks. Can you believe it? Japan! We'll be there for a whole month, maybe more. It's actually a business trip for Ned, but we're going to make a vacation out of it. Can you imagine? Me, in Japan? I can hardly believe it! Ha, I'll have to learn to speak Japanese. I'm so excited. I've been shopping like crazy. I need all new clothes. Oh, this is just wonderful. Maybe we'll even climb Mount Fuji! Can you picture me, your mother, on top of Mount Fuji? I hope you're doing OK. I worry about you, you know. I'm worrying where you are right now. Give me a call when you get a chance, just so I know you're OK. Then I won't have to worry. OK? Well, I'd better be going. Ned and I are off to a big business dinner with some fancy friends of his, and we don't want to be late. Well, OK, love you! Don't forget to call. Bye! Oh, honey, I almost forgot. Ned says he can get you a job in the States if you want. He says he has a lot of 'connections,' whatever that means. Oh well. You think about it, OK? Gotta go. Love ya. Bye!"

Benjamin filled Barney's dish to appease the pitiful and persistent begging, popped a large bowl of buttered popcorn for himself, and finished his weekend in front of the television set, watching a rerun of the movie *Titanic*.

Hours, threading themselves into days, are weaved together by minutes as the second hand of time sweeps them all into endless tomorrows that perpetuate this lineal expanse in the fabric of the true reality, a reality that has been locked from our grasp. The second passes; the minute passes; the hour passes; the day, the week, the month, the year…All were moments of a present; perhaps all "are" moments of a present, a present that we are allowed to visit only once, in this existence.

Worlds spin, endlessly rotating round and round as they simultaneously revolve around their suns, which move on their own paths through the cosmos, carrying us all into a newness, into an unfathomable newness. We all take our seats and ride the traveling merry-go-round, reaching for the golden ring as we spin ourselves dizzy, never fully understanding the meaning or the goal, not completely. "Even if a wise man claims he knows, he cannot really comprehend it." So, onward we ride, hurling along within a momentum, a momentum as wondrous and mysterious as a birth, as creation itself.

Benjamin's life mingled with the seconds and minutes, fusing itself into their brief existences, pressing itself onto each hour, leaving its impression, leaving its imprint, whether it be forgotten or remembered or, perhaps, recorded somewhere in the files of eternity.

His workdays accumulated into a decrescendo and then instantly melted into weekends of freedom and bliss, as the cycle repeated itself time and time again. Taconite made its way out of the mines and onto ships. Workers grumbled at their respective stations. Managers mapped their strategic plans, laying out the groundwork for the future. Bowling tournaments were played. Carburetors were repaired. The drywall job progressed during most weekends and whenever ambition rose out of the misty fatigue of the remainder of the workday. Eventually, though, the living room was sanded and primed, awaiting the final act: the paint.

Paint is an interesting article. It coats and protects while it reflects a color of the spectrum, a color programmed by its composition, its makeup, its genetics (so to speak). The color that it projects provides personality, provides character. This essence can create or enhance a particular mood, a particular emotion, affecting the consciousness of the room, bringing it to light, bringing it to life, and in turn, affecting the consciousness of the people inhabiting the room. In a way, choosing just the right color for a room can affect a person's destiny, or at least alter it in some way, whether it be dramatic or a trifle. Therefore, choosing a color should not be taken lightly, but with a deep deliberation. A scrupulous owner or painter should choose wisely.

Paint also has a devious side to it; it has the ability to hide things from view: for example, a water stain, indicating a leaky roof; or a crack in the plaster, indicating a shift in the foundation. A coat of paint can gloss over the walls of an inferior building, projecting a healthy look of integrity, but in fact, it creates only the illusion of newness, a facade of strength and stability when underneath lies imperfections, hidden from the naked eye.

Benjamin's building was strong and sound. He built everything with only quality materials. And if he was ever in doubt of the integrity of something he was doing, he would seek advice from a trusted professional and proceed with confidence. He did not really dwell on the color of the paint. He gave no thought to projecting a mood or anything of the kind. He didn't really think about it at all. He assumed all along that the room would be white, not an almond color or an off-white, but white—pure, bright white. He simply liked a bright room, full of light, full of beautiful light. And, because the color white reflects all light, it was the only natural choice; there were no other considerations.

One Friday evening, after work, he stopped at a hardware store and purchased the necessary supplies: brushes, rollers, roller pan, paint, masking tape. He also stopped at a fast-food joint to quickly appease any
approaching hunger that might distract him from his anticipated work.
Upon arrival at home, and after the ritualistic "greeting of the dog," he
immediately began the painting process. The protective masking tape
was carefully adhered around the window frames and moldings of a
small portion of the house that was not remodeled but needed a fresh
coat of paint. The new drywall area needed no masking tape because
there were no moldings or accents in place as of yet, which drastically
diminished the time spent administering the cutting-in process. Rolling
was the tricky part, simple but tricky. The paint had to be applied in such
a way as to not leave any telltale lines in order to give the appearance of
unblemished smoothness. Benjamin worked steadily and diligently at his
task. By late evening, the deed was done, the first coat anyways. He sat
among the glistening walls, wet and glossy, admiring all that he had done,
his work, his creation, and he saw that it was good. A satisfaction dwelled
within, a joy, a contentment, a sense of accomplishment. These were the
spiritual fruits of labor, fruits that can only be achieved by the person
who actually performs the work, good work.

Barney seemed to also admire the work. She realized a change, that
something was different. She sensed something new, but really didn't
know exactly what it was; nor did she care one way or the other. In fact,
the smell of the new paint was rather overpowering and somewhat of
a nuisance. However, she wagged her tail in approval out of respect for
her master.

"What do you think, girl? Just like the Taj Mahal? Yup, just like the
Taj Mahal. Our palace is taking shape. Our kingdom is taking shape—the
Kingdom of Frisk. How's that for a name? Kingdom Frisk. I'm the king,
of course. You can address me as 'King Benjamin' from now on. And you
can be the...the peasants."

Barney wagged her tail with delight. Benjamin, pleased with his audience, continued his proclamation using a royal British accent.

"As your king, I do solemnly swear to rule honestly and justly,
always to look out for the best interests of my loyal subjects. And as

a reward for any subject who demonstrates unwavering loyalty, I shall award each such individual with a royal gift. Sir Barney, it has come to my attention that you have demonstrated such loyalty. It has been unequivocally proven by your unfaltering support of this drywall project, which was so recently completed at the Palace Frisk. Although you did absolutely no physical work on the project, I hereby commend you on your encouraging spiritual support. Your encouragement has played an intricate part in fostering a positive attitude toward this endeavor, which in turn was instrumental for its success. Therefore, with no further ado, I hereby award you with your choice of royal gifts. Sir Barney, peasant of the flea, prepare to make your choice. Would you like a treasure chest filled with the finest gold and silver collected from the Orient afar? Or would you rather prefer a royal... hot dog?"

Upon hearing the magic *h* word, Barney whined with anticipated joy, prancing on her hind legs, whimpering with delight.

"I see," said Benjamin in stately fashion, still administering the royal accent. "Let it be known to all subjects of this kingdom that the peasant, commonly known as 'Barney of the Flea,' has chosen her reward. She has rejected the trappings of societal wealth and chosen instead to enjoy the sustenance of the moment by celebrating her achievement to the fullest, by dining on the revered and highly prized royal hot dog." Benjamin marched to the royal refrigerator and retrieved the royal cuisine. Barney howled with frantic giddiness.

"And for choosing so wisely, I, with all the kingly powers vested in me, declare that from hence onward, the lowly Barney of the Flea shall be raised to a position in this kingdom that is representative of her apparent royal character. I therefore declare the peasant, Barney of the Flea, to be hereforthly addressed as 'Duke Barney, Earl of the Squirrel.'" King Benjamin allowed the royal hot dog to fall from his royal fingers. Duke Barney, hysterical with anticipation, devoured the entire mass immediately, licking the spot where it hit the floor. With the royal ceremony concluded, the king and duke retired to the royal beanbag, basking in the ambience of their glistening kingdom as they drifted into a blissful sleep.

The morning sun crept over the horizon, beaming its awakening rays through the windows of Palace Frisk, shining its warmth on the goodly king, who lay in his slumbers, still upon his blue throne. The white walls greeted him a good morning as the remnants of a happy dream danced into oblivion. Sensing her master's wakeful state, Barney pawed his dangling hand for attention. Benjamin, not looking, moved his hand over and on top of the duke's head, gently rubbing the back of her ears. Then he stretched the sleep out of his body by raising his arms upward. He noticed a splotch of white paint on the back of his hand, glistening paint, wet paint...wet paint! Benjamin sprang from the beanbag, perplexed. He stood in awe as he gazed about his kingdom, temporarily speechless. There, before his eyes, were white splotches of paint all over the floor, throughout the house. Footprints. Paw prints. He looked at the half-empty roller pan, lying on the floor, and then at the duke's new white shoes.

"Barney!"

From the tone of the king's voice, the duke knew that her nocturnal artistry was not appreciated. And the ever-reddening hue of his majesty's face forecast a demotion to a lowly serf. Barney ran into the kitchen for safety, shelter from the storm, leaving a trail of white tracks.

"No!" screamed Benjamin. "Stop!" He opened the front door and motioned with pointed finger. "Get out!"

Barney cowered in the kitchen, unwilling to confront the wrath of the ungrateful, once-benevolent king. Benjamin marched into the kitchen, reached under the table, and grabbed the dog's collar and dragged her resisting paws across the floor toward the door, leaving four white skid marks on the linoleum. The king dragged her out the door and slammed it shut, banishing her from the kingdom completely. Barney placed her wet front paws on the door, just to make sure it was closed. She was a bit confused by the day's events, but quickly dismissed the whole affair, electing to take advantage of the situation and patrol the grounds for any sign of the enemy. With nose to the ground, she trooped about the yard, sniffing for any telltale signs.

Benjamin's anger only increased as he attempted to scrub off the freshest paw prints, which seemed to be scrambled everywhere about the house. He questioned the wisdom of owning a pet. "What good are they?" he mumbled to himself. "They get you in trouble with the neighbors. They chew up your furniture. They lay out land mines in the yard for you to step in. What utility are they? None, that's what. The only thing they do is provide companionship; that's it. I should've gotten a hamster or something of the sort." Deep in his heart, Benjamin knew it was his fault for leaving the semifilled paint pan on the floor, but the anger had temporarily mastered parts of him, and it had to play itself out. He cleaned up as many paw prints as he could. A great majority of them were too dry to come out. He looked over his spotted living room, which had seemed an illustrious palace just hours before. He sank in his chair as the fragments of his anger dissolved into nothingness. Actually, the dog tracks looked rather interesting, rather unique. He amused himself with the idea of leaving them there, sort of as a conversation piece for guests. He imagined Barney traipsing about the night before, like a canine Van Gogh, deliberately creating a masterpiece as he slept nearby, unaware of the great painter's creative forces at work. He laughed out loud. "Oh well," he said. "I better get Picasso's paws cleaned off and get her back into the house before she gets into more trouble."

He opened the front door, finally allowing the joy of the morning into his house and into his day, half expecting to see the dejected duke on the porch. The porch was barren. The yard was quiet. A squirrel scampered across the green grass of the lawn. Benjamin walked behind the house, searching for his dog, as a growing feeling of guilt gnawed at him. He wanted to formally forgive Barney for her misdeeds, to make her happy again and set things right between them. However, any action to grant forgiveness on his part would have only been a masqueraded attempt to forgive himself.

"Barney," he yelled, "where are you, girl? Barney!"

A woman suddenly appeared, briskly walking into the drive, almost running; it was Cindy Granger. She did not notice Benjamin standing in the yard as she bounded to the front door, furiously rapping on the wood with her clenched fist. Benjamin inwardly laughed to himself. "What next?" he thought. "It seems that Rembrandt must have taken her art out into the neighborhood, to expand her boundaries. It seems she has gained some recognition." Cindy continued pounding on the door, frantically, while Benjamin stood in silence, pondering the new predicament. He eyed up the new, black bathrobe that she was wearing, looking for any fresh tears. The blackness of her robe accentuated her bouncing blond hair. The robe was tightly clad at her waist, revealing her womanly silhouette.

"Can I help you?" said Benjamin, startling Cindy as she quickly spun around.

Benjamin's inward smirk vanished as he realized that the expression on Cindy's face was not of anger as he had anticipated, but of shock or fear. She looked into his eyes, pausing before she spoke. The moment hung, suspended, stopping time. Benjamin's countenance palled.

"Your dog has been hit by a car," she blurted.

"What?" said Benjamin, stunned.

"Your dog's been hit by a car, right in front of my house."

Benjamin turned, briskly walking to the roadway. He did not run. He held his composure, as the shock settled in. He battled to hold a tight rein over the explosion of emotions that had just been blasted out of his sealed safe, breaking the lock and roaming wildly.

"She's over there, in the ditch," Cindy said and pointed. "I saw the whole thing. I was sipping a cup of coffee and just happened to be looking out the window when I noticed a dog chasing something—a squirrel, I think—right out into the street, right in front of a white van. It happened so fast, all in an instant. The van didn't even stop. It happened so fast. I can't believe they didn't stop. I ran out and saw that it was your dog. She's over there."

There, in the green grass, lay Barney. Her body was bloodied and contorted but alive.

"Oh, Barney," gasped her master, trembling. "Oh, Barney…"

Upon hearing her master's voice, the dog tried to move her head, to meet his eyes with hers.

"No, girl, you stay…just stay…It's OK, Barney…We'll get you home, girl. We'll get you out of this ditch."

Benjamin tenderly moved his hand under her twisted body. The dog writhed with pain. He pulled his hand back.

"I'll need a box of some sort…or…or something to lift her with."

"I'll get a box," said Cindy. "I have one in the house." She got up to retrieve the box.

"Wait," said Benjamin. "Cindy, would you stay here with Barney. I'll go get a blanket and my truck. We can slide her onto the blanket and then lift her onto the tailgate."

"Yes, of course," she replied. "Go ahead."

Benjamin ran toward his house, as Cindy gazed upon the dog. She cringed at the sight. In places the fur was gouged and peeled back, exposing the raw meat of twitching muscles. One hind leg was almost completely reversed. Drips of blood oozed out of her nose. She noticed the white paint on her paws. "Hello, Barney. Remember me?" she whispered. "It'll be all right. You just stay there. You're a good girl. You just stay there." She placed her hand on the dog's neck, resting it there, somehow creating an intimacy, a reaching out. Barney gazed ahead with glassy eyes, unable to turn her head, but aware of the connection.

The pickup spun out of the driveway and backed up to the ditch. Benjamin unlatched the tailgate and grabbed an old wool army blanket. He spread it out next to Barney.

"We'll have to slide her onto the blanket. She's not going to like it, but it has to be done. I'll put my hands under her head and front quarters and pull her on, if you'll just help her back legs along."

"What should I do? Push?" asked Cindy.

"No, just lift the back end a little. Try not to move the legs, just lift a little bit, just so they don't drag."

Benjamin pulled Barney's body onto the blanket, while she weakly groaned.

"OK," said Benjamin. "So far, so good. Now, if you'll get on one end of the blanket, we'll lift up and place her onto the truck. Ready? OK, lift. There, we did it. Thanks, Cindy."

"Benjamin, should I run home and call the vet, to let them know you're coming?"

Benjamin thought briefly, shaking his head. "No, Cindy. There's no sense in that. I'll take Barney home…with me."

Cindy's eyes met Benjamin's. "Go ahead and drive her home. I'll ride in the back here, with her."

Benjamin complied, driving slowly, at a crawl, trying to jostle Barney as little as possible.

At the house, he backed the truck up to the front porch, exited the cab, and walked into the house, retrieving an appropriate-sized cardboard box. "We'll set her in this box, blanket and all." Benjamin set the box on the porch as the two lifted the blood-soaked blanket and its cargo off the truck and into the box.

"Maybe we should call the vet," said Cindy.

"No," replied Benjamin. "There's no sense to it. Besides, it's Saturday and they're probably closed."

"We could try," she pleaded. "We should do something."

Benjamin folded the excess blanket ends that drooped over the edges of the box inward, covering Barney's trembling body, only exposing her head. "Oh Barney..." he said with his hand resting on her head. "You're a good girl, aren't you? Yeah, you are. You know you are, don't you? Sure you do. You're a good a girl." Benjamin silently stayed there for a long time, kneeling next to the box, flooding with memories.

Cindy didn't know what to say. She felt awkward. She turned away, inadvertently peering at the slightly opened door of the house, which had two distinct white paw prints on it. She opened the door completely and gazed upon the additional white paw prints adorning the floor, piecing together what had taken place.

"Benjamin...Benjamin?"

"Hmm? Wha—Oh...Cindy..."

"Benjamin, do you have any cleaning solution for these paw prints on your floor? I could..."

"What? Oh...Oh no...no, Cindy. I—I really appreciate everything you've done. I really do. Thank you so much. Thank you. But I have to ask you to leave now. I have to ask you to go. I really appreciate all you've done, though. I really do. Thank you so much."

She walked over to him and hugged him. In the embrace, Benjamin felt himself slipping over the edge as his emotions attempted to overpower him. He fought back and quickly turned from her, to hide his face. Cindy paused for a moment and then turned and walked home.

Benjamin stayed there a long time, with his hand lovingly on Barney's head, speaking soft words, nostalgic words laced with sensitivity, words reflecting shining moments of their history together. Barney was quiet at first, but then seemed to be agitated. She began to whimper in a weak, gravelly howl. The sickening noise subsided only briefly, intermittently between breaths. The dog was suffering. Benjamin tried to console his best friend, but his comforting words failed. He attempted to reposition the dog in her box in hopes of reducing her pain, but to no avail. The grinding noise grew unbearable. Benjamin rushed away from the porch and into the kitchen, trying to force himself not to listen, yet simultaneously straining to listen. He thought of his idiotic anger. He blamed himself for his stupidity in leaving the filled paint pan on the floor in the first place. He dwelled upon his selfishness, torturing himself with emotion and guilt, as Barney lay moaning, agonizing toward the inevitable. Benjamin tried to get a grip on himself; he tried to be a man; he pushed away his emotions with all his inner strength, only to have them flow around him, engulfing him again. It was like trying to hold back a river. He needed help, help to dam up the emotions. He resorted to anger. "Get a grip, damn it!" he spoke out loud. "It's just a dog! These things happen all the time. Get off your ass and do what's right; don't sit here and cry like a blubbering baby. You owe her. To be strong…you owe her."

He firmly rose from his chair and marched to the shed behind the kitchen. He opened a door to a small storage closet where he kept various sporting goods, such as fishing poles, snowshoes, and a double-barreled shotgun. He fumbled open a box of twelve-gauge shells, took two, grabbed the gun, and loaded it. Slamming shut the door to the closet, he walked out onto the porch.

"How you doing, girl?" he asked.

Barney was still uttering the same sickly drone, her eyes glassy and drawn.

Benjamin leaned the gun alongside the house, gently picked up the box, and walked it behind the house, next to a white pine tree. He then

walked back to the front of the house and retrieved the shotgun. On
his return, he picked up a shovel that was lying in the grass. He began
to dig a hole next to the tree, a deep hole. Barney had always liked that
tree. She'd chased many a squirrel up into its branches. She'd always
had a lot of life in her, a lot of vigor. One time she'd chased a raccoon
up that very tree, barking ferociously like a vicious warrior, until the
coon came growling down the trunk of the tree, chasing her whimpering
carcass into the house, where she ran to the safety of the window and
continued her renewed ferocity. Benjamin paused from his task as he
inwardly laughed at the memory; then, remembering his grim endeavor,
he soberly continued shoveling.

With the grave dug, he stuck the blade of the shovel in the ground
to hold it in place. Then he sat next to Barney, whose sickening moans
had subsided to a weak wheezy noise. Benjamin just looked at her, wishing she would breathe her last, wishing death would take her, hoping
death would relieve him from the weight of his grueling mission. But
death did not take her. She painfully lingered. The seconds crawled.
Benjamin opened the breech of the double-barreled shotgun, removed
the shells, and then closed it and pulled the front trigger. He opened the
breech again and looked at the exposed firing pin; it was the pin for the
right-side barrel. He replaced just one shell in the right-side chamber
and closed the breech.

Barney's wheezing grew shallower. Benjamin sat waiting for hours
as the vigil went on and on. At one point, she seemed to quit breathing,
but it was just a pause. As long as she wasn't showing signs of suffering,
death would be allowed to take its natural course. So the vigil continued.
Benjamin prayed that death would come soon. His mind wandered to and
fro, mixed with emotions. He realized what the blast from a twelve-gauge
shotgun would do, but it would be quick, complete, and instantaneous. If
the time came for it, he would place the end of the right barrel one inch
from the back of Barney's head, take very careful aim, and then pull the
trigger while simultaneously closing his eyes. Immediately after the act, he
would turn away; it was important not to look. He didn't want that final,
gory image imprinted in his memory, to haunt him forever. Hopefully, the
gruesome scenario would not have to be played out. Death seemed like

such a strange entity, as well as life. It was rather bizarre. What was the meaning of it all? What was the sense? Barney began to groan again. Her raspy gurgling grew intense. She tried to move her body. Benjamin gently touched her head, speaking kind words in a feeble attempt to stifle the suffering; however, the dog writhed in agony while attempting to move her twisted limbs, struggling for breath, gurgling deeper toward inevitable death. Benjamin could stand it no longer. He ran away from it all, into the house, closing the door behind him. But no door could be closed on the situation. He could only hide from it, only turn his head from it. His mind was fastened on his dog, outside, suffering—alone. And here he was, a coward, too weak to help her, to help her exit this world. This was a time when she needed him most. "Cindy was right," he spoke quietly. "I should have taken Barney to the vet. The vet would have put her to sleep...But Barney hated going to the vet. She would rather be home." Thoughts and guilt congregated and mixed into an emotional soup as he paced the floors. Finally, he threw the door open and marched to where Barney lay. He hoped with all his heart, body, and soul that she would be dead, at peace. But she was the same. He knelt next to his dog.

"Love you, Barney," he said.

He stood up and pointed the right gun barrel directly behind the suffering dog's head and closed his eyes.

Turning from the scene, Benjamin numbly walked away, through the deafening quiet and into the house as if floating within a misty existence, as if known reality had ceased, yet lived on only as shards of thoughts, mixed and mangled into a live, fluctuating ball of dulled emotions. He mechanically cleaned and oiled the shotgun and then returned it to its place. Drifting to the bedroom, he fumbled through the dresser drawers, retrieving an old bedsheet. He walked to the base of the white pine tree, where the body lay, careful not to look into the box, and draped the sheet over the whole mass. Then he slid the shovel under the box, steadying it with one hand, and slid it over the hole, allowing it to fall into the earth from under the sheet. Then he gently placed the sheet into the hole, reaching down and tucking it around the cardboard coffin. He stood up and bowed his head and then shoveled the loose mound of dirt into the hole, ending the funeral.

The quiet house haunted, as evening shadows darkened the gloom, gradually wiping away visible images, unleashing, all the more vividly, the invisible images of the mind, the ghosts of this world, apparitions that, perhaps, masquerade as memories. Downward, these ghosts pulled Benjamin, spiraling him deep into the dull bleakness of the depression known as grief. He allowed the ghosts to pull him. He did not resist; he had not the strength. There he allowed them full reign, to consume him, following each ghostly thought through its spooky corridors, allowing the realities of emotion to devour his will. There, he helplessly stayed, wallowing in the black pit of despair, oblivious of any way out.

Light burst forth in the room. The overhead light had been turned on.

"Hello, Benjamin."

It was Cindy Granger.

"I knocked, but you must not have heard me. I noticed your lights were off and your truck was still in the driveway. I just thought that—that maybe you might need some company. You know, not be alone." She knew, by looking at Benjamin's expression, that his pet was gone. As a pet owner herself, empathy poured from her heart, compassionate and true. She imagined where he must be right now, mentally trapped in the pit, far away yet physically here in this material illusion we call reality. She knew that his share of time in the blackness was inevitable, but she intended to offer some condolence, some comfort, anything to help him bear the brunt of the grief, until time dissipated it enough to be accepted and managed, boxed and placed on a mental shelf. Sympathy drew her to him, demanding she offer herself.

"Oh, Cindy," said Benjamin waveringly. "C'mon in. Please, sit down. Can I get you anything, something to drink?"

"No, thank you," she replied. "Uh, how are you doing?"

"Me? Fine, fine. I'll be fine. Don't worry about me. You sure you don't want anything to drink, coffee maybe? I make a great cup of coffee.

Sorry for the messy house. Haven't had time to clean up those crazy paw prints yet. Isn't that something? She must've stood right in that paint pan and then traipsed through every room of the house while I slept." Outwardly he laughed at the thought. Inwardly he fought to suppress a tide of emotion, welling up like a tsunami. He averted the storm by changing the subject. "I'll go make us some coffee. We can have coffee. That'll be good."

Cindy, sensing his struggle for composure, allowed him his space as he walked toward the kitchen. She could hear him fumbling with the coffee filters and running the water. He did not emerge from the kitchen until the coffee was done.

"There you are," he said while handing her a steaming cup. "I'm sorry, it'll have to be black. I'm out of milk, and I'm out of sugar. You'll have to forgive me; I'm not much of a grocery shopper."

"That'll be fine. Thank you," she said, noticing his shaking hands and red eyes. "Do you want to talk about it? I think you should talk about it. It's a hard thing; I know. I remember when my last cat died, Mr. Whiskers, I about fell apart. I know the place you're in now. And I know that there is nothing I can do to keep you from walking through it. You have to walk through it. But it's important that you look at it squarely and feel it. You have to deal with it, accept it for what it is. And then move on."

"That simple, huh?" Benjamin quipped.

"No, it's not simple. It's hard—very hard. My advice to you is not to turn away from it, not to pretend you're above it. You will feel like—"

Cindy stopped abruptly, suddenly realizing that Benjamin had recently lost his father and must be more acquainted with the grieving process than she could possibly be.

"Feel like what?" snapped Benjamin. "Hollow? Like a huge void exists in your soul? Like a black cavern has been cut through your stomach? Like half of you is in hell, while the other half of you exists only to feel the pain of that hell? Is that how I'm supposed to feel? Is that the deal? That whatever or whoever we love eventually gets ripped from us? So we can live in torment for a while, until we get used to the idea that our loved one is dead, dead and buried in the cold dirt, while we get on with our meaningless lives, only to end up dead and rotting ourselves, so the people who love us will have to go through this same hell? What's the sense? Why have emotions anyways? It's like this: I had a dog; I treated her well; she's dead, end of story. Deal with it. Forget about it. Get on with it."

"You're hardening yourself to cope with the pain," she said meekly. "And yes, we must deal with it, but we must never forget. We cannot. As time passes, we cannot forget the love. It's the love that is what's important. The love generated between you and your father, between you and Barney. The pain you feel now is great. It is great because your love was great. The love bound you to your father, as well as to your pet, like different threads forming a fabric, unifying into one garment, one flesh. And now part of you has indeed been ripped from you, and it is painful. But the love remains with you. The pain will pass, but the love will remain. You must never forget, never forget the love. Keep the love strong by keeping the memories in your heart. And who knows? Maybe in our last days, we will be reunited somehow, perhaps through that love we carry with us."

Benjamin wept.

Cindy put down her coffee cup and embraced him deeply, forging the fabric together, creating, perhaps, the beginning of a new garment.

VI

The Awakening

The sun rose the next morning, as well as the many mornings after. Its great beams of light illuminated an entire world, but its hopeful rays did little to penetrate the blackness of Benjamin's universe. From the core of grief, he could see no sun; the bright center of his solar system was no more. He groped in the blackness like a planet with nothing to orbit, lost in a vast space of nothingness. Other familiar planets of his life—home, work, and even friends—seemed somehow alien to him, as if it were they who had changed. They seemed distant, even superficial, as they went on with their lives, spinning in their own foolish orbits, revolving around a transient center of their own creation, destined toward the inevitable conclusion.

Benjamin wandered aimlessly through the universe. He did not realize it, but he was a planet seeking a center, an orbit, a purpose, something to revolve around. Death had separated him from the gravitational force of the centers that had held him in his orbit. Without a solid center, there was no gravity to keep him on course. He was a planet vulnerable to the gravity of other objects, other planets, other suns. Any new light that would appear on his horizon now, in his current state, would pull him, drawing him into its gravity, possibly forming an entirely new solar system.

A month or so had passed since the accident. Gradually, the days seemed brighter, but the silent nights continually unleashed their familiar ghosts, haunting his memories, unwilling to weaken their grip. His life was in limbo, between two worlds. He had traveled through the darkest trails leading upward out of the pit; however, he was only halfway up the incline.

Cindy stopped by from time to time, just to check up on him, usually after work, as long as she didn't have many papers to grade. At first Benjamin politely accepted her visits only out of duty. He really did not want her company; he didn't want any company, wanting only to be left alone to wallow with his ghosts. However, she persisted. One night she brought over two bottles of wine and some homemade tacos. She christened the evening, proclaiming it "bullshit" night. That evening they were to put inhibitions aside and just enjoy each other's company, chatting about anything other than something "normal," which she dubbed as "boring." The wine was to act as the social lubricant for the experiment. Benjamin played along out of respect and hunger. As the evening progressed and the wine loosened the tightness of the tongue, they found themselves speaking of otherwise forbidden topics, hidden topics, topics that all people consider but keep locked securely in their closets, shrouded from view.

"What do you do for sex?" Cindy said bluntly, as the second bottle of wine was well on its way to depletion.

"What do you mean?" asked Benjamin, temporarily stunned by the sheer impact of the question.

"I knew you were going to ask that." She laughed. "Every time you ask people a question pertaining to their 'hidden truths,' they usually respond with a 'what' question of some sort. I suppose they do it to buy time, time to think about how to respond. Then you have to repeat the question, which will make them feel noticeably uncomfortable, and they will respond by asking me that same question, turning the tables on me, which means they will not reveal any hidden truths about themselves until I reveal a hidden truth first. Then we trade hidden truths—tit for tat. It's sort of like playing a dare game."

"Well, I think it's foolish," said Benjamin. "Some topics of discussion are private, and sex is one of them."

"And why is that?" she asked, looking him in the eye.

"Why is what?

"Why is sex such a forbidden subject? I mean, why does it have to be? People treat it like it's a taboo or witchcraft or something dirty to be ashamed of, which is silly when you really think about it. Everybody does it—well, almost everybody. Everybody thinks about it, fantasizes about it. Yet few are willing to talk about it openly. A handful of people might dare to talk about it in the third person, but hardly any are willing to speak about it in the first person—you know, like specifics."

"What do you mean 'specifics'?" probed Benjamin, smiling uncomfortably.

"Well," she offered, "I mean, like specific thoughts or fantasies a person might have while experiencing sex. What are his or her turn-ons or turnoffs? What they think about, you know, when they masturbate, how they masturbate, that sort of thing. You know, everything—just be open, honest, truthful."

Benjamin squirmed in his chair. "OK, I'll be truthful with you. I honestly do not feel comfortable discussing such a topic with you—not with you or anyone, for that matter. If I were to discuss such things, and I stress the word *if*, it would be with a person I was very close to—you know, like a girlfriend, certainly not with a casual neighbor."

"My, but it seems like we've touched a nerve." She giggled. "Your response was predictable—textbook, in fact."

"What do you mean 'textbook'?"

"Another 'what' question," she said and glowingly laughed as she filled both their glasses with the remainder of the wine. "Oh, I've been reading, studying about sex, the sex drive, reproduction, that sort of thing."

"Why?" he asked.

"Why not? It's an intricate part of life, all life, yet it's mysterious, don't you think? I mean, what draws a male and female together. Even now, here we are, sharing time, drinking wine together, a male and a female. You could be drinking wine with your work buddies, but you're not; you're here with me, with a woman. It would be silly not to wonder if those ancient, mysterious forces are not at work, hidden underneath our superficial social restraints."

"Social restraints," said Benjamin, "are what keep out the chaos; it tames the animal instinct; it tames the primitive. Social restraint provides order, so we can live together as a society, in some sort of harmony. Think about it: would you really want to live in a world without social restraint? It would be like the days of early civilization, the days of the conqueror. People would just take what they wanted, when they wanted. We would have to build castle walls around our houses to keep out the chaos. And speaking of sex, without social restraint the male conqueror might just grab a woman by the hair and do as he pleased." Benjamin emphasized the last sentence to affect Cindy in such a way as to cause her to rethink her topic.

"Maybe that's what women want, secretly," she said reflectively.

"You've been reading too many textbooks," Benjamin said and laughed sarcastically. "OK, you go ahead and tell me what kind of crazy sex theories your books have taught you. I'm all ears."

Cindy was a bit unnerved by his cynicism, but she brushed it aside. "All right," she said, "here's what I've pieced together."

"You mean this isn't going to be directly from a textbook?" he asked.

"It's what I've tentatively concluded from my study of various sources, Mr. Smart Ass. Now, do you want me to continue?"

"Sure, sorry. Go ahead."

"First of all," she began, "the mating process normally affects both the male and female after puberty. The female is then attracted to the alpha male. She knowingly or unknowingly seeks the dominant male. That is just the plain simplicity of it. However, in our crazy society, it is difficult to determine how to define 'dominant.' In high school, it might be the captain of the basketball team. In college, it might be the boy on the debate team or maybe the one with the new car. If the girl is a rock and roller, it might be the guy who plays in a band. If the girl is a Bible thumper, it might be the nice guy in Bible class or the guy studying to be a preacher. You see, our society has complicated the role of the 'dominant' male. In the days of prehistoric humans, the dominant male was simply the most physically and mentally fit, the alpha male. But today, the dominant male is the male who is dominant in the woman's particular social sphere of interest. Therefore, she is attracted to males in that particular category and will probably be willing to accept the best available one for her mate. Of course, the physical qualities of the male are still a factor, playing a significant role in the selection process."

"So," Benjamin laughed, "we are being 'selected,' like specimens?"

"Sure, I think so. The men or boys parade their tail feathers in front of the female, showing off, tempting them with their physical appearance, their material wealth, their social standing, their power, as the woman chooses the best out of what is offered. And that's the cold truth of it, without getting into any complex scenarios. And as far as the sex drive of a man, it's rather simple and basic. He is simply drawn to the alpha female who is in her childbearing years, and that's it."

"Alpha female?" asked Benjamin.

"Yes, the most physically and mentally fit. This is what attracts the male. The only prerequisite is that the female must be in her childbearing years. Therefore, if she is too young or too old, there is no sexual magnetism."

"You actually believe all that stuff you read?" quipped Benjamin.

"Hey, did you ever hear of any young, beautiful models marrying an old, dried-up coot who was poor or insignificant, like some old guy who works at your plant? No, of course you don't. But you know it happens all the time to old men who are either rich, famous, or powerful. 'Why?' you ask. Because women are attracted to the old geezer's alpha-dominant element, which I believe is usually the power, maybe the fame. Tell me this: can you think of any old, dried-up woman marrying a young man? No, because the man has no attraction for a female who is not in her childbearing years. Of course, she can have plastic surgery, to keep the attraction alive."

"Looks like you've got it all figured out," said Benjamin. "What prestigious scientific journal did you derive that theory from?"

Cindy blushed. "I didn't say I studied any scientific journals. It was just what I derived from reading various books on the subject."

"Like what books?" pried Benjamin.

"Well, like *Wuthering Heights*, for example," she said defiantly.

"*Wuthering Heights*!" roared Benjamin with laughter. "That's a romance novel!" He about buckled over with giddy mirth. "*Wuthering Heights*!"

"Tell me, Benjamin, is it your habit to belittle your guests by doing your best to be a sarcastic ass?"

Benjamin looked into her eyes and saw no sign of anger, but instead, a firmness. Cindy was standing her ground, marking the territory of her social domain. She projected strength, and her strength magnified her countenance, beautifully transforming her into a goddess. In an instant, before his eyes, she had completely changed. He gazed in awe, noticing her pursed lips, her perfect cheekbones, the smoothness of her skin, a sudden majesty about her, a mysterious aura that captivated him, drawing his attention, drawing him...

"Cat got your tongue, Mr. Frisk?"

"Uh, no. What? I mean...It's just that...No, no, go ahead, please. You were saying?"

"I was saying," she said firmly, "that the 'romance novel,' *Wuthering Heights*, accurately mirrors an example of the theory I have proposed to you. You see, when the main character, Catherine, was a young girl, she fell passionately in love with a young boy, Heathcliff. He was strong, young, and handsome, but poor and uneducated. He was the dominant male in her small social sphere. However, as she matured, her social sphere grew and changed. Now social standing was important. She then was attracted to a rich, wimpy guy. You see, in her eyes, the wimpy guy was the alpha male in her new social sphere. Social prestige, wealth, and power trumped the physical aspect. So she married the rich guy, leaving the ignorant Heathcliff to wallow in heartbreaking sorrow. However, Heathcliff was not ignorant in matters of love. You see, he understood what directs a woman's passion. He understood my 'dominant social sphere' theory. He knew what females were attracted to. So he went out and became rich, as well as a prestigious landowner. He then confronted Catherine's husband in such a way as to show her that her husband was a coward. Do you see what he did? In that instant, Heathcliff had proven his dominance over Catherine's husband by wealth, prestige, and even physical strength. Heathcliff became the alpha male again. You see?"

"So," said Benjamin, politely pretending to have followed her narrative, "she dumped her husband and ran off with Heathcliff?"

"No," said Cindy. "Actually, she found herself caught between two worlds, between her social responsibilities and her natural, sexual instincts, between her chosen family and her alpha male."

"Whom did she choose?" asked Benjamin.

"She didn't," said Cindy. "Being caught between the two worlds tore her apart emotionally. She was too weak. She died."

"Yes," said Benjamin. "Her will was too weak."

"What do you mean?" asked Cindy.

"It all boils down to a person's will," explained Benjamin. "A person has to be disciplined and get a firm grip on his or her willpower to overcome the temptations of this world. Take sex, for example. Sex is a strong biological hunger that needs to be fulfilled; it's almost as strong as a person's hunger for food. However, as long as one is disciplined, one can control one's urges and temptations, by fortifying one's willpower."

"And how does one fortify one's willpower?" asked Cindy.

"That's a good question," said Benjamin as he pondered it. "That may be *the* question. Maybe we all have a natural amount of willpower to guide us and act as sort of a defense or a wall to protect us from various temptations. We just should be careful not to do things that cause our walls to weaken."

"What kind of things?" asked Cindy.

"Well, things like drinking wine, alone with an attractive woman," he blurted out, not realizing what he had said until the moment he finished saying it.

"Oh?" she said and smiled. "So, you think I'm attractive, do you?"

"I didn't mean…I mean…What I meant was—was that people should think twice about drinking in certain circumstances. The alcohol weakens their protective walls. That's all I meant to say."

"So, you think I'm not attractive," she said with a smirk.

"I didn't say that. Would you like another glass of wine?"

"We're out of wine," she said, laughing. "Are you trying to change the subject? Or are you trying to pull my walls down with more booze? Oh, never mind. You seem to have a lot of hidden truths that you're not sharing. Maybe your protective walls are too high—too high to let in the sunlight."

"Sunlight, huh?" said Benjamin, looking directly into her eyes. "And I suppose you are the sunlight."

"I might be," she said, returning his penetrating gaze.

The moment seemed to be suspended, reaching a pinnacle of intensity, like reaching the crest of a hill, waiting for direction, waiting for a choice—like destiny itself depended on the subsequent moment. Benjamin's emotions welled up through the cracks in his walls, intoxicating him, directing him to allow himself to roll down the hill, let gravity take control of him, with no restraint.

Benjamin stood up, not breaking his stare. "I think you're attractive," he said, "very attractive."

She stood up and came to him, silently. She pressed her lips to his. His mind immediately exploded with sensation—the fragrance of her blond hair, the softness of her lips, the feel of her shoulders, her waist, and her arms around him. He pulled her tighter into the embrace, fusing their bodies together, melting into her, feeling her breasts pressing into his chest. Erotic passion welled throughout his being, primitive, consuming, greedy. He pulled her tighter as their tongues meshed, deeper into each other. Delirious with pleasure, he slid his hands down her back, over her hips, and lower, over the seat of her tight jeans, cupping her smooth buttocks, pulling her, meshing his wanting groin with hers, crazed with an increasing fervor, building up toward an intensity of no return. With his hands still firmly in place, he lifted her as she wrapped her legs around his waist, fusing their clasping bodies all the more, both desperate to unify into each other, to merge, to integrate, to amalgamate into one flesh. He laid her on the sofa, still embraced, severing any final threads of restraint, unleashing the unbridled passion of nature, allowing it to engulf and obsess both their souls completely as their bodies simulated the sex act, though fully clothed. Breathless and panting, they pulled their greedy mouths apart and thrashed at each other's clothes. Benjamin devoured her neck as she ripped the buttons off his shirt, feeling the skin of his chest. He unbuttoned her white blouse, exposing the hidden white softness underneath. She raised herself up and unclasped her black bra, allowing it to fall from her like a dark veil, revealing her intoxicating breasts, as he placed his greedy mouth over them while unbuttoning her jeans and sliding them off. He reached between her legs, warm, wet, probing, throbbing. He slid his head down into the mist, lapping, sucking, nearly exploding with ecstasy. He looked up through it all, seeing Cindy's erect nipples dancing as she squirmed, while he simultaneously reached down, unbuckling his belt and dropping his pants. Holding her waist, he pulled her to the edge of the sofa as he lifted her legs. Cindy gazed between his legs, reached out, and held his manhood briefly before directing it into her, pushing her groin onto him, as he began spastically thrusting into her with increasing momentum, uncontrollable momentum. She began to softly scream spasmodically as she neared the edge of release. Benjamin, sensing her orgasm, pounded all the more furiously, pushing himself over the edge as his semen blasted into her with convulsions of blissful climax, as they both fell into completeness, together, embraced wholly, as one.

That one act dismantled any known barriers that may have existed between them and opened a door to a new bridge that connected them both. Upon that bridge, each could now cross voids otherwise unattainable. The two lay naked on the sofa together, talking softly, laughing, speaking of anything, speaking of everything, basking in the afterglow, touching, kissing, recognizing this newborn feeling between them, welcoming it as it surrounded them, uniting their spirits again and again.

Afterward

The morning sun ushered in a new day, filling the world with its light, offering its joy to those who merely have to accept it into their hearts to experience its rich fullness. Benjamin awoke as one born again, joyfully accepting that light deep into his inner being. As he lay awake in embrace on the sofa, his eyes followed the blanketed curves of the sleeping lover who lay nestled in his arms, gliding his hand over her skin as to ensure the reality of it all. She was beautiful. Everything about her was beautiful—the way she slept, the way she breathed, the way her hair fell over her eyes. Why had he not noticed these things before?

He reached up, brushing her golden hair to the side, touching her face, feeling her skin, awakening his sensuality yet again. He kissed her on the neck as he delicately arose from the sofa, careful not to wake her, accidentally exposing her nudity as the blanket slipped to the floor. He covered her again, as she sleepily opened her eyes to his, hazily recognizing the moment, smiling as if caught somewhere between a dream and reality. He kissed her on the lips, deeply. She responded, melting into its softness.

"Go back to sleep," he whispered, kissing her again.

She complied without saying a word, allowing herself to drift back into sleep's sanctuary.

Benjamin dressed himself and made a pot of coffee. His mind was captivated, held firmly under the sensual influence of the passionate evening that had taken place just hours before, conjuring distinct images and impressions, tingling his senses. He allowed his mind to drift into these images, reliving the ecstasy, allowing the reunion all the freedom it desired. There was no restraint. His walls lay in rubble as he joyfully peered into the possibility of a new world.

Pouring a cup of coffee, he sat out on the porch, watching the well-risen sun make its way to its climax. His mind swam with thoughts of the present and future. What would today bring? What would tomorrow bring? Everything had changed. His entire life had been altered, overnight. It was not solely because of the sex. No, the sex was instrumental in the change, but it was something more, something wonderful. Benjamin drifted into the past, toying with thoughts of his first sexual experience. His girlfriend at the time was well versed in sex, and he was frightened out of his wits. He knew that she expected him to be aggressive in such areas, but he couldn't bring himself to actually do anything. The celibate months passed as they dated, creating an ever-increasing pressure. Girls seemed so...so "nice" to him, like sweet flowers. The sex act did not seem to fit into his scenario of what love should be between a girl and boy. His impression of such a love fell more along the lines of a fairy tale. Holding hands and kissing was sweet and seemed to fall neatly into his definition of "making love," accentuating the beauty of the girl, dreamily transforming her into a princess, a Cinderella. But sex was something altogether different, something that shattered his idea of fairy-tale love. Thinking of performing the actual sex act with his girlfriend did not conjure joyful pictures of birds and butterflies dancing in his mind; it was something different, something hidden, something lustful, something secret and forbidden. He was not foreign to sexual fantasies at the time. He occasionally acquired pictures of naked women from his school buddies, who had torn them out of men's magazines. He hid them in his bedroom, secretly unfolding them at night. He knew what he was supposed to do with a girl, but he couldn't make the connection between his sexual fantasies and the reality of a real, live girl. The sexual fantasies conjured by the naked pictures were erotically stimulating; however, the reality of actually doing it seemed frightening, even silly. In fact, the whole idea of reproducing in such a fashion seemed bizarre. He couldn't imagine his parents doing it, nor his grandparents. What did preachers think about when they did it with their wives? What went through their minds? Birds and butterflies? Were his sexual fantasies the same as theirs?

One night, he and his girlfriend were at his parents' house, kissing and flirting with each other as they had done before. She asked if he wanted to take her to his bedroom, making it apparent what she wanted to take place. Shielding his frightened nervousness and pretending to be "a man," suave and debonair, he said, "Sure, I do!" acting like he had been waiting for this chance all along. She lay on the bed while he pretended he knew what he was doing, attempting to "masterfully" take off her clothes, while locking tongues, praying secretly for an erection, an erection that evaded him under the pressure. However, he focused his concentration with all his inner strength, managing to produce a partial erection; he quickly took off the remainder of his clothes, jumped on her, and with her brief guidance, began and finished within a minute or so. Even though the sex had been less than good, it was the fact that he'd actually done it that he reveled in. The barrier had been broken.

Since those days he'd gradually managed to adopt the idea of sex into his notions of fairy-tale romance, attempting to mesh both concepts together as he matured; however, he could never mesh them completely. He could adopt the idea of sex into a man–woman relationship, but sex was something uniquely its own, somehow separate from true love.

Benjamin, awaking from his thoughts and his third cup of coffee, realized it was already noon. He went into the kitchen, opened a can of orange juice, took some bacon and eggs out of the fridge, and began cooking breakfast. Soon the aroma of smoked bacon drifted through the house, luring Cindy into consciousness. She wrapped the blanket loosely about her and sauntered toward the kitchen.

"Good morning," she said, standing in the threshold of the kitchen.

Benjamin spun around, a bit startled by her immediate presence, looking toward her, scarcely believing the reality of it. She was smiling, wrapped up like a geisha doll. Any makeup that she had been wearing the night before was gone. Her blond hair was knotted and ratty; strands of it hung over her left eye. She was beautiful, gorgeous, more beautiful now than ever before—more beautiful than anything he had ever seen or experienced. Light seemed to radiate out from her smile, smiting him, rendering him speechless.

"It's not polite to stare," she quipped. "I don't look that bad, do I?"

"No…oh no," he said. "You're…I mean…You really look good…I mean…Would you like some breakfast—bacon, eggs, and toast?"

"Yes, please! I'm starving," she said. "I seemed to have worked up quite an appetite," she added, provocatively.

Cindy walked to him and hugged him, kissing him on the mouth as they embraced. For Benjamin it was as if the passion of the night before instantly re-created itself into a semblance of its former intensity, building as he felt her intimate closeness. She smilingly interrupted the embrace, whispering in his ear, "I think the bacon is burning."

Benjamin turned from his passion, laughing as he turned off his burner.

"How do you like your eggs?" he asked. "Scrambled, overeasy, or sunny-side up?"

"Overeasy, please. I had no idea you were a chef."

"I'm not, but I can scramble up a pretty good breakfast. There's some coffee left; if you'd like, help yourself. I hope it's still good; it's a couple of hours old."

"Sure! I'm just not myself unless I have my coffee. Hmm," she said, tasting the coffee. "If you don't mind, I think I'll make another pot."

"Yeah, go ahead. Coffee's in the fridge, and the filters are next to the bread box."

Cindy laughed while making the coffee, as Benjamin set the table.

"What's so funny?" he asked.

"Oh, nothing, I just had a silly thought, that's all."

"Oh, c'mon," he said. "Out with it. Or do we have to get two bottles of wine again?" he said and smiled.

"Oh, I just wondered if this is what married people do. You know, share their nights, get up, and share breakfast. Do you ever wonder what it would be like?"

"What, being married? Not really. I assume it would be like everyone else's marriage: wife, kids, a pet or two, nothing special, just living a normal life."

"Did you ever think about having your own family?" she asked as she sat at the table while Benjamin set her breakfast before her.

"I can't say that I dwell on it," he said while sitting across from her. "I guess I've always assumed I will have a family someday. I mean, it just seems natural, like it will just happen on its own. Do you want jam for your toast?"

"No, thank you," she replied. "I like to break the bread and dip it in the yellow blood."

"So do I," he said and laughed. "I wonder if everyone does that with their toast and eggs. Or are we just weird?"

"Benjamin, breakfast is delicious. You're a good egg cooker. They're done just right."

"Thank you. I'll make you more if you like. It'll only take a minute."

Cindy smiled. "I'm fine," she said. "You know, it's sort of strange... the way we humans eat...I mean, like what we humans eat...like eggs, for example. We are eating the embryos of another being. We are eating babies. These four eggs we are both eating would have been four baby chicks, all fluffy yellow and peeping, running around the barnyard, scurrying after their mother. And here we are eating them, not even considering what we're actually doing."

"We're carnivores," responded Benjamin.

"I know," she said. "But it seems so...so ghoulish."

"Well," he pondered, "it is ghoulish, I suppose. When you think about it, we feed off the living. We strip plants of their seeds, their nuts, their babies, eating their offspring, as well as the plants themselves. The animals, we murder and feed on their recently dead carcasses, labeling the meat 'fresh.' The word *fresh* that we see in the supermarket means 'freshly murdered.' It sounds rather unsettling when you think of us as no different from a pack of wolves, killing and eating another being's flesh to perpetuate our own lives."

"Are you about finished?" said Cindy.

"Almost," he replied. "Just have to finish my bacon."

"I was referring to your morbid conversation!" She glared.

"You brought up the subject," he retorted.

"I was talking about eggs...about life. Somehow you managed to twist it into a depressing discussion of death."

"No, Cindy, it was you who started it with your talk about eating fluffy yellow chickies."

"No, you started it by bending my comment about eating eggs solely into the topic of death, not giving any thought to the positiveness of what I was saying!"

"You were talking about eating babies, about being ghoulish. I just expanded on your topic. You see, it was all your fault!"

"It was not my fault! How can you say it was my fault! My God, you are the most...the most..."

"I guess you were right earlier, Cindy. Maybe this *is* what married people do." Benjamin laughed.

Cindy laughed, too, while they both quietly finished their breakfast.

"Would you like another cup of orange juice or coffee?" asked Benjamin.

"Yes, I do love my coffee, but stay there; I'll get it. You want some, too?"

"Sure, if you're pouring."

"Benjamin, you have a nice house; it's homey. I like it."

"Thanks. I like it, too. Needs work, though."

"I really like what you've done with the living room," she said as she poured them both a fresh cup. "A little too white, though. Did you ever consider an almond color or something a little less…bright…or something?"

"You think so?" he asked.

"Oh, yes," she said, "an off-white color with borders, maybe flowers or something cheery, with matching curtains…and some plants. You don't have any plants, do you? I haven't seen any."

"Well, no, I guess I didn't even consider plants."

"Oh, yes, plants are essential for a home. They give a feeling of nature, a feeling of life. Benjamin, show me all of your house. I haven't seen it all yet. What do you have upstairs? Oh, never mind, you can show me. I'll get dressed first; then you can show me, OK? Will that be all right?"

"Sure," he said. "There's not much to see, but you're welcome to see it."

"Splendid!" she said as she snuggled the blanket about her, picked up her coffee cup, and walked out of the kitchen and into the living room. Benjamin got up from the table, following her.

"Do you mind?" she said. "I could use a little privacy while I change."

"Oh—oh sure," said Benjamin absentmindedly. "You know, I've already seen about all there is to see," he added, smiling.

"Benjamin," she said while turning and kissing him on the cheek, "there is a time for everything and a season for every activity under heaven, a time to embrace, and a time to refrain—a time to look and a time to keep your eyes to yourself."

"OK, OK, I get the picture." He turned back into the kitchen, sipping his coffee. "I didn't know you were religious," he said. "Was that a quote from the Bible, or did you make it up?"

"Most of it was; check for yourself," came the reply from the other room. "And yes, I guess you could say that I am religious. I mean, I believe in God and love and all that, don't you?"

"Sure, I guess. Everything had to come from somewhere."

"Benjamin, did you see my bra? I can't seem to find it."

"On the floor."

"What?"

"I said, it should be on the floor somewhere."

"Well, I don't see it."

"You want me to come in there and find it for you?"

"No, I'll just go without."

"And flaunt yourself in front of me like that?"

"Oh, shut up. There," she said while entering the kitchen. "Better?"

"Actually, I sort of liked you in the kimono," he joked.

"OK, I'm ready. Sir, you may start the tour!"

"Madam, if you'll step this way," he said using a dashing British accent. "This is, of course, the living room, of which I believe you are very acquainted. This is the sofa of dreams, used exclusively for...Well, I shan't say—discretion renders me mute on the matter. Moving right along, this is the master bedroom. Pay no attention to the articles of clothing scattered about and the unmade bed. You see, the maid is on strike...very unfortunate."

"Why is that, sir? Do you not pay her her due?" said Cindy, happily playing along with the charade, mimicking her own version of the British accent.

"Yes, yes, it seems she demands more shillings, talking of unionizing. Preposterous—totally unreasonable."

"It's hard to find reliable peasants these days," said Cindy. "They all seem to want a slice of what *we* have. How silly of them. Whoever gave them such a foolish notion? I mean, the nerve!"

"And this, madam, is the spare room. Note the exotic luster of the light as it reflects from the surface of the cardboard boxes stacked in the corner there, and pay strict attention to the color scheme of the paneling—genuine wood veneer."

"Oh, yes," said Cindy as she opened a box revealing some old Christmas decorations. "This is a smashingly grand room."

"Madam!" commanded Benjamin. "If you could possibly contain your ecstasy by keeping your hands to yourself, it would be appreciated. Do you think these precious treasures, mere trinkets, are here for your amusement? How dare you!"

"Oh, forgive me, kind sir. The grandness of the moment captivated me so completely, I just—I just...Oh, forgive me. I shan't let it happen again."

"See that it doesn't. Now, then, shall we move along to the upper wings?"

"Let's shall," she said with a smile.

The two walked up the stairway as Cindy marveled at the spectacular decor.

"How many lavish apartments are on this level, sir?"

"There are two grand ballrooms and one somewhat smaller room, for guests; however, there is only one lavatory. Quite a blunder on my part, I'm afraid. I should not have purchased a manor with such a barbaric accommodation for the upper wing. I worry so…about what the guests must think."

"I should say so!" she gasped. "This would never do. My, my, the clutter. Sir, I had hoped to rent the upper level from you while I was in London, but these rooms, as well as the lavatory facilities, are out of the question. In fact, I am appalled that you would even dare to show me these rooms in the conditions they are in. They are filthy! Fit for rats! Certainly not fit for a queen such as myself."

"But, madam, the maid…"

"Tut, tut, don't be blaming everything on the maid, my good man. Good God, take some responsibility!"

"If Your Majesty would like, I could have these rooms sanitized and freshened. I would gladly welcome your presence into my humble castle. It would be my sincerest pleasure."

"Hmm, the rooms seem a bit small," she said with her nose in the air.

"With all due respect, Your Majesty, there is only one of you and three suites to choose from."

"Well, has it occurred to you, my good man, that I may have a family?"

"A family!" said Benjamin. "Of course, your family. And how many will be arriving?"

"I'm not quite sure at the present," she reflected. "One, maybe more, I'm not sure."

"Not sure of how many are in your family?" asked Benjamin.

"Well, if you must know, kind sir, I am in a family way," she said as she felt the quality of the draperies.

"Oh, I see!" beamed Benjamin. "You're expecting! Splendid, just sple—" Benjamin's face whitened as he stood like a statue.

However, Cindy went merrily on with the game. "Yes, the children will love it here. I do believe that with a little work—with a lot of work—the upper wing would make fine bedrooms for any prince or princess, whatever the case may be. Wouldn't you say, sir? Sir?"

"Cindy," Benjamin said solemnly, dropping the British accent.

"Sir!" she said abruptly. "Please address me as 'Your Majesty,' and kiss my feet as you do so. I command it—as your queen!"

"OK, Cindy, knock it off. It's not funny. The game's over."

"Funny? Game? Whatever do you mean 'game'?" She giggled.

"Last night," he said. "You know what I mean."

"Yes," she said, dropping her accent. "I know what you mean."

She let the moment linger, allowing it to ripen.

"Well?" he said.

"Well, what?" she teased.

"Cindy, don't fool around."

"I think it's too late, Mr. Frisk, for not fooling around, don't you think?"

"Cindy, you're on the pill, right?"

"These are fine draperies you have here. I like the colors," she said with a smile.

"Cindy."

"Does it matter if I'm on the pill?"

"Does it matter? Does it matter? Hell yes, it matters!"

"What if I said I wasn't on the pill? What if I was pregnant? What would you think then?"

"What are you saying? Just tell me if you're on birth control or not."

"Not till you answer the question."

"What? About you being pregnant…What would I think? You want to know what I would think?"

"Yes, I do. What would you think, Benjamin? I mean, really, what would you think?"

Benjamin paused, allowing his mind to catch up with his emotions as he pieced together the fragments of his thoughts. Cindy did not speak as he thought, allowing him his time. She stood with her back toward him, staring out the window, waiting for his answer.

"Jesus," he mumbled. "I never...I mean...I just never really thought...you know...about actually being a father...me, a father. It seems surreal. I mean, I thought about it before, but not seriously."

Cindy waited by the window, allowing him all the time he needed.

Benjamin imagined what his life would be like as a father. He envisioned the room with pink or blue walls, lined with teddy bears, filled with a child's laughter and bedtime stories. He looked at Cindy's back as she stood in front of the window and the dazzling sunlight shown around her silhouette. Shining like an angel, she was beautiful in every way he could imagine. Her beauty seemed even richer as he visualized her as a mother, cradling a baby in her arms, breastfeeding while softly singing, projecting the very essence of love into their infant child. There would be dinners around the supper table in the evening and stories of how everyone's day went. Christmas trees and birthday gifts danced through his mind. "A family," he thought to himself. "My family...my wife...my son or daughter!" At that moment, he realized that a family was exactly what he longed for, what he was born for. It was the life he wished to live: a life as a family man, a life with a wife and children, a life with responsibility, with purpose, with love. And what better purpose of life could there be in the whole world than to raise a child, to nurture him or her as he or she grows, bringing him or her up through a household of love to become a being of joyous light to lighten the world?

"I would welcome it," he said out loud and with confidence.

Cindy did not turn away from the window as they both stood with their thoughts. Finally she turned toward him. He noticed her blushed cheeks, streaked wet from tears. Instantly, he knew that she wasn't on the pill. The reality of the implication swam over him like a deep sea. The moment held, as she sought for words to speak.

"Benjamin," she said softly, "I haven't had a relationship with a man for well over a year; it's closer to two, actually. He was a good man, a smart man. We met in college. I wanted to be a schoolteacher because I love children. He wanted to become a lawyer because he loved money. Oh, I didn't believe he was in it just for the money at first. I deluded myself that he was in it for some noble purpose, perhaps to represent the poor or oppressed, to give them a voice, to stand up for justice in the face of evil, that sort of thing. I was naive. His goal was to become a corporate lawyer. 'That's where the money is,' he would say. I had dreams that we would marry and start a family, but he always avoided any conversation that headed in that direction. 'Oh well,' I thought. We were young; there was plenty of time. But he changed, or I changed; I don't know. I came to realize that we wanted different things out of life, completely differ-ent things. I remember," she said, laughing through the tears, "trying to encourage him to entertain the thought of having children, to become a father. I'll never forget what he said. I remember it clearly. He was working at his desk, as I rambled on about how nice it would be to have children, to have a baby and our own house. He kept scribbling on his stupid papers, not even looking up. He said, 'A person would have to be out of his mind to want children.' I brushed it off, smiling and saying, 'Oh, surely you would like a cute little baby one day, a child of your own.' He put down his pen and looked up from his desk and into my eyes and said very coldly, like ice, 'Cindy, I would never want a child; I would hate it.' Can you believe it? He actually used the word *hate*! How could anyone be so cold, to even say it. I knew then I could never be with a man like that. So I broke off the relationship. And you know what he said? He said he was glad—that it was for the best. He said he couldn't envision being with a silly schoolteacher who was wasting her time on a bunch of snotty-nosed brats. He said if I had any sense, I should quit the idea of teaching for peanuts and get a real job, to afford a real life. That's what he said.

"Anyways, I finished my degree, took on some part-time teaching jobs, and then came here, complete with a new job but with the same dream. It's a rather impossible dream to have, without involving a man. However, I've been wary to start a relationship again. I've never dated since. And when one isn't dating, it's really not necessary to be on birth control pills, now is it? However, I do realize that unplanned things may happen. And I knew what was happening last night. I'm not a stupid girl, even through the wine." She paused, still staring out the window. "There's always the morning-after pill; it works best if taken within twenty-four hours after sex. It's common these days—no big deal." She turned toward the window again, looking out into the light.

"I see," said Benjamin.

"Do you, Benjamin? Do you see? Do you really see?"

"Why me?" he asked.

Cindy stared out the window, as in a trance. "You're a good man. You work hard every day and then come home and work on projects. You like it; you enjoy it—to work with your hands. When you came over for pizza that night...You remember? We walked through the rooms of my house together, and you dreamed of how I could remodel each room and put on additions. I was dreaming, too. I guess that's where it started. You're also kind. The night you stepped on Muppet and she scratched and bit your ankle." She laughed. "I noticed the blood, but you didn't complain. I bet you wanted to strangle that cat! But you kept your composure, like a gentleman. You're also a compassionate man. You loved your dog almost like she was a child of your own. I saw you cry, even though you turned away from me. And most of all, I think you're honest. You say what you think. There's a sincerity about you. I admire that."

"Cindy," said Benjamin firmly, "I know this may sound crazy to you, and I know that it seems like I should be overwhelmed at what has transpired between us in the last twelve hours or so, and I realize that you may not think I could have possibly thought this thing through, which I haven't. But I know me. I know when I know something. I feel a strength when I know something about me—a truth. And I know that I will be true to that thought. I just know it. You have to trust that about me. And I know that I do not want you to take any kind of morning-after pill. I hate the thought of it! I do not regret last night in the least. I'm glad about it. And I welcome whatever comes from it. And I hope with all my heart that you and I would welcome it together. I would be a good father, to the best of my ability. I don't just promise that; I know it. I would be true to my child, always, no matter what. I know this. I just do. I would love a child more than anything in the world. It's what I want. I think it is always what I've wanted. I just didn't realize it until now. We could live here. This could be the baby's room. No, wait, the baby should be closer to us. We'll turn the spare room downstairs into the baby's room. I could get started on it right away. It'll be wonderful. And you... You would make a great mother. I know you would. I can see it in your eyes: the love is there. When you speak of children, the love reflects in your eyes—you shine. There would be other children...five...ten—who knows?—a whole house full of kids. We'll have to consider what school to send them to...and college funds. It would be just great. We would be a family. Just think, our own family!"

Cindy turned into him, sobbing as she embraced him and his dream. "I would want that more than anything," she said, kissing him again and again. Going downstairs, they sat on the sofa together, conjuring dreams, painting illusions, choosing names. Rebecca if it was a girl; they both loved the name Becky. They were unsure about a boy's name. Cindy seemed to like the name Seth. Benjamin wasn't sure. What he was sure of was his overwhelming feelings that seemed to grow by the minute for Cindy. He wanted to tell her that he loved her, but he didn't know how to approach the words. He was afraid it would sound superficial because everything between them had happened so quickly. What he had proposed upstairs was nothing short of marriage, but the word *marriage* had never actually been spoken; however, it was what he assumed. He wondered if his assumption was mutual, at least in the way he had envisioned it in his mind.

"Cindy," he said, allowing her to finish a thought about bassinettes, "what I said upstairs, about becoming a family and living in this house together..."

"Yes?" she said, laughing. "Don't tell me you're getting cold feet already?"

"Oh no, never! Not me, anyways. But I just want to make sure we are on the same page here. You know, upstairs, when I said 'family,' I meant family as in husband and wife, you know, as in married."

"Why, Mr. Frisk," she exclaimed, "are you suggesting marriage? Is this how you propose to a girl? Is this your idea of sweeping me off my feet? Quite unsatisfactory, to say the least! Frankly, I am quite appalled at this barbaric maneuver and consider it a blemish on your character," she said and smiled with delight.

Benjamin got down on his knee in customary fashion, as she regally awaited his words of love and commitment.

He held her hand as he gazed into the wondrous blue sea of her sparkling eyes.

"Cindy," he began, "I realize that we've only known each other a short time. And it scares me that this wondrous joy that I'm feeling right now, though it feels like love, may be just an intense infatuation—an infatuation that many couples mistake for love. Whatever it is, it's wonderful. I believe it's a beginning of love, a glorious door leading toward a higher love. I don't know, but I feel it. I feel it when I look at you, almost like you are that door, that beautiful door. I want to say that I love you, but somehow the words do not seem valid; they seem cheap, like a cliché. I think it is more accurate to say that I *will* love you. And I will; I know I will—more and more every day. There will be laughter and pain and arguments over eggs at breakfast," he said and smiled. "But all these things will only temper our love, creating a deeper, richer love. I believe that love is a verb; it's something you do. And I promise you—I pledge to you—that I will love you always, every day of my life. And also, may my pledge to you go through you and rest on any and all children we may have together in the future, God willing, so that our love will grow together in the garden of a family, as we travel through our years, growing old together, forever, into eternity." Benjamin paused. "Cindy, you see what I am. I am no more—just a simple man with a simple dream, but a dream laced with the riches of love, real love, family love. Cindy, will you marry me?"

Cindy's wet eyes sparkled all the brighter as a tear gently formed and began its journey down her cheek. She kissed him, temporarily unable to speak. She leaned away from the kiss, wiped her eyes, composing herself. "Benjamin," she said, "I have no eloquent speech for you, but here goes: I believe you to be strong...your willpower, I mean; it seems as strong as iron. The words that you've just spoken are beautiful, and I believe them to be true, and I believe that you will be true to them. I truly do. However, I am not as strong as you. I know this. I am not a perfect person; I have my days. But I share your dream. I will be a good mother; in that I am confident. I adore children, and they will be loved deeply. That is my pledge to you; in that I am firm. As far as my feelings for you go, well, right now, I adore you. I really do. Is this feeling love? I don't know; I can't say right now. I believe, as you believe, that this feeling we share is indeed a door toward love. And I would gladly walk through that door with you, as your wife, if you'll have me. Truthfully, that's all I can promise."

Benjamin thought about her words, considering her proclamation. "Cindy," he said with solemnity, "marriage is serious; it is for life. I firmly believe that. What you have just told me is not really a commitment of lifelong marriage, but more like a commitment to *try* to be married. However, I believe you have spoken sincerely and with truth. That will have to be enough for me." While speaking these words, Benjamin noticed a strand of black fabric hanging from under one of the sofa's cushions as he continued his narrative. "Cindy, I wish I had a wedding ring to give you, to seal my pledge of marriage, but I do not. However, I do have a token of love for you, if you will accept it. It is a token to remind you always that as far as our love goes, may our cups be filled and runneth over." With that statement he placed her black bra on her lap, as he bowed in reverence.

Temporarily stunned, Cindy slapped the bra on top of the praying monk's head, as the two playfully and laughingly fought, rolling on the floor, celebrating their joy, ending in embrace, induced, consumed, with an aura of intensity, powerful and deep, as the two lay enchanted, within the wonder of it all.

"Benjamin?" said Cindy. "What's on your palette for today?"

"You are," he said with a smile.

She returned his smile, kissing him on his cheek. "Let's do something special."

"Like what?'

"I don't know…something special, just the two of us."

"Hey, I know!" he said. "We could take a ride up in the backcountry. I know of a secluded little lake; it's beautiful, it really is. I go camping there a couple times a year. It's like heaven. Been going there since I was a kid, with my family. It's a special place to me. You would love it there; I know you would."

"What would we do when we get there?"

"I don't know—hike, swim, lie naked on the beach, do it in the sand." He smiled. "Whatever we want."

"Right!" she said, laughing. "What if someone should see us, naked on the beach, I mean?"

"The lake is secluded; hardly anyone goes there, a few hikers maybe. If anyone sees us, I don't think they would mind." Benjamin smiled.

Cindy kissed him sensually on the mouth as her mind entertained the erotic scenario. "Actually," she said, "I was thinking of doing something a little closer to home."

"Such as?"

"Such as...go shopping."

"Shopping?" exclaimed Benjamin. "I'm not much of a shopper. Anyways, what's so special about shopping? You out of groceries or something?"

"No, silly, I was just thinking that we could go and look for...wedding rings. That's all."

"Oh," he responded as he thought deeply.

"Benjamin," she suddenly said emphatically, "I want to get married as soon as possible—next week if we can."

"Next week? You're kidding! I was thinking more along the lines of a few months, at least, or maybe a—a year, you know, to see how things line up...Next week!"

"Benjamin, I don't want to wait. We could have a small wedding, just friends, no big ado, just us. We could get a marriage license and a preacher and be married next Saturday."

"Cindy, I really don't think it's wise to rush into this any more than we already have. We need time to think."

"Think about what?" she asked confidently. "Do you plan to change your mind?"

"Well, no—no, never. I'm sure of that, but I think we need time for our lives to adjust, time to allow the pieces to fall into place. This is all so—so new. I mean, you're probably not even pregnant...I mean...not that it matters...I mean..."

"Benjamin, would you marry me if I was pregnant?"

"Of course, I would. You know that."

"And if I wasn't?"

"Well, yes, but I don't see the need to rush into it, especially if you're not pregnant."

"Oh, I know it's irrational," she said, her eyes ablaze with the firmness of iron. "I know it's crazy, but I don't care. I'm on top of the world right now! Oh, Benjamin, I've never felt so happy. I want to be married as soon as possible and start a family as soon as we can!"

"But Cindy, it would be—"

"Benjamin," she said, cutting him off, "I have little desire to *get* married. I want to *be* married. Do you understand? I don't care about the engagement. I don't care about the wedding; I mean, you know, the party part of it, with all the traditional hoopla and ceremony, walking down the aisle, the dress, the show. I just want to be married, to share breakfasts in the morning, cups of coffee on the porch, our days, our nights, our children. Oh, I know it makes sense to wait, but life has knocked on our door. Let's grab hold of it, embrace it, and shake it, take it, while it's intense and fresh. Let's live it, deliberately. We didn't plan this, but here we are. Let's inhale it, allow it to intoxicate us and revel in it to the fullest extent possible. Let's not wait, please."

"What type of ring did you have in mind?" said Benjamin.

Cindy gleefully kissed him over and over again. "A big one," she said dreamily. "With a huge diamond in the center, symbolizing us as one, and little diamonds, like five or six, set around the larger one. Oh, it will be beautiful and expensive—at least a million, maybe two," she said, laughing.

"Hmm," he said, "I would have to work a lot of overtime to pay that off."

"Oh, of course!" she said with all seriousness. "You see, Benjamin, that's how marriage works: You shower me with expensive gifts and do all the breadwinning. I, on the other hand, stay home and figure out ways to spend that bread, which, in turn, keeps you busy and out of trouble. Every woman knows this. Isn't the notion of marriage divine?"

"Oh, is that how it goes?" he said.

"Yes," she stated with all sincerity. "That about sums it up. What about you?"

"What? My definition of marriage?"

"No, silly, my definition is the one we'll follow. What about your ring? Anything particular?"

"Hmm," he said, "I guess it will have to be big enough to fit through my nostrils."

"Ha! Good idea," she said, laughing. "Now, seriously."

"Well," he said, "I just want a plain gold band, but one that's durable, maybe one that's made with a gold alloy of some sort, for strength, to keep its shape. I want one that'll last forever."

"That's sweet," she said.

"And practical," he added. "There's no sense in getting an expensive ring for me and throwing ourselves deeper in debt, since most of my working life I will be paying off your ring."

"But I'm worth it," she quickly added. "Every penny! Benjamin, believe me when I tell you that my heart will go out to you while you are working and sweating, doing your best to fend for your beautiful wife, while I watch soap operas, polishing my ring, planning what you can cook for dinner when you arrive home."

"Yes," said Benjamin, thinking of the night before, "you're worth it."

She gazed into his eyes. "I was kidding, you know…about my ring. I just want something nice, something sincere. I believe in wedding rings—the idea, I mean."

"I do, too," said Benjamin as he kissed her. "Well, shall we depart in my blue chariot, my princess, soon-to-be queen?"

"Let's shall, my goodly prince!" replied Cindy, reviving her regal British accent.

They walked out of their new home hand in hand, as novel beings of light, completely transformed, distinctly different from the two people who'd entered the house's portal the evening before. They drove off into their future, meeting it head-on, embracing it with the intensity and fervor and wonder that only young lovers taste, and they drank deeply from the cup presented before them, savoring the richness of its wine, a wine seasoned with an intoxicating enchantment that sparkled about them like glittering snowflakes, as in a dream.

VII

At the Plant

The days melted into each other just as Benjamin melted into Cindy, and she into him, mingling and meshing into a joyous unity. Even Benjamin's workdays seemed brighter, as if the work itself became purer, refined with meaning, with purpose. He worked all the more diligently, whistling through his days, emanating an aura of happy optimism, shining like a beacon, puzzling his coworkers.

"OK, Ben, what the hell gives?" asked Mark during their break in the plant's lunchroom, as the other men forged through their sandwich-laden lunch pails, lending their ears toward the birth of a new topic.

"What?" questioned Benjamin, genuinely bewildered.

"These past few days you've been hummin' and whistlin' like a goddamned tweety bird, volunteering us for the hard jobs, workin' like a madman. I can hardly get you to take a break!"

"Maybe I'm just happy to be here, working in this fine establishment, with all of you good men—the salt of the earth. Who wouldn't be happy?" Benjamin said and laughed.

"Damn it, you did it again. That's the bullshit I'm talking about," stammered Mark.

"Did what?" Benjamin said, smiling.

"OK, Frisk, what the hell's goin' on with you? You hit the lottery or something?"

"He probably got a piece of ass last night!" piped Jerry Winters, as he gnawed at a bologna sandwich.

Mark accepted Jerry's keen summation of the situation as highly plausible. "So that's it!" he stated confidently.

Benjamin just smiled, a little embarrassed and dreading the inevitable initiation process that was now imminent.

"So, you found a hot one, did you? That explains it!" said Mark. "Anyone I know?"

The lunchroom erupted with comments and suggestions aimed at providing Benjamin with wise advice in matters of love and the opposite sex.

"What? Did I hear right? Benny's got a woman? Well, goddamn it; it's about time! You might as well suffer like the rest of us!"

"Oh, he ain't sufferin' yet. He's probably just thinking 'bout that little patch of fur he been diddlin'. That's why he's been so giddy. Got his hand in the cookie jar."

"You mean *her* cookie jar!"

The room exploded with laughter as the men pounced on the fresh topic, continuing the initiation process.

"Better check your teeth for hair."

"Funny he has any energy left."

"Yup, his little head is doin' the thinkin' now."

"Oh, I bet it's doin' more than thinkin'."

"That true, Benny? You givin' her the ol' trouser snake?"

"Yup, he's givin' some gal the ol' toboggan ride."

"That true, Ben? You givin' some girl free rides on the ol' baloney pony?"

Benjamin quietly ate his lunch, allowing the men to get it out of their system. It seemed to be standard lunchroom protocol: whenever a worker was found out to be in a new relationship with a woman, the ribbing would have to ensue until the men had their allotment of fun. It was rather crude and barbaric; however, it was their way of showing approval, of showing acceptance. Usually, in such a circumstance, a person in Benjamin's position would comment on the jests thrown his way, which would only encourage the mob all the more. Therefore, he allowed the jocular banter to play itself out before he spoke. He just smiled as he slowly finished his lunch.

"Look at him," said Jerry Winters, "smug as a bug in a rug. He's get-tin' 'er, all right!"

"Yup, he's hooked—hook, line, and sinker—and he don't even know it yet," joked another man.

"I don't think he cares, Bob. Hell, I didn't care either, back when I was chasin' skirts. A good set of boobs and a firm ass—mmm…Goddamn it, that'll take away a man's sense, his reason—just like a buck in rut."

"Next thing you know," said another man, "he'll do something fool-ish, like get married. Then the party'll be over, and the work will start."

The men laughed all the louder, jubilant in their merrymaking.

"Saturday," said Benjamin with authority.

The laughing dwindled and ceased, as the confused gladiators pon-dered the victim's strange statement.

"Today's Thursday, Frisk," said Jerry Winters. "The boy's so fucked out, he's delirious—don't even know what day it is."

A few lingering snickers filtered through the room, as the men waited for an explanation.

"Well?" said Mark, staring expectantly at Benjamin.

"Getting married Saturday," said Benjamin nonchalantly.

"That's bullshit! You're kidding. You never mentioned that you even had a girlfriend. You're so full of shit your eyes are brown!"

"And," said Benjamin looking back at Mark, "I need a witness for the ceremony. It'll be two o'clock Saturday. Can you make it? I'd really appreciate it. I know it's sudden notice, but that's just the way it unfolded. What do you say?"

"Oh, shut up! You're just trying to spoil our fun."

"No, Mark, I'm serious."

"OK, OK, we'll lay off. You don't have to be so cocky about it. We were just having a little fun is all."

Benjamin laughed. "Believe it or not fellas, you've hit the nail right on the head. I'm getting married Saturday whether you believe it or not. Cindy's her name. And you're right, Bob, I've fallen hook, line, and sinker, and I love it."

Mark sat wide-eyed with his mouth open as the notion hit home. "Son of a bitch…He's serious."

"Cindy's my neighbor," explained Benjamin. "We haven't known each other very long, but it all came together this weekend. She's really great. And we're getting married. End of story."

Mark sat in amazement, stunned. "Ben," he finally said, "please, don't take this the wrong way, but are you out of your fuckin' mind? People don't meet one minute and get married the next! You've got to back out...or back off...slow it down...or—"

"Mark," Benjamin cut him off, "will you be a witness on Saturday or not? Cindy and I set this up with a preacher yesterday, and he says we need two witnesses. Cindy's asking one of her girlfriends at work, and I'm asking you. What do you say?"

"Jesus, Ben, I'm sorry. I just didn't...you know...think that—"

"You got that right, Mark," piped Jerry Winters, cutting Mark off. "You just didn't think."

The room erupted with an uneasy laughter, as the weight of the news blanketed them.

"Yeah, Ben, sure, I'll be a witness. I just...I mean...This is just so...I mean...It's awesome, I guess."

"Thanks, Mark. I'll let you know the particulars tomorrow." Benjamin got up from the table and walked out of the stunned lunchroom.

As the door closed and Benjamin's footsteps drifted safely out of hearing range, the wry statements began to resurrect themselves.

"Poor bastard," began one man, "walkin' to the gallows with a smile."

"He'll be pullin' his pecker again within a month—guaranteed."

"Dumber than a box of rocks. The guy finally gets some steady fuckin'. Why the hell ruin it by marrying her? Don't make no sense at all."

"Hey, he's gotta learn—just like the rest of us learned."

"Yeah, a few years under the ol' ball and chain will cure 'im."

"You got that right. I bet he won't be whistlin' like a shit bird then!"

Just then, Jeremiah Akmin, who was one of the senior workers, respected for his sound morals and good judgment, stood to address the men. The men immediately quieted down. Jeremiah rarely spoke foolishly and usually held his tongue during such proceedings.

"Now, you boys had your fun with it, the way you always do. But from now on, you just let the boy be. There ain't a damned man here that doesn't wish he was in Benjamin's shoes, and you know it. A feller fallin' in love with a woman is a damned precious thing, and if that woman gives 'er back, it's worth more than all the gold on this earth. Young Benjamin here's a damned good man, and he thinks he found that gold. And as far as he's concerned, he did find that gold. Hell, we probably all found it at one time, but some of us might have let it slip away—not paying attention, not appreciating what we had. Tell you what I'm gonna do: I'm gonna march out of this here lunchroom and find Benjamin and congratulate him, wish him well. I suggest you boys do the same." On that note, Jeremiah walked out of the lunchroom as the men sat in reverent silence, reflecting on the solid truth of his words. Then, periodically, one by one, they filed out.

VIII

Wedding Day

The wedding day finally arrived. Cindy and Benjamin had been busy all week, making arrangements, making plans, and moving furniture from her house to his house—to their house. As the days passed, they were ecstatic, giddy, feverish with anticipation, like children eagerly waiting to open their presents on Christmas Day.

The couple had shown restraint and agreed to sleep in their own respective beds until the wedding night, abstaining from sex. This proved to be difficult. After an evening of planning the wedding and calling people and moving furniture, the night always ended the same, embracing them with a cavernous passion, consuming them, engaging them in every way, short of actual sex. In this fashion they tortured themselves. The abstinence from sex was Cindy's idea. Benjamin respected her commitment toward the traditional notions of marriage, and the noble attempt to make the wedding night more passionate with their fasting. However, each evening, as he and Cindy dangerously flirted precariously on the slippery slope of passion, his footing slipped as he allowed the erotic sensations to devour him. The feeling of her lips, her skin, her body, her darting tongue touching his was an erotic torture beyond his control. His temporary vow of celibacy, he would have gladly and greedily broken, as the ecstatic hunger crumbled his will. It was Cindy who would break it off, right when he was near the edge, when they were both near the edge. Then she would stop the climb in a desperate attempt to lower the escalation onto a safe plateau, only to resume the climb once they arrived. Finally, she would pry herself away and go to the door, where the couple would continue the glorious torture again, flirting with ecstasy, with one hand on the door. One last deep kiss would elevate them both to the pinnacle of no return, as Cindy gently, but forcefully, pushed him away, quickly making her escape, fleeing from nature's ravenous grip. Benjamin would watch her rush off into the night, feverish with a jumbled, lusty knot of sensual desire deep inside his being. In this fashion, they continually tormented themselves, as the nightly separation broke the bonds of passion, leaving their wanting bodies unfulfilled, but filling their hearts with a craving anticipation, consuming them with a deep longing that engulfed them completely. Benjamin, dazed and delirious immediately after her departure, would take an ice-cold shower in an attempt to shock himself out of the overpowering desire to alleviate passion's grip manually. In this fashion he remained completely true to his celibate oath in every way.

Saturday's welcome light flooded through their worlds, waking them into their wedding day, the day of their dreams. Both of them, although alone in their respective beds, seemed united in spirit—a joyous spirit that could not be described with mere words. They both lay there, basking in the joy, unable to contain it within their bodies. Sunlight dazzled out of their eyes, it emanated outward from their countenance, transforming the world into an Eden. It was raining outside. From the looks of it, it would rain all day. To them, the rain seemed as sparkling glitter, as it gracefully danced through the heavens, falling dreamily as sliver flecks of stardust to the greenness of the life-covered earth, providing sustenance to all life as it continued its ancient, miraculous cycle, a cycle of life that they were a part of, a cycle of birth and rebirth.

Benjamin got out of bed and made some coffee. He poured himself a steaming cup and looked out the window, into the soft, gentle rain, as it glided down in a misty haze, coating the trees, the grass, everything to a glistening luster. He loved rainy days. There was a tranquility about them, a calmness, a serenity that seemed to sing to his soul. He hypnotically gazed into the crystal droplets, as one who gazes into a crystal ball forecasting the future. "Next year, in this very room," he thought, "there will be two gazing out this very window, hopefully three." Warm illusions of family quelled up inside his mind, forming into happy daydreams, only to evaporate and then amalgamate themselves into a new, richer illusion, more fantastic than the first. Maybe they would have twins…or triplets. Maybe they would just have one healthy child and try for more as soon as possible…and then another after that and after that…ten perhaps… maybe fifteen." Warm cookies, Easter egg trees, footsie pajamas all pacified his visions as the falling rain sang its watery lullaby.

Suddenly, the phone rang, immediately sending the chimera scattering into oblivion. Benjamin shuddered, thinking that the call might be from his mother. He'd put off notifying her about the wedding. Because she was in Japan, there was no way she could make the wedding, and if she knew about his plans, she would just be cynical about the whole thing, questioning Cindy's character, questioning their judgment, their sanity. At best, she would try to persuade him to wait a year or so, so she could attend the wedding properly, laying a guilt trip on him about him being her only son and all of that. Benjamin did not want her interference to disrupt both his and Cindy's euphoria. "Oh, not now," he muttered to himself as the phone rang on and on. Finally, he could stand it no more and picked it up. "Hello?"

"Still in bed, sleepyhead?" came Cindy's sweet voice, sweeping him back into his fairy-tale state of mind.

"Oh, Cindy! Thank God, it's you."

"You were expecting one of your other fiancées on our wedding day?" she said, laughing merrily.

"I just had a premonition that it might be my mother."

"Maybe you should call her. You have lots of time; it's only seven thirty."

"Hmm," he said, "I'll wait. I'll tell her next week. She'll freak out."

"I imagine she will," said Cindy. "Oh, Benjamin, I can't wait. Did you see the rain? Oh, it's beautiful. Everything's shining like it was just painted—just for us. Lisa and Denise are going to be here in an hour. We're going out to get our hair done and get all spiffed up. Oh, I can't wait. I just can't wait."

"Hey, I'll cook us all up some breakfast. You can all come over here when they get there," said Benjamin, anxious to see Cindy.

"What? And see me before the wedding? No way, José. The groom isn't supposed to see the bride until the ceremony. You know that; we talked about that."

"Well, I just thought that breakfast wouldn't—"

"Benjamin," she said, cutting him off, "N-o, no! Besides, I don't think I could handle it again. When I got home last night, I had to take a cold shower for half an hour," she said and laughed.

"Really? So did I," he said, joining her laughter. "I had to...I mean... I just had to...I just—"

"I know what you mean," she said. "So, did you make it? I mean, are you still a virgin since last weekend, you know...in every way?"

"Well," he replied, "I made it, but just by a thread. What about you?"

"Last night? Yes, I made it. Thanks to the cold shower, I made it."

"What about the other nights, you know...after...*the* night?"

"I'd rather not say," she said, breaking out in guilty laughter, brighter than ever.

"What?" said Benjamin, merrily stunned. "What about your big speech about fasting and building the anticipation until the wedding night and all that?"

"Well, what can I say? I did try," she said, giggling. "Don't worry, there's plenty of anticipation built up for tonight. Oh, I just can't wait—to be married, I mean. Benjamin, I'm so happy; I could just burst. You're not going to be late, are you? You better not be. I couldn't take it. Get there at least a half hour early. Did you call Mark? Are you sure he knows the correct address and the right time. You didn't sit on the suit I ironed for you last night, did you? And make sure your tie is tied properly. And—"

"Whoa!" stated Benjamin. "Slow down. Everything will be fine. Just don't worry about me. We'll be there on time. I promise."

"Oh, I just want it to be nice, Benjamin. I want it to be simple, but nice."

"It will be," he said, "as long as we are married."

"That's sweet. Oh, my God! Denise just pulled into the driveway, and I'm not even dressed yet! Oh, I've got to run. Benjamin, oh, I can't wait."

"OK, OK, you better get going, or you'll be the one late for the wedding!"

"Ha, you're probably right about that! OK, I'm going. Oh, Benjamin, I love you."

Benjamin's tongue instantly tied itself in a million knots. It was the first time Cindy had declared her love for him verbally. He stood, with the phone to his ear, dumbfounded by the impact of those sweet, honeyed words.

"You still there?" said Cindy. "You didn't fall on your head, did you?" she said and laughed. "Please, Benjamin, don't say anything, and don't repeat those words just because I said them. It would cheapen everything, OK? Gotta go. Bye."

The Reverend's Speech

Benjamin stood there with the phone in his hand, basking in the sheer delight of hearing those sweet words and, more importantly, believing them to be true. Regaining his composure, he set the phone down and walked back to the window, sipping his coffee, staring into the dazzling silver flecks of liquid crystal as his mind wandered into the rain itself, into a billion drops of wonderful dreams. His thoughts eventually drifted toward a conversation that he and Cindy had with the preacher earlier in the week. He had asked his father's pastor, Reverend Daniels, to do the officiating, thinking that, because he was affiliated with the family, he might be willing to perform the ceremony on such short notice. The reverend's acceptance was conditional; he and Cindy were to meet with him to go over some "considerations," as he called them, before they were to be married before God and man. Of course, they were more than happy to accommodate, thinking the meeting to be a mere formality, with the preacher congratulating them and encouraging their happiness and diligently confirming the importance of the wedding vow, that sort of thing. Benjamin reflected on the preacher's countenance as the meeting began. He did not seem happy, nor encouraging, but rather skeptical—cynical, in fact.

"So you think you want to get married, do you?" began the reverend, looking over the top of his glasses, almost glaring. "Don't speak," he commanded, "until I tell you to speak."

Both Benjamin and Cindy were taken aback by the gruffness of his tone, retreating into muteness, bound with a tingling of fear.

"Benjamin, Cindy, I am an old man in your eyes. Fifty-seven: I must appear to you as an ancient relic. But with these gray hairs comes wisdom. Many a young couple have sat before me, in the very chairs you sit in now. And I have gone over the seriousness of the commitment that you plan to partake in, the finality of what you're embarking on here. The protocol is that I tell you the usual particulars of marriage, as the happy couple just sit there and nod their heads like a couple of morons, thinking this is nothing more than a boring formality. Then they comment on my words, trying their best to be clever to say things that they think I want to hear. Then they leave, and everything I've said is soon forgotten the moment they leave this building. Look at you two—just young twerps, both of you. You think you're in love, I suppose. They all do." He laughed. "Every damned one of them. What? You never heard a preacher use profanity? Is using the word *damned* profanity?"

"Well…" began Benjamin.

"Quiet!" yelled the preacher. "Don't you dare answer any of my questions or make any comment of any kind until I explicitly ask you to speak! Hmm, now, where was I? Oh yes, the word *damned*…Couples, not unlike yourselves, continually come to me and stand before the altar of God professing the wedding commitment; some are sincere, some are not. However, over fifty percent of marriages fail in this country. Fifty percent! So fifty percent of marriages—marriages not unlike your marriage—will end in divorce. Those couples will break their promise to each other; they will break their promise made before their family, friends, and the state. And most regrettably, they will break their promise made before their God—a promise they themselves mutually committed to before God Himself! Do you realize the implications here? Seriously, do you think God will just say, 'Oh well, they just wanted to go their separate ways,' and then forget about it? To tell you the truth, I don't know what He would do. His mercy is vast—but His anger is to be feared! Do you two have any idea how the Lord feels toward divorce? Well, do you?"

Benjamin and Cindy sat mute, terrified to utter a word.

Reverend Daniels glared at them, shoving a black Bible in front of them. "Pick it up," he commanded. "Turn to Malachi, the second chapter; read verses fourteen and fifteen aloud."

Benjamin picked up the Bible and fumbled through the pages, totally lost yet afraid to ask any questions. Reverend Daniels allowed the minutes to creep by, glaring at their obvious lack of biblical knowledge, allowing them to desperately scramble through the book, allowing them to feel the embarrassment of their ignorance. After some time, he noticed that they'd finally found the book of Malachi, but they had forgotten which chapter and verse.

"Chapter two, verses fourteen and fifteen," he said with disgust. "I'll give you some background. The Lord God is ticked off at these people, and because of the Lord's anger, their lives have grown miserable, and they can't figure out why. Now, go ahead, read it together."

"'You ask why?'" they chanted. "'It is because the Lord is acting as the witness between you and the wife of your youth, because you have broken faith with her, though she is your partner, the wife of your marriage covenant. Has not the Lord made them one? In flesh and spirit they are his. And why one? Because he was seeking godly offspring. So guard yourself in your spirit, and do not break faith with the wife of your youth.'"

"Good, good," stated Reverend Daniels. "Now read the next three words out loud. Do it now!"

"'I hate divorce,'" they said.

"Who hates divorce?" stammered the reverend.

"'I hate divorce,'" repeated Benjamin and Cindy, "'says the Lord God of Israel—'"

"Yes, yes!" yelled the reverend. "He *hates* divorce. He hates it! Do you two understand that? Can you? Do you know what divorced, or nearly divorced, people say when I ask them what went wrong with their marriage? Do you? They look at their shoes in shame and say, 'I don't know. Maybe it was this. Maybe it was that.' They're not sure—can't seem to put their finger on it. Malachi says it all; they have broken faith with their spouse in some way. Yet they can't understand that. And here I am again, counseling yet another couple before they get married while they sit here in an infatuated stupor, taking my words lightly. Therefore, I am not going to speak to you about the great blessings of marriage—the great joys. That is going to be your doing. I have compiled a list of scriptures for you to look up—together. And don't just read them—think about their implications." He handed Benjamin the list. "Now," he said, "I have one question to ask of you. And before you answer, I want you to think deeply about the question and then answer truthfully. And be genuinely serious about it, as if God would strike you dead on the spot if you weren't sincere. And don't you dare give me some crap that you think I want to hear. You got that?"

They both nodded, wide-eyed, at the sheer impact of the reverend's forceful persona.

"Why do you want to get married?"

The couple looked into each other's eyes, knowing exactly what to say, but afraid to say it immediately. Finally Benjamin spoke up. "Reverend Daniels, Cindy and I know exactly why we want to be married. You asked for the truth, and I'll give you the truth. We've been dating for only a week. Are we infatuated with each other? Sure, we are! I imagine that all couples who enter into marriage are. However, it isn't just the feeling between each other that pulls us together. It's much more than that. It's about family. We want children, many children—our own family. We realize that the intensity of what we feel right now may be a bit superficial and fade somewhat, but even if the emotional facade evaporates, the love will remain, there in our hearts and within our family, our children, and there it will grow. I can't tell you that I'm a great Christian or anything. You've seen us fumble through the scriptures. I can't speak for Cindy, but I didn't even know that Malachi was a book in the Bible, let alone what it said about divorce. But I can tell you this much. I agree with what the Lord said. I hate divorce, too; believe me when I say that. And I would do everything in my power to be true to Cindy. And about that scripture verse, where it says that God created marriage because He wants godly offspring. Well, that's exactly what Cindy and I are founding our marriage on. I'm not sure exactly what 'godly offspring' are, but if it has anything to do with loving and caring for your children and bringing them up in a good and solid home, then we are on the same page." Benjamin hesitated before continuing. "And, since we're being truthful, as we should be…"

Benjamin's gaze turned away from the reverend and into Cindy's eyes. As he paused in his speech, she sensed his intended words and continued the professing of truth with her own words. She turned an iron gaze toward the reverend.

"The truth is that there is a slight chance that I may be pregnant. We had participated in sexual activity just one night, last weekend, without the use of contraceptives. We could have taken steps to prevent a pregnancy the morning after. However, we discovered our love and desire to start a family. And honestly, I don't think I could have. I…we want to be married and raise a family in love. I truly hope I am pregnant, but even if I am not, I…we intend to pursue that path."

The reverend was temporarily stunned by the directness of their bold statements, immediately accepting their words as valid truth.

"I see," he said meekly as he mulled over their words, allowing the minutes to tick by. "Tell me," he spoke contemplatively, "what is your battle plan? You may speak freely."

"Battle plan?" repeated Benjamin, looking into Cindy's puzzled eyes. "We aren't sure what you mean by—"

"Oh, come on, man!" blurted the reverend with a burning fire in his eyes. "Don't be naive. It's a war out there, and the enemy doesn't play fair. Guerilla tactics—that's what he employs! That's what you're up against. The enemy will lie in wait; he'll find a chink in your armor and then do his best to infest you like a disease, attacking with all the ferocity of a starved lion after a lamb, especially when you're alone and vulnerable. He'll rip you limb from limb, devour you, devour your spirit. Then your empty shell of a body will wander the earth in desolation, void of love, void of God. Do you two have any idea what I'm talking about here? Do you?"

Benjamin almost answered, but decided against it.

"A battle plan is what you need!" continued the feverish minister. "A defensive plan—yes, a defensive plan would work best in your case. Defense! We don't know when or where the enemy will strike, but I can assure you that he will be trying. You'll have to be on your toes twenty-four-seven. He'll tempt you with the usual: pride, money, power, the works—and the big one these days, sex. And don't think for a second that you won't fall prey to it, that you're above it! Even the greats succumbed under the enemy's devious attacks: David, Solomon, Samson. As Christians, we firmly believe that sex should be thoroughly enjoyed between a man and a woman, within the bounds of the marriage covenant, for the procreation of children and for the bliss associated with it. However, there are many out there in the world who would love to have sex with you, to fulfill their own selfish lusts, with little regard for your spouse, your marriage, your family, and your soul. Are these not the very things you hold most dear? Are these not the very things you would long to protect with your very lives? Don't be fooled by these wolves in sheep's clothing. They think only of themselves. If they truly thought of you, they would consider your family, your soul, and how much destruction would occur to them as well as to you, by tempting you away from the noble path. And don't think for a moment that you are immune to lustful thoughts for a person other than your spouse. We all have minds. We all think. We all imagine and dabble in…oh, let's say…dangerous thoughts. But beware! The snare has been laid out before you. Defense! Think defense! Cindy, when that handsome man is at work, the one who seems so kind and attentive to you, asks you to go out for a friendly cup of coffee, think defense! Benjamin, when you see that sexy little brunette by the water cooler and you suddenly decide to walk over there and say an innocent hello, think twice. Would you have thought about saying hello to some guy at the water cooler? Why the pretty little brunette? Defense—think defense! Any fantasies that you might conjure up, take home to your marriage bed. Relish the physical with each other; keep your marriage pure; keep your souls pure. You two are both young and seem to be strong…strong willed. Tell me, do you think you can win over the enemy? Do you think you can keep your marriage pure? Feel free to speak."

"Yes, I think so!" Benjamin said.

"Cindy?" asked the reverend. "What about you?"

"Yes," she answered.

Reverend Daniels paused, staring into their eyes with a glare so penetrating that it elevated the gravity and seriousness of what he was about to say.

"Herein lies the problem of humankind," he said directly. "You think you can do it all by yourselves. Well, you can't—not on your own. You need God! You need Christ! You need the Holy Spirit! Only He will protect you. Only He is your defense. Only He...If you embed yourselves and your children into the protective arms of our Lord, you will be safe; you will live richly in spirit and love. However, the good Lord has given us the glorious gift of free will—free will. It's all up to you. Embrace Him. Stand firm in His precincts. Dine on His words! Allow them into your stomachs to nourish your soul, and allow their power to course through your veins. If you do, God will bless you; He will bless your marriage; He will bless your children and your children's children. It's up to you. It's all up to you. And not just one of you—both of you. Now, then, you have the list I've given you to help you start off in a positive direction. That's all I have at this point. Benjamin, Cindy, I may have sounded harsh just now, but it is a serious business you embark upon. The immense joy you have now is just a taste of what could be in store for you. But you have to guard your marriage. I like to think of marriage as sort of like a delicious soup, and every day you put something into that soup to make it more flavorful, making it taste even better than before. However, if something rotten is placed into the soup, it could taint the whole batch, giving it a putrid flavor that will make you vomit. And how does one get a putrid flavor out of a soup once it's been added? Do you have any questions?"

The couple looked at each other, shaking their heads, not thinking of anything they could possibly say that wouldn't sound completely foolish. "No."

Benjamin thought of how they'd felt after the meeting, as he looked into the rain, how they'd laughed during the drive home to his place. How quickly they had set aside the minister's words. He walked into the bedroom, shuffling through the scattered bits of paper on his dresser, where he was sure he'd placed the list of scriptures that Reverend Daniels had given him. It didn't seem to be there. He checked the pockets of the clothes he'd had on that day. Nothing. He thought that maybe Cindy had taken it. He glanced at his watch. "Oh well," he said.

Church Service

The church service was short; the whole ceremony lasted no more than fifteen minutes. It was very simple and straightforward. Benjamin and Cindy stood before Reverend Daniels, along with the two witnesses, Mark and Lisa. Cindy's friend Denise was the only other person in the room, sitting quietly in the front pew. The couple declared their commitment, their promise, publicly, before the people, before the state, and before their God. In their hearts, they knew that this promise was unlike all others. It was not just a legal contract that bound them by a marriage license; it was also a moral contract, a contract of character and integrity, a contract of love professed before every known thing in the universe, both visible and invisible. It was a contract of commitment, of committing their spirits to each other. It was this spiritual aspect that bound them, the binding of their hearts and minds, their souls, "forever, in sickness and in health. Till death do we part—forever."

The reverend's last words fell warmly on their hearts like a long-awaited homecoming: "By all the powers vested in me, I pronounce you man and wife! Benjamin, you may kiss the bride."

Benjamin looked into Cindy's sparkling blue eyes, and she into his, as they embraced the moment, melting into each other as their two spirits mingled into one flesh. Tears of joy blossomed as they kissed, the birth of their love for each other blooming into a radiant flower, baptizing them into the joyful beginnings of their holy state.

Reverend Daniels smiled inwardly as the couple embraced, noticing the distinct aura of love that emanated from the couple, filling his heart with hope. As they embraced, he raised his hand over their heads, giving them his blessing, and then concluded the ritual. "What God has brought together, may no man put asunder. Mr. and Mrs. Benjamin Frisk, may you walk with the Lord forever. Amen." The reverend shook both Benjamin's and Cindy's hand, finalizing the formal ceremony. Lisa and Mark exchanged hugs with the married couple, melting any remaining tension into celebration.

Denise was bawling like a baby as she rushed to hug Cindy. "Oh, it was beautiful," she sobbed. "I wish you all the best in the world. Both of you," she added, hugging Benjamin. "OK," she stated, regaining her composure, "it's time for pictures. We need lots of pictures."

Afterward, they all laughingly splashed through the rain as they ran to their cars and drove to Lisa's place, where she and Denise had prepared a celebratory reception in honor of the newlyweds. A handful of friends and acquaintances welcomed them into the streamer-laced apartment, showering them with congratulatory hugs and kisses. The inquisitive guests demanded a full account of how they'd met and fallen in love, because all of them were still in a state of shock from the immediacy of the whole affair. Benjamin and Cindy each merrily commented on their particular perspectives of how destiny's hand had led them into each other's arms, while everyone listened attentively, sipping champagne and nibbling on hors d'oeuvres. Their story ended with the details of the wedding ceremony and the emotional thoughts that had been going through their minds at the time, bringing most of their audience to tears, as they again professed their love for each other.

Lisa raised her glass for a toast. "Ben and Cindy," she began, "may your days always be blessed with good times and happiness, just as it is now. To Mr. and Mrs. Frisk!"

"To Mr. and Mrs. Frisk!" everyone chanted as they each lifted their glasses and drank.

The party went on into the evening, with everyone casually mingling and chatting with each other, allowing the wine to loosen their tongues. Mark was gladly allowing the wine to get the best of him, as he grew loud and a bit obnoxious. However, he was gleefully embraced as the evening's "live entertainment." It grew quite obvious that Mark was putting the moves on Lisa, as she toyed with the attention.

As the evening wound down, Benjamin sat on the sofa, sipping yet another glass of champagne; his eyes were fastened on Cindy, who was giggling with Denise at the other side of the room. He watched her facial expressions, her smile, her earlobes—each decorated with a single, glis-tening diamond, accentuating her beauty. Her wedding dress was just an ordinary white dress that barely covered her knees, exposing her naked legs, smooth and firm. Her neckline was accentuated by a delicate gold chain, which hung down toward a teasing hint of cleavage.

Cindy turned her head toward Benjamin. Their eyes met, connecting them both, connecting their thoughts. She came to him and kissed him.

"Let's go home," she said.

"Home," Benjamin thought warmly to himself. "Home!"

They said their good-byes and thank-yous, as the congratulated cou-ple made their escape. The rain was pouring around them as they ran through the night toward Cindy's car, hand in hand, laughing. Neither spoke much during the ride home as they made their way through the deluge. The frenzied windshield wipers barely kept up as they slapped back and forth at high speed, splashing the liquid away as more streamed from the unending heavens. It was raining harder than ever as they pulled into the driveway. Benjamin turned the ignition switch, elevat-ing the sound of the pulsating rain as it pounded all the louder, like a primordial drumbeat, beckoning them both. He turned to Cindy and kissed her, softly at first, but as the kiss developed, it devolved into an animalistic craving as the two meshed tongues and began clawing at each other's clothing, overcome with lust. Cindy greedily fumbled with his shirt buttons as he unzipped the back of her dress, sliding it down her bare shoulders, as she wiggled it off completely. Benjamin lunged toward her, over her, as she lay back on the front seat. The rain was beating at a furious pace as Benjamin unclasped her lacey bra, exposing her white breasts. He greedily sucked the erect nipples as he pulled off her pant-ies, reaching between her warmness as he returned his mouth to hers, deepening himself into her, consumed with fire. Cindy reached into his unfastened trousers, tugging him free as she positioned herself in the cramped car. Benjamin released himself from her, ripping his pants from his body as she lay moaning, watching him, spreading her legs to him, as he watched her writhe in wanting delight. He hovered over her in an attempt to mount her, but the cramped quarters denied him access. Frustrated with greedy passion, Cindy slid up onto the passenger door allowing him more room while accidentally pulling the door latch. As the car door flew open, the rain gushed in on her face and breasts, shocking her into reality as she screamed with laughter. Benjamin, delirious with consuming passion, near the edge, advanced onto her. She kissed him deeply as she fought free of his grip, running out into the rain. "Come and get me!" she screamed and laughed as she ran through the downpour. Benjamin ran after her, across the yard and in the back of the house, both completely naked. She allowed him to catch her as the rain pounded around them, building the intensity between them to the point of no return. Then she ran away again, laughing as she danced away, toying on the verge of ecstasy. He ran after her as a madman, consumed with animalistic desire, breathing heavily. He slipped on the wet grass, tumbling to the ground. Cindy turned toward her fallen pursuer, approaching him, and lay on top of his nakedness, wrapping her mouth onto his, reaching down and guiding him insider her, as the rain pounded their glistening bodies, faster and faster, fusing them into oneness as they crossed the threshold of bliss together, melting into the rain itself, quenching their passion into completeness.

Afterward, they lay on their backs feeling the cool grass about them, laughing as the rain bathed them.

"Shall we get out of this moat and retire to our chambers, my queen?" Benjamin said, laughing.

"Oh, let's shall!" Cindy said with a smile.

They held each other's hand as they walked lovingly through the purity of the rain, through Eden, to the entrance of their home, to the entrance of their eternal life together, clean and whole, virgin, stopping briefly by the door and embracing each other.

"I love you, Cindy," said Benjamin gently.

She kissed him. Then they walked through the doorway, together.

IX

Married Life

Through the night, the rain subsided as the morning sun shone forth its warm glory, chasing the last of the darkness toward the west, causing a faint haze to suspend over the glistening ground as the dewy earth dissolved its wet clothing into mist. Nature's orchestra erupted from the skies and leafy limbs as birds chattered harmoniously in chorus, celebrating the day. Butterflies flitted gracefully through the calm, lighting on the greens, contrasting their colors all the more spectacularly. A robin hopped across the lawn, searching for worms to tug on, intent on feeding the chirping mouths waiting at her nest. The lush grasses and trees thankfully drank deeply from earth's cup, which had been so generously filled. Nature's harmony buzzed as the bees hovered from flower to flower, collecting their nectar, competing with the iridescent hummingbirds, which magically darted through the air, chasing each other. Water-laden puddles mirrored blue, rippled only by a happy frog or two, greedily hoping for yet another mosquito. In the distance church bells rang out, announcing the arrival of the Sabbath, the holy day, awakening the town's sleepy inhabitants, beckoning them to participate in the spirit that dwelled among them, beckoning them to look, beckoning them to see the glory of God's hand in all creation.

Benjamin woke first. As he lay in their marriage bed, he observed his sleeping wife. "So beautiful!" he thought. He wondered where she was in her dreams and if he was with her there. He longed to will himself into her dreams as he caressed her neck with his lips, tasting her smooth skin tingling with traces of perfume, as a flower. She briefly woke from the attention, smiling as she felt his closeness. Then she pulled herself completely out of sleep's grip and into his eyes, melting into him. Her body and kiss felt like warm butter liquefying into his, awakening their desire once again. Through the open window, nature's orchestra continued its concert, as Benjamin and Cindy fervently joined the symphony, melding their instruments into a crescendo of happiness, ushering in the joys of a new day.

Afterward, they lay in bed, chatting and laughing, reminiscing about the night before.

"Oh, Benjamin," said Cindy, "it's going to be a beautiful day; it *is* a beautiful day. I'm so happy I love you. Hear the birds singing? I feel like—like we're in Oz, like everything is enchanted. Do you feel that way?"

"I feel hungry," he stated. "I could fry us up some enchanted eggs for breakfast."

"Ha, ha, very funny," she said, smiling dreamily. "Maybe you should cook breakfast and serve your queen in bed. And while your hand is feeding me, I'd prefer that you sprinkle rose petals over me. You do have rose petals, don't you, Benjamin?"

Benjamin thought for a second. "I can pick you some dandelion petals from out on the lawn. Will that do, Your Highness?"

"Weeds?" gasped Cindy. "You would shower your queen with mere weeds?"

"Oh, but, Your Majesty, these happy little wildflowers, which bear the bright color of the sun, radiate their yellow warmth and joy into the very heart of the beholder, accentuating the joys that already reside there. Please, my queen, find it in your heart to accept the simple dandelion as a symbol of joy, representing my joy of love for you."

Cindy kissed him. Benjamin smiled at her, got out of bed, and walked to the kitchen as Cindy dreamed of bright yellow dandelion snowflakes dancing about her.

"Cindy, we're out of eggs," echoed Benjamin's booming voice of reality, scattering Cindy's yellow snowflakes into oblivion.

"That's OK," she said as she got out of bed. "I'll just have cereal."

"Cindy, we're out of milk."

Cindy laughed to herself, realizing that neither of them had bothered to think of groceries. "Benjamin?"

"What?"

"Let's just go to McDonald's, to the drive-through, and grab some breakfast. Then, if you want, we could run over to Lisa's apartment and see if she needs a hand cleaning up; her place must be a mess. It was awful nice of her to put on the reception for us. It's the least we could do."

"Sure!" said Benjamin. "Sounds good to me."

"Then we could go grocery shopping together. Wouldn't that be great? Just like married people. I'll cook you up dinner tonight. How'll that be?"

"Beans and oatmeal?" he joked.

"Yes! How did you guess? I had no idea you were so clairvoyant!" she jeered back. "Actually, I was thinking of Mexican. I make a mean burrito."

"Sounds great," he said. "I'll choose the wine."

"Good," she said. "Choose whatever you like, as long as it's white zinfandel."

Benjamin laughed heartily.

They each showered and dressed and then walked out into the freshness of the day. The passenger door of Cindy's car was wide open, and the front seat was soaked with rain. Her white dress was crumpled on the floor, along with his clothes. Various articles of undergarments were strewn about abstractly.

"What went on here?" said Benjamin, acting quite puzzled.

"I don't know," said Cindy in a serious tone, "a robbery perhaps?"

"Perhaps," said Benjamin, picking up the black panties. "Whatever it was, there must have been a struggle; this article of clothing is ripped."

"Shall we call the authorities?" questioned Cindy.

"I think it best we do just that," he answered. "It's obvious to me that whatever happened, foul play was certainly involved."

"I agree, Detective," she said as she picked up his underwear. "Foul play was definitely involved."

They both gathered up the clothes. "I'll take this evidence into the house, for future study," said Cindy laughingly.

"And I'll get a blanket for the seat," stated Benjamin, "to cover the crime scene, until we have more time to investigate this matter a little deeper."

And thus the day began as they rolled off into it, as free and merry as the birds that sailed through the air above them, singing their joyous song, as an ode to life.

The Accident

After breakfast, they headed for Lisa's apartment, speeding through the busy streets of the downtown district, sipping hot coffee, while happy pedestrians dotted the sidewalks, enjoying their Sunday. Some were shopping, some biking, some jogging; others were just enjoying the sunshine. The whole world seemed happy.

Suddenly, Benjamin lurched, hitting the brakes and simultaneously slamming into a baby carriage that appeared out of nowhere. The impact threw the crumpled carriage and its contents ahead of the car as a white van slashed through the intersection, smashing into the wreckage, obliterating it, before speeding out of sight.

Dazed, Benjamin looked at Cindy, who was shocked speechless. A woman was screeching hysterically on the street corner. "Killed! Killed!" she was bawling. "You would have been killed!" she said as she approached the car. "Are you hurt? Are you all right?" she asked.

Benjamin and Cindy paused to answer, unable to comprehend what had just taken place. "We're—we're fine," he said.

"Oh good!" beamed the woman, smiling jubilantly. "It's such a sunny day. I love sunny days. I go now. Bye bye." She turned to leave.

"Wait!" shouted Benjamin as he pulled the car to the curb.

"Hello," said the woman. "Is it your birthday?"

Benjamin and Cindy noticed the woman's tattered clothing. She appeared to be in her late twenties. Her dark, oily hair was held back with a purple scarf, except for her long bangs, which she constantly brushed away with her hands, which were adorned with plastic rings on every finger.

"It is, isn't it? Your birthday, I mean?" she repeated, smiling radiantly.

"Lady," said Benjamin, "what the hell just happened here?"

She abruptly slapped him across the face. "I won't tolerate profanity, young man! I just won't!"

"I'm sorry," said Benjamin. "Ma'am, did you see what happened here?"

"Where?" she asked.

"Here," said Benjamin, trying his best to restrict his frustration. "I just hit a baby carriage with my car."

"Really?" she said. "How odd. I had a baby carriage once, but it's gone now."

"Ma'am, it must have been your baby carriage that I hit!"

"Really? So that's where it went to. Oh well. Maybe it'll come home to me someday."

"Lady, what was…uh…what was in that baby carriage of yours?"

"Shh," she whispered while looking suspiciously from shoulder to shoulder. "I'm not supposed to tell."

"Was there a baby in that carriage?" he asked blatantly.

"Oh noooo," she said, laughing heartily. "We don't have babies." She laughed all the heartier at the thought. "My God, how would we have babies? Tell me." She added, "Is it your birthday today?"

"Ma'am," said Cindy, "I'm afraid there was an accident. It seems that we've hit your baby carriage with our car. We are worried that a baby might have been in that carriage. Please tell us what you can about this accident, please."

"Accident?" She smiled contemplatively. "Oh, it was no accident. Now, if it's not your birthday, whose birthday is it?"

"Ma'am," said Cindy, "please tell us what you did with your baby carriage; it's very important."

"Oh yes, the baby carriage. I remember. I pushed it in front of your car. Yes, that's it. I remember! Oh, it's such a nice day, isn't it?"

"Ma'am, why did you push your baby carriage in front of our car? Please, think."

"Oh, let's see…Oh…oh yes, it was to save you from the collision. Oh, it was a dreadful collision. I'm so glad I was allowed to save you from it. Consider it a present for—for your birthday."

"Ma'am," said Benjamin, "tell us about the collision, please. Take your time."

"Oh, it was dreadful…wasn't meant to be…We heard you, though, Benjamin. That's why I pushed the baby cart in front of your car—to stop the collision."

"But it didn't stop the collision. We did hit the baby cart."

"Shh," she whispered, looking about her suspiciously again. "It was the only way to get you to stop before the…Oh dear, I had better be going. Oh my, but aren't you the handsome couple," she said, smiling brilliantly. "I'm so happy for you and your birthday. I'm so happy." She turned and whisked herself away down the sidewalk.

"Wait!" shouted Benjamin futilely, as she disappeared from view.

A police cruiser pulled next to the curb, flashing its blue-and-red strobes. An officer got out. Benjamin recognized him; it was Sergeant Franks.

"Well, well, Mr. Frisk," said the sergeant. "We meet again. May I ask why you're parked here, next to the curb?"

Benjamin explained the accident as best he could.

"Hmm," said Sergeant Franks. "Peculiar…Baby buggy, you say? White van slammed into it after you collided with it?"

"That's right," said Benjamin, "broadside, at a high rate of speed. Smashed it to smithereens, and he didn't even stop."

"I see," said Franks. "What you're telling me is that that van ran the stop sign at the intersection here. I suppose it would have broadsided your car if you hadn't stopped."

Benjamin and Cindy froze as the reality of the sergeant's words hit home.

"Can you describe the van?"

"Just a white van…It happened so fast, like a blur," said Benjamin. "It was—"

"It was a white commercial van," continued Cindy. "The advertising on the side read, 'Health Surveys,' something like that."

"Are you sure?" questioned Franks.

"I'm positive. In fact, I think it was the same type of van that hit your dog, Benjamin. I'm sure of it."

"Did you get the woman's name?"

"No," said Cindy as she described the woman. "She just walked away. She seemed unbalanced, not all there."

"There're lots of homeless people in this city," said the sergeant. "It's common for them to use carts to haul their belongings around. Homeless women like to use baby carriages. I suppose baby carriages look more—more appropriate than a shopping cart."

Sergeant Franks took their complete statement, as other officers came to assist holding back traffic and collecting the bent, mangled pieces of the baby carriage, checking each piece thoroughly for any signs of human remains.

"How's she look?" said Franks to an officer as he finished the incident report.

"All clear, far as I can see," replied the officer.

"OK, folks, that's it. You're free to go. We'll let you know if we get a line on that van. Have a nice day."

Benjamin and Cindy went over the accident again and again as they continued on their way, finally arriving at Lisa's apartment. Benjamin noticed a vending machine across the street.

"Cindy, go on ahead. I'll run across the street and get us a couple of Cokes, since our coffees ended up on the floor."

"I'm sure Lisa will have something to drink," she said.

"I don't want to be a mooch," he said and smiled. "Go on ahead."

"Make mine a diet," she added as she headed up the stairs to Lisa's place, excited to tell Lisa of the strange accident.

As Cindy approached the door, she noticed that the door was opened a crack. Thinking that Lisa was already busy cleaning up, she barged right into the empty living room. "Hey, Lis!" she called, walking toward the kitchen. Suddenly, the bathroom door opened and out walked Mark, totally nude, facing her. Cindy froze in her tracks as the awkwardness of the situation stifled any words. Her eyes inadvertently darted down to his midsection. He saw her gaze and made no attempt to cover himself.

"See something you like?" he sneered.

Cindy spun around, totally embarrassed.

"What did you say?" called Lisa's voice from the bedroom.

"You've got company, Lisa!" called Mark as he wrapped himself with a towel and went into the bedroom.

Cindy could hear muffled voices from behind the closed door. She thought of just leaving and headed toward the door. However, Lisa came out before she could leave, wrapping her robe about her.

"Cindy?" she asked in surprise.

Cindy turned around. Her face was blushed crimson. "I—I—I'm sorry. The door was opened. I thought you were cleaning. I—we came to help clean up. I'm sorry. I didn't—Oh, my God, how embarrassing!"

"Oh, my gosh!" said Lisa. "The door was unlocked all night? Wow, I'm glad no one walked in on us. They would have gotten an eyeful," she said, laughing.

"Yeah," said Cindy, still exasperated, "I just got an eyeful."

"Mark told me," giggled Lisa. "Can you believe the, you know, the size?" she whispered. "My God, it's—"

"OK, OK," said Cindy, fighting the imagery that popped into her thoughts, "spare me the details. I'm embarrassed enough as it is."

Lisa giggled. "I'll tell you the details later."

Benjamin walked in with the Cokes, noticing Lisa's robe. "Hi, Lisa! Just get up?"

"Hello, Benjamin. Hey, you two make yourselves at home while Mark and I get dressed." Lisa turned and walked into her bedroom.

"Mark?" asked Benjamin.

"Don't ask," said Cindy as she began taking down the wedding decorations, attempting to regain her composure. Benjamin helped her, a little in shock at the idea of Mark being with Lisa. To him, Lisa seemed a bit out of Mark's league. She had been enrolled in school as a premed, but recently switched her major to law, and Lisa was gorgeous: black hair, dark eyes, distinctly feminine features. He couldn't imagine her being with Mark. Mark seemed so crude, so basic. And she seemed so refined and sophisticated—above him.

Soon, Mark and Lisa joined in the cleanup.

"Hi, Benny, old chap!" Mark said with a smirk. "Bet you're surprised to see me here."

"A little," said Benjamin—an understatement.

Mark laughed. "It was raining so hard I didn't want to leave and get wet. But we got wet anyways, didn't we, Lisa?"

"Oh, shush," said Lisa, smiling. "You're embarrassing everyone."

"I was em-bare-assed, that's for sure."

"Mark, have you no manners at all?"

"None," he said, laughing.

Benjamin and Cindy told their story of the baby carriage accident as the four took down decorations and cleaned the apartment. Cindy and Lisa conjured up cryptic theories as to the meaning of the mysterious affair, settling on the idea of destiny.

"If that baby carriage wouldn't have stopped us," contemplated Cindy, "we would have been broadsided by that van. And at the high rate of speed that he was going, we would have probably been killed. That's what that woman was screaming. Remember, Benjamin? 'Killed! Killed!' she was screaming, like she actually saw us being killed. It's like she stepped back in time to prevent it."

"Quick," said Mark, "let's hurry and finish up. We've got to find that woman. She could tell us what the winning lottery numbers are for next week."

"Ha, ha, very funny," said Lisa, smiling. "We were just considering the possibilities, for the sake of conversation. It's not like we really believe in time travel or anything."

"Maybe the woman was like a guardian angel or something," said Cindy, "watching over us, protecting us."

"Oh, c'mon," exclaimed Mark. "Give me a break!"

"Benjamin?" said Cindy. "Do you remember when that woman said, 'We heard you, Benjamin'? She distinctly said, 'We heard you, Benjamin.' She said 'we,' yet she was alone."

"Let me get this straight," said Mark. "You guys got killed in an accident, but the angels heard you praying—before you died—and sent down a bag lady from heaven, turning back time, mind you, to prevent the accident. And," he continued, "this all-powerful celestial being was so scatterbrained that she didn't even know what day it was. I'm sorry, Cindy, but I just don't believe in any hocus-pocus. If anything, it was a fortunate coincidence—nothing more."

"Mark," said Cindy, who was noticeably perturbed at his directness, "I'm just saying that the whole situation was strange, to say the least." Cindy suddenly reveled in a thought. "Benjamin," she said, "how did she know your name?"

"What do you mean?" he asked.

"That woman, she said your name. She said, 'We heard you, Benjamin.' She said your name. We never told her your name. You remember?"

Benjamin tried to think back. "Cindy, I'm not sure what she said. Maybe you casually spoke my name, and she picked up on it."

Cindy thought hard. "Hmm, maybe," she said doubtfully. "Oh, I suppose it was just a coincidence."

"That's right," stated Mark. "Everything can be rationalized. There's no such thing as spooks and spirits and all that crap. Like there's a God or something, sitting on a huge white chair on top of a fluffy cloud, spying on us. I just don't buy it."

"You're an atheist?" asked Lisa.

"No," he answered. "I'm Mark. And you're Lisa. And you're Cindy. And you're Ben. That's all there is to it. If there is more, I don't see it."

"Mark," said Benjamin, "a person has to believe in the Lord—that's all there is really. He's the only thing that really makes sense to me. It's, you know, love."

"Love?" Mark laughed. "So, we get created, bust our ass to make a living, and then die at the end. Where does the love fit in?"

"Well," said Benjamin, "we live, we learn, we love. We temper ourselves with this life; it prepares us for heaven, you know, eternity. So dying is just a door to the other side."

"Woohoo! What have you been smoking?" Mark laughed. "You know, for centuries people have conjured up different religions to supply answers to the unknown. I guess people feel they need to know what they don't know. So since they can't know, they make something up and fit it nicely into their little societies, to appease everyone and make the ball go around."

"So what's your philosophy on life, Mark?" asked Lisa.

"Live as best you can. Take your opportunities as they come. And make opportunities to take. It's all up to me. I can either be a sorry sap or someone who lives. I choose to live."

"What about helping others, helping the community, relationships, love?" asked Cindy.

"It's all up to me, whatever I choose. Just don't pin that God business around my neck!" replied Mark, who was getting noticeably upset.

"Well, I agree with you there, Mark," said Benjamin. "It's all up to us to choose—free will, I mean. We all have choices. But if you walk in the will of God, you will make the wise choices, directing your life toward something fulfilling."

"Can we change the subject?" yelled Mark. "I didn't know I was going to get a sermon."

"Hey!" said Lisa, changing the subject. "Let's go uptown for lunch—Mark's treat!"

"My treat?"

"Sure!" she laughed. "This can be your opportunity to show love to your fellow man and woman, by buying us lunch. And, who knows? Maybe it will get you into heaven."

Mark laughed uneasily.

Benjamin looked at Cindy, and she at him, inquisitively reading each other's facial expressions like two mystics reading tea leaves, determining the other's thoughts without words.

"You guys go ahead," said Cindy confidently.

"Oh, come on," prodded Lisa. "It'll be fun. We can go to Kali's. They have a buffet that will tempt you to death. It's absolute ecstasy! You've got to try it."

Cindy, considering the enticement, looked questioningly at Benjamin again. He turned away from her gaze.

"No, thanks, Lisa," said Cindy. "Maybe some other time. We sort of have plans."

"Oh well. OK," said Lisa, sounding a little disappointed. "Some other time, then. Thanks for stopping by and helping to clean up. It would have taken me all day by myself."

"Thank you for throwing the reception. It was great. That was really nice of you."

"My pleasure!"

To the Beach

"Whew!" said Benjamin, as he and Cindy got in their car.

"What?" Cindy asked.

"Oh, nothing," he said as they motored away.

Both he and Cindy quietly thought to themselves about Lisa and Mark being together. How odd it'd seemed when they first arrived, not to mention shocking, but in the few short hours they'd spent cleaning the house, it seemed natural, casual, like they had been a couple for years.

"Benjamin, let's drive to the beach."

"The beach? That's a two-hour drive. What about groceries? Dinner? Burritos? Weren't those our plans?"

"Plans have changed," she said and laughed. "Oh, please, it could be like a honeymoon. It's such a beautiful day. It would be romantic. We could walk barefoot in the sand and search for shells and just—just *be*. We could just be. Doesn't that sound lovely? To just be…with no distractions, no responsibility, just for a day. Let's not even think. Let's just do it. Please, Benjamin, please say you will."

"Sure," he said. "If that's what you'd like to do, I'm game. We can go home and get some—"

"Let's not go home first; let's just go," Cindy pleaded jubilantly. "Right now, with nothing but ourselves."

Benjamin thought deeply about Cindy's apparent flare for spontaneity, causing him to wonder about how many things he did not know about his wife. However, he admired her for her positive attitude. It seemed to kindle a joy within him, and the joy was elevated when he pleasured her in any way. Yet he himself was a realist, more on the conservative side.

"Do we have enough money for gas?" he said.

"Who cares?" she said with a laugh. "We're free as the birds in the air, and they don't have any money. However, I do have my credit card."

"To the beach."

The day flowed onward, like a lazy river, calmly streaming its way through the shallow eddies and winding currents of each temporal moment, which lashed themselves together into the delicate raft known as "life." Benjamin and Cindy flowed with it for a day, allowing the current to take them wherever it may, as free as the birds in the air.

It was late in the evening when the birds finally came home to their nest, thoroughly cleansed and exhausted by their day under the sun. They both tumbled into bed, quickly falling into a deep tranquility, at peace with the world in each other's arms, as sleep swooned within, caressing them with poetic thoughts of gentle sea breezes, cool blue waters, warm sands, and a setting orange sun that was now casting its celestial pathway directly to them alone, beckoning them, as they willingly walked together across the waters into its bright colors.

X

Life Goes On

The morning rose out of the mists of sleep, painting itself onto the world, shrouding the heavens from view, fastening itself into the current of time as the birth of a new day blossomed illustrious and fresh, bloomed into noon and then ripened into evening, evaporating the sky's blue illusion, exposing a glimpse of universal reality, a reality that is incomprehensible, filled with unfathomable oceans of darkness, spangled with giant floating orbs of violent energy, which all vanish from view as the sun re-creates its blue cloak for another day.

The days passed effortlessly, ending as simply as they had begun. Each day seemed a festival, a celebration, as Benjamin and Cindy's appreciation for even the most simplest of things grew robust, accentuating the seemingly trivial into profundity as each thought passed through the transformational love that they shared with one another. A simple cup of coffee together in the evening was a cherished moment, as they shared stories of their workday, their contemplations, their hopes and dreams, their philosophies, expanding the moment into a brilliant richness of reflective emotion and substance. As the days combined into weeks, their roots grew deeper and deeper, flourishing together, entwining each within each, extracting spiritual nourishment seemingly from existence itself.

Their joy borne for each other was only deepened and matured by the advent of the fertile seed discovered to be growing inside Cindy. Her countenance mellowed into an ethereal radiance, an aura of mystery. Oh, how her eyes shone with wisdom and contentment as the miracle of life embraced her! Benjamin watched his wife ripen through the months, expanding into two beings, yet bound together as one. She positively glowed with the warmth of motherhood; she wore it as a shining robe. She was spectacular in Benjamin's eyes. Nothing he had ever seen or felt compared to the radiant love emanating from within her, captivating him. She was beautiful.

The blessed months passed as the expectant couple jubilantly dreamed only the happiest thoughts of parenthood. The spare room was converted into the baby's room, complete with a stimulating plethora of colorful baby paraphernalia gifted from friends and completed by the adoring parents, who always seemed to find themselves in the baby aisle each time they went shopping. Each day seemed to grow richer and richer with meaning and purpose. The idea of "family" centered itself within their perspectives as life's sole importance, and they reveled in it, consuming it completely. Only one slight flaw blemished their seemingly indestructible dreams: it was Benjamin's mother. She was rather taken aback by the abrupt news of not only their quick marriage, but the quick pregnancy. Benjamin had avoided calling her for weeks after the marriage, until Cindy was found to be with child. Then he knew that he could not delay the inevitable any longer. The phone call was torturous, but had to be done.

"Hello? Benjamin, is that you? What's happened? Are you all right?"

"I'm fine, Mom. How's Japan?"

"Japan's fine. Why are you calling? You never call. Are you sick? Is everything all right?"

"Everything is great, Mom. It really is."

"Are you sure? You know how worried I get. And I do worry about you so. And, yes, Japan is wonderful. I know I didn't call these past few weeks, but I've been so busy. Oh, there is so much to see and do here. It's just unbelievable. And the people here have been so good to me. It's like I'm a celebrity. Everyone stares at me when I go out. They love Americans here. Oh, Benjamin, guess what? I'm learning Japanese! Can you believe it? Me! Speaking another language? Here, listen. *Gakkarida*, Benjamin. That means that I think you're special. No, wait. Hmm, I can't seem to find it in my book. Well, it means something!" She laughed. "Oh, Benjamin, you would like it here; it's so exciting. Ned and I are going to Mount Fuji in three weeks. I'll send you pictures. Can you imagine your mother as a mountain climber? Oh, I know it's not like Mount Everest or anything, but it is to me. Oh, you should have seen...Ned and I went to a traditional Oriental concert last night. It was spectacular! Oh, the geishas had on gorgeous costumes exploding with every color of the rainbow. They were dancing onstage in a peach orchard of some kind with billions of peach blossoms falling about them. It was beautiful, exotic. I was crying by the end of it. You know how emotional I get at performances. I just loved it. Oh, I know I should have called, but I just got carried away with everything here. Ned says that he may be stationed here for a year, maybe longer, which is OK with me, but I do miss you and worry about you so much. I don't know if I can stand it that long. You are OK, aren't you? I mean, you're not just saying it, so I won't worry, are you? Please tell me you're not."

"No, Mom, really, everything is great here. In fact it's better than great."

"Oh, good. I'm always so relieved when I hear you say that. Then I don't worry so much. Oh, my God, Benjamin, you'll never guess what we're doing tonight. We're going to Osaka Castle! Oh, it's magnificent—at least it is in the brochure. I think it's some sort of temple or shrine that they turned into a museum or something like that. I'll e-mail you some pictures of it if I think of it."

"Yeah. Mom, I do have some good news."

"Oh, good. It's always nice to hear good news from you, Benjamin. Oh, I miss you so much. It's really nice to hear your voice and to know everything is OK. I can feel more relaxed, more comfortable with myself. I'm so glad you called. You know, sometimes I think of calling you, but then I don't. And you know why? Because I fear that something bad might have happened to you; then I'd worry. I'm so glad things are good for you. I really am."

"Well, Mom, I—I got married a couple of weeks ago."

"Good, that will keep you out of trouble," she said, laughing. "Oh, Benjamin, I hate to cut our conversation short, but I really need to get myself ready. Ned will be home to pick me up in less than an hour. I'm so glad you called; I really am."

"Mom."

"Yes, honey?"

"I really did get married a few weeks ago. Her name is Cindy."

There was a long pause.

"Mom? Mom, are you there?"

After another pause, she said, "Oh, God, you're not kidding, are you? Oh, my God. Oh, my God, tell me you're joking. Please tell me you're joking."

"Mom, I know this is a shock, but it happened—sort of quickly. I love Cindy, and we were married. And that's it. Mom? Mom? Uh, Cindy's pregnant. We're going to have a baby. We just found out yesterday. Mom? Will you say something?"

After another pause, she sobbed. "Benjamin, how could you do this to me? How could you do this to me?" She was crying uncontrollably. "Oh, my God. How—how could you let this happen? Now what am I supposed to do? How am—How am I supposed to be happy now?"

"Mom," he said, "just enjoy yourself in Japan. Stay there as long as you like; have fun; go climb Mount Fuji. I just called to let you know, that's all; just to let you know. I love Cindy, and we want to have a family. It's a dream come true for me—for both of us."

"Oh, my God," she bawled, "you have no idea…You have no idea… Benjamin, I had hoped for something better for you. I had always hoped for something better. That's all I've ever asked for you. And now this. Oh, my God, this is like a nightmare."

"Mom, I knew this would be a shock for you. That's why I didn't call you before the wedding, and that's why I waited until now to call you. It was weak of me to keep the truth from you for so long, but you have the truth now, and you're going to have to face it! I hope you find it in your heart to accept it—to accept us."

"Benjamin, I really can't deal with this right now. I need time to sort this out. My head is swimming. I'll call you in a few weeks, after I've had time to think, time to get this in perspective. OK? How does that sound? OK, then, I've got to go. Bye."

Benjamin felt relieved when he hung up the phone, like a weight had been lifted from him. Cindy had been eavesdropping from the kitchen as he spoke with his mother, completely aware of his apprehensions.

"Well? How did it go?" she asked.

He laughed. "Better than I thought."

"Are you OK?"

"Oh, yes, I'm fine. I'm great. Sometimes the truth is difficult, but once it's loosed, there is no pressure. Right now, I feel like I've been purified or something. I mean, I've been worrying about this hidden truth for weeks now; I'd lie to myself and say it didn't bother me, but it did bother me. It sort of gnaws at you. And the only way to rid yourself of it is to do something horrendously unpleasant, which is to tell the truth, knowing the unsavory ramifications. I mean, I knew my mom would be bummed out and disappointed in me. And after I told her the truth, sure enough, she was bummed out and disappointed in me, and that does hurt. But it also feels great to get back on the right track, back on the road of truth. Somehow, I feel clean. Right now, I don't have any secrets, no worries gnawing at me. And even if my mom rejects us for eternity, it's OK because we are on the road of truth, and that's a good place to be. And besides that, it's good that we are married and want a family. It's certainly nothing to be ashamed of. Sometimes I wonder about people who have hidden truths that are, you know, wrong. How hard it must be to come clean with those."

"What do you mean?" asked Cindy.

"Well, let's say a person did something very wrong, like cheat on a spouse or rob a bank or even kill someone. And let's say he or she got away with it. Nobody ever found out. But that person knew what he or she did. That person would have to live with the fact that he or she is despicable in the face of society. Other people would think of him or her as filth if only they knew the truth. So, a person like that would have to either live with the lie and feel dirty and guilty for the rest of his or her life or come clean but face the fire of the ramifications. I mean, he or she could go to prison or face the death penalty; that would be the cost of coming clean, of purification. What a dilemma those types of people have! The best is to stay on the right track in the first place, stay in truth; that way the pitfalls will be avoided."

"Benjamin," asked Cindy, "do you think your mom will accept me?"

"It doesn't matter. I mean, it will matter as far as her involvement in our lives, but it doesn't matter as far as what we can do about it. We've told the truth; now it's up to her. As far as we are concerned, we can offer and encourage her to participate in our lives, but it's up to her to accept us as we are."

"OK, Mr. Philosopher," said Cindy. "Hypothetically, let's say that your mom accepts us fully and wants to live next door and help raise our children. And let's say she's over here twelve hours a day and driving us crazy. Then what?"

"Then we just tell her the truth and let the chips fall where they may."

"But aren't some truths best kept hidden? You know, to keep the peace?"

"Well, I think that holding your tongue is prudent in many cases, as long as it doesn't turn into a lie. When you have to lie to hide a truth, that's when it becomes wrong."

"Benjamin," said Cindy with a noticeable nervousness in her voice, "I sort of—sort of…Well, I haven't been truthful."

Benjamin just stared at her, feeling the tension, waiting for the explanation, for the confession.

"Benjamin," she began, "do you remember when I said that I wanted to cook dinner tonight? Well, I lied," she said reflectively and reverently, as if deeply moved. "I'd rather that *you* cook dinner," she said, giggling. "And you're right, Benjamin. It's refreshing. I feel *so* purified. The truth has set me free! Free at last, free at last!" She hysterically laughed. "How's that for coming clean?"

The chase that immediately followed the confession began with two pairs of wild, giddy eyes separated by the kitchen table, as Cindy used the barrier to ward off her aggressor. If he would go one way, she would go the other, keeping the table between them, until he began climbing right over the table, at which she screamed with delight and made a run for the living room and then the bedroom, where he almost had her, but she managed to squirm from his grasp and run into the bathroom and lock the door, out of breath from laughing. She wouldn't come out until he promised to leave her be, reminding him of her delicate condition. He promised, and she unlocked the door and walked out, only to have him resume the chase.

"You said you wouldn't!" she screamed with laughter as he caught her in his arms.

"I lied," he said.

Happy Birthday

Months had passed. Benjamin's mother eventually accepted the situation, although reluctantly, as the young couple's love for each other flourished and matured. Cindy's midsection grew as round and ripe as a striped melon, ready for harvest, as the anxious couple awaited the day of birth with anticipation and desire. The suitcase had been packed for two weeks as the due date arrived and departed with no indication of any labor pains.

Finally, the telltale pains did come, and the couple rushed to the hospital. They had been practicing this moment for months, growing in confidence as time passed. However, as Cindy's pain increased, the confidence diminished and melted into apprehension. Benjamin did his best to coach Cindy, to encourage her, trying to be the rock that she could focus on. The doctor said it would be a while before the baby came and then left the room, leaving the nurses in charge. Cindy's pains grew intense, seemingly unbearable. Benjamin grew helpless, and out of that helplessness came forth an intense frustration. As his wife screamed and writhed in pain, he frantically read the faces and eyes of the attending nurses, growing certain that something was wrong, listening to each muffled word that one nurse would say to the other, imagining that those words held a negative meaning. The nurses would periodically assure both of them that everything was fine, that this was natural. The words of comfort would temporarily ease their worries, but the next skin-wrenching jolt of pain would explode any notions of comfort into oblivion. Each slow hour screamed with pain as Cindy's sweaty body convulsed violently. Hour after hour passed, steeped in torment. She was weakening, craving sleep, but the pains kept pounding at her, ripping at her insides, demanding she remain conscious. Hour after hour passed, as Cindy's screams became weaker, and her words delirious. Benjamin tried his best to comfort her, but it was as if Cindy was in another place, a place he could not access. He held her hand as she screamed. Her voice grew hoarse and garbled.

"Where in the hell is the doctor?" screamed Benjamin at the nurse.

The nurse did not answer. Benjamin read her eyes. Something was indeed wrong. Fear tinged him and then surged through him like an anesthetic, numbing him into a ghostlike state, surreal.

"Mr. Frisk. Mr. Frisk?"

"Wha—Uh, what?" said Benjamin.

"Mr. Frisk, you'll have to step out of the room," said the nurse, looking quite grim.

She guided Benjamin out into the hall, quickly pointed to the waiting room, and then darted back into Cindy's room. The doctor and two other nurses rushed past Benjamin and into the room, closing the door behind them. Benjamin placed his hand on the closed door and prayed with his entire mind, body, and soul that God would spare his wife and child, pleading for Him to guide the physicians, to intervene. He stood by that door for an eternity, yet the passage of time did not exist for him there. Out of the infinite, he felt something pull him back into the physical world: a patting on his leg. He looked down into the face of a child—a little girl, no more than seven years old, who was looking up at him.

"Hello," she said, smiling. "Why do you have your hand on the door?"

Benjamin just stared at her, not knowing how to respond, temporarily confused at the sudden change in thought, feeling off balance, dazed. She looked into his eyes, expectant of an answer.

"I can't go in," he said. "I have to wait."

"I have to wait, too," she said. "But it's OK. Mr. Jeepers keeps me company. As long as Mr. Jeepers is with me, I don't feel sad." She held up a stuffed teddy bear, worn ragged from use. "Mr. Jeepers says that you're a good person. I think he likes you. Don't you, Mr. Jeepers?" She held the stuffed toy to her ear as if it was whispering to her. "Mr. Jeepers says that you're scared, and it makes him sad that you're scared. He wants you to be happy."

Benjamin crouched down to her level. "I don't think Mr. Jeepers can help me, but I think it's nice that you have such a thoughtful friend. And do you know what? I think that you are thoughtful, too. Now, tell me, who are you waiting for? Are you waiting for your parents?"

"Oh no," responded the little girl, "they are here, with me. They are sad, too, just like you."

"And why are your parents so sad?"

"I think it's—it's...I'm not sure. I think it's because I have to go away."

"Where are you going?"

"Mr. Jeepers says that I shouldn't worry about that and that I should be happy, and Mr. Jeepers is always right about things like that," she said matter-of-factly. "He is the bestest friend in the whole world."

"I bet he is," smiled Benjamin.

The little girl held the stuffed toy to her ear again. "Mr. Jeepers says it's time for me to go," she said as she turned to leave.

"It was nice talking to you," said Benjamin. "Thank you. I feel much better."

The little girl smiled up at him as she began walking down the hall, with her toy to her ear. Benjamin watched her walk away, alone, as a deep sadness crept into him. The little girl turned to him and waved. "Mr. Jeepers says to tell you, 'Happy birthday,'" she said and then disappeared around the corner of the hallway.

Suddenly, the door to Cindy's room opened, and the doctor approached Benjamin. "You have a healthy baby boy!" he said. "The nurses will let you know when you can go in. Mr. Frisk, you're wife has been through a lot, much more than the average first delivery. However, I expect her to make a full recovery, but she does need her rest. When the nurses allow you to go in, just comfort her as best you can and let her sleep. And, again, you're baby boy is just fine. Congratulations."

"Thank you. Oh, thank you!" said Benjamin, shaking the doctor's hand.

Oh, what a weight had been lifted! He felt as light as a feather, as he paced anxiously back and forth in front of the door to his wife's room, with his mind racing forward into the future, expanding into rambling thoughts of joy, as the celebration of the new life began its journey. A nurse asked him to please go in the waiting room to have a cup of coffee and relax, for it would be a while before he was allowed to see his wife. Benjamin conceded, but it was difficult to contain his joy. He held the nurse by the shoulders and kissed her on the mouth. "Thank you," he said as he walked toward the waiting room. As he approached the waiting room, he noticed a doctor leaving, and upon entering, his happy state immediately abandoned him as he beheld a man and woman who were embraced in sorrow, crying hopelessly. Benjamin bowed his head in respect as the couple made their way toward the door. The woman was so distraught that she could barely stand, as her husband held her along. She was clutching something firmly to her breast as if it were life itself. Benjamin's emotions collapsed into numb fragments when he realized what the woman was holding so dearly: it was Mr. Jeepers. Benjamin fell into a chair as he watched the couple leave shrouded with grief, which spilled over onto him, trumping his happiness and scattering it away as the heavy wind blows away specks of dust. He sat in deep contemplation. He folded his hands and prayed. He prayed for the couple who had just left. He prayed for Cindy and his son. He prayed for all the people he knew. He prayed for everyone in the world. He prayed for everything in the world! He thanked the good Lord for all things, both happy and sad, and he also prayed for strength, strength for all people, strength for everyone to weather through all the trials of this life.

"Mr. Frisk. Mr. Frisk? You may see your wife now. Please be quiet; she is sleeping. Allow her to sleep as much as possible. It'll be a few days before she'll be able to go home. Your son is in the maternity ward. When you're ready, just come to the nurses' desk, and we'll have someone take you to see him. He's a beautiful, strong, healthy baby boy," said the smiling nurse.

"Thank you. Thank you so much," said Benjamin.

Benjamin sat by Cindy's bedside, holding her hand, as he let go of reality, joining her in the mystical world of dreams. His dream flowed through his hand and into hers and hers into his, merging into a fullness that completed itself with the advent of another tiny pair of hands, unifying the trinity into one. Oh, how the light of a family shines brilliant!

Oh, how solid is the love that is strengthened by three chords! Can anything created on earth compare to the indestructible love of family? Even death cannot destroy or even penetrate such love; death can only enforce it, crystallize it. Oh, life will cast its trials into the fabric, tearing holes in the garment, but love will mend the rips and cuts, transforming the old garment into newness, stronger and more beautiful than the old. Oh, may the glorious chords of family fuse into one rope, bound tightly with the spirit, strong and stout, capable of spanning the entire earth and reaching into the heavens themselves. Such a love is real. Such a love is secure. Such a love is a foundation on which to build a house, a home—a home that will weather any storm, be it rain, snow, or stormy gale, a home that is built upon the rock, the rock of family. Oh, what joys await those who embark on this noble path. Oh, what contentment will bloom in the heart of a mother, a father, a child, when they are in concert as one, laced together and bound in love. Such a love for each other will cast its brilliance in the heavens as the brightest morning star, rising higher than anything in heaven, to the pinnacle and beyond. There, alone, it will shine solely, independently, with glory, forever and ever!

Cindy opened her eyes on her sleeping husband, recollecting fragmental thoughts of the delivery, still far away. She gently squeezed his hand, as he awoke into her gaze. His smile reassured her that everything would be all right, that everything was fine. She smiled weakly, closed her eyes, and drifted back into sleep.

As the hours passed, Cindy grew stronger. The baby was brought in, and the family was united for the first time. Cindy looked upon the child in her arms with wonder and delight, as she hummed a lullaby, fascinated with the creation of life at her breast. Benjamin absorbed the aura that emanated from mother and child, complete, and within each other. An enormity of joy consumed him, so much so that a tear streaked his cheek. Little Seth shined in their eyes like a sparkling star, radiant and lovely. When the nurse came to take the baby back to the nursery, Cindy had to muster all her strength to let him go. She longed for the day they could go home, as a family, and that day came.

Growing Up

Benjamin and Cindy flew through their days as effortlessly as birds gliding on a sea breeze. Little Seth grew in size as the happy parents grew in
wisdom, shedding many of the adolescent notions of love and adorning
themselves with the richness of love's maturity, growing richer every day
as a fine wine. There were many endless nights of crying and teething,
taking turns sleeping, taking turns checking, taking turns rocking—all
done under the umbrella of love. Little Seth was the absolute finest child
in their eyes, as are all children in the eyes of their parents. He complained
very little and smiled very much. Simple pleasures abounded, joys of
unspeakable delight, such as playing a simple game of peekaboo, causing
little Seth to laugh uncontrollably. The giving of this joy was reciprocal,
reflecting it all back to the giver sevenfold. As the years passed, suppertime turned into a sacred event, a time to share the activities of each day,
to assess the important issues of life, to reaffirm accomplishments and
goals. It was a time to share and bond as a family, and bond they did as
the days and months formed into years.

Seth's third birthday came and went. Benjamin reflected on the birthday party. Mark and Lisa were there, as well as Denise, and two parents
and their children from Seth's day care, which Denise ran. It was a happy
day. At bedtime, when the day was over and Benjamin tucked his son
into bed, he asked him what his favorite present was. Seth thought for a
minute and said that his favorite present was that Jill and Peter had come
over to play with him. They were his best friends and were inseparable at
the day care center. Benjamin kissed him and told him a bedtime story.

"Dad?" asked Seth, wide-eyed and not a bit sleepy. "Where do babies
come from?"

Benjamin was a bit shocked by the question. He was not prepared
for anything quite so direct. He chuckled to himself. "Why do you ask?"

"Jill says she's going to have a baby brother; that's why her mom is
so big, because there is a baby insider her. Dad, will Mommy ever get big
and have a baby brother?"

"Well, Seth, I suppose she could…one day. Would you like a little
brother? Or a little sister?"

"Would I have to share my toys?"

"Oh, yes," said Benjamin. "We would all have to share."

"I would share my toys, but not my Legos. Jill says that babies shouldn't play with Legos; they might eat them."

"OK, Seth, night-night time. Give me a hug. Love you."

Benjamin smiled inwardly at the innocence of his son. He and Cindy had not spoken of more children since the day that Seth was born. He had tried to bring it up on numerous occasions, but she always avoided the issue. At the hospital the doctor had a serious discussion with both of them. He advised that any further pregnancies might prove to be difficult, even dangerous, however, not impossible. The doctor suggested that future tests would probably be necessary to determine any options before entering into a pregnancy. Cindy was shaken deeply by the difficult labor and never mentioned the horrendous hours before Seth was born.

Benjamin set his alarm clock and got into bed. Cindy was reading.

"Seth really liked playing with Jill and Peter," said Benjamin, trying to nonchalantly bring up the subject. "Seth was wondering where babies come from."

"Oh?" said Cindy, smiling. "And what did you tell him?"

"I told him that a man and a woman have to have sexual intercourse by the man inserting his penis into the wom—"

Cindy hit him with her pillow. "You did not!" she said and laughed.

"I think he was just curious," said Benjamin. "Apparently, he and Jill were discussing where sisters and brothers come from, you know, since Jill's mom is pregnant. He said that Jill's mommy is so big because there is a baby insider her. Then he asked me if *his* mommy would ever get big, with a baby insider her." Benjamin looked into his wife's eyes. He had never brought up the subject so directly. He was confronting Cindy, waiting for a reply, waiting for an indication, a sign showing which direction they were destined to as a family. The choice to have more children would have to be up to her. It was she who would have to endure another delivery; it was she who would face all the possible dangers and perils. How could he pressure her to have a child? What if anything would happen to Cindy? No, he must not pressure her, forcing her against her will. She must come to the decision herself. Cindy knew in her heart that Benjamin longed for more children. He was a good father, a good husband, caring and kind. He did his very best to provide for his family in every way. She felt his love toward her and their child as a person feels the warmth from the sun. There was no question of his love—none.

Cindy turned away from her husband and set her book down, lying with her back toward him, in silence. Benjamin got into bed and placed his hand on Cindy's shoulder; she bristled at his touch. He immediately sensed the tension, sensed the coldness. Reaching over to the lamp stand, he turned the light out. Both he and she lay in silence, alone in the dark, with their eyes wide open.

The days continued their onward march, rolling through the years as casually as a breath, one after the other. Seth's first day of school arrived suddenly, as if the five previous years of his life had all happened in only a week. Seth was happy and confident about going to school. Benjamin pretended to be the rock of stability and encouragement for his son, but in truth he was apprehensive. This was the first time that his son would be totally entrusted to strangers. All the previous years, Seth was always left with people who were known to the family, completely trusted. Now, Benjamin and his son were waiting for the foreign school bus on the curb. Seth would be on his own, swimming in a sea of other children, other adults. The yellow bus swallowed up his son and drove away, as Benjamin watched on until it drove out of sight. He felt separated, like part of him was missing, hollow. He shrugged it off, packed his lunch pail, and drove to work, lost in contemplative thought. He was thinking of his determination to put Seth in a Christian school and was glad that Cindy had finally agreed to his demands. It was really the only thing that he insisted on; however, the tuition was quite substantial, and Cindy did not see the justification of spending money on a private education when they were already paying taxes to support the public school, in which she was a teacher. For months they argued, always civilly, but nonetheless strained. Benjamin dismissed all of Cindy's logic and reason, holding firmly to his beliefs that a child needs a strong moral foundation, steeped in the virtues that Christianity seemed to represent. She would counter that the public school focuses on a moral foundation, through the teaching of ethics, sociology, teamwork—everything necessary for a well-rounded education. Benjamin stood firm, stubbornly. Nothing she could say would change his mind. He had been taking Seth to church and Sunday school for the past year, getting him ready for a religious school. Cindy accompanied them from time to time, but usually enjoyed having her Sunday mornings to herself, as a quiet time to grade papers or catch up on school lessons.

In a blink of an eye, Seth was in fifth grade and about to embark on a summer youth retreat with his teacher and classmates. They were to spend a week at a 4-H camp, which was an outdoor facility, located remotely in the hills. Seth was excited about going, yet a little worried about spending an entire week away from his parents. Benjamin realized that he would probably get homesick, but felt that Seth needed to taste life on his own, to understand that life abounded outside his parents' world. However, it was heart wrenching to watch him get into his teacher's van and drive off—away from them for a whole week. The solemn parents waved good-bye, already homesick for their child. As the van rounded the curb, a red sports car pulled into the driveway; it was Lisa and Mark.

"Hey, dudes!" they called and laughed. "What's happenin'?"

"Oh, nothing," said Cindy. "Seth just left for a week of summer camp. We came out to see him off. What are you two up to?"

"Well, we knew Seth was leaving, so we thought that you might need some cheering up. We came to invite you two old married sticks in the mud out for an evening of chaos and mayhem, you know, fun. You do remember what fun is, don't you?" Lisa said, laughing. "We're going out to Kali's for an evening of dinner, dancing, drunkenness, and debauchery, in that order. They have a really great rock band playing tonight. It'll blow you through the roof! What do you say? Pick you up at sixish?"

"No, thanks," said Benjamin. "I don't really feel like partying or anything."

"Oh, come on! What else are you going to do tonight—sit around the house and mope?"

"No," said Benjamin. "Maybe get a movie, popcorn."

"Oh, come on!" coaxed Mark. "It'll do you good to get out of the house for a change. For Christ's sake, go out and have some fun! Live a little! Take your wife out and put a smile on her face; she's dying to go. Isn't that right, Cindy?"

Benjamin looked at his wife, who didn't answer but smiled dreamily, with glistening eyes.

"You see?" chirped Mark confidently. "What did I tell you? She wants to go out and give 'er! Lisa was right; you guys need some time out on the town—blow off some steam. So what do you say? Sixish?"

"Sure!" said Cindy. "I'll be ready with my heels on!"

"Great!" said Lisa with a smile. "I knew that *you* would. Be ready at six—sharp! See you then."

XI

Problems

Benjamin watched the red car speed out of sight as Cindy abruptly turned away from him and marched into the house. Benjamin was a bit stunned that his wife had not considered his wishes as she knowingly went against his will. Her statement to Mark and Lisa had been a proclamation, an act of defiance.

Cindy was at the sink when Benjamin arrived in the kitchen. She was washing the dishes as he nonchalantly browsed through the refrigerator, pouring himself a glass of milk, wondering how to approach the subject. His thoughts mingled with notions that perhaps it would be best to just go out with Lisa and Mark, and give Cindy a break from their home life and just do something different. Maybe Cindy just needed a reprieve from everything. In the past few months, he'd noticed a subtle change in Cindy's character. She seemed happy on the surface, but somehow a little melancholy at the same time. She had been spending a lot of time with Lisa, shopping and girl talking. Secretly, he did not care for Lisa or even Mark. He felt that they were a negative influence. They seemed to chase after things that were contrary to the family values that he cherished so dearly.

Benjamin sat at the kitchen table, drinking his milk. He sensed the tension in Cindy.

"Cindy," he began, "if we go out tonight—"

"We?" she snapped while simultaneously spinning around like a pouncing wildcat. "We?" she repeated. "I thought you had plans to sit on the couch and watch a stupid movie!"

"Well," he stated, "I just thought that we would rather—"

"We?" she snapped again. "There was no 'we' in your reply to Mark when he asked *us* to go out with them. You did not even consult me in your decision to decline Lisa's invitation! You just decided that *you* didn't want to go. You did not think of what I wanted to do, not one bit!" Cindy turned her back toward him again, plunging her hands furiously in the dishwater.

Benjamin thought deeply before answering. Perhaps it would be best to just walk away and let her cool off. He had never seen her so angry before. After some consideration, he thought he had better appease the situation by agreeing with her; after all, he could empathize with her perspective.

"Maybe you're right," admitted Benjamin. "I guess I just assumed that—"

"Well, don't assume! And don't you ever answer for me. I have a mind and voice of my own. Don't you ever forget that!"

"Cindy, I admit that I probably should have—"

"Probably?" she snarled. "You just go watch your movie tonight. I'm going out!"

"Cindy, I'll go out with you. I just thought—"

"No!" she hissed. "I don't want you to go. I know you don't want to go, and Mark's right: you'd just be a stick in the mud. You hate going out and having fun. And on the ultrarare occasions we do go out, I can't have a good time knowing that all you want to do is to go home. Lisa was right!"

"Lisa?" snapped Benjamin. "So that's it! What else has Lisa been filling your head with?"

"You just shut up about Lisa!"

"All that Lisa and Mark do is drink and party. I've even heard stories at work—"

"Shut up! Just shut up!" Cindy slammed a dinner plate on the floor, smashing it into a billion fragments as she turned from the sink with fire in her eyes, pointing straight at Benjamin, gritting her teeth hatefully. "Don't you ever say anything bad to me about Lisa. Do you hear me?"

Benjamin sat there with his mouth hanging open, stupefied, as Cindy knelt down and began wiping the broken fragments together in a heap.

He quietly got a dustpan and a rag and knelt down by his wife, helping her with the task. Cindy began to cry, breaking into as many fragments as the broken dinner plate, hiding her eyes with her hands as the tears flowed like rain. Benjamin cleaned up the mess. Then he touched his wife on the shoulder. She shuddered, as her body stiffened. She got up off her knees and plunged her hands back in the dirty dishwater, with her back toward her husband, scrubbing the dishes furiously, adding more soap, and then scrubbing them again. Benjamin did not know what to do or say. He thought it best to just leave her be. Perhaps things would sort themselves out as the day progressed. He left her there at the sink; he walked out of the room and out of the house.

He needed time to think, time to absorb what had just happened. He and Cindy had what he considered a perfect life, steep in family values. The three of them went through their days happily; however, it was now glaringly apparent that Cindy was not as happy as he had thought. What had changed? Was it him? Had he grown complacent toward her feelings? Had he become old and boring in her eyes? What could he do to correct things, to get things back on the right track? These things he pondered as he walked off into the day, awash in thought.

He stopped and looked about him. The sun was high in the sky. The birds were singing merrily. It was a fine day—the birds and squirrels certainly seemed to be enjoying it. Continuing on, he spotted a black mass of something up ahead on the side of the road, a dead animal of some sort. It turned out to be what was left of a cat; it had apparently been run over numerous times, and from the looks of the dried body, it was a few days old. The bloodied carcass wore the remains of a mangled white color. Benjamin bent down, shooed away the flies, and removed the collar, which bore a brass nameplate stamped with an address and the name "Sassy." The address indicated on the nameplate was only a few blocks away. Benjamin headed in that direction. As he neared the address, he noticed colorful posters dotted about the neighborhood that read "Missing...Black Cat...Reward." He was looking for house number 177. The house numbers were decreasing by twos as he walked: 185...183...181. Two houses up ahead, he noticed a little boy sitting on the porch steps; he was about the same age as Seth. He stopped for a moment, put the collar into his pocket, and then proceeded.

"Hello there," said Benjamin.

"Hello, mister," said the little boy.

"Are your parents home?"

"My dad is; my mom doesn't live here."

"Could I speak with your dad?"

"Sure, I'll go get him." The boy left and quickly returned, saying, "He's on the phone right now. Says he'll be out in a minute."

"OK, I'll wait," said Benjamin as he took a seat on the step, adjacent to the little boy.

"I'm waitin', too," said the little boy. "Been waitin' for my cat to come home. Been gone for over a day and a half, but she'll be home today for sure."

"I see," said Benjamin, not knowing what to say.

"Her name is Sassy. She's really a nice cat, but she has a mind of her own. She was always happy staying inside the house, but then all of a sudden, she wanted to be outside. So we let her out, and she hasn't come back since. But she'll come back today. I just know it."

"How can you be so sure she'll come back?" asked Benjamin.

"'Cause I been prayin' all night long, and the angels is gonna find her for me and bring her back. And because we is her family. She'll come back to her family. Yup, today she'll come back home."

"What's your name?" asked Benjamin.

"David."

"Glad to meet you, David. My name's Benjamin."

"Glad to meet, Mr. Benjamin."

The two shook hands like gentlemen as the screen door to the house creaked open.

"Yes, sir, what can I do for ya today?" said David's father.

"Hello, my name is Benjamin Frisk, and I was wondering if I could have a few words with you—alone." Benjamin looked seriously into his eyes.

David's father noted the aura of seriousness. "Go in the house, David."

"But, Dad, I—"

"Do as I tell ya, now. Get in that house 'fore I tan ya good."

"Yes, sir."

"Now, what's this all about, Mr. Frisk?"

Benjamin pulled the tattered white collar out of his pocket. "Came across a black cat that was hit by a car, a few blocks down the way. Took the collar off; followed the address."

"Oh, Lord," said David's dad as Benjamin handed him the collar. "That cat meant everything in the world to that boy. It'll break his heart. Well, I might as well go tell him. Damn that cat anyways! Been a house cat for years; then all of a sudden, somethin' got in its head…like it just had to. Well, no sense whinin' 'bout it. Might as well go tell him. You say the cat's a couple of blocks down thataway?"

"Yes," said Benjamin. "She's on the side of the road, right in front of a big white house with pillars in the front."

"That'd be ol' Judge Farland's place. Well, I s'pose I'll go tell David, then get a shovel and drive down there."

"The—the body is…well…It's been there a while. And it's…Well, let's just say that it might be a good idea for the boy not to see—"

"That'll be up to David," said his father. "He's got a right to look life squarely in the face. Too many people turn their heads away from unpleasantries, bury their heads in the sand…don't learn a damned thing…pretend everything away. David's young, but he needs to know; he needs to see."

"See what?" said Benjamin a bit defensively. "His dead pet flattened to a mangled heap?"

"To see the truth," said David's dad.

The two men shook hands. Benjamin thought of making his way home by an alternative route as he departed, but decided against it. As he approached the pillared house, he stopped to look upon the black mass of fur pasted to the pavement. He observed flies aggressively buzzing, hovering over the body, feasting on the flesh, penetrating the now-sunken eyeballs; he noticed the maggots squirming, gorging themselves without restraint, lustfully enjoying the banquet. He thought about how sleek the cat must have looked, how much life must have ebbed from those eyes only a couple of days earlier…of how little David must have hugged it and loved it with all his heart, body, and soul. And now it was food for the worms, lying in a lifeless heap, never to return to the land of the living. And why? Just because it had made one bad choice? What unseen force had coaxed it away from David, from the one person who loved it so dearly? From the one person who'd cared for it and protected it? If only it would have remained content, content to stay home with the family who loved it. Benjamin turned his eyes away from the decomposing corpse and wandered toward home, deep in philosophic thought. Life was surely a mystery, he thought to himself. As far as he was concerned, the most important virtue in life was discipline. A person needed to discipline him- or herself from all the foolish, superficial desires of the flesh. The body powerfully persuades the mind to do things that are knowingly unhealthy for a person, both physically and psychologically. Yet the tools of persuasion that the body uses are so difficult to rise above. The second greatest virtue is that of appreciation—to appreciate and be thankful for all that we have, at all times. However, humankind had always proven itself to only be temporarily appreciative and thankful, usually in a cyclical fashion, with appreciation always manifesting itself out of a contrast of some sort, compared with something like a difficulty or hardship or oppression.

Perhaps this was why negative things happened: to create a compare/contrast scenario, ushering in appreciation for the positive, declaring what indeed the positive of any situation was. Perhaps Cindy had become immune to appreciation for their family life together. Perhaps she needed something with which to compare and contrast her married existence. Surely she would realize that her family life was the true treasure. Surely the love of family would trump everything and usher in a deep appreciation for her chosen existence within her family. Appreciation, then, ushers in contentment, and with contentment, happiness. Yes, thought Benjamin, it all hinged on comparing, contrasting, and choosing the right course—the right course home. He turned into his driveway, refreshed with a new perspective.

Cindy was reading on the sofa as he entered the living room. She did not look up from her book or acknowledge him in any way. Benjamin didn't really know how to break the tension. He certainly did not want an emotional escalation to erupt as it had earlier. However, to remain quiet seemed ludicrous. He needed—*they* needed—to reconcile the friction between them. They needed to talk about it.

"Shouldn't you be getting ready to go out?" asked Benjamin. "It's almost five o'clock."

"Not going," she replied coldly.

Benjamin knew he was on thin ice. He could think of nothing to say to defuse the situation. She was still angry, and the act of not going out with Lisa and Mark automatically dumped the blame on him—like he was the source of her unhappiness, like he was the negative. Where was his neat little compare/contrast theory now? This complicated things immensely. His feeling of confidence vanished and was replaced by an uneasiness, as he ventured out on the ice.

"Cindy," he began, "I've been thinking. Maybe you're right. Maybe you should go out with Mark and Lisa by yourself."

"No, I'll just stay here like a good little wife, maybe bake some cookies," she said sarcastically, not removing her eyes from the pages.

He sat down on the sofa, trying to make eye contact with her, as she pulled her legs up next to her body, seeming repelled by his very presence.

"Cindy," he began again, "you spoke the truth earlier. You said that I hate going out and having fun. And you're right in a way. It all hinges on the definition of the word *fun*. You know better than anyone that I enjoy going out and doing things like…well…shopping or dinner, movies—you know, family-type things. But it's true that I don't like going out drinking at clubs and that sort of thing. I never did. Even in high school, it seemed that all my friends couldn't go out and have a good time unless there was alcohol involved. Oh, I went along with them; I drank, threw up on my shoes, had a rotten, miserable time, and then told everyone how 'cool' it was, just like my buddies. I guess I was trying to be one of the guys. But I truly hated it. To me, life is great just the way it is. To be drunk diminishes the experience of life. Instead of crisp, clear life, it makes it diluted, fuzzy, even depressing. I used to think that I was weird, like I was the only one who felt this way. And sometimes I still feel like I'm the only one who feels this way. Even today, at work in the lunchroom, guys talk about how much booze they've consumed over the weekend, and they speak of all the 'fun' things they did. Well, those 'fun' things they brag about seem asinine to me. It's like they enjoy acting like total assholes, like they would rather live their entire lives in a drunken state, or at least be drunk at every opportunity. The fact is that I've sort of alienated myself from the whole party scene. I like to be in control of my existence, to feel my senses to the fullest, not to be drugged into a numb stupor. I would love to go out to a concert or even dancing. What I hate is not really the going out; it's the drinking, or 'partying,' as it's called. A few drinks is fine, but getting bombed is what I hate. And I've heard Mark's stories at work. I just don't thi—"

"And you think I'm going to go out and get bombed and turn into an alcoholic?" Cindy snapped.

Benjamin immediately realized his blunder. "No, no," he pleaded, "it's not that. It's just that—"

"I know exactly what you think it is," she said quietly, her eyes fastened on her book. "You don't trust me—that's exactly what it is. You think that I'm going to indulge in a little fun and allow it to corrupt me or some such nonsense. For God's sake, I am a teacher. Don't you think that I can handle a night of silly fun? What? Am I supposed to stay in this house for the rest of my life, planning trips to Disney World and playing canasta with the ladies on Friday night? Well, if that's what you want, that's what you'll get, but I'll be miserable. And you're right, too. You're right about Lisa. She's opened my eyes. And I'm seeing things much clearer lately. The fact is that you don't trust me. All that garbage you just spewed out about drinking: you sure seemed to enjoy all the wine we drank when we first met. Tell me, was that all a lie? Did you really hate the time we spent together, under the influence?"

Benjamin felt the noose of Cindy's logic tighten around his neck. "Well," he said, pausing to buy time to think, "when we drink, we do it responsibly. And I certainly enjoy it; you know I do—"

"Oh?" she questioned. "First you say you hate drinking; then you say you enjoy it. I guess the world should just revolve around you, and I should only do things when and where you think it is appropriate."

Benjamin looked at his wife as she stared directly at the book in front of her. She was impenetrable. Her mental walls had been forged and laid, stone by stone. Why hadn't he noticed this before now? He had always assumed that Cindy was united with him on their path of life, but perhaps she had deviated from the road. Oh, she was still there physically, but not spiritually. And if the spirit isn't there with the body, the body will have no choice but to eventually decay into a lifeless, loveless, depressed heap of flesh, only resembling a mirrored image of what once was.

"Cindy, you know that I love you, don't you?"

She did not answer nor look up from her book.

"I'm going for a ride downtown. Probably stop for a bite to eat and then get a movie for later. You want to come along?"

Again, she did not answer nor look up from her book. He walked out of the house and got into his pickup, motoring away down the road. He was shaken by the impossible confrontation with Cindy. There was no appeasing her. She did not want him to go out with her, and she did not want to go without him, and she did not want to stay home. What she wanted was for him to *want* to go out and party. That was the one thing he hated to do. That was the one thing he could not do. And besides, it was dangerous, a slippery slope, a place of temptation and lewdness. And he did not want Cindy to go out and party either. Actually, that statement wasn't totally correct; he didn't mind if Cindy went out and partied, but he did not want Cindy to *want* to go out and party. But she did want. Why did she want all of a sudden? Benjamin's thoughts turned to Lisa and how Cindy had been spending more and more time with her these past few months. He thought about the stories he had heard at work about Lisa, stories told in the lunchroom when Mark was not present. He wished that Cindy wouldn't want to associate with Lisa; however, she obviously was associating with her, and it was driving a wedge between them. Maybe he was making too big a deal of this. Maybe Cindy was right—that it was a trust issue, that he should just trust his wife. Perhaps that would be the best course of action, to just trust Cindy and hope for the best. After all, she was a responsible adult, a respected schoolteacher. Was he worried that she would become corrupted in some way? Was this whole conflict with Cindy a manifestation of his own insecurities? Benjamin questioned himself and his morals, holding them up to the fire of his own scrutiny. Perhaps he was scared—scared that Cindy would like the partying life, that she would see that the fruit of that tree was pleasing to the eye and good for food, and that she might even eat of the forbidden fruit. Perhaps jealousy lurked at the foundation of his thoughts. Everything seemed to hinge on his trust. Cindy was right! He did not trust her fully. Secretly, he feared she might be led astray if her protective shield of restraint was diminished, and alcohol is certainly a popular restraint diminisher. Benjamin remembered that first night they had spent together and the two bottles of wine Cindy had brought over. Why two bottles? Benjamin's mind was racing into a jumble of thoughts and scenarios, fusing into a mass of unintelligible mayhem. He mustered all his mental power to break free of the landslide of thoughts, distancing himself to assess a summary of his deliberations. He did not understand his wife's perspective on this issue, that was for sure. And it would seem that he did not completely trust his wife when it came to drinking and partying. Perhaps it would be best for him to accompany her to these idiotic outings, where grown people act like retarded morons for an evening. But he would hate that, and she would know that he hated it. And she would eventually hate him for hating it, as she'd already alluded to. And besides, if he went along with her, it would be sort of a lie. He would be chaperoning his wife, like a constable, making sure she acted appropriately; he would be playing the role of an overprotective parent. She would despise him for that. If he demanded she stay home, she would despise him for that, too. No matter how or which way he looked at the problem, there seemed to be only one solution, and that was for Cindy to go out and decide for herself. He decided not to address the issue. He would not encourage her to go out nor discourage it. Cindy knew how he felt. He would leave the choice up to her.

Benjamin drove up to a fast-food joint, ordered three hamburgers and a Coke, and then drove to the city park. He sat on a bench, overlooking a small, lazy stream, while munching on his supper. Swans and ducks graced the mirrorlike river, as the waters gleaned their feathery reflections and duplicated them as two different beings, one on each: one real and one an illusion, with reality reversed. Some floated with the current; some swam against it. Benjamin imagined how furiously the ducks must be paddling against the current. But the struggle was hidden from view, well beneath the water's surface. The only image that he saw was the graceful gliding. He finished his last hamburger, crumpled up the paper bag, and deposited it in the trash. Walking down the sidewalk through the park, he sipped on his Coke, mesmerized by the beauty of nature—the trees, the sunshine, the thousand shades of green. How simple life was; it was as natural as rain. How do people get so pulled away from the reality of life? Why do we complicate the simple truths of life? Why must people corrupt themselves with foolishness of one sort or another? Benjamin noticed an old man with a young boy, no older than seven. The grandfather was teaching the boy how to cast a bobber out into the river. After a fumbled cast by the boy, the two sat on a large rock with their eyes glued, anxiously waiting for the bobber to magically dance to life. Benjamin remembered the days of his youth, when he and his father used to go camping and fish offshore. He remembered the joy of just being there, even when they caught no fish at all. There was a secure blissfulness about family life that seemed to make sense, to provide purpose, to provide reason for life—for everything. Without it, what would life be? Just an attempt to make the self happy? To entertain the self? But how? By some foolish game or sex or drugs? Would these things truly make a person happy? Or just paint a superficial illusion of temporary happiness while allowing oneself to get duped into the pit of despair, laughing merrily as you plunged deeper and deeper? Benjamin took a seat on an old log jutting out from the riverbank. He noticed a stone next to his shoe, half embedded into the sand; he kicked it loose. Picking it up and brushing the loose sand off it, he observed speckles of quartz glimmering among black-and-white flecks of some substance, probably just granite of some sort. It was beautiful; even the shape was beautiful, not perfectly round—more egg shaped but flatter on one side. The rock felt cool on his hand. He tossed it high in the air. "Phluck!" sang the water as the stone broke through its surface, causing perfect rings to ripple out from the center of its impact, sending intermittent waves to every shore, impacting everything within range. Even the ducks fifty yards away were affected by the ripples, but they hardly noticed the effect as they nonchalantly went about their business.

It was 6:00 p.m. Cindy had either called the whole thing off, or Mark and Lisa were at his home at this very moment, probably coaxing her to go with them, justifying to her why she should go with them. Benjamin thought deeply, trying to justify his own role in all of this. Again, he came up with the same conclusion: it had to be her decision. She alone had to defeat herself.

The sun was sinking over the horizon, casting long shadows on the water. The frogs were beginning to rehearse for the nightly chorus. Various insects were hovering over the surface of the water. A mosquito landed on Benjamin's hand. He watched it penetrate his skin and grow plump on his lifeblood and then fly away, leaving an itch that was near impossible not to scratch. He focused all of his concentration on that swelling patch of skin, mentally fighting the urge to scratch it, fighting the body's demand for relief, testing himself, testing his willpower, determined to win this contest with himself. Of the two contestants, who would be the victor? It was imperative that he win, that he rise above. But the desire was so strong—and constant. Benjamin did not mentally turn from his desires and attempt to alleviate the pressure by trying not to think about it. Instead he focused his attention directly at the thing, dissecting the very essence of what was happening and purposely feeling every drop of agonizing *want*. It seemed to him that it wasn't so much the strong desire that was difficult to fight, but the constantness of it. It was not so hard to muster the willpower to fight his desire temporarily, but the constant gnawing of it—that is what would break him. He thought of prisoners of war being tortured with pain until they gave in. How ironic it was to be tortured with pleasure. All he had to do was to scratch the itch. It would feel like heaven, and the relentless longing, the hunger, the desire would be alleviated. He began to think that the experiment was foolish, that he should just scratch it and be done with it. What could this possibly prove? Just do it! It was just a natural thing. Why fight against nature? After all, he was just feeling a common, natural reaction of the body. Why fight life? Benjamin laughed at himself and reached over to scratch the itch, but stopped short of doing so. Then he saw what had almost happened. He saw the other—hiding in the shadows. It was he who was deviously using his own logic against him.

Benjamin shuddered at the crafty deceit employed by the enemy. It had almost worked. "Damn you!" he said as he hopped off the dead log and marched to his pickup truck, furious with himself for almost being duped. He spun off into the dusk as the itch left him. He had won the battle, but only by a thread. And this skirmish was only that of a simple mosquito bite. How much more difficult it would be to confront the enemy on a battlefield where the intensities are complex, hidden, camouflaged, and constant. As Benjamin drove toward the video store, he thought of Cindy, riding into battle alone. The thought jolted through him like cold lightning. He pulled over on the side of the road to think. Then he swung the truck back on the road and headed toward home. He was hoping dearly that she had stayed home. She would still be angry, but he could deal with that. He could deal with anything, as long as she was with him. Perhaps it was not solely a "trust" issue, as he'd been deluded to believe. Perhaps he'd been fooled by the enemy. Perhaps it'd been a cunning ploy just to get her away, to get her alone and vulnerable. He should have stayed with her at all costs. No, it wasn't just a simple trust issue at all; it was an issue of the will, a test of the will. Trust only fused itself into the issue of Cindy's will, fastening itself into the scenario like a virus. Whether she could maintain the battle was not relevant; it was the fact that she was going into battle with little armor, with little reinforcements. He should have been her reinforcements. Two cords make a stronger rope than one.

Gone Out

By the time he pulled into the driveway, it was well after seven o'clock. He walked into the house hesitantly, desperately hoping that she had stayed home. The house felt cold and awkward. In the air, he could taste the mingling fragrance of Cindy's perfume. He noticed that the book Cindy had been reading was lying across the room in a heap on the floor. She was gone. An unsettling frustration dangled in the pit of his stomach, similar to the feeling of dangling over the ledge of a cliff. He questioned himself. Should he drive to the nightclub and find her? Or would it be best to wait? He thought of that mosquito bite. It would have been best to prevent the mosquito from biting in the first place. He took a quick shower and got dressed, all the time trying desperately to remember the name of that nightclub. It was Kathy's or Katy's, something like that. He scanned the phone book. Kali's! That was it, on Sixth Street. He tore out of the driveway toward the battlefront, all the while questioning his actions. What would happen when he got there? Would she accept him? Could it be that what he was doing was actually just giving in to the whole affair because of his own weakness? Was he jealous? Was he afraid that his wife might enjoy the company of someone else more than his? He imagined Cindy dancing with some stranger at the nightclub, dancing close, the stranger smelling her scented skin, feeling her hand in his. And what scared him more was the thought of Cindy liking it. Benjamin mentally heard the mischievous buzz of mosquito wings, resembling a suppressed, sarcastic laughter, eerily echoing as if coming from another world.

He pulled into the parking lot of Kali's, looking frantically for Lisa's red sports car, but all the vehicles looked dark in the dim lighting. He circled again. Nothing. A ray of hopeful relief settled about him. Perhaps they'd decided not to go to the nightclub. Maybe they'd decided to just go to Lisa's apartment. Maybe Cindy had been noticeably distraught because of their disagreement, and Lisa had thought it wise to comfort her or something. He thought of driving home and waiting for her. But what if they were not at Lisa's place? Where would they have gone? He drove to the other side of town, cruising slowly past Lisa's parking space. Her car was not there, and the lights were not on in her apartment. Where could they be? He had no idea. Perhaps Cindy was home by now; it was well past nine o'clock. Maybe they'd just gone out for dinner and a drive. Yes, that was probably it. She would be home by now, probably wondering where he was. Maybe she was worried about him. Of course, in her present mood, she would never let on that she was worried. He headed for home, somewhat confident that she would be there.

But his heart sank as he pulled into the driveway. The house was dark. Where could she be? "Damn it!" he swore to himself as he entered his home, flicking on the lights and sitting on the sofa. The house was so quiet—hauntingly quiet. His family was not there; without them, the house was just a hollow building, void of the warmth and love of a family. "How odd life is," he mumbled, as his thoughts drifted into the past.

Before he'd met Cindy, this house had been a home, even though he'd been alone. Even though alone, he'd been comfortable; even though alone, he'd been happy and content. Life had been so simple then—just him and Barney.

He walked over to the front door and opened it, smiling at the two white paw prints that still graced its surface. He had never removed those two paw prints, even after all these years. He remembered his pet dog, caressing each memory fondly and delicately, remembering the emotions associated with each one. Loving a pet is unique in its own right. The love is unconditional in a way. No matter what the pet does, it does not diminish the relationship. Sure, there might be anger at times, but it is so easy to forgive a pet, because they know not what they do. In fact, it is somewhat easy to forgive people when they do something wrong, but don't understand fully what they've done; children are like that. How hard it is to forgive a person who does something wrong and knows very well what he or she has done and the damage caused to others by the impact of the sin rippling across the social waters. Of course, if the person is deeply and truly sorry, he or she can be forgiven almost anything. But the deed will never be forgotten, buried perhaps but not forgotten, never forgotten, always lying there in its tomb as a blemish, as a scar of impurity, forever branded into the memory, but not necessarily branded into the soul. No, forgiveness can make the soul clean again, but that kind of forgiveness does not come from others; it comes from within, with the self being the conduit to an ultimate forgiveness. "Oh, for Christ's sake," he said, shaking himself out of his thoughts. What was he thinking about? He and Cindy just had a simple little misunderstanding; married couples cannot agree on everything. Was he overreacting? Cindy would be home at any minute, and they would kiss and make up, and their lives would fall back into place. After all, they were a family, and they loved each other; they could surely weather a little storm such as this. Benjamin turned on the television and flicked through the channels, settling on a rerun of an old western. He liked the old western programs; it was always easy to tell the good guys from the bad guys, and the good always triumphed over evil. The conclusions always left him feeling fuzzy and warm, confident that as long as a person was righteous in his or her beliefs and actions, life would always turn out for the best. Even though it would not necessarily be easy and there might be some difficult times here and there, it would always turn out for the best. He went to the kitchen and popped himself a large bowl of popcorn, grabbed a soft drink, and sat in front of the television, trying his best to pretend that he was engrossed in the movie, attempting to dilute the crouching thoughts that were dashing about in his brain. During some brief intervals, he actually managed to distract himself enough to temporarily forget his current dilemma, but only for a moment. Then his thoughts would burst through the barrier and flood back into his consciousness, filling his heart, which tingled with sickening apprehension. He found that he had to force himself to watch the movie, forcing his head deeper into the sand, constantly glancing at his wristwatch as the seconds ticked, one by one by one, slowly creeping, one by one by one.

It was midnight. He and Cindy had never stayed out past midnight! Of course, they always had the babysitter to think of. Was she doing this to punish him? To show him her independence or something? Cindy had been acting a bit reserved the past few months. It was really nothing. He had just assumed that because she had been spending more time with Lisa, her mind was on girl things, or whatever it is that girls talk about together. Perhaps he should have inquired more. Perhaps he should have offered to go along with her. Perhaps he was not as good a husband as he had assumed. Perhaps everything was indeed his fault.

Suddenly, he heard a car door slam outside. He quickly situated himself in a casual position on the sofa. He would pretend that he hadn't missed her at all, but he would act pleased that she was home. He would hug her and then kiss her. She would tell him how the night went, over a glass of wine. Then they would kiss again, this time more passionately as their spirits would reunite again as one. Everything would be all right now, now that Cindy was home. Benjamin felt guilty and ashamed for not trusting his wife, not trusting her will. But his guilt was trumped by the joy of her return home, home to him, home to her family. Everything would be fine now. A fulfilling peace settled about him as he waited for the front door to open, as he simultaneously suppressed the urge to run out to the driveway and fling his arms around his wife.

Minutes passed. The door did not open. She must be saying good night to Lisa and Mark, probably hashing over the night's events or discussing something else of no concern. Perhaps they were talking about him and his reluctance to go out and have "fun." The minutes passed. What the hell was she doing out there? For God's sake, she'd just spent the entire evening with those people, you'd think she would have had her fill of them by now. The minutes inched on. Oh, damn her anyways! Why in the world is she sitting out in that stupid driveway? Benjamin glanced at his watch; it was after one o'clock. He got off the couch and crept over to the window, peeking around the curtain. He could not see a car in the driveway, but the glare from the living room light prevented a clear view. "Oh, what the hell!" he thought as he marched over to the front door and swung it open. The driveway was barren except for his pickup truck. A nauseous wave of anxiety swept over him like an emotional tsunami, crashing down around him, encompassing him with its smothering weight. He had been mistaken; Cindy had not come home after all. She was still out. Lord knew what she could be doing at this hour. If they'd gone out to a nightclub, she would probably be drunk, and her guard would be down; her restraint would be diminished; she would be vulnerable. "Goddamn it! What the hell is she doing? I can't believe this!" he yelled out loud with clenched fists. Benjamin paced the floors as one who was lost and roaming the earth, going back and forth and getting nowhere, while wild scenarios conjured themselves out of the abyss, painting fantastic scenes of horrid possibilities, possibilities that he had never thought of before. Maybe he'd overlooked their car at the nightclub. Maybe they were still there. His thoughts turned to driving down there again, but it was nearing one thirty; by the time he got there, it would be closing time. He might miss them. And what if she came home while he was out looking for her? She would know that he'd gone out to spy on her, and she would hate him for it. Maybe he could just call the nightclub. No, that would be useless; the only way an employee would know whether Cindy was there would be to have her paged or something. Maybe he should call Lisa's place. He could pretend that he'd just woken up and noticed how late it was and was simply concerned for Cindy's safety because she wasn't home yet. However, she would know; she would know that he was just checking up on her. Maybe he could just make the call and then hang up if someone answered; then he would at least know where she was, that she was indeed safe. But on second thought, Lisa's caller ID would give him away. Benjamin paced back and forth furiously. One thing was for certain: he could not stay in this house one more minute. It would drive him crazy! He devised a plan. He would drive a few blocks and use the old pay phone in front of the post office; then he'd call Lisa's house. If someone answered, he would at least know where they were. Perhaps that would provide him some relief.

Out Looking

He flew out of the house and sped out into the night once again. He wasn't sure whether the phone was even there anymore or whether it was in working condition if it was there. But it was no matter; it just felt good to be doing something instead of sitting alone, stagnant, with his thoughts tormenting him. At least now he had a reprieve, a small diversion to avoid the brunt of his rampaging emotions. He pulled up to the phone and paused, questioning himself, examining his motives. Was he jealous? Was this jumbled-up glut of emotions that he was feeling born out of jealousy? Yes. Yes, it was. He was jealous. Benjamin thought deeply about this. Is it wrong to be jealous? Should he be ashamed for feeling jealous? He examined the concept of jealousy, mentally sifting through its known definition, desperately trying to confirm and justify his course of action. He was perplexed. On one hand, the concept of jealously is associated with envy, which was wrong. But, on the other hand, jealousy was a feeling of apprehension when a person was fearful of losing another's love, or perhaps fearful if that love was in jeopardy. Wouldn't that be a good thing? Wouldn't it be right to feel apprehension if someone you loved might be traveling on a dangerous road? Doesn't God Himself state that He is jealous? Benjamin got out of the pickup and made the call.

The phone rang once, twice, three times. "Damn it," he swore. The answering machine would kick in at any second…four…five…

six. "Liiiiiiisa?" It was Cindy's laughing voice. Benjamin froze solid at the sound of her voice. "Hellllllllooooooo?" She giggled. "Who the hell is it?" came a man's voice from the background. Then the connection went dead. She had hung up. Benjamin stood there, like a statue. His mind was ablaze with fire and electricity as he churned in a frustrating sea of emotional agony. What the hell was going on? Cindy was at Lisa's apartment, that was for certain. But Lisa was not there. And some man was there. Was it Mark? The voice could have been Mark's, but it was difficult to be sure because there'd been music playing in the background, disguising his voice somewhat. It probably was just Mark. Yes, that was it. Lisa had probably gone out, maybe to Mark's place to get something, while he and Cindy waited for her to come back to the apartment. That would explain why Cindy had answered the phone by saying Lisa's name; she was obviously expecting a call from Lisa. Yes, that was it, or something like that. Benjamin felt relieved as he accepted his scenario. He sat in his pickup and thought about the entire evening. What an emotional ride he had been on! What horrid feelings had quelled up in him, feelings like he had never experienced before. He hoped with all his soul that he would never feel them again. Maybe he had been wrong. Maybe he should go out to the nightclubs with Cindy and make the best of it. Perhaps he was acting too righteous or something. What's wrong with going out and having a little fun once in a while, blowing off a little steam? It certainly would be better than repeating the agony of this evening. Benjamin thought about driving home. But what would he do there? He certainly couldn't get any sleep, not until Cindy was in his arms. And there was an element of uncertainty about the whole affair that would starkly flash across his mind intermittently. "Why play any more waiting games?" he thought. "Why not just drive over to Lisa's place and get it over with." He could come clean, just tell Cindy what a fool he had been and throw himself at her mercy. By the tone of her voice on the phone, she had been drinking a good deal; alcohol always made her giddy, glowing, and mellow. She would accept him, and everything would be right again. Yes, that's what he would do. He drove off into the blackness toward Lisa's place.

Upon arriving, he circled the parking lot looking for Lisa's car. It was not there. He noticed that the lights were on in the apartment as he approached the front door to the building. He walked slowly down the hall toward Lisa's door. He was a bit apprehensive, a bit nervous. Looking down, he noticed two buttons lying on the carpet. They seemed familiar. He picked them up and examined them. They were white with a faint red cross in the center. Weren't these the buttons from Cindy's blouse? The one he had gotten her for Christmas? Yes, they had to be. A paralyzing numbness enveloped him. Questions exploded in his mind, corrupting his thoughts, turning his stomach to the consistency of crawling ants and his legs to Jell-O. He approached Lisa's door, which was open, just a crack. He heard wild music emanating from within, mingling with other sounds, animalistic sounds, lustful sounds. A woman's groans spasmodically grew in pleasurable intensity. Benjamin recognized the voice. He quietly pushed the door open as he stood like a corpse.

In their entwined passion, they did not even notice him standing there. She was on top of him, greedily straddling him, lustfully meeting his thrusts to the brink. The swing of the door rapped the wall. Mark lifted his head slightly and looked down Cindy's shoulder and over her pounding rump into the appalled face of Benjamin.

"Holy shit!" shouted Mark, instantly pushing her off him, as she confusingly spun around, in awe at the sight, not fully realizing what she saw. She stared at him, as she sat there on the couch, naked; her breasts glistened with Mark's saliva as both husband and wife stood mute as if spellbound. Mark was scrambling to get his pants on. "Holy shit," he said again, looking at Benjamin and quickly turning off the music, not knowing what he would do next. The quiet seconds ticked on like an eternity. Cindy made no attempt to cover herself. They just looked into each other abstractly, dazed.

"Ben," Mark blurted, "I'm—I'm...It's just that...I mean...We just..."

Benjamin raised his open hand to Mark, silencing him, without taking his eyes off the naked body in front of him, a body that physically resembled his wife in every detail, but the spirit that was in that body was alien to him. Time had ceased. Existence had ceased. All that remained was the blandness of a mix of putrid emotions that puddled themselves into a weary form, resembling disgust.

"Get dressed," he said. "We're going home."

His words, his voice, the voice of her husband broke the spell, and her eyes were opened, and she realized her nakedness. She covered herself from his eyes with a small blanket that was draped over the back of the couch.

Benjamin repeated himself. "Get your clothes on. I'm taking you home."

Cindy turned her eyes away from him and blankly gazed ahead of herself, into nothingness. "Home," she said in a weak, guttural voice, barely audible. "Home is gone now…"

There were approaching footsteps in the hall. Benjamin did not turn away from his wife to see who it was.

"Oh, my Go—" said Lisa as she immediately assessed the obvious situation.

Mark put his shirt on and lit a cigarette, not saying a word.

Cindy stared into a netherworld of black-and-white images, void of color, void of emotion, blank with emptiness, vacant.

"Cindy!" Benjamin commanded angrily. "Get your clothes on! Now!"

Cindy did not move nor acknowledge him in any way. She was far from him. She could hear his words, but they sounded weak and distant. An immense chasm separated them, an uncrossable chasm. Their bodies were in the same room, but their spirits were worlds apart. Hers was drifting, drifting away from him, drifting farther into the abysmal current, which pulled her farther and farther away, widening the chasm between them, furthering the distance.

Lisa quickly took charge of the situation. "Mark, you better leave."

Mark looked at Lisa, and she at him, reading each other's thoughts. He nodded in agreement, picked up his shoes, and walked out the door, not saying a word. Lisa's attention turned to Cindy. "Benjamin, go in the kitchen," she said as she gathered Cindy's clothes.

"I'm not going anywh—"

"Go in the kitchen!" she repeated with authority. "Give her some time. Give us some time."

Benjamin reluctantly went in the kitchen, which was really an extension of the living room. He could clearly see and hear both of them, who were only a few yards away.

"Cindy?" spoke Lisa softly. "Cindy, honey? I want you to stand up, and we'll walk to the bedroom together, and we'll get you dressed, OK? Cindy? Did you hear me, honey? Stand up. Come on now. That's it. OK, now let's go to my bedroom. Let me help you. That's it. You're doing fine."

Cindy staggered toward the bedroom, clutching the end of the blanket to the base of her neck with both hands, allowing it to drape down, covering only her front half. Lisa held on to her shoulder and arm, steadying her as she swaggered along into the bedroom. The door closed.

Benjamin sat at the kitchen table, stunned, immobile. He was in shock, unable to assess anything, unable to think, shattered, in total annihilation. He just sat there with a glazed consciousness, numb. Maybe an hour passed, maybe two—it didn't matter; nothing mattered. His world had instantly changed in a moment. The defining shapes of existence were not true; they were not reliable any longer. Everything had been turned into an illusion. Everything he had known, everything he had trusted to be true, was now just an image representing what once was. Had it ever been what he'd thought it was? Was his life only a belief, created in his own mind by the way he perceived it? Was this reality? Or was yesterday reality? Yesterday was a world away, a universe away, never to be revisited again—only a memory now, only a numb memory of what he'd thought existed at the time. Out of his inebriating psychosis, he saw the ghost of Lisa in front of him, mumbling words incompressible to him; he puzzled at the sound of her voice and the fuzzy form that beheld itself in front of him as it reached toward him, forever toward him, grasping his shoulder with power and might, shaking his foundation.

"Men-chur-men...men-gur-men...meg-jur-men...Benjurmen... Benjamin!"

"Wha—" Benjamin snapped to with a jolt. Lisa was shaking him.

"Benjamin! Get a hold of yourself!" Lisa said firmly, like iron, yet quietly. "Listen to me. Cindy's going to stay here. Do you hear me? Do you understand? Cindy is going to stay here with me. I'll drive you home. OK? Benjamin? Benjamin!"

"What? No, no...Cindy's coming home with me. I'm going to—"

"Benjamin!" Lisa spoke sternly. "Cindy is in no shape to go anywhere at this moment, and I'm not going to allow her to go anywhere. Do you hear me? She needs time, and so do you. Nothing will be solved tonight. Now, you're in no shape to drive. Let me give you a ride home."

Benjamin stared in bewilderment. Lisa assumed that he was drunk. He was perplexed by the irony.

"Lisa, I am not drunk. I haven't touched a drop all night...unlike yourself," he added sarcastically. "I'm—I'm sorry, Lisa. I didn't mean that. I'm sorry. You must be just as devastated as me. I mean, with Mark and..."

Benjamin stopped speaking, unable to finish his thought.

"Benjamin, please. Just go home." She helped him up from his chair with her hand on his sleeve, gently coaxing him toward the door.

"No. Wait!"

Benjamin stopped, sensing that something was out of place—that something was wrong. Lisa seemed to be taking this too easily, too casually. Suspicion welled up within him. "Why are you so compassionate toward Cindy? Do you know what they did? Do you know?" he blurted. He looked sharply into Lisa's eyes for the first time since she'd arrived. His mind flashed through the promiscuous rumors he had heard about Lisa at work. Where had she been this evening? She did not seem to be emotionally fazed in the least, knowing the fact that her good friend and her boyfriend had been having sex at her very apartment while she'd been out. She should be furious with Cindy—and Mark, too. It was as if she just accepted it all, like she knew, almost as if it had been arranged, and she knew. Benjamin looked at her skeptically, unwilling to believe his thoughts, but her eyes were like iron, cold and black.

"You knew," he said. "You knew what was going on here, didn't you? Didn't you?" he yelled.

"Go home, Benjamin," she said, glaring at him.

"Where were you while Cindy and Mark were here alone?"

"Go home, Benjamin," she said while lighting up a cigarette and sitting on the couch, fully realizing that he had no intention of leaving.

"Well?" he demanded.

"Well what?" she said angrily. "What do you want me to say? That I was out delivering Girl Scout cookies to my dear old aunt or something? Is that what you're so anxious to hear, some sweet little fairy tale?"

"How about the truth," he said, glaring.

"The truth?" She laughed sarcastically. "You don't want the truth! You want to live in a fantasy land where all the houses are made of gingerbread and gumdrops, and all the little boys and girls are happy and dream of sugarplums and daffodils. You wouldn't want the truth to corrupt your sweet little Eden, now would you? Oh, how silly of me; it must've slipped my mind. I guess the truth already *has* found its way into your pitiful little utopian bubble, now hasn't it?"

"Just answer the goddamned question!" Benjamin hollered, his face blushing red with anger.

"What's the matter, Benjamin? Getting angry with me? Why would you be angry with little old me? Why, I wasn't even here when you wife was getting f—"

"Shut your damned mouth!" yelled Benjamin, clenching his fists and trying desperately to master his rage.

Lisa laughingly crushed out her cigarette. "What's the matter, Benjamin? I thought you wanted the truth." She giggled in an evil tone. "I just repeated a truth that you already know for a fact, and you're ready to strangle me. How will you handle *all* the truth?"

"You just tell me everything, and do it now, or I swear I'll—I'll—"

"You'll what?" she prodded. "Kill me? Is that what you're feeling, Benjamin? The desire to murder? You do feel it, don't you? Don't you? It's welling up inside you, building in intensity. It's like an orgasm, really," she sneered. "It keeps building up, needing release. Or so I've read. You want to know where I was tonight? Well, I'll tell you. The three of us went clubbing. I met some guy and ended up at his place. Mark and Cindy got a cab and came back here. I told them not to wait up for me, but to leave the door unlocked, that I would only be a few hours. I don't like to sleep overnight with them. If you sleep overnight with them, they sometimes get the idiotic notion that you care about them. Men are so stupid; it's unbelievable really. Anyways, I had to come back to give

Cindy a ride home, you know, after they finished. Had to keep the illusion going; keep the walls up in that gingerbread house."

Benjamin's anger raged wildly, foaming violently, intensifying by the second.

Lisa laughed at him to his face. "Oh, that's not all, Benjamin. You did want *all* the truth, didn't you?" Her upper lip sneered as she stared at him with disgust. "This isn't the first time—Cindy and Mark, I mean. They've been banging each other for months."

"That's a damned lie! You're nothing but a goddamned liar!"

"Oh, don't be so self-righteous. It's not the first time a wife had an affair on her *Leave It to Beaver* husband. Think about it: school gets out at three, and she gets home at five thirty or so; then there's always a few conferences or meetings or special events that teachers go to in the evenings, always something—"

"Shut your mouth. You're a lying—a lying—"

"What? A lying what? Go ahead, say it! Go ahead. You think you're so damned good. Well, look at you now. How does it feel? How does it feel to hate? You've never felt it before, have you? You stupid ass! How does it feel? How does it feel to sit home and watch *Peter Pan* on TV while your wife is getting fucked?"

"Shut up! Just shut up!"

He attacked her in a furious rage, thrusting her onto the couch with both hands around her neck, squeezing uncontrollably, snarling like an animal through gritted teeth.

"Shut up! Shut up!" he repeated again and again as he stared into her black eyes. In a fraction of a moment, he jumped away in horror, away from Lisa's gasping, coughing body. He had seen in her eyes a reflection, a reflection of evil, an evil so monstrous that its intensity blotted out the sun. In that fraction of a moment, Benjamin recognized the evil that was himself, in him, consuming him and devouring him. He just stood there, amazed and confused, as the spirit left him.

"Go home, Benjamin," pleaded a shallow voice from the shadowy hallway that led to the bedroom. It was Cindy, standing there in darkness, vaguely indistinguishable. "Just go home," she repeated drily.

Benjamin wondered how long she had been standing there. He stood by the door, but did not leave; he couldn't. He could not walk away from his wife.

"I can't," he said in a fashion similar to a man who has just discovered a sudden revelation about himself. "I cannot leave here without you. I just can't. Come home. Come home with me. Come home to your family. We can work through—"

"I can't believe this crap!" snarled Lisa, with one hand on her neck, as she regained her composure. "It about makes me sick." Lisa lit up a cigarette and poised herself on the couch to watch the disgusting show.

Benjamin did not let Lisa's words affect him. To him it was as if she was not even there. Only Cindy mattered now. If only she would come to him, out of the darkness into his light; only then, perhaps, she would be safe—perhaps *they* would be safe.

"Cindy," he said quietly, "go get your things. Let's go home."

"I can't," said Cindy as if in another world. "I can't go home. I don't have a home anymore. It's gone. It's all gone. It's just a house now, an empty shell, just a scrapbook of what once was."

"Cindy," he said, "listen to me. You're not thinking straight right now. You're not making sense. We have Seth. We have a family. We can get through this. We can get through anything."

"You can, Benjamin. You can get through anything. But not me. You have to leave me. You just have to. I want you to leave me. I want to stay here."

"I will not leave you here!" he stated firmly as he looked directly at Lisa, who quietly smirked and rolled her eyes as she made love to her cigarette.

Cindy's ghost disappeared into the bedroom in submission, as a sense of temporary relief filled Benjamin's heart.

"She's mine now," sneered Lisa triumphantly. "She'll never return to you—never."

"Cindy is my wife, and she *is* returning to me."

"Only in body, only in body," said Lisa, grinning.

Benjamin did not wish to respond to her. It would only provoke an argument or invite an unwanted anger to revisit him. He was content for now. Cindy was coming home with him. That was enough for the moment.

"She can't survive in both worlds," said Lisa quietly, matter-of-factly. "Even if she stays with you, she'll just go through the motions, day after day, like a machine, day after day as the months turn into years, ever so gradually sliding into a mild depression. Then deeper and deeper she'll slide, shrouded by a cloud of guilt, not so much the guilt of what she did, but the guilt of what she wants. Nothing can erase her want now. She's tasted the forbidden fruit. It's in her now. She is spiritually separated from your seemingly utopian relationship. She can never go back to Eden. You'll have to think about that. You'll be alone there: you in your world and she in hers. But you don't have to be. It's up to you, Benjamin. She can never go back to your world, but you can go to hers and join her there, join us there. You just have to accept it, accept us. It's just nature. Come with us; break free of your prison." Lisa rose from the couch and walked in front of him, reaching out to his face and gently turning his eyes to hers; she put her arms around him, kissing him sensually on the mouth. He stood like a stone, unmovable. She laughed erotically. "You will think about it, Benjamin Frisk. In the days ahead, you will think about it." She walked to the kitchen and poured herself a glass of wine. "I need a drink, and so do you," she said as she filled another glass. She offered the wine to Benjamin with a silent gesture, but he did not acknowledge her or her offering. "Suit yourself," she said and laughed before gulping down his drink. "Ahh," she said, with a grin. "Oh, Benjamin, you silly little insignificant man, why fight it? Why spend your whole life fighting it? Why not enjoy your days? Have some fun? Live a little? Hell, everyone else is!" She laughed sinisterly and then drank her entire glass in one swallow.

XII

Ten Years Later

"Hello?"

"Hi, honey. It's me. Just calling to touch base. How've you been?"

"Oh, hi, Mom. I'm doing good, and you?"

"Oh, fine, just fine. How's Seth doing?"

"Great, just great. He seems to really enjoy living on his own—hardly ever calls home anymore. I was a little apprehensive about the transition, you know, from living with me, going to his hometown community college, and then moving away to the other side of the world with a new job and new place, you know, a totally different situation."

"Ha, ha, Benjamin, I would hardly say that he is on the other side of the world. He's only four hours away, you know."

"Yeah, I know, but it seems farther."

"Well, I hope he comes to his senses and goes back to college. Whatever possessed him to go into construction? Such a waste! A dead-end job, if you ask me. He should hit the books and make something of himself."

"Oh, Seth and I had many discussions on the subject. He says he wants to work with his hands, to create, make something tangible, useful, something that will last. That's why he got into masonry. He says that something about laying bricks seems solid, purposeful. And he loves it."

"Well, I think he has bricks in his head. In twenty years he'll have debt up to his nose and a bad back to boot. Then what?"

"Oh, he'll be fine. He just wants to get out and stretch his wings a bit, taste his independence. I'm sure he will go back to college once the infatuation of the new job wears off. Anyways, I'm glad he's happy and moving along with his life. It sure seems strange here without him."

"I bet you're feeling lonely in that great big house. It must be awfully quiet without Seth and all his friends rumbling through the place."

"It sure is! It seems like a library or something, maybe more like a museum. Actually, I just came back from looking at apartments, you know, something smaller and a little closer to work, something easier to maintain and cheaper to live in. Hell, I don't need much, certainly not a big house like this. Guess I shouldn't have added on so much. Kind of seems silly now, looking back."

"Well, it's always a good idea to move ahead, and it makes good sense to move closer to your work. By the way, how's the new job going?"

"Ha! New job? Mom, I've been there over five years now!"

"Oh, you have not! It can't be that long ago. I was still with Ned then. Let's see. It must have been…Hmm…Good God, maybe you're right. It doesn't seem like that long ago."

"Well, it was more like four and a half years ago, something like that. I guess I'm not sure myself. Anyhow, the job is going fine. In fact, I even got a promotion out of the mailroom."

"Out of the mailroom? Isn't the whole post office a mailroom?"

"Ha, I mean that I was promoted out of the mail-sorting room and into a clerical-type job—even have a small office now."

"Oh, Benjamin, that's great. It sounds so…safe."

"Safe?"

"Oh, you know how I worry. And it's comforting to know you're not involved in a dangerous occupation, like that other job you had. I'm so glad you accepted Ned's offer; at least he was good for something."

"You ever hear from him—Ned, I mean?"

"Why on earth would I ever want to? Let his spoiled-rotten kids take care of the old coot! Besides, he was getting senile way before the stroke. I mean, the relationship was deteriorating with his age. Oh well. I just don't think about it. Besides, I have Don now. He drinks a little too much, but what can you expect for a bar owner? And he's fun—for now anyways. Oh, Benjamin, by the way, you should drive out and visit us. I know it's a long ways, but there is someone you should meet."

"Mom, not again. Please."

"She's pretty, for her age, and she is separated right now, and she is *loaded*. Her husband is some sort of do-gooder executive for the World Health Organization. If you want, I could orchestrate a meeting or dinner with—"

"Mom, listen to me. No! N-o, no!"

"Oh, honey, I only want what's best for you. You know that. Besides, who's going to take care of me in my old age? Heaven only knows how long Don will hold out, the way he drinks. Why, if you and Alicia hook up, you could move out here and—"

"Mom."

"Oh, I'm only kidding. You know I am—about Don, I mean. I'm not kidding about Alicia."

"Who?"

"Alicia—she's the girl I was telling you about. She is really worth pursuing. In fact, Don and I had her and her husband over for a bit of a social a few months back, and she noticed a picture of you and Seth. She asked a few questions."

"Oh, good God, Mom, stop it! If I want a girlfriend, I'll—"

"You'll what? Benjamin, it's been a long—"

"Mom, listen: just stop it and leave it alone."

"You mean, it has left you alone, don't you?"

"Let's not get into this again, OK? For one thing, I would never go out and pursue a girl who was separated from her husband. In fact, you should be doing everything in your power to reconcile their marriage. Hell, everybody should, including Alice!"

"Alicia."

"What?"

"Alicia—her name is Alicia. You said 'Alice.'"

"Whatever."

"Oh, honey, don't get angry with me. I only want what's best for you, you know, so I don't worry. That's all. You know that."

"Yeah, Mom, I know you do. We just have a different idea of what's best, I guess."

"Oh well, you can't blame me for trying. Anyways, I had better get going. It's karaoke night at the bar, and I usually help out."

"I didn't know you could sing."

"Ha! Me? Sing? I sound like a rusty hinge. No, I don't sing. I usually help the girls serve drinks if they get too busy. You know, help old Donald out—prime the pump a little."

"Well, OK. Have fun."

"Always do. OK, then, I better get going. Benjamin, do take care of yourself, and be careful. Love ya. Bye!"

"Bye, Mom."

Benjamin suddenly felt the need to get out of the house, to go for a walk or a ride or something, just something, not knowing exactly what. With Seth gone, his home seemed to have morphed into just a house, a mere structure. Right now it seemed like a vault, a dungeon. He wanted escape; he needed escape.

Locking the door behind him, he looked out into the world, a world of choices, as well as a world of chains. It's funny how a person feels free to make choices when the vast majority of people continually make choices as predictable as the setting of the sun, which was indeed setting. Benjamin stared into the brilliant oranges and scarlets emanating from the crimson center, thinking of its energy and the vast splendor of it all, relating the whole heavenly display to his relevance in the grand scheme of things and how people long to be as free as the light itself, but instead are tethered to their social situations as well as to their immediate geography. The whole world beckons to be discovered, offering itself for participation; yet we remain planted in our clay pots, stationed on our individual windowsills of life, forever peering through a transparent glass barrier, wondering where a particular road or pathway may lead, but never experiencing the journey. Thus, life becomes a waiting game of chance, waiting for some exhilarating sparkle of life to fall into our laps, to arrive by some divine intervention, as our allotted time ticks away minute by minute, never to be retouched,

only to be revisited by memory—that is, if there is anything significant to remember. Still as a shelved seed, we wait in our geographic
pots, conformed to our surroundings and conforming still as each year
strengthens the tether or adds yet another link in our chains. Is fear
to blame? Is it cowardice that prevents us from forging forth into life
and furthering the creation—whatever the circumstance or outcome?
Or is it our underlying goal to make our own nests as comfortable as
possible, comfortable and safe—a job, retirement, medical benefits, a
tasteful headstone, a tear or two—then forgotten?

The sinking sun glazed a pallor on the immediate surroundings with
a surreal wash of Technicolor, almost like the world was an imitation
of sorts, just a series of snapshots, like frames from a movie reel that
endlessly repeats itself simultaneously for every player in the picture,
regardless of time or place or dimension of thought.

Benjamin shuddered, chilled to the core of his soul as his mind
flirted with the vastness of the incomprehensible, shaking him back
into the present, still transfixed on the very spot where the sun had
disappeared from view, yet he knew it was there, just as bright as ever,
somewhere, but not here, not now. Now, it was the beginning of evening, his evening, and the heavens would get blacker still, as the night
played its hand.

For some odd reason, a strange feeling of anxiety quelled from
within, as if it were a fear, a fear of the inevitable night, of the inevitable darkness that he was destined to live through. Instinctively, he
got into his car and drove toward the dimming sky, as if being drawn
into it by an unknown force, mechanically pulling him along like a
horizontal gravity, pulling him farther and farther into the dimming
sky, forever toward the remaining flickers of light. He imagined the
impossibility of driving as fast as the earth could rotate, always staying in the light, never to taste darkness again, but that could never
be. Everyone has their allotted portions of light as well as darkness,
always a contrast of which to foster awareness, to compare, to assess,
to choose.

The light was gone now.

After many unknown turns and curves, Benjamin found himself on a freeway, heading straight into a direction of which he knew not. Yet he continued to drive on, into the black. Only the names on the road signs looked familiar, but eventually even they became strangers; yet he trudged onward, through the blackness of night, driving toward a nothingness, driving away from a nothingness, engulfed in nothingness.

The barren road edged on like a flat dividing line through an arid desert. Repetitively, the center line strobed black and white, as memories flashed like an old film, mesmerizing the pilot of the rolling vessel, hypnotically taking control of reality. It was like only the road itself was moving as the stationary car remained geographically fixed. Only the aimless tires spun as on an endless treadmill, droning a constant hum from the inevitable friction of movement. The bland sound was evidence that life continued around him, just outside, just past the metal skin of his capsule. Inside, he was separate from the world, like being inside a one-man submarine with his periscope headlights searching the bleakness of the open ocean for a rescue ship, or at least a desert island on which to take refuge, only to turn away at any hint of their approach.

Suddenly, the world clanked and sputtered, jolting Benjamin into a slight panic as the treadmill coasted to a whisper, void of the engine's drone.

Out of Gas

"Out of gas!" Benjamin exclaimed as the car rolled to a silent halt on the shoulder of the unknown.

Instantly, a thousand thoughts meshed through Benjamin's regained consciousness. Where was he? Did he have a map in the glove compartment? Where and when had he passed the last gas station? He cursed himself for being so stupid as to not recognize that his gas tank was on "E" and must have been for some time. What a predicament this was, stuck in the middle of who knew where, in the middle of the night. He wasn't even sure of the name of the highway, and he hadn't met any other cars for hours.

"My God," he mumbled as he looked at his watch. It was exactly 12:53 a.m. One in the morning! He'd been driving all night! What was he thinking? He searched the corridors of his mind for any remnants of his little excursion, but could only recall a surreal numbness of the highway, like in a trance. Well, he surely wasn't in a trance now. In fact, it felt like he had just woken up from a deep sleep, sort of refreshed actually. A glimmer of positiveness welled up within him; however, the weight of his current dilemma immediately quashed the brief spark of optimism, leaving a path of frustration in its wake.

The night's liquid blackness seemed to rush into the car as Benjamin opened the door, the darkness engulfing him, claiming him as its own. He exited the car and stood in the night's grip, closing the metallic door, sealing him either out or in—he couldn't tell which. A spangling of stars etched overhead provided a welcome contrast to the blackness, as well as a bit of comfort from the bleakness. Turning in every direction, he noticed no horizons at all; there were just the stars above his head and the earth below his feet—just up and just down. Those two things were for sure. They were something that he could depend on. The very essence of that thought seemed to foster a feeling of contentment that ushered in a welling sense of confidence, although slight. It was as if—

"Ooowwwoooo!" screamed a noise out of the black, immediately exploding the blackness to life, instantly spinning Benjamin around in a contorted spasm of jolting fear, as if a lightning bolt had struck him directly.

"Damn it!" he cursed into the blackness where the coyote must have been or was still. Perhaps it was a pack of coyotes? Hungry coyotes? Or wolves? Could it have been a wolf? Maybe it was circling around him, ready to lunge at the back of his neck. Maybe they were all circling him, ready to pounce any second. Fear unleashed its imaginative flurry of white-fanged, snarling ghosts, ripping and shredding raw flesh amid futile screams of helplessness.

Benjamin instinctively clawed through the black for the safety of the car's door handle, frantically feeling the smooth finish of glass...lower then...to the right...There! Locked! Locked? He tugged at the door again and again. "Locked!" he spouted in disbelief, automatically jumping on the hood of the car, scrambling over the windshield and onto the roof, screaming in an uncontrollable, guttural growl that was not born of rage or fear, but more out of instinct, like that of a primordial spasm of vocalized defensive intent, making it known to his attackers that he would fight to the death. There, crouched atop the car roof, with gritted teeth, poised like a samurai, he screamed into the blackness, simultaneously turning to address all sides, full circle.

"C'mon!" thrust forth his voice. "C'mon, damn it!" he repeated. But out of the blackness came only silence. He imagined the wolves licking their chops, waiting for an opportune moment, wearing him down. Or... Were there any wolves at all? Perhaps the howl he'd heard had originated from a lone coyote that had inquisitively yelped out a blast just to test the integrity of the curious intruder who had invaded its domain. Benjamin's mind conjured all sorts of thoughts and scenarios as he stood, defensively crouched, scanning the situation, eventually focusing on the stupidity of his ordeal. First he drives into the middle of nowhere, in the middle of the night, and runs out of gas. Then he locks his keys inside his car, which was his last link of safety protecting him from the elements of the world. He pondered his predicament. He could find a stone and break a window, gaining access to the car; that would provide shelter. However, he was still out of gas, but at least he would be safe. Safe? Safe from what—his imagination?

Some time passed before Benjamin felt comfortable enough to sit down on the roof of the car, in the lotus position, taking care not to allow any appendages to dangle over the edge—just in case.

As his tsunami of emotions ebbed, so receded his thoughts, back into the ocean, flowing backward like a retreating tide, filling his mind with a fullness, as the currents shifted and eddied in and out of abstraction.

Was not life the strangest of entities? A total mystery? Why was he here? Why are we here? Why are we born at all? Why do we die? What is the purpose of life? Is there not some higher purpose? Why must we live as we do, encompassed in our own situations, embedded into them like thread into fabric? Does not a person's specific situation allow him or her only actions within that specific situation and only it? Thus, our situation is an intricate part of our destiny, but only a destiny imprisoned in that specific situation. If so, what if a person forcefully threw him- or herself into a different particular situation, perhaps a situation that was not particularly on his or her social map or akin to his or her dogmatic routine? Would he or she then change the course of his or her destiny? If so, what prevents a person from doing so? After all, why not change your destiny if the path that you are on seems undesirable or mundane? As long as the change in course has integrity…Yes, of course! Perhaps the path, the path toward wisdom, toward enlightenment, requires a conscious effort to discover the dogmatic thought and situation in one's mind and life, and then take action to change that situation, thus placing oneself, even forcing oneself, into a situation that would ultimately be bathed in an effort that was laced with integrity—integrity and virtue. Yes, virtue. Then, no matter what would happen, the path would prove positive and noble, thus worthy, whatever the outcome. Therefore, any step into the future, with integrity and virtue as the soul's compass, is the best that we can do.

However, what prevents a person from doing so?

At that moment, a coyote howled somewhere in the distance.

"Fear!" said Benjamin. Fear is the barrier. Fear is the entity that holds people fast to their current, dogmatic situations, preventing them from moving ahead toward a nobler pursuit, a nobler path, toward Eden. Fear is like a flaming sword, guarding the entrance.

But is not fear a necessary mechanism, designed for self-preservation, for protection to keep us safe? Of course that is true, but too much safety can cause us to stagnate, like a prison, preventing us from participating in the fullest of experiences, experiences that we may never taste—all because of fear. And why not experience the whole buffet of life that one has the opportunity to experience, as long as the venture has integrity and virtue associated with it?

But how does a person avoid or alleviate fear? Is it even possible? It's possible, but not probable. Any new venture into the unknown would have some level of fear associated with it. What, then, is needed to thwart the stifling effects of fear? Courage, for one! It would be silly to pretend that the fear associated with any new endeavor did not exist. However, it would be mandatory that courage be administered in order to trump fear, to overcome fear, to win the battle. But where does one find this courage?

Benjamin's thoughts focused, and as they focused, they deepened, ushering him into a tranquility, a peace, a place of uncharted clarity. There in the center was a well, a well of living water, as pure and clear as crystal.

A faint light manifested itself directly before Benjamin, who was still sitting statuesque in the lotus position. All of his attention was focused on this new illumination—the horizon at last! The birth of morning was baptizing the skies with joyous hints of light, of beginning. Benjamin, facing east, welcomed the embrace of a new dawn and a new perspective.

Mining Gold

"Howdy!" boomed a voice out of the desert, startling Benjamin, instantaneously evaporating his mental ecstasy to remnants of a fleeting dream scattering into oblivion. There, walking toward him, seemingly out of the sun itself, was a man, an old man and what appeared to be a pack mule loaded with supplies of some sort. The man wore a long-brimmed hat that was turned up in the front, covering most of his grayish hair, but totally exposing his weathered face and lengthy, white beard. As he came closer, Benjamin could hear an audible clanging sound jingling from the mule, no doubt from the metal pans or pots that were hanging off the mule's pack. Benjamin noticed the man's attire, which consisted of a long-sleeved flannel shirt and jeans that were worn in the knees; the rips were patched with a green fabric of some sort. The old leather on his work boots seemed well broken in from years of use, but the leather itself was sound, and the soles looked brand new. He reminded Benjamin of something or someone, but he couldn't pinpoint what or whom. Actually, the old man and mule looked like they'd just stepped out of a western.

"Howdy!" the man repeated.

Benjamin, rather dumbfounded while beholding the strange spectacle before him, could do nothing but stare in disbelief, wondering whether this was a mirage.

"What, are ya deaf? Ain't p'lite not ta say howdy back to a feller that said howdy to ya!"

"Uh, howdy," said Benjamin.

"S'pose yer probably gonna think it tain't any uh my biznuss, but Martha here been pester'n me to find out why you is uh sittin' atop this here motor carriage like a buzzard sittin' on a fence post. Ya see, we was havin' breckfust over yonder there, not more'n seven stone throws thataway when we spied ya. The queerest sight we ever laid eyes on—well, 'cept that time when...Oh never mind 'bout that. Now, where wuz I? Oh yeah! After me an' Martha spied ya, Martha got ta thinking that you might be a sign."

Benjamin, still somewhat in a mild state of shock, was currently in the process of absorbing the reality of the anomaly standing before him. "Your mule talks to you?" he said skeptically.

Suddenly, the beast began braying and kicking wildly with the pots and pans clanking madly as the old man grabbed the mule's tether in an attempt to calm her down.

"Naw, naw, Martha, calm down. Naw, he didn't means it. You know he didn't; he jest don't know no bedder. You know he don't; he cain't he'p it. Naw, that's bedder," soothed the old man as the animal reluctantly grew more passive with each word. "You'll hav'ta pardon Martha here. She's mighty sensitive 'bout bein' called somethin' she ain't. Ya see, Martha here is full-blooded donkey and is a might touchy 'bout her line. I'll hav'ta asks ya to refrain from usin' the *m* word round Martha from here on out, if that'd be pleasin' to ya."

"The *m* word?" thought Benjamin. "Oh!" he said. "Oh, sure, mister, I just thought that...Well, I didn't know exactly what...I mean...I'm sorry if I—"

"Ya hear that, Martha?" said the old man sympathetically. "Feller says he's sorry. Cain't hardly help but forgivin' a feller who's genuinely sorry, now can ya?"

For a moment, Benjamin sincerely hoped that Martha would indeed forgive him, and then he smiled inwardly at himself, once the reality of the situation resurfaced.

"What's that?" questioned the old man, looking intently at Martha, as if expecting her to speak. "Well, o'course I's a-gonna invites him to breckfust. Cain't hardly do no otherwise." Turning toward Benjamin, the old man spoke. "Might as well get down off'n that motor carriage and have yourself some breckfust. We's just camped over yonder a spell. C'mon naw; Martha gits a bit unsettled when she ain't had her breckfust."

The old man and Martha turned in the direction of their apparent origin. Benjamin, still dazed by the strangeness of his situation, obediently left his perch atop his metallic, man-made vessel and followed. They walked about a hundred yards. There, Benjamin saw a fire of burning coals, with a kettle in the center and what looked like bread warming alongside the fringe. There was also an open bag of grain.

"Well, young feller," said the old man, "rest yer weary bones next to the fire, and I'll dish ya up a plateful of beans. They's a might spicy, but me and Martha, we likes 'em flavorful. If they's a bit too hot fer ya, just take a swig o' ol' 'double H' from this here canteen, and it'll quench the fire."

The old man unfastened a rustic, pouchlike container from Martha's pack and set it between himself and Benjamin. Then he proceeded to dish up a heaping plate for his guest and himself while Martha nudged into the bag of grain.

"One thing about beans," said the old man, "they's fillin'. They not only get a feller through; they stick with 'im. Now, young feller, where'd you say you was a-headin'?"

"Well, I honestly don't know. I was just going," thoughtfully said Benjamin as he began his meal. "Didn't really have a destination. And then I just ran out of gas."

"Hmm," said the old man as he savored his mouthful. "These is the best beans ever. It's Martha's recipe. The trick is that you cain't overboil 'em; they gotta have some firmness to 'em, some texture. Then you add the spices and let the whole shebang simmer. Then, when it's almost done, ya add a pinch of brown sugar—kind of mellows the sharp edges." The old man took another bite. "Ya say ya didn't have a place ya was a-headin' to. What about now?"

"What do you mean?" said Benjamin.

"Well," replied the old man, "where ya wanna head to now that yer here, where ya are?"

"I suppose I'll have to try to head back home."

"Back to where you come from?"

"Well, sure," replied Benjamin between mouthfuls. "I've got nowhere else to go."

"So, yer gonna go back to what you was a-drivin' away from?"

"Well, I wasn't driving away from anything. I just went for a drive and lost track of myself, you know, just lost track of—"

"You lost track, huh?" stated the old man. "Me and Martha ain't like that at all. We knows what we's after and where ta find it."

"And what are you and Martha after?" asked Benjamin.

"Gold!" solemnly stated the old man, and he meditatively paused and stared into the burning coals laid out before him.

"Gold?" questioned Benjamin, the reality of his word seemingly evaporating the old man's reflective state.

"Yup, gold," he repeated. "Me and Martha is prospectors. We's been lookin' for gold fur as far back as time was born."

Benjamin observed the seriousness in the old man's face and the exactness of his words. In a way, Benjamin admired the old man for having a purpose, a goal that provided a destination to strive for, even though it was just a goal of money. He smiled as he mentally pictured the old man in a business suit, living in a penthouse suite, after he struck it rich. "Think you'll ever find any?" Benjamin said, grinning, while simultaneously noticing a rising intensity of heat on his tongue that made his eyes water.

"Find any?" exclaimed the old man. "Why, we're findin' it ever' day. We's the richest prospectors ever walked the face of the earth. And you know whut? We get some of our purest right here otta the desert! Ya just gotta know where ta look and how to mine it. It's really just a matter of process: findin' it, seperatin' the gold from the chaff, and then refinin' it. Yup, me and Martha been at it fer ages, and we still git a thrill when it all works out. Course, sometimes things don't always turn out the way we hope. But it's not fer lack of tryin' on our part. Say, young feller, yer lookin' a might peculiar, a bit flushed. Yer face is getting redder'n them beans is hot. Ya better take a splash of some uh my aerated double H. It'll tame the sharp offen yer tongue."

Benjamin gladly drank deeply from the odd-looking canteen, soothing the acidic burning in his mouth. "Wow," he said after drinking his fill.

"Those beans sneak up on a person. Honestly, I didn't even notice how hot they were until just now."

"Well," said the old man, smiling, "sometimes a feller gots ta be careful what he puts on his tongue."

"Forgive me," said Benjamin, "but I find it hard to believe, you know, that you can find and have found gold. I mean no disrespect, but it's a lot to take in. I mean, we're in the middle of the desert! And I'm sorry, but you do not appear to be a picture of wealth." Benjamin felt that now-familiar intensity of heat returning on his tongue and instantly reached for the canteen.

The old man broke some bread off the warming loaf and mopped up the rest of the beans from his plate, thoroughly and thoughtfully savoring the uniqueness of his simple banquet. After a long while, the old man set down his plate and turned to his four-legged companion, who was contentedly munching with flecks of grain glistening on her muzzle.

"Martha sez we best quit jawin' and git goin' iffen we're gonna make any headway. Can't help you out with yer motor carriage, bein' you is otta fuel. But we'd be more'n happy to guide you otta this here desert you're in here. Martha sez she's willin', too; she seems ta taken a shine to ya. Course, we ain't followin' the flat road that you was on, mind ya."

"Jeez, I don't know," said Benjamin. "I hate to leave my car and go traipsing off into the desert."

"Traipsin' *otta* the desert," corrected the old man.

"It's not that I don't trust you," balked Benjamin. "It's just that I'm sure I can handle it myself. I mean, someone is bound to come along, and I just can't leave my possessions—my car, I mean. I know it sounds odd, but right now, my car seems to be a sense of security, and to leave it would be difficult."

"Well," said the old man, "most of'en the hardest things in life are the most rewardin'—in the long run."

"It just doesn't make sense. I mean, it isn't logical to—"

"It's up to you," said the old man. "Me and Martha gots ta git. Yer surely welcome to follow along; we'd genuanly appreciate yer company."

"No, I'm sorry. I can't. I'll just wait for a car to come along. I do appreciate your offer, though. I do thank you—and Martha."

"Well, suit yerself, young feller," said the old man as he scrubbed clean the bean kettle with dry sand and tied it to Martha's pack.

For some odd reason, Benjamin seemed to feel a connection to the old man and Martha. It became more pronounced, knowing that they were about to leave him. Perhaps it was just that he welcomed the connection with humanity during this particular predicament in his life, stranded alone in the desert. Whatever the reason, he sensed a longing to follow the old man, even though it made little sense to do so. He knew, deep in his heart, that he couldn't—wouldn't—go along, yet he absorbed the idea and imagined a journey with the old man, a journey out of the desert, heading toward a noble destination by day, listening to the old man's stories around the campfire in the evening, sleeping humbly under a blanket of shining stars at night. Such a journey would be food for the soul! And what stories would the old man tell? He surely was a unique individual. And to get to know him more intimately would probably be interesting, if not a complete treasure—something to remember and reflect on for the rest of his life. This was an opportunity, an opportunity to step out of the box and live, deliberately. All that he had to do was abandon his car and follow—so simple, yet so difficult. It would be an easier task to thread a large rope through a tiny peephole.

"Well," said the old man after he finished securing the kettle, "that about does it. Martha sez she's anxious to git along and mozey on down the trail. It's always nice seein' ya, young feller, and it's been real plea-sureful for me and Martha ta serve ya breckfust. But the old haymaker's climbin' higher, and me and Martha gots ta team up with 'im."

"Team up with whom?" puzzled Benjamin. "Team up with the sun?"

"Why, shore," said the old man, laughing. "He gots ta shed some light so's we can sees where the gold is and where it ain't. Cain't hardly 'speck us to find any gold in the dark, now can ya?"

"No, I guess you're right," said Benjamin, smiling. "Well, it's been nice sharing your company, and again, I surely thank you for breakfast."

"Aw, 'twern't nuthin'," said the smiling old man. "You woudda done the same iffen the sitchyation wudda been flipped round the other way. Like Martha always sez, ain't no use ta livin' iffen a feller cain't be a-helpin' out folks positive-like, even when they need a kick in the pants. Well, we best be off." The old man and Martha turned toward the east and headed into the rising sun.

Benjamin felt somewhat hollow as he watched them walk away, like the old man was solid and he was superficial, like he needed the solid food that the old man provided for sustenance, and without it, without him, the world would be unfilled. It was a strange feeling that didn't make any sense, and Benjamin suddenly felt a need to prolong the connection.

"Hey!" Benjamin yelled. "I'm sorry I couldn't go along. I really am!"

The old man turned, barely visible, with the body of the sun brilliantly encapsulating their sparkling silhouettes. Benjamin held his palm horizontally over his eyes to shade out the sun's intensity, while squinting to one side of the tremendous radiance. The old man seemed to hold up his hand, acknowledging Benjamin's words. He and Martha then turned back toward their destination and continued onward. Soon they disappeared completely as if absorbed by the sun itself, leaving only waves of the sun's energy radiating from the sands of the earth.

The Rescuer

As the sun rose from the horizon and began its ascent into the heavens, a new day dawned, its hopeful beams breaking onto the world. Benjamin stood in reverent silence as he pondered the morning's significance, still mentally connected to what had transpired. His meditation was broken, however, by the sound of a familiar hum. There, in the horizon, opposite the sunrise, came into view an approaching car. Benjamin ran out to the roadway, waving his arms in desperate fashion, signaling the driver to stop.

The car slowed and came to a halt as Benjamin gratefully approached the driver's window, which was opening wide, revealing the face of a young woman.

"Hello! Car problems?" she said with a smile.

"Oh, thanks for stopping!" said Benjamin, grinning. "I sort of ran out of gas. And I was wondering if you would be good enough to give me a ride to the nearest town or call for help if you have a cell phone. I'd really appreciate it."

"Out of gas, huh?" she mused. "I ran out of gas myself once, right about in this same area. It turned out that my gas gauge was stuck on full. I bet that's exactly what happened to you, wasn't it?"

"Well, no," replied Benjamin, embarrassed. "My gas gauge was right on empty. I was just too preoccupied—just too stupid—to notice. I just wasn't paying attention."

"Well, fear not!" she said and laughed. "I am here to rescue you! The fact is that since I was once in the same predicament as yourself, I always keep a full can of gasoline in the trunk. I don't want to spend another night in the desert filled with sneaky coyotes prowling about. But first, I'd like to see your driver's license, if you don't mind."

"Driver's license? Sure. What for?" questioned Benjamin as he fumbled through his wallet, extracting his identification.

"Just precautionary," she answered. "I'll just call work on my cell to let them know where I am and who I'm with."

"That's sensible," said Benjamin, approvingly handing her his license.

"Benjamin Frisk," she read. "You're quite a ways from home. Please excuse me while I call work; it'll only be a sec."

She closed her car window while Benjamin waited for her to make the call.

"There," she said as the car door opened and she extended her hand to Benjamin. "Marty. Marty Gratchett. Nice to meet you, Mr. Frisk."

"Believe me, the pleasure is all mine," said Benjamin, smiling as he vigorously shook her hand. "I can't believe my good fortune. I mean, that you have a can of gas. I mean, what are the odds?"

"Looks like it's your lucky day, Mr. Frisk." She beamed, happy to help someone out and happy to be the conjurer of joy. "Like I said, I was in your shoes at one time." She opened the trunk, and Benjamin extracted the gas can as she explained. "I travel this desert road to work nearly every day, so I carry the extra gas, just in case. And that's the initial reason that I got a cell phone."

"You sound like a practical, level-headed girl. I admire that," said Benjamin as they both walked over to his vehicle and he began to fill the tank.

She laughed at Benjamin's impromptu assessment of her character. "Well," she explained, "I am actually sort of the reverse of that. In fact, the real reason I carry the gas and cell phone is because I have been conditioned to do so."

"Conditioned?" asked Benjamin.

"Yes, by my parents and friends at work. They say that I'm too— well, too something. They just worry about me, worry if I'm safe. Hence, the phone and the gas, and the 'call if I meet a stranger' protocol. You see? Now they can have peace of mind. And what's wrong with peace? I love peace myself. And I find it, too—all over the place. Hey, maybe that's why I don't move closer to my job. Because I find it peaceful to drive through the desert. Don't you find it peaceful to drive through the desert? I certainly do. I love it. And you know what? I'm always heading into the sun. It's sort of positive—uplifting."

"Heading into the sun?" Benjamin asked as he drained the last drops of fuel into his tank.

"Yup!" she merrily exclaimed. "I live on the west side of the desert, and my job is on the east side of the desert; I'm always following the sun. In the morning I'm heading into the sunrise, and in the evening I'm heading into the sunset. They call me the 'Sunshine Girl' at work. They say, 'She always has the sun in her eyes.' Of course, they usually say that after I've done something that didn't quite turn out like I expected. But hey, a person has to try new things, new ideas, you know, to move ahead, to grow. That's where I think I'm most helpful at work—to create new ideas, new enthusiasm for living. Did I tell you where I work? No, of course I didn't. How could I? We've only just met." She laughed. "I work at the Sunrise Mission. I'm a counselor. It's really a great job. I work mainly with teens, but I am willing to work with anyone. I just love people. Do you love people, Benjamin? Of course you do. Everybody loves people. That's what makes it. It just does. You know, I can't believe that I get paid for what I do because I enjoy it so much. It's like getting paid to have fun. That's why I donate a lot of my income. Somehow it doesn't seem right to keep it, almost like it isn't really mine, like I'm just the caretaker of it or something. Ha, isn't that the truth! I am a caretaker, or a caregiver. But, you know, a person who gives gets back what she gives in a way. It's like…"

Benjamin had filled his tank some minutes ago and was quietly listening to Marty ramble merrily on without a care in the world. He was amazed at her positive energy and equally amazed at her apparent joy for talking. She'd hardly stopped speaking since she'd gotten out of her car! And it didn't seem likely that she had any intention of stopping at all. As she gleefully continued her artful communication, Benjamin was astounded with the aura that surrounded her countenance. It was rather unexplainable. Her smile and her intensity seemed to emanate an elation, an encouraging elation. There she stood before him, radiantly beaming with joy for no apparent reason, other than the simple joy of communicating with another human being. Benjamin absorbed the essence of the pleasant anomaly that gleamed before him, noticing the sunlight dancing off her hair and sparkling off the gold cross from her breast. He was quite amazed at how off he'd been in his first impression of Marty and was equally amazed at the constant flow of words that seemed to endlessly continue, like a river.

"And that's how I learned to play the piano, and I've been playing ever since. I just love music, and singing. Do you like to sing, Benjamin? Oh, of course you do. What a silly question to ask someone. Everyone likes to sing, although some people are reluctant to sing because they have inhibitions about themselves. Don't you think so? About inhibitions, I mean. I don't think that I have many inhibitions at all. I mean, as long as a person is intending to do something good, why be self-conscious about it? I mean, it's like one of the keys to life is to be able to open the door to—"

"Keys!" blurted Benjamin, instantly extinguishing Marty's thought.

"What?" asked Marty, a bit startled by the suddenness of the interruption.

"My keys!" repeated Benjamin. "I accidentally locked them in my car. I almost forgot. After my car stopped, I got out, shut the door, and must've hit the electronic door lock or something. Oh, man! I bet you're wondering how one person can be so dense."

"Oh, don't be silly," said Marty, smiling. "These sorts of things happen to people every day. It's just life. I call them pepper flakes. They spice things up a bit, don't you think so? I think so. I think that many problems that people have are not problems at all, just ramifications of circumstance coupled with the reality that people aren't perfect and make mistakes. You know, it's like when I was little, my grandma used to—"

"I'm sorry," said Benjamin, canceling Marty's nostalgic memory. "Could I bother you once more and borrow your phone to call a garage or something? I really hate to bother you. You've already done more than I can say. And I feel terrible to hold you up, you know, on account of my irresponsibility."

Marty puzzlingly gazed at Benjamin in awe, like she couldn't fathom why he would feel that he was a bother to her, when, in fact, she embraced any opportunity to help anyone as a wondrous privilege. However, she clearly saw that he was troubled, and her heart went out to him.

"Why don't we try my key?" she said, smiling.

"No, it'll never work," replied Benjamin. "Our cars are not even the same make. And I've worked on many ignition switches, and I've never seen any key that ever matched."

"Never say never," said Marty, smiling. "Unless you say that it *never* hurts to try to do something good, even if it seems silly. Don't you think so, Benjamin? Oh, of course you do. Who wouldn't?"

Marty optimistically proceeded to approach the driver's door of Benjamin's car while rummaging through her purse for her keys. Upon extracting them, she noticed a shiny object slightly protruding out of the sand, directly under the driver's door. As she focused her eyes upon the object, she realized it had to be Benjamin's key. So she pretended to accidentally drop her keys and retrieved both her keys and the found key without Benjamin the wiser.

"Mr. Frisk," she stated with an air of supreme confidence, "you just have to have faith!"

She turned the lock and the door opened.

Benjamin stood flabbergasted in jaw-dropping amazement.

"It's a miracle," he said. "You're a miracle. I can't believe it. I just can't. I've never seen...I mean, it's almost impossible that...Wow, I'm amazed. Here I am in the middle of nowhere, and along you come and not only give me fuel, but provide the key to put me back on the road. How can I ever repay you?"

"You already have," said Marty jubilantly, basking in Benjamin's joy, which projected out to her, warming her like energy from the sun itself. "But it wasn't my key that put you back on the road,' it was your own key. I saw it lying in the sand when I approached your car and thought I'd give you a start." She laughed at her little jest. "You must have dropped your key when you got out of your car."

Benjamin laughed. "I guess I must have. Marty, you're a lifesaver. I really feel the need to repay you in some way."

"Oh, don't be silly," she replied. "I'm sure that you would have done the same if the situation had been reversed. I'm just glad to be of service."

"Well, at least let me pay you for the fuel," pleaded Benjamin.

"I won't hear of it, Mr. Frisk. What you can do is help someone else when the opportunity arises, you know, keep the positive flow going." Marty extended her hand as a farewell gesture.

Benjamin took her hand. "Thank you, Ms. Gratchett. Thank you for everything."

"You're most welcome, Mr. Frisk. Now, I'd appreciate it if you would start your car, just to make sure everything is in operating order. I'd hate to drive away and leave you stranded again."

Benjamin started his engine.

"There," said Marty, smiling as Benjamin's engine came to life. "You're good to go and off to a fresh start!"

"Thanks again," said Benjamin.

Marty smiled all the more gleefully as she accepted his thanks, walked back to her car, and drove off into the sunrise, as content as a shining star in heaven. Benjamin sat in meditative silence as he watched her disappear straight ahead into the blazing horizon of the morning's light. He then slowly drove his car across the road, intending to turn around completely. However, he stopped in midturn, with his car perpendicular across the road. For some strange reason, Benjamin felt disoriented. He knew where he was; he knew who he was. However, he wasn't sure of his direction, and he felt a need to be sure. He needed solidity, yet pondered the end result of such a course. And there he stayed, lost in the doldrums of flux, until the approaching traffic forced him to move from his static position and proceed in one direction or the other.

The End

About the Author

R. D. Berg lives in a tiny village in northern Michigan. He lives mainly in a house with a door, two doors, actually. The front door is just for show—it opens to the outer world; however, it is hardly ever used unless absolutely necessary. There is a county roadway just outside the door. Cars and trucks traffic by periodically. The backdoor opens toward a different world altogether, more of a private world. There is a garden just outside the door. The garden is ripe with nostalgic tomatoes, zesty onions, and a few melancholy weeds. From this very garden, Mr. Berg found the various ingredients to compose his novel, *Mr. Frisk.*